Praise for Michael Amos Cody's *Avalon Moon*

"With wolves across the river and murder in the high meadow, *Avalon Moon* knows exactly how to raise the hair on your neck. Move it to the top of your book queue."

—BestThrillers.com

"A deliciously gothic tale stitched into a brutal murder mystery. As a serial killer stalks the mountains of North Carolina, Cody's precise language shifts effortlessly like light through the trees—from lush gothic poetry to gritty Appalachian realism. Facing ancient gods and hungry beasts in the deep woods, the reader can't help but dread a darker truth: evil is only ever a breath away.

—Andrew K. Clark, author of *Where Dark Things Grow*

"A crime novel featuring a new entry to the list of Most Bone-Chilling Fictional Serial Killers ever committed to paper. Or to e-book. Whatever. The influence of Poe and Hawthorne, at their bone-chilling creepiest, can be felt egging on the unfolding of the story, one eerie development after another. A taut, skillfully crafted thriller."

—Whiskey Leavins, author of *Low Angle Shot*

"*Avalon Moon* relies on vivid, inviting storytelling and precise language to lure you in, and once you're caught in Cody's prodigious literary talents, it's hard to escape.... A book you'll think about long after you've finished the story on the page."

—Bobby Mathews, author of *Magic City Blues*

"The Appalachian town of Runion is threatened by a serial killer, wolves, and ghosts—literal and figurative—in Michael Amos Cody's propulsive new novel, *Avalon Moon*. The tension and constant sense of danger kept me turning the pages, but the heart of the book is the large cast of believable characters. All are rendered with insight, compassion, and humor, and they continued to linger in my thoughts long after the novel's satisfying conclusion."

—Peter McDade, author of *King Cal*

"A richly atmospheric crime novel set in the mountains of western North Carolina. Calling to mind the early Appalachian work of Cormac McCarthy cut with the chill of Stephen King.... A beautifully written thriller that immerses readers in a world where the landscape is as compelling and enigmatic as the killer they seek."

—Mark Powell, author of *Lioness*

"A story that has the dark and haunted feel of an old-time Appalachian ballad. Literary echoes of writers such as Samuel Taylor Coleridge and Charles Brockden Brown add to the novel's richness and make *Avalon Moon* an exceptional addition to the genre of Southern Gothic fiction."

—Ron Rash, author of *The Caretaker*

"A delicious slice of Appalachian Gothic, filled with mystery and intrigue, and layered with a compelling cast of characters, malevolent to endearing. Rich with mountain folklore and a centering nod to Artemis, Goddess of the Hunt, Cody's novel is a page-turning who-done-it you'll find yourself flying through. But do slow down. Breathe! There are so many tasty layers, and you're gonna want to savor every bite."

—Cathy Rigg, author of *That Which Binds Us*

"Michael Amos Cody delivers a thrilling and tense Appalachian noir in his latest novel *Avalon Moon*. By turns suspenseful and evocative, this story of a killer on the loose will keep you up at night. Deftly written, with a sharp ear for dialogue and a faultless sense of place, Cody affirms his position as one of the most exciting writers of crime fiction in Appalachia today."

—Charles Dodd White, author of *How Fire Runs*

Avalon Moon

a novel

Michael Amos Cody

Lake Dallas, Texas

FIRST EDITION

Requests for permission to reprint material from this work should be sent to:

Permissions
Madville Publishing
P.O. Box 358
Lake Dallas, TX 75065

Author Photograph: Sam Barnett

Cover Design: Jacqueline Davis

Cover Art: "Shaun's Strange Land." Oil Pastel by Shaun Power.

ISBN: 978-1-963695-67-0 paperback, 978-1-963695-68-7 ebook
Library of Congress Control Number: 2026932895

For Tamara Baxter and Tess Lloyd
First Readers

Tuesday, March 4, 2014

ONE

Gabriel Tanner

"Editor of and chief contributor to a country weekly" never made my top ten list of things I wanted to be when I grew up. For the longest time, I had only one item on that list—*Rock Star!* I toyed with adding a second item, maybe being just a hit-making songwriter, but the songwriting I did throughout the 1980s was so closely bound up with the *Rock Star!* idea that I couldn't pull the two apart. If I didn't become the next Bruce Springsteen, which I didn't, I was unlikely to become the next Bob McDill—ditto on the *didn't.*

So, with the *Rock Star!* phase of my life gone grumbling into my dreams, I left Nashville in the hot gut of August 1990, retreated, tail between legs, to Runion, my hometown in the North Carolina mountains, and the following January entered Runion State University, where I double-majored in English and Journalism. I took a part-time job as student reporter and all-around grunt for Sheldon Dean's *Runion Recorder.* A couple years after I graduated, Sheldon decided he was tired of writing and offered me a full-time position as editor, keeping only the title of "General Manager" for himself. I accepted.

And so it came to pass that on a cold evening in early March, on the darker side of twilight, I drove toward the Lonesome Mountain end of Genesis Road, planning to swing around the back way into Runion. On regular mornings going to work, or any other time I was in a hurry, I drove down to the French Broad end of Genesis and took the river road up a short hill and onto Main Street, but I was dreading two hours minimum of sitting in a meeting at the Madison County Cooperative Extension Office complex, housed in the recently renovated Old Mill on Mill Street, and taking notes for a regular report to appear in next week's paper. The room would be stuffy with heat and humanity, and to be honest, I was lollygagging.

This year's March was looking like a lion-lamb version—*in like a lion, out like a lamb*. We expected to wake up the next morning to some serious snow and ice courtesy of Winter Storm Ulysses. The fields on my left and the woods on my right seemed to hold their breath in anticipation.

I rolled to a stop at the T-intersection where Genesis Road dead-ends at Jewel Hill Road, with Lonesome Mountain ahead and to my left, dark against the sky. My new Honda hybrid sat quietly, and still not used to its workings, I thought it might have died but relaxed when no warning lights appeared. Even though the temperature was in the upper thirties, I opened my windows and—with no other traveler sitting at my bumper and politely honking, as our mountain folk do—sat at the intersection with my eyes closed and my skin alive to the chilly air. I heard a few of last summer's still-tethered leaves shivering in the boughs overhead and something scurrying through the underbrush in the woods off to my right. I think I could've engaged the emergency brake and gone to sleep, but I opened my eyes, suddenly uneasy and unsure why.

The headlights shown across Jewel Hill Road and lit the lower part of a hillside pasture beyond. A few head of cattle midway up the slope stood at the edge of the light and grazed on pale grass.

Not one to be unnerved by a bovine presence in the twilight, I strained my senses to catch and identify what raised hairs along my forearms and around the back of my neck.

To my left, a field rolled away in successive swells toward a wooded ridge standing blackly against the sky. Runion lay on the other side of that ridge, but somewhere between the town and me, yips and cries rose from the gathering dark. These joined together into an eerie howl of various voices that twisted around one another, broke apart, and swelled together again.

Coyotes.

When I was growing up in these mountains, coyotes existed only in old TV westerns. But they were voice-over actors only, strictly behind-the-scenes. They were soundtrack features. Technicians of ambiance. Nothing said a cowboy was alone in the darkening wilderness like the distant howl of a coyote. The cowboy would raise his eyes from the campfire and sit still and listen for a moment, alert to the wild. But it was never the coyote itself that frightened him. Maybe the coyote's cry was a reminder of his loneliness and vulnerability—that if such a critter could be out there in the dark, then anything could be out there.

But in recent years, coyotes had loped out of the faded glory of Hollywood's western and into our world, maybe crossing the Mississippi around Memphis and moving steadily east across Tennessee until they reached Appalachia and Runion. They were seen trotting along the edges of regional four-lanes or lying dead on twisting mountain highways. They stole cats and small dogs just beyond the lights of back porches. That evening at the stop sign, they yipped and yapped and cried somewhere out on the verge of a Runion farmer's field.

Still, I thought, *at least they aren't wolves.* Wolves, of course, were a different story. Send up the howl of a wolf into the night, and the cowboy would become focused on the beast, not on loneliness or vulnerability. The wolf's howl menaced, threatened. Eyes might shine at the edge of the campfire's light, followed by snarling close-ups. Then enter the legend of the wolf mixed with a man, and the beast achieved cinematic glory, jumping genres from westerns to horror, something coyotes could never quite pull off.

When I pressed the accelerator, the Honda whispered to life, and I turned left toward town. If I sat there much longer, I would be late for the extension meeting, during which one item on the agenda just happened to be related to the beasts of my T-intersection musing.

Theery Johnson, the county's first female extension agent, a recent NC State graduate, was moving along the line of windows, her straight ponytail of red hair swinging back and forth across broad shoulders as she threw up the sashes. With the air flowing almost too freshly, she faced the room and flashed her bright smile, spoke to a couple of the farmers in attendance, drew herself a cup from the coffee cistern, and took a seat at the table in front of the gathering. As attendees noticed her there and began to fill the folding chairs, she called the meeting to order.

"Let's all stand for the Pledge of Allegiance," she said and stood to face the flag.

While everybody remained standing, Rev. Amos Thorn provided a prayer of invocation, followed by a moment of silence. Then the preacher exited as the men settled into their seats with creaks and grunts and nose-blowing. Theery moderated a few moments for public comments regarding minutes from the last meeting, which were briefly discussed and unanimously approved.

"All right," Theery said. "Our first and main agenda item this evening is the new wolf sanctuary being established on Christabel Island. As you know, most of the central part of the island is taken up with the house and its grounds and the orchard and its buildings." She paused, as if expecting to be interrupted, but while some stirred in their chairs, nobody said anything. "Our guest tonight is Mr. Spellman Anderson, owner of Avalon Orchards and the island, who's gonna tell us a little bit about what he's doing over there with the wolves and then try to answer any questions we might have."

Spellman Anderson IV left the wall by the doorway where he'd been leaning with arms crossed over his thin chest. As he made his way to the front of the room, his narrow face wore its perpetual serious expression. This countenance didn't seem in keeping with his collar-length and wavy silver hair, which he kept tucked behind his ears and didn't cover with either cap or toboggan, as most of his audience covered their pates. He sat down in the empty chair beside Theery.

"Thank you, Ms. Johnson," he said and scanned the faces in the crowd. "And thanks to all of you for coming out tonight, given the weather that's forecast to arrive in the next few hours." He stopped and took a sip of water from the glass on the table in front of him, drew in a deep breath, and began. "I'm guessing that most of us in this room have a special place in our hearts for animals. We have them in our homes and on our farms. We get a special thrill when we see them in the wild, even if the next thing we do is run from them or shoot them or shoot them and then run."

A few of his listeners cracked a smile, but Anderson didn't.

"So, as Ms. Johnson said, we have set up a modest wolf and wolf-hybrid sanctuary on my island."

Anderson was a good speaker with a clear, rich voice. His delivery tended to sound somewhat formal in its syntax, maybe something to do with the IV attached to his name, but he softened this formality with a friendly Appalachian drawl. He'd leaned just slightly on the *my* of "my island," not enough to draw unwanted attention to it but enough to emphasize that Christabel was indeed his island—and, according to the good old USA's understanding of such things, his to do with as he pleased. Something else colored his speech, however, something I couldn't precisely define, but I supposed it could be traced to his having grown up on that island in the middle of the river, with its touch of isolation and its odd history.

"I have three enclosures, which is relatively limited for such a sanctuary. One on the north end of Christabel is some eighty thousand square feet. That's the biggest—"

"A little under two acres," Theery Johnson said. "Sorry, Spellman."

Anderson nodded and continued. "Another is adjacent to the orchard on the opposite side from Avalon Cottage and the third is on the highland at the south end. Each of these is approximately an acre. We have four red wolves at present—one pair in the highland enclosure and one in the smaller enclosure adjacent to the orchard. But when we're at capacity, we'll be providing sanctuary for eight wolves and wolf-hybrids."

"What the hell's a wolf-hybrid?" Bob Tweed asked and caught his cap by the bill, lifted it, scratched at his receding hairline, and lowered the cap again.

"Let's all hold our questions until Spellman has finished with his talk," Theery said with a smile.

"It's a cross between a wolf and a domestic dog breed," Spellman answered anyway. "Sometimes referred to as a wolf-dog." He took another sip of water. "Now, each of my enclosures is surrounded by a seven-foot-high chain-link fence and includes three structures. They have pool houses, raised or multi-level platforms, and aboveground or underground dens. If the wolves aren't from an area like ours, we'll try to provide them with a versatile habitat that'll help them be as comfortable as possible."

I saw more grins break out among those sitting in the folding chairs, but these had little sense of humor in them. I heard "comfortable" grunted a couple of times. Somebody stage-whispered to a neighbor, "I didn't know they played pool," and a couple of roughhewn farmers actually giggled and one snorted.

"As for the wolves themselves," Anderson continued unflustered, "the ones we have now and those that will come afterwards have been bred in captivity. They've been in people's homes as pets. Some will have been breeders for kennels and wolf-puppy mills. Or they've been on display in roadside attractions out west or down in Florida. Or been in zoos that need to replace them every so often with younger animals. They've imprinted on humans and can't go into the wild, even if they were born there, so we're just trying to provide a sanctuary for them, especially the older wolves, to prevent their being killed and let them live out their last days in relative comfort."

I stood by the open windows, alternately watching Spellman Anderson and the twenty-three men facing him and Theery Johnson from the rows of folding chairs. I jotted down the names of the men I knew and took notes on what Anderson said. When I wrote the report for the paper, I would also provide our readers with a brief description of the island, its geography and position in the river, how it's accessed, a bit of its history. I knew some about that last item, although not as much as I would've liked. But I figured that I could learn more when I followed up with a visit to the island tomorrow—or soon, depending on the weather—to see the enclosures and the wolves that were already there.

Gene Fredericks, former county extension agent, now retired and working in real estate and insurance, stepped through the door and took the place that our speaker had earlier occupied against the back wall.

"All the animals we rescue," Anderson was saying, "will have full breed and medical documentation on file in the Avalon Orchard office. We're focusing on the endangered American Red Wolf, but we'll probably have a gray or two as well from time to time. And all of them, except for a pair of younger Reds, will be spayed or neutered as soon as they arrive, if they haven't been already." He took a deep breath and turned to Theery. "That's about it, I suppose."

The folding chairs creaked and scraped as the men sitting

in them shifted their bodies after having to sit and listen when they would rather be socializing.

"Thank you, Spellman," Theery said. She then scanned the faces rowed in front of her. "I'm sure y'all have some questions"—a couple of hands went up immediately—"but remember that Mr. Anderson has every right to create this sanctuary for rescued wolves. So, we're not here to debate that or to pass judgment or to give any sort of approval. This is just information. Transparency, as they say these days, so that the idea doesn't get started that this is some sort of secret venture." She looked over toward me for some reason and then again glanced through the faces in front of her. "Now, Mr. Anderson has agreed to entertain questions from the public, so ask 'em if you got 'em."

Danny Davidson stood up first. "I live over on Piney Ridge, almost directly up the mountain from the south end of your island, and I'm wondering how much noise we're likely to get from this sanctuary. I've got little kids that'll be scared shitless if they heard a pack of wolves a-howling."

"Thank you, sir," Anderson said. "The fact that these wolves are captive-bred means that they'll make very little noise. We've had four residents for about a month now, and I haven't heard the first howl. I'm guessing that you haven't either. I'll definitely keep your concerns in mind, should the noise level raise with the addition of more residents or with changes in the weather. I'm not sure if either of those will make any difference, but only time will tell."

"Probably won't hear the wolves as much as we hear the coyotes," my old friend Mel MacOde said to Danny Davidson and the crowd in general. Other than my wife, Eliza, Mel was the only friend from high school—all the way back to first grade, actually—that I saw around Runion on a regular basis. He turned to Anderson. "Spellman, do you plan to have the public coming over to see the wolves?"

"That's a good question, Melvin," Anderson said. "As you all know, we offer some orchard experiences for local school classes at various times of the year, particularly around harvest. My child, Ariel, is working on some wolf-related ideas and educational materials that can be incorporated into the school visits." He stopped as his throat seemed to clench, and he winced visibly. He then drew a quick breath and picked up his water glass. "I say 'child'—she will be twenty-seven this year." His voice again shook to a stop at "this year," and he took another sip of water.

I couldn't help but feel like the pause was to recover from an apparent emotional rush related to Ariel, a beautiful and mysterious character rarely seen even by those who were regular visitors to the island. I found the idea that she might be drawn out into a more public life through these wolves strangely exciting, and I think others in the room felt a tinge of the same.

"But there are bigger sanctuaries around, Melvin, and not too far away," Anderson said, recovered from whatever had tightened his throat moments before. "I don't foresee a lot of outside interest being drawn to it."

After a moment of restless quiet, Theery asked if anybody had another question, but her little speech about this meeting's being just for information seemed to have taken a good deal of steam out of the room.

Ben Frisby remained tense, which wasn't surprising. He seemed tense and angry at the world all the time about something or other, at least in my limited knowledge of him. He and his boys—Billy, who was here with him, and Benny, who was off who knows where—had been implicated several years ago in an act of vandalism that today we'd call a hate crime against the Fredericks family and their gay son Mike, long dead from AIDS by this time. The Frisbys kept to themselves and away from the authorities as much as possible. Ben stared at Spellman Anderson IV and didn't turn to his son Billy, only nodded almost imperceptibly.

Billy thrust himself up from his folding chair.

"So, what happens if something happens and they get out?" he said and sat again with such a heavy swagger that I thought his chair might fold on down to the floor.

Theery stared at Ben and Billy for a moment and then turned to look at her guest.

"Well, sir," Anderson said. "I can answer that in a couple of ways, if you will. First, these enclosures won't be easily escaped from, but I understand your concern. Lots of unforeseen things might happen, I suppose, that could compromise the fencing. But remember that the wolves will still be on the island, and it's unlikely that they would make their way off of it." He scratched lightly at his pointed chin. "Second, remember that these wolves are all more or less tame. I don't think they would either seek escape or know what to do if they did find themselves outside their enclosure. They might just come up to the porch of the big house and stretch out for a nap."

"But they're still wolves, right?" Eddie Fore said without standing or raising a hand, appearing to expend all his energy in those few words and a furrowed brow.

"Well, yes, but I'm not sure what you mean by that."

"I mean that they're still killers."

Theery Johnson spread her fingers on the tabletop.

"Let's not mistake an animal for a legend, okay, Eddie?" she said, working hard, it seemed, not to sound like somebody talking to Transylvanian villagers armed with torches and pitchforks. "Wolves have gotten lots of bad press for lots of years. But these shouldn't legitimately bother us any more than the animals in Chief Saunooke's Bear Park bother the tourists over in Cherokee."

"That place shut down last year," Mel said. "The Cherokee Bear Zoo's still operating, but I think the community elders would like to see it gone, too."

The room seemed to take this in but still focused on Spellman Anderson, waiting for a response.

"Look," he said with a sigh. "I'm all in on this venture, and I believe in it. But I would never have considered it if not for Ariel." Again he stopped for water and drank the last swig in his glass. "Not many of you know Ariel. Probably none of you. But she's my only child, and she wants this badly." He looked around at the faces in front of him but avoided looking at Gene Fredericks. "Who would not do something good like this if his only child really wanted it done."

All of us in the room now clearly avoided looking at Fredericks, whose only son Mike still seemed to be the only lost child belonging to this group of men.

"Ariel wanted it for some reason," Anderson added. "I have the means to do it, and I've done it."

"Thank you, Mr. Anderson," Theery said as she finally glanced toward Gene Fredericks and watched him slip out the door. "Let's take a five-minute coffee break and then get on with our next agenda item."

In the hallway outside the meeting room, I shrugged into my jacket and caught up with Spellman Anderson in the parking lot. He was looking from side to side as he walked and stopped when I called his name.

"I hoped I would be able to catch Gene," he said. "I wanted to tell him—" He stopped and looked around again.

I knew what he meant, or thought I did, but I didn't know how to respond. "I was wondering," I said. "Could I come over to Christabel sometime soon and take a look at what you've got going over there?"

"Would this be an official newspaper visit?" he asked.

"It doesn't have to be," I said. "I'll be writing up this meeting as part of my usual business, of course, so the extension report will come from what just happened inside."

"Fine."

"I'd just like to come over and take a look at things, jot down a few notes, maybe take some pictures for my files. But if you'd like something specific written for the paper, I'll be glad to do a feature." I shoved my hands into my jacket pockets, looked up at the blank sky, and then turned back to Anderson. "That's up to you."

He looked around the parking lot as if Gene Fredericks might have reappeared.

"Fine," he said again. "But hold off on the feature for now. Maybe we can do something when residents are at capacity and we are ready to receive visitors."

"All right," I said.

"So come over to get your notes and pictures whenever you like," he said. "If you are interested, we serve lunch in the house at exactly noon. I never know what is on the menu for any given day, but I can testify that it is always good."

"That sounds perfect," I said. "I better get back inside, but if you don't mind, and if tonight's storm doesn't shut us down, I'll come over around ten o'clock in the morning and wander the island for a while and then eat lunch with you."

"Very good," he said and, with a last glance around the parking lot, turned to his vehicle.

Back inside, I found that talk had turned from the wolf sanctuary to the coyote population, and Theery Johnson was trying to explain recommendations for control.

"We're at the height of their mating season right now," she said. "So, the males are really aggressive." She paused and shot a hint of a smirk at the men arrayed in front of her. "The folks in Raleigh recommend a campaign of neutering once mating is over."

"Theery, they're killing our stock," Bob Tweed said. "They ain't fuckin' 'em."

The room exploded in laughter, and Theery collapsed against the back of her chair, covering her face with her hands but laughing along. During the uproar, Deputy Davis Boyce stepped into the room, looked around, and wiped a palm across his mouth.

Andy Campbell stood up as the laughter died down. "Bob, with a mind like that, we ought to run you for mayor or sheriff."

"How's about we don't?" Deputy Boyce said from the back of the room, and everybody turned that way.

"Welcome, Deputy Boyce," the county agent said. "Is everything all right?"

"It is for the moment, Ms. Johnson, but that storm's looking like it's coming straight at us." He again wiped his mouth with a palm. "I just dropped in to say it might be wise to cut the meeting short so's everybody gets home all right."

"Well, I think Mr. Tweed has already cut us up," Theery said and looked around at the gathering as Deputy Boyce slipped out of the room. "So, if there's nothing else?"

Mel MacOde came over and stood beside me while his fellow farmers made their way out of the room, many of them still laughing and repeating Bob Tweed's one-liner. The two of us then helped Theery fold chairs.

"You've got a birthday coming up on Saturday," Mel said.

"Reckon so," I said. "No way to avoid it."

"Joining the ranks of the fifty-fives."

I folded four chairs and carried them, two in each hand, to the cart Theery rolled from a corner to the center of the room. "Do you feel that old, Mel?"

He set the last four chairs on the cart and fisted the small of his back, leaning into it. "Most of the time I don't," he said with a grin.

We told Theery good night and left the room together. Both of us looked up at the sky as soon as we walked out the Extension office's front door.

"Sure looks like a snow sky," Mel said.

"It does," I said. "We might be a little snowed in come morning."

"Might be," he said as we shook hands and headed for our vehicles. "Hey, listen, Ezra's coming up on the Ides of March.

Why don't you and Eliza come over to the farm in the afternoon and stay for supper?"

"I'll have to check on her schedule, but that sounds fun," I said. "Ezra doing okay?"

"About like usual." He grinned and shook his head. "Rich and confused."

"Is he still caregiver for that old wrestler?"

"Homer Alexander," Mel said. "But I don't think it'll be that much longer. He's in pretty bad shape."

"How old is he?"

"I think seventy or seventy-one? I take it that he's lived pretty hard and fast at times." Mel yawned and stretched. "And then there's the beating a body takes in that line of work, even if it is mostly fake."

"Man, at fifty-five, seventy-one seems not so old anymore."

"I heard that," Mel said and then broke into a proud smile. "Ezra's kind of amazed us all."

"You've been an awesome friend to him, Mel."

"Well, I love the guy."

"I know you do," I said. "It'll be good to see him." I opened my car door and then spoke over the roof. "Take it easy, Mel. Give my love to Caroline."

"Will do, Gabe," he said. "Same to Eliza."

I checked in with her as I drove Mill Street toward the *Runion Recorder* office on Main Street. All was well at home on Genesis Road, although she seemed a little anxious about my being out with a snowstorm on the way. I said that nothing was falling yet and that I'd be home in an hour or less and that I loved her. I made a U-turn at the north end of Main and parked outside my office. The air felt a little colder and a little moister here closer to the rivers, and I pulled up the collar of my jacket before I crossed the sidewalk and unlocked the door. Then I took one last look up at the blank belly of clouds and went inside. Because of the early end to the meeting, I decided to write up my brief report and add it to Thursday's edition. I was sorely tempted to add some version of Bob Tweed's joke just to see if anybody actually read these things, but I resisted. After writing about two hundred words, I fit it into the layout and emailed the edition to the printer. I texted Eliza that I was headed home—a text complete with a blown kiss emoji and a heart—and then stepped out onto the sidewalk to find snow falling straight and steady on Runion's Main Street.

Wednesday, March 5

TWO

Winter Storm Ulysses had been underway in the Runion area for three and a half hours when the man rolled his vehicle to a stop in the middle of a dip in Pump Gap Road and turned off the lights, including those on the panel. He sat still, staring ahead into the darkness until he could differentiate between snow-ghosted air and snow-covered ground. Then he eased off the road into a field on the right and crept the vehicle diagonally up toward the treeless ridge, but before topping the rise, he arced left and down and rolled to a stop in the deep shadow of the tree line at the field's upper edge. He clutched to shift to neutral and set the emergency brake, turned off the ignition and pulled the keys and lay them in the ashtray. He reached up and back and flipped a switch to deactivate the interior light. Then he leaned forward and reached down to pull a lever near the floor that released the back hatch, then eased his seat back. Being careful not to press against the steering wheel and sound the horn, he removed boots and socks. With a sock pushed into the top of each boot, he set the pair in the passenger-side floorboard. After drawing a deep breath and releasing it slowly, he opened the door and stepped barefoot into snowy grass, where he stood listening to wind filled with falling snow and felt the few thick flakes that passed through the leafless limbs above settle on his hair and melt through to his scalp. The unblemished dark blue to his left meant the snow was deeper in the open field, and he picked out a site some thirty yards away, six yards or so on the near side of a copse of trees and accompanying underbrush that stood alongside Pump Gap. He looked at the spot for a long moment and then, with the door still standing open, made certain all his pockets were empty and stripped off his clothes, folding each piece and stacking all in the driver's seat. From a pouch located on the interior panel of the door, he pulled yellow rubber gloves and put them on and then closed the door without latching it.

At the rear of the vehicle, he raised the hatch and stood still, again feeling the snowflakes kissing his head and shoulders, back and buttocks, and picturing the bodies beneath the tarpaulin. After another moment, he took the tarp's near edge in both hands and began gradually pulling it away, like a magician's big reveal in slow motion. He stepped back and to his left, and shaggy heads, pale chests and arms and legs and feet appeared. He spread the tarp on the snowy grass and stepped forward onto it.

The man lay on the left, the woman on the right, not even their hands touching, as separated and unaware of each other as strangers asleep in adjacent motel rooms. She was thin and bony, angular at every point where it's possible for a human body to be angular. But she was muscular as well and in life had been much stronger than expected. Her skin was darker than that of the one who lay like a bear beside her, although the graying brown hair that swirled across his torso made that difficult to tell in the snow-glow of the night. Big in chest and belly, thick in thighs and calves, he lay as if he might suddenly snore loudly and roll over with his back to the woman. In life his hands had been meaty and calloused and his voice mountain-brash but almost childish. Yet, strong as he was, in the end he'd proved easier to overpower than she.

He grabbed her cold feet and backed away, pulling her free of the vehicle and letting her fall partway on the tarp and partway on the grass. With some pushing and pulling, he maneuvered her fully on top of the tarp and then dragged her out into the open and across the field to the plot he'd picked, feeling the snowflakes on his skin multiply when he moved from under the trees, as if he'd walked into a swarm of frozen mosquitos. He reached the plot, dropped the end of the tarp, took it up again by one side, and rolled her off into the snow. He then positioned her on her back, briefly cupped a hand over each small, cold breast, and then pushed her legs together. He stood looking down at her a moment, then at the copse of trees and the road, standing still and looking and listening. After another moment, he picked up a corner of the tarp and returned to get the other one.

He crawled into the back of the vehicle and mounted the man. He straddled him for a moment, knees and shanks pressed against the chilled softness of the dead's hips, his warm genitals flaccid atop the dead's cold package, and then he leaned down to press against him—cheek to cheek, chest to chest, belly to belly. From that position, he eventually raised up, clasped his hands behind the man's neck and pulled hard—one time, two times, three—until he raised him to a sitting position. Holding him up, he scooted backwards on shins and knees until he could stretch one foot to the ground and then the other. He maneuvered the man's body until the thick calves and feet hung toward the ground. He drew one deep breath and with a grunting bear hug, a jerk and a twist, he landed on top of the man on top of the tarpaulin. He lay there a long moment, pressed against the cold body and breathing hard, feeling the touch of falling snow from the back of his head to his ankles. Once he caught his breath and his heart rate slowed, he raised up and, bracing both gloved hands on the man's belly, got his feet under himself and stood.

When the two bodies lay in the snow, lay farther apart than they could in the back of the vehicle, he lay down on his back between them—shoulder to shoulder with the man, hand in hand with the woman—as if he would stay and share their sleep. But he forced his eyes to remain open and blinked against every snowflake that touched his lashes.

When he could tell that snow had begun to accumulate on the bodies, he rose from between them, gathered the tarp into his arms, and returned to the vehicle. He opened the driver-side rear door and took out a large, fully stuffed garbage bag and set it beside the back tire. Then he reached inside again, took out a sixty-four-ounce container of creamy peanut butter and a spatula, and returned to the bodies, dragging the garbage bag behind him.

He knelt in the snowy grass beside her and removed the lid from the container and hung it on the big toe of her left foot. Then he dipped the spatula and spread peanut butter over her feet and up her legs, the thin layer of snow melting and somewhat thinning the paste as he worked. He left the pubic triangle unsullied, hoary with snowflakes, and applied the peanut butter thickest on her breasts and face and hands. He stood up and moved to the side of the man and knelt and began with the forehead, covering the startling blue eyes as if the peanut butter were spackle. He carefully worked the spread around and around into the swirls of hair that covered the body's chest and belly, applying it slowly and thickly to fingers and penis and scrotum and thighs before continuing over the knees and down the shins to the feet. He collected the lid from the woman's toe and screwed it back onto the nearly empty container. Then he licked the spatula clean and laid it and the container together beside him in the snow-covered grass.

He stood and opened the garbage bag and removed handful after handful of loose straw and released each to drift down onto the bodies like the falling snow. When the bag was empty, he picked up the spatula and peanut butter container, dropped them inside, and without a backwards glance, returned to the vehicle parked against the dark tree line.

THREE

Ariel Anderson

I could not sleep and found myself wide awake at some few minutes past three o'clock. I lay still beneath the comforter that kept my body warm while, at the same time, I balanced the chill of the room on the tip of my nose. The sense of cold intensified with the hush of snow at the window, heard between periodic blasts and howlings of wind. Even though the moon in its waxing crescent phase was hidden and the sun was yet some hours from rising, my room glowed with the same seemingly sourceless glow that fell from the vast, featureless face of the storm called Ulysses.

The glow of snow? I wondered.

I recognized that my evening reading was more to blame for my poor sleeping than was the frightful weather outside. I spent the hours before retiring to bed poring over a brief manuscript I had recently discovered in the attic—secreted away in a desk that must have been built in place like Odysseus's bed in Ithaca, as it seemed too large to have been moved up there after construction of Avalon Cottage. The handwritten document was in the form of a journal covering roughly one month and extending to eighteen pages, not counting the top page, which was a letter dated the fifteenth of December in the year eighteen hundred. Even though this letter was in the same hand as the manuscript, it was not part of it—that is, not a cover letter or an introduction. Rather, it was the author's request that the manuscript, mysteriously gone missing at the time of his departure from here, be returned to him in Philadelphia should it be found. Whether mislaid or stolen, the manuscript had obviously been secreted away by some inmate of Avalon and not returned as requested.

I could not disentangle myself from the tension and terror that arose from the story narrated in those pages. I could not tell who the author was or how trustworthy his perspective and telling might be, but I knew I was reading a tale of horror that had taken place on this island and in this house where I had spent the whole of my life. Long I lay awake and attempted not to listen for the snarling of the beast the manuscript claimed to have prowled Christabel Island in the autumn of eighteen hundred, only two or three years after the small Pantisocratical community's settling here.

At last, I arose in the blue glow from the window, dressed myself in warm clothes, and descended the stairway. I donned a red cloak and cowl that made me feel like a woman of mystery in a Gothic novel or, better yet, a maiden in a fairy tale. I stepped out into a snowy dawn, intent on pushing through the drifts to feed our resident wolves. I filled a satchel with the bodies of catfish and squirrels and took the hard road first, climbing up to visit Demeter and Iasion in Wolfpen One. The snow was not as deep as I had expected, just under a foot, I supposed, and not as heavy as it might have been either, so the walking was relatively easy. Before long, I stood beside the fence where Father had removed a few metal strands to make a kind of feeding window, and there I spoke the names of the wolves.

"Demeter? Iasion?"

Nothing happened immediately, but after a moment the pair loped towards me through the snow, having emerged from separate hiding places, neither of which I could detect in the blanketing whiteness. As they approached, I pushed the bodies of two catfish and two squirrels through the fence to them.

With only brief snarling and snapping at each other, they chose their first course—Demeter a fish and Iasion a squirrel—and moved apart. But before bending their heads to their cold repast, each stood and stared at me with yellow-gold eyes that seemed to glow in the blue dawn.

"Yes," I said to them. "I will leave you to it." At that I turned to move down the hill toward Wolfpen Two, glad that the wind high in the evergreens masked the sound of cold flesh being torn from cold bones.

I emerged from the woods that separated Wolfpens One and Two and stopped in my snowy tracks. Even from a distance, I could see that something was amiss. A trail of blood as vivid against the snow as my cloak and cowl in this blue-tinted landscape began some twenty feet inside the fence and moved in a jagged line that disappeared where I knew the lip of the enclosure's underground den to be. As I approached, a faint trail seemed to extend from the fencing to the point where the blood began, but new snowfall had blurred it sufficiently to make me uncertain it was there at all.

I stood a moment at Wolfpen Two's feeding window, but I did not speak the names of these wolves—Atalanta and Milo. Instead, I moved around to my left, to the locked gate, and dug keys from the inside pocket of my cloak. I hesitated for a moment, recognizing that this was not the best of ideas, but then I unlocked the gate and began pulling it open against the drift of snow along its bottom. Part of my recognition of this idea as ill-considered was the realization that I should leave my burden of fish and squirrels outside the enclosure, so I dropped my satchel in the snow before stepping inside and pulling the gate closed behind me.

The low rumble of a growl reached my ears when I was yet several feet from the den. The next sound I heard was my own beating heart beating hard. I looked down at the trail of blood in the snow and imagined my own blood mixing with it, refreshing it. Ever perverse, however, I pulled apart the skirt of my cloak and dropped to my knees and hands and began a slow crawl forward, wanting only to see both sets of glowing eyes so that I would know both wolves were present and well.

A second growl joined the first, confirming that both wolves were indeed present, but as of yet I heard no movement of either escape or attack.

Finally, after long moments with my bare hands aching in the snow and the knees of the blue jeans I had tucked into the top of wool-lined snow boots soaked, I reached a point where four rounded yellow-gold eyes locked on mine.

The growls took on an urgency that matched my heartbeats and the rush of blood in my ears.

With the sun risen behind the eastern clouds, just enough light fell into the den to reveal the hump of a carcass and a fluffy striped tail.

How or why a raccoon found its way inside the enclosure, I could not imagine, but once I knew that poor beast to be the source of the blood, I lowered my gaze and bowed my head and backed away from the den.

Milo emerged from the darkened enclosure, his muzzle still reddened from his breakfast. He did not approach but remained standing and watching me.

I kept my eyes lowered, but I did not turn away. Instead, I slowly stood and backed to the fence and found the gate. Then raising my gaze and keeping watch on Milo, where he still stood without making any motion to approach or attack, I slipped through the gate and closed and locked it. Then I paused for a moment, breathing deeply and feeling increasingly shaky with cold and with shock at what I had just done.

Not wanting my father to venture out into this weather, I braced myself with prayers to Artemis and then walked the perimeter of Wolfpen Two in search of how the raccoon had gained access to its horrible but well-deserved death. I inspected several spots closely, yet I could not find an obvious point of encroachment. Before long, I returned to the gate and shouldered my satchel, knowing that I had been gone too long and that Father and Mother would worry. I decided I would return the remaining fish and squirrels to the cold larder and then, after breakfast, tell the tale of the raccoon's misadventure and report my inability to locate its point of access.

With the next few minutes settled in my uneasy mind, I readjusted the satchel on my shoulder and turned to make my way through the orchard toward Avalon Cottage. The strangeness of the episode at Wolfpen Two, the inexplicable presence of the raccoon, the animal violence indicated by the trail of blood, the growls of Atalanta and Milo—these returned my mind to the old narrative I had read and mulled over, puzzled and shuddering, through many of the hours just before and just after midnight. As I passed between rows of winter-naked apple trees, I could not evade the feeling that eyes followed me. Strangely, I suppose, I hoped that those eyes belonged to the wolves I knew and to no one or to no thing I did not know.

Sunday, March 9

FOUR

When the shadow stuttered the gray-green light that glowed in the corner of his eye, he glanced at the window but saw nothing. He turned back to his book, not reading again but holding his breath and listening. *All quiet*, he decided, *and all well.* Perhaps the shadow had been that of the red-tailed hawk recently hunting this side of Five-Finger Mountain. He began to read again.

> *... One of them, in truth—it was he with the blood-stain on his band—seemed, unless his gestures were misunderstood, to hold the parchment in his immediate keeping, but was prevented, by his two partners in the mystery, from—*

"Mr. Reeves?"

At the first syllable, he closed the book on his finger to hold his place and lifted his head to listen. The voice sounded small and distant, but as distinct as if she stood just outside the door.

"Plumer Reeves?"

Quick and quiet he rose and in the space of a breath stood a step inside his open front door, where he held back in shadow and looked out, seeing nothing at first. The mountainside was still, unusually soundless, and he rebuked himself for not having taken notice of the deep quiet before.

"Are you Plumer Reeves?"

He tracked the voice and spotted a face like an early blossom on the yet winter-bare pink-shell azalea across the yard.

Eighteen-, nineteen-year-old girl, he thought.

But after the gentle glow that surrounded his reading roost, he found it difficult to keep her in focus at this distance in the harsh bright-white light reflected from the remnants of last week's minor blizzard that had conspired with an accompanying period of below-normal temperatures to keep the mountains—his front yard included—mostly covered since, despite this day's warmer blue skies.

"I am," he said and stepped through the doorway to stand squinting on the porch. "And who might you—"

He lost the face as she disappeared with no glimpse or whisper of movement. Holding his breath, he scanned the tree line and listened, but he seemed again alone on his mountainside.

The flesh on his arms and at the back of his neck goosed and stood hairs on end.

"Livvy," she said from thicker undergrowth uphill to the right. "Livvy Goforth."

"I'm pleased to meet you, Miss Goforth," he said. "You can call me Plumer."

"Livvy."

"We have unusual names in common, Miss Livvy," he said.

No response returned from the mountainside quiet.

Then, "Just Livvy."

She seemed to be making her way back to the freer spaces beneath the trees directly in front of him, but he still couldn't get a fix on her.

"All right," he said.

"I hear you help folks. Help 'em with sundry troubles."

She didn't stutter, but he heard something halting in her voice, as if it were unaccustomed to much use.

"Finding folks and such like," she finished.

This time he couldn't even tell where her voice came from, and his head momentarily swam with vertigo. He opened his eyes wide and sniffed and touched the doorframe with his left hand. "I try to help when I can," he said. "But right now, I can't even find you."

"I'm right here," she said with a sudden playful exasperation that somehow conjured her as she appeared down the yard to his left, in the shade of the tin canopy that covered his wood pile.

His flesh prickled again.

Strands of long, golden blonde hair drifted across her face with a breeze he couldn't feel from the porch. She wore a too-big jacket of old denim over a knee-length black shift. Her calves were bare, and the tops of her brogans barely showed above the sun-bright patch of snow in which she stood.

She brushed the hair from her face. "Uncle Terry's dead, and I need you to find him for me."

Again, the clarity and presence of her voice struck him, as it should have been muted by the snow or tugged away by the breeze that kept her blonde hair in gentle motion.

"Uncle Terry?" he asked, remembering she'd said her last name was Goforth. "Terry Goforth from up Lonesome Mountain? He's your uncle?"

"Yes, sir, he was."

"Did you walk all the way here from Lonesome?"

"Yes, sir, I did."

Plumer palmed down his black beard. "Will you come in and warm yourself, Livvy?"

She brushed blond wisps from her face again. "Reckon I will if it's all right."

"It's all right," he said as she started toward him across the snow-covered yard. He held the screen door wider as she came up the steps without a single clomp from her brogans. "I'll fix us some tea."

She stomped slush from her feet at the threshold and walked past him into the living room. "Tea's fine," she said, "if you ain't got coffee."

"I have coffee." He smiled to himself and scanned the edge of the yard and woods. Then he closed the door and turned to find her standing straight and grave, facing him, with hands clasped in front of her.

Something over five and a half feet, he reckoned. "Sit anywhere you like, Livvy," he said. "I'll put the coffee on."

As he stepped into his kitchen, she followed.

"I don't sit much, except on my front steps and at my kitchen table."

He went about preparing the coffee, smiling to himself again. "Well, it's a tad chilly to sit on my front steps, so you can sit here at my kitchen table if you like." He heard neither a response nor a scraping of chair legs, but when he half turned, she already sat at the table, hands invisible in her lap and green eyes watching him. He froze for just a moment before forcing himself to turn back to the coffeemaker.

That's Kayla's.

"I should sit another place," she said.

"What? No, you're fine," he said, but as the coffee began to drip and he turned again to the table, she'd moved to a seat he couldn't remember anybody sitting in before. He put a hand on the back of his usual chair as another wave of something like vertigo momentarily blurred his vision and flashed through his head from ear to ear.

She watched him slide back his chair and sit down.

"You said Terry Goforth was your uncle," he said.

She raised an eyebrow.

"You said 'was' like he isn't anymore."

"Well, he still is, I reckon, even though he's dead."

"But you said you wanted me to find him."

"I do."

"Okay, well, how do you know he's dead if you don't know where he is?"

Her eyes finally left his as she dropped her gaze to the yellow

Formica tabletop. "I know," she said and pushed strands of her long blonde hair behind her ear. "Just do."

He studied her profile and, despite her age and height and gravity, saw the girl in it. "All right," he said. "It's all right." He drew a deep breath, leaned backwards and right, and balanced the chair on one back leg—*Kayla doesn't like*—and released the breath as he swiveled to his left and set the chair back down on all fours—*didn't like*—and braced his palms on his thighs and stood. "When was the last time you saw him?"

She turned to meet his eyes again. "When he left the house last Tuesday, right after lunch, and he ain't been back."

Plumer tried to situate this day in relation to last Tuesday.

"Today's Sunday," she said. "It's going on a week."

He turned and took down two coffee mugs from the cabinet above the coffeemaker and poured each three-quarters full. Then he drew and released another breath to steady himself, turned, and set a cup in front of her.

"Thank you," she said.

"I have sugar and milk if you want either."

"No, thank you."

He sat down in his chair again and rested his forearms on the tabletop and held his cup between his hands. "Maybe he got snowed in somewhere."

"No."

He lifted his cup to sip and looked at her over the rim. "So, you live with your uncle Terry?"

Her eyebrow raised again, and she seemed about to smile. "He lived with me," she said and leaned forward with head bowed. She let her eyelids close and drew in a deep breath, as if praying over her coffee. After a moment, her eyes opened again, and she seemed to lose herself in thought or maybe in her own reflection from the steaming black surface. Then she raised the cup and took a sip. "Big Granny give me the house when she walked on." She gently lowered her cup to the tabletop.

Plumer tried to see her uncle in Livvy's profile. He'd gone to school with Terry Goforth from first grade to sometime during the tenth, and he remembered the boy as often laughing and sometimes drooling, chubby and perpetually red-cheeked. He'd been smart in some ways, most of which didn't have to do with books. He always seemed to need to be touching a body—from holding hands on buddy-system walks to the lunchroom and on field trips to scuffling on old gym mats and in the playground grass, from playful pokes and bear hugs in the locker room to bullying shoves and punches in the Methodist graveyard after school. And then he'd dropped out when he turned sixteen, and all the fondling and fighting stopped as far as Plumer was concerned.

"Big Granny was your grandmother?" he said.

Livvy looked up from her coffee. "No, sir. My great-grandmother."

"Would that be Nettie Goforth?"

"Yes, sir," Livvy said. "Big Granny's real name was Agnes, and she begat Elizabeth, called Betty. Betty begat Annette, called Little Nettie. And Little Nettie begat me, Olivia called Livvy."

He smiled but couldn't remember an Annette Goforth in the grades just ahead of or just behind Terry and him. "So, if you don't mind me asking, where's your mother and your grandmother?"

"Gone," Livvy said. "Neither lived here past the age of twenty."

"I'm sorry to hear that."

"They're just gone, Plumer. Run off. Could be dead, I reckon, but I don't think they are." She downed the last of her coffee and stood up. "It's Uncle Terry that's true dead and needs finding."

Plumer stood, picked up both coffee cups, emptied his in the drain, and set them in the sink. Then he turned. "If you don't think he's snowed in somewhere, what makes you think that he's not just run off like his sister and mother did?"

Livvy stared at him, again pushing a strand of hair behind her ear.

"Okay, I'll see what I can do," he said. "You told me Terry left after lunch last Tuesday. Did he leave by himself, or did somebody pick him up?"

"By himself, in our old Ford." She began buttoning her denim jacket. "A pickup."

"Color? Tag number?"

"Not much color left except rust. But I reckon it used to be navy blue." She pulled her collar up around her ears. "Don't know about the tag." She walked to the doorway between the kitchen and the living room. "Thank you for the coffee and for finding Uncle Terry."

"Let me grab my keys," he said. "It'll be black dark and lots colder before you get home on foot."

He stepped through the doorway from the kitchen into the bedroom and then back again, keys to his Jeep in hand. "Livvy?" He continued through the kitchen and the living room, to the front door, and out onto the porch. "Livvy?" He saw fresh footprints that went straight from the bottom of the porch steps across the yard past the Jeep and into the trees. He held his breath, looked and listened. But he could catch neither sight nor sound of her.

Gone. He felt again the brief swirl of vertigo that had accompanied her strange visitation.

FIVE

The man sat with his right elbow braced on the bar at Cowboy's, a lounge on Old Mars Hill Highway. With his right hand wrapped around a warming bottle of Budweiser, he scanned the room, careful to let his gaze drift without apparent thought and without hardening into a stare at any of the few patrons present on a late Sunday afternoon.

The bartender stood with his back to the barroom and his eyes on the Thunder/Lakers game. At the opposite end of the bar, a young woman sat in front of a screen and played a video game. Two men in caps and flannel shirts open over big-bellied T-shirts played the middle of three pool tables. Their women sat at a nearby round-top table, smoking and chatting and watching the back and forth between their men. Beyond these four, a drum kit and a dusty Peavey amplifier sat on the stage where a lank-haired young man in jeans and a long-sleeved T-shirt put together a karaoke machine for later in the evening. Everybody had a bottle of beer within reach.

"Shit," the young woman at the video game said as the machine emitted an echoey Vincent Price laugh. She stood, wiped her palms on the ripped thighs of faded blue jeans, and walked in the man's direction. Wavy red hair fell loose around her shoulders and breasts, vivid against her black T-shirt. Her eyes moved down and up his body as she approached but stopped short of meeting his.

Late twenties, early thirties, the man thought. He loosened the grip on his beer bottle and straightened his back.

"Shit," the bartender said. "Come on, Durant."

Without breaking her subtle sashay, the red-haired woman set her beer on the bar beside the man's and passed by him and out through a door to his left.

He looked down at her half-empty bottle, glanced up at the basketball game on TV, at the profile of the bartender, and then turned to the pool players just as one of the big bellies leaned over the table and clacked the eight-ball into a side pocket.

"Shit." The other tossed his cue onto the table top.

"Don't rip my felt," the bartender said without turning from the game.

The pool players' women blew smoke up through their bangs and mashed out their cigarettes in the same ashtray.

The amplified voice of the lank man on the stage said, "Test, test." With the microphone in his right hand, he leaned over the system controls and adjusted a knob with his left. "Testing."

Keeping an eye on the eyes around him, the man reached slowly into his shirt pocket, drew out a small white pill, and dropped it in the redhead's beer. Then he wrapped his hand around his own bottle and continued watching the room.

After a few moments, the door at his left elbow opened, and then the redhead stood beside him, smelling of cigarette.

He turned to look at her profile and saw a wisp of smoke drift from between her parted lips.

"This place is dead," she said and turned to look up into his eyes.

"I was expecting more of a crowd," he said. "After people have been cooped up by the storm."

"They'll probably come out for karaoke."

"Probably."

"Thanks for watching my beer," she said as she mounted the barstool beside his. "You didn't, like, put anything in it, did you?" She took a swig before he could answer. She pulled the bottle from her lips, looked at it, then set it down again and held out her hand. "Kandy Wood."

He shook her hand—"Nice name"—and released it. "Nice name for a nice girl?"

"Nice woman," she said. She took his hand again and turned the palm toward her, then placed the heel of hers to the heel of his, looked at them together for a moment, and shook her head. "I'm married, and I've got a kid."

"Where are they?"

"She's with my mom, and Fish's in jail." She took another swig of her beer. "Prison, I guess."

"Fish?"

"Yep. Fisher Wood, serial sex offender." She turned the beer bottle between both hands and then began peeling off the label in strips. "Peeping tom, indecent exposure, and criminal trespassing." When the man didn't comment, she added, "Serial asshole, too."

"You've got a right to be angry."

"I am so fucking angry," she said. "Pardon my French."

They sat together without speaking until both finished the beers.

"How forward—" She stopped and blinked and cleared her throat. "How forward would it be if I said I wanted to get out of here with you?" She fed two strips of torn label into the mouth of her nearly empty bottle. "If I said, like, I want some fucking revenge sex?"

He took out his wallet, removed a ten, and flattened it on the bar. "How forward would it be if I said you can take all your anger out on me?"

"Damn." She slid off the barstool to her feet and grabbed a fistful of his shirt. "Damn," she said again. She looked up at him through half-lidded eyes. "Let's go."

Monday, March 10

SIX

Gabriel Tanner

As it turned out, I couldn't visit Christabel Island for almost a week, on the Monday after the storm. Ulysses had snowed and iced us in for all of Wednesday. Eliza and I enjoyed an energetic oversleep in our house on Genesis Road and then fixed ourselves a sweet-and-savory brunch of fried chicken and waffles with butter and maple syrup. Fortunately, we didn't lose power, so she was able to catch up on some of her recorded shows through the afternoon and I was able to make some progress on the weekly update to the *Runion Recorder* website, taking breaks to play my guitar and work on a new song I was writing.

On Thursday, the main roads were mostly passable, and I made my weekly run to the printer to pick up the hard copies of the newspaper. When I got back to town, the *Recorder*'s one full-time reporter, Eden Mackenzie Lane, aka Edie-Mac, our handful of Runion State interns, and I distributed papers to the post office, commercial locations around Madison County, and coin-operated newsracks in the towns. Eliza was able to reschedule a couple of the Wednesday cancellations for Thursday evening, so I stayed late in my office on the other end of Main Street from her salon, getting a jump on a couple of pieces for the following week's edition. I called it a night when she showed up and pecked on the front window with a key, and we rode home together.

By Friday evening, the snow had melted from everywhere but shaded spots and north-facing slopes, and on Saturday, we took most of the day to celebrate my fifty-fifth birthday. I wrote some in the morning while Eliza did a couple of heads at the shop. After we finished our work, we ate lunch with my mother in Jewel Hill before driving to Asheville, where we caught the last matinee showing of *The Grand Budapest Hotel* and then hurried to Weaverville to meet my cousin Cutter and his wife Rendy for supper at Stoney Knob Café.

Sunday, we enjoyed a rather less energetic sleeping in, and the rest of the day followed suit: breakfasting on buttered toast and coffee, listening to '80s music on Spotify, making tuna sandwiches for lunch and drinking our last bottles of Cold Mountain. We spent the warmest part of the afternoon on the deck, where Eliza cut my hair, trimmed my beard and eyebrows, and clipped tufts from my ears and stragglers from my nostrils, where men my age are prone to get hairy. Then I played guitar and sang for her until we went to eat supper with her mother. Afterwards, we barely made it into bed before we were asleep.

Monday morning found me early at my desk, where until ten o'clock or so I pursued a few mostly routine tasks. I began tinkering with the layout of the week's edition and then edited some community pieces emailed to me over the weekend. Dr. Caldwell Rowe, Runion State Professor of History, sent the third installment of a piece on the massive French Broad River flooding that happened on the third of March in 1902. The RSU office of Student Activities & Organizations submitted a final brief article describing alternative spring break opportunities and soliciting last-minute financial support for some of these. An email from Runion High included items covering everything from the previous week's athletic events and results to the next week's lunch menu. I downloaded all these to a single file named for the upcoming edition and then emailed a couple of regular contributors to remind them of looming deadlines.

"Somebody's here to see you," Edie-Mac said from the doorway.

I looked up from the computer screen. "Who is it?"

"Plumer Reeves?" she said, looking at somebody out of sight for confirmation. Then with a nod, "Yes, Plumer Reeves."

"Thanks," I said. "Ask him to come on in."

The man who stepped into my office appeared to be about half a generation younger than I was, maybe around forty. I judged him to be somewhat under six feet tall—maybe five foot nine or ten. He wasn't skinny, but he also wasn't even in the same area code as my two hundred forty-five pounds. His full beard and the hair brushed back from his face and just touching his shoulders were black. He wore a cotton button-down shirt that was beige and collarless, its tails hanging over the waist of brown herringbone wool trousers. Except for the Columbia hiking boots with their red laces, he looked as if he could be a model in a vintage clothing catalogue, but he carried off the whole outfit as if those were his everyday clothes. He approached my desk and switched a matching herringbone tweed newsboy cap to his left hand.

"Mr. Tanner," he said as I stood up.

"Mr. Reeves," I said as he shook my hand. "Have a seat."

"Thanks." He lowered himself onto one of the cushioned ladderbacks I provided for guests and interviewees.

I sat back down and swiveled my chair from facing the computer to facing him. "Kind of hard to believe we were snowed in just a few days ago," I said.

"Yeah, it's spring all of a sudden." He glanced around my office, at the walls and the shelves.

"What can I do for you, Mr. Reeves?"

"Plumer," he said. "One *m*, no *b*."

"All right, call me Gabe." I saw Edie-Mac disappear from the doorway and realized that this visitor would delay our staff-of-two meeting that was scheduled for ten-thirty and mess with both our schedules for rest of the day. "What can I do for you?" I asked again.

Edie-Mac reappeared in the doorway and interrupted. "Mr. Reeves, Gabe made coffee this morning if you want some. It should still be pretty good."

"No, thanks," he said. "I don't intend to take up much of your time."

"You're not asking me if I want some?" I said.

"Ha, good one, boss," Edie-Mac said. "I promised Eliza I'd keep an eye on your caffeine intake." She disappeared from the doorway.

Smiling, I turned back to Reeves, who sat unsmiling and stiff. I adjusted my position in the chair and tried to remember what I knew about this man, which turned out to be more than I realized—that he lived somewhere high up on the northwest-facing side of Five Finger Mountain, the side opposite Mel's MacOde Farm; that he'd married local artist and art teacher Kayla Logan early in the 2000s; that she'd disappeared on her forty-first birthday in 2012; that he'd been cleared of any wrongdoing related to her disappearance; that folks often sought his help to find their missing people and stuff although, strangely, he'd never been able to find his missing wife. I hoped none of this showed on my face. "What can I do for you?" I asked a third time.

"Do you know the Goforths up on Lonesome?" he asked.

"There are a lot of Goforths in the vicinity of Lonesome."

"Terry Goforth, about my age, and his niece Livvy."

"Well, about the best I can say is that I know of them, but I don't know them." I pulled at the beard on my chin a moment. "I'm pretty sure I was in school with a Betty Goforth, but I want to say that she got pregnant and dropped out before we graduated." I continued tugging at the gray whiskers. "I ran across mention of their matriarch, Agnes—Nettie, I think they called her—several times recently during some research in our archives. She was quite the community leader for a time."

"Terry's gone missing," Reeves said. "And Livvy came to my cabin yesterday to ask me to find him."

I leaned forward and put my elbows on the desk and lay my forearms alongside each other. "Well, I've heard you have a gift for that kind of thing." Before I could think how it might sound, I added, "Generally."

Something flared up behind his eyes but disappeared just as quickly. "Yes, generally," he echoed, almost whispering, and then leaned forward as well. "Have you heard anything about Terry?"

"Not a thing," I said, feeling a bit relieved that we hadn't gotten hung up on my mistake with the word *generally*.

"I don't take your paper," he said. "No offense intended."

"None taken."

"Does he show up in your pages a lot? I'm wondering about the crime blotter, if you still include that."

"He has, but I wouldn't say he's a regular inhabitant."

"What do you know about Livvy?"

His sudden change of focus stopped me for a moment. Then I answered, "Not much of anything, really." I heard the soft arpeggio of tones that indicated the arrival of an email. "What do you know about her?"

He braced his hands on his knees as if ready to stand. "She's an odd bird," he said. "But I'll have to see her again to get a better idea of just how she's odd."

Not how odd she is but how she's odd, I thought.

Then he rose from his chair, and I followed him up. He didn't turn to go but stood with an arm across his chest and his bearded chin cupped in a palm. "She says that Terry's been gone for almost a week and that he's dead."

"What?"

"She says he's dead, and she wants me to find the body."

"What—" At first, I couldn't figure how to finish that thought. Then, "What makes her say that?"

"I don't know," Reeves said. "I tried to get her to tell me, but she wouldn't. Or couldn't."

I heard the soft tones of another email's arrival. "If he's been missing almost a week now, we ought to let the sheriff know," I said. "Maybe tell Davis Boyce first."

"Yeah, I reckon I'll walk across the street and see if he's at his desk."

"So, you're taking the case?"

"I'll at least look around. Ask around."

I pulled my phone from my pocket. "Do you have a number where I can reach you if I happen to learn anything?" I picked up my business card from a tidy stack on the desk and handed it to him.

"I'll get in touch with mine after while," he said and extended his hand.

I shook it, and he turned and left without another word. I heard Edie-Mac say something to him as he passed her desk, but I didn't hear what she said or if he responded.

Then she appeared in my doorway. "Quick meeting today?"

"Sure," I said and motioned her in.

But she disappeared from the doorway as she'd done earlier—to retrieve something from her desk, I figured—and returned with her laptop and a half cup of coffee she handed across the desk to me. "I won't tell if you won't." She winked. "But let's not make this a habit."

After our brief meeting, I put my desk in order and was about to head out for a bite of lunch before my visit to Christabel Island and Avalon Orchards when I remembered the two emails that arrived while I'd been talking with Plumer Reeves. I jiggled the mouse to wake up the screen and read the subject line of the item topping my inbox—"Buncombe County Sheriff's Office Seeks Missing Woman."

The message identified the woman as Dolly Ham, a custodial worker at UNC-Asheville. She lived in an apartment on Breckenridge Parkway in the New Bridge area of Buncombe, but she'd last been seen at the Ingles in Mars Hill on Sunday, the second of March, wearing blue jeans and a black leather jacket over the top of a white taekwondo dobok with a blue belt. She'd been missing for just over a week. The accompanying black-and-white photo, dated the previous October, showed a thirty-seven-year-old woman with short hair spiked above a narrow face and a half-smile that hinted at some dental problems. Her stats included green or hazel eyes, the spiked brown hair, a height listed as 5'10", and a weight of one hundred forty-seven pounds.

I didn't usually put such items in the print edition of the *Recorder*, given that they usually resolved themselves before the weekly could have any effect on the search. But I made myself a note to upload the photo and a summary to the online version after I finished on Christabel Island.

"I'm headed upriver to Marshall," Edie-Mac called from the front office. "See you tomorrow."

"All right," I said. "Be safe." I heard the front door open and close.

I returned to my inbox and clicked on the other new item, this one with the subject line, "FOR IMMEDIATE RELEASE: CASTING ANNOUNCEMENT – THE COVE to Film in Hot Springs/Runion, NC Area 6/21 – 7/18." The email came from Tona B. Dahlquist Casting, and the message was short. The much-anticipated film adaptation of novelist Ron Rash's *Serena* was set to be released within the next year, and an unnamed production company appeared to be getting busy on an adaptation of Rash's most recent novel *The Cove*, which, I remembered, is set in Mars Hill around the time of World War I. The call was for "classic faces of Appalachia," people who could easily assume the look of mountain and smalltown folk from a hundred years before.

That won't be too hard, I thought, and pictured somebody like Plumer Reeves fitting the call to a tee.

The notice included an email address to which interested folks might send two cellphone photos, one close-up and one full-length, along with name and number, age and address, height and weight, sizes for shoes and clothing, and descriptions of any visible markings—born with or paid for—they might have.

They also wanted buckboard wagons, if anybody had one or two forgotten under layers of barn dust. And, of course, they would need horses to pull them and to ride in the streets of an early twentieth-century Appalachian town.

I heard the front door open and close again and guessed that Edie-Mac had forgotten something. I pushed back my desk chair, wondering about the casting call and whether or not Eliza and I might do to *swell a progress* and maybe *start a scene or two*, surprised at how easily T.S. Eliot's words came back to my fifty-five-year-old mind.

A body—stocky and somewhat short and decidedly not Edie-Mac's—suddenly stood in my office doorway.

I startled for half a second before I recognized him. "Jubal," I said. "What brings you down from the Ivory Tower?"

"The usual," he said, his smile flashing in the middle of his immaculately trimmed and graying beard. "A growling stomach."

"Like calls to like." I stood and smacked the sides of my belly with both hands. Then, "Hey, I just got something you and Caldwell might be interested in." I began telling him about the casting call, but he interrupted.

"Caldwell will want to do it for sure," he said. "But the production company already got in touch with me about working on the film."

"Really? Doing what?"

"Apparently the novel has a flutist that plays a big part in the story, and they're hiring me to coach the actor, whoever that's going to be."

"That's awesome, Jubal," I said. "They're paying you?"

"They offered fifty dollars an hour for whenever I'm on set."

He rubbed a palm across the short-cropped hair on his pate. "I had no idea how much to ask for."

"I wouldn't have known either," I said. "Have you read *The Cove*?"

"I was going to ask you the same thing."

"I haven't," I said. "I've read most of Rash's other novels and a couple of his short story collections, but not this latest one yet." I bent to the mouse and put the computer to sleep. "I wonder if they'd want to hire Eliza as a stylist."

"Maybe," Jubal said. "I think I'll swing by the campus library and see if they have the book." His eyes twinkled, and he bounced his brows up and down a couple of times. "Maybe," he said again and patted his belly. "But first things first."

"Stonehouse, Rio Burrito, or Pizzeria?"

"I'm feeling pizza and a salad bar," he said. "Okay with you?"

"Again, like calls to like."

SEVEN

Plumer Reeves drove his Jeep up Lonesome Mountain Road, looking for the Goforth place. He didn't have an address, so he was checking for names hand-painted on mailboxes. As he approached the Islamic Center on his right and slowed to take it in, something caught in the corner of his eye. He looked up to his left and saw Livvy Goforth sitting on the front porch steps of a weathered board-and-batten farmhouse. He braked hard and swerved right into the upper entrance to the mosque, swung down through its parking lot, and pulled across the narrow two-lane into Livvy's roughhewn driveway, stopping the Jeep just off the blacktop rather than following the drive up to the right and behind the house. He geared to reverse, pulled up the emergency brake, cut the engine, and got out.

"You should've waited until today to come see me," he said as he climbed the homemade stone steps from the driveway to the small front yard.

Livvy looked at him and tilted her head slightly, pulled a few strands of her straight golden blonde hair from across her face and tucked them behind her ear. Today she was barefoot and wore faded, straight-leg blue jeans and a green Runion High Ridgerunners sweatshirt.

"You would've had better hiking weather," he said, arriving at the foot of the steps up to the porch.

"But you wouldn't have been home. You've been gone all morning."

Plumer froze for a moment and then smiled. "I probably would've been there if you hadn't come yesterday."

A smile thinned her lips. "There's that, I reckon," she said and patted the step beside her. "Come up."

He climbed the steps and turned and stood a few moments to take in the mosque from this vantage point, thinking how, apart from mostly minor detailing, it seemed not nearly so strange as many in the community thought it to be. Then he pinched both legs of his trousers, hiked them up, and sat. He stretched his left leg straight down the steps, kept the right leg crooked, and clasped his hands around that knee. "There ever any problems over there?" he asked, indicating the mosque with the flick of a finger.

She didn't respond at first. She turned and looked at him. "They had some trouble early on from a few folks. Big Granny and me never had a problem with them, and those early troubles were soon put a stop to. They're good people."

He wanted to ask how the problems had been stopped, but her tone didn't invite such questions. "What about Terry?" he asked instead. "Did he get along with them?"

"He never had any real problems with them, but that didn't stop him fretting as if he did." She still looked at Plumer. "Lord knows what he heard out yonder from them he hung out with and the television he looked at in this tavern or that." She lifted her face toward the sky and closed her eyes. "That's where he took up fretting that they'd done something to him or were about to."

"Anything in particular recently?" Plumer said.

She took a deep breath, turned her face toward him again, and opened her eyes. "Not with the Muslims," she said. "Here lately he's been scareder of Democrats and liberals than of them yonder or even of communists, haints, and monsters."

"You don't have a TV?" he said.

"Do you?"

"Fair enough," he said. He let his own gaze roam beyond the mosque to clouds that mimicked the shapes of the blue ridges layered into the distance. He picked out the last ridgeline on the near side of the French Broad and the first on the far side, beyond which stood Five Finger Mountain. "You didn't really walk all the way to my place and back yesterday, did you?"

"I ain't telling."

"Fair enough," he said again. He bent his straight leg and planted both feet on the step two below his seat and leaned forward, bracing his forearms on his thighs and staring for a moment at the sparse grass in the front yard. "I don't think I've seen Terry, except at a distance, since he quit high school. What was he like these days?"

Livvy braced her palms against the step they sat on and stretched both legs straight out in front of her, bare feet touching and toes pointing toward the crescent moon atop the mosque. Then she drew her legs in again and assumed a sitting position that mirrored his. "He was lonely," she said. "He's been lost and mixed up ever since Big Granny died, and that's been almost seven years ago." She bowed her head and released a bead of bubbly spit that fell between her thighs and landed with a pip on the step between the one she sat on and the one she planted her feet on. "And he was confused." She raised her head again and looked toward the horizon. "I think he couldn't understand why his mother and his sister had left him here and why Big Granny left the house to me." She paused. "And there was other, private stuff he was wrestling with, but he never talked to me about it."

"I guess all that would be confusing," Plumer said. "For a guy his age not to be the man—"

"I don't think age is such a big thing," she said and stood suddenly and brushed off the seat of her pants.

He rose to his feet, too.

"And I don't think being a man is either," she added and turned to face him. "I owe you a coffee. You want one?"

Only a single vehicle passed from the time he'd arrived until they were seated on the steps again, coffee cups in hand—a dusty silver pickup moving slowly up the mountain. The driver had been looking toward the mosque, so Plumer hadn't seen his face.

"You don't get much traffic up this way," he said.

"Lonesome Mountain, Plumer."

"Fair enough," he said a third time and sipped his coffee. "Do you know who your uncle hung out with these days?"

"We didn't talk much, and he never brought anybody here to the house. I figure he knew less and less people these last few years." She leaned back and set her cup on the wood floor of the porch. "I think more and more he went around with strangers."

"Strangers? In Runion?"

"Reckon not. Maybe all the way in Asheville or maybe along the interstate from Mars Hill over into Johnson City."

Plumer tried to conjure an image of the teenage Terry Goforth he'd known almost twenty-five years before as a grown man just into his forties. He could picture the pack Terry had run with and how, like Livvy suggested, it dwindled as guys got married or moved away or grew up or died. He tried to picture Terry with a girlfriend, a woman, but he couldn't do so, having no memory of him with a crush on any girl in junior high or high school. He thought it possible that the death of Nettie Goforth—the only parental figure and steadying influence in the life of a sensual mountain boy grown to a sensual manhood—might have opened a deep well of desire and released something that Terry could neither understand nor control.

"You ought not be thinking along such lines," Livvy said with her eyes on the car that had appeared at the front door of the mosque.

Startled from his reverie and the direction it was taking, Plumer looked at her profile and saw that she didn't appear angry or tense. "Well," he said, "if you think you know what I was thinking, then they might somehow be thoughts you've had yourself." He turned and put his cup on the porch beside hers.

"You and Terry have lived here alone together these seven years since your great-grandmother passed on?"

"Like I said, you ought not to be thinking about what you're thinking about." She waved at the tall dark-skinned man who had unfolded from the car in the gravel lot across Lonesome Mountain Road. When the man smiled and waved in return and then unlocked the front door and went in, Livvy turned to look at Plumer. "I'm not a thing to be messed with, and Uncle Terry's been long aware of that."

For a moment, her green eyes held something he couldn't identify, and he felt a freezing like fear in the pit of his stomach. But then her eyes changed and warmed him.

"You need not be afraid," she said and looked again toward the mosque.

He remembered the strangeness of yesterday's first meeting—how she'd moved through the woods beyond the edge of his yard without any sound or so much as a shaken bough or bush, how she'd seemed to disappear when their meeting was over, and how, in between arrival and departure, she seemed able to sense or maybe even read his thoughts, as she seemed to have just done again.

"That was Dr. Baddour that went in over there a minute ago," she said. "He was the first one I met fifteen years back of this when they moved in."

"I know him," Plumer said. "I like him." He took a deep breath and blew it out through his nose. "Listen, I hope you don't mind, but I spoke to Deputy Boyce before I came up here."

"I don't mind."

"He said you need to file a missing person report. Said he'll go ahead and put out the word about the missing truck."

"All right, I'll go down there tomorrow."

"Walking?"

"It ain't that far," she said. "And it's all downhill."

"I could come up and give you a ride," Plumer said. "Or I

could pick you up in town after you do the paperwork. Maybe we could begin to look around a little bit."

She reached back and picked up her cup and then sat for a while without responding to his idea or saying anything else. Then, "I want to talk about something, but I'm gonna get another cup first. You want a refill?"

"Better not. I'd likely be up half the night."

Without another word, she stood, scooped up his empty cup as she rose, turned, and moved toward the front door. "Be right back. Holler if you change your mind about the refill." Then she disappeared into the house.

Another car pulled into the lot across the two-lane. One squat young man emerged from the back seat and went into the mosque. Two others remained in the front seats with the windows rolled down. In quick succession, seven more vehicles arrived, each carrying from one to four occupants, who likewise remained where they were with the windows open. Then a man began to sing inside the mosque, a haunting melody of long-held vowels and intricate trills through intervals odd to Plumer's ear. All the car doors seemed to open at the same time as the screen door behind him opened, and the men passed into the mosque, several of them turning to wave at Livvy as she returned to her place beside him on the step. With a nod to her, the last man pulled the double doors closed.

Livvy sat quiet for a moment, holding her cup with both hands and sipping the coffee. "It's Dhuhr prayer," she said at last. "The midday prayer."

Plumer sat and listened to the distant drone of men's voices speaking together in measured phrases. He couldn't make out the words, not that he would have known their meaning even if he could hear them clearly.

"You lost somebody, too," Livvy said. "Like the way I lost my grandmother and mother. Not knowing if they're dead or alive."

He looked at her. "If you don't know whether Betty and Little Nettie are alive or dead, how can you be so sure about Terry?"

"I told you, I just know." She turned to look back at him. "And you just shied from what I said."

He saw the way her green eyes caught the slant of early afternoon light and thought how different their effect from his memory of Kayla's silver-blue eyes that had sparkled like stars or airplanes in the night sky, like ripples of sunlight on flowing water. Kayla's eyes—the eyes of an artist—observed and absorbed. They could be distant. They could take his measure and see through him to the canvas. Livvy's eyes glowed like those of a predator in the night woods, like a porchlight left on until dawn. The eyes of a hunter, a seeker, they watched, tracked, and pursued. He'd already learned that they could be inscrutable. They could burn through his defenses and see into him rather than through him.

He cleared his throat and wished he'd accepted that second cup of coffee. "Yes, Kayla," he said. "She left me almost two years ago."

When he said this, she turned her gaze away, back toward the prayerful stillness of the mosque.

"Did you know her?" he asked.

"Knew of her, I reckon, but didn't know her." She paused and then continued. "Uncle Terry spoke of a Kayla some when I was little, I remember."

"He did?"

"Love dreams, you know," she said. "A crush of sorts." Without turning, she offered her coffee cup to him. "Sip?"

He was surprised at the warmth the cup still radiated, took a slurpy sip and found it hot but not scalding.

The sound of the men at their unfamiliar prayers still washed over them, now and then punctuated by staccato riffs of birdsong. Whenever the breeze swung around to come down from higher up Lonesome Mountain, it carried the solid chug of a tractor.

"Tell me," he said and stopped.

She turned to him. "What?"

"I don't know how to ask it."

She looked away as the double doors of the mosque opened and the small group of men began to stream out. All seemed to acknowledge her in some way: a brilliant smile in a dark face, a wave, a nod, a slight bow. She returned these with a smile and nods of her own.

Plumer glanced back and forth from her profile to the men getting in their cars and wondered about what he saw. He thought the exchange could be neighborly and decided certainly an element of that existed in it. But it also seemed ceremonial in some way that he couldn't quite apprehend. The moment contained something sociable, and yet it felt somehow akin to their prayers, too.

When the doors were closed and locked and all the cars from last to first were gone, her voice again startled him out of his reverie. "You want me to tell you if your Kayla is alive or dead."

He realized he still held her coffee cup and handed it back to her.

She took it and sipped. "I can't do that."

"Why not?" He stood and moved somewhat stiffly down the steps and into the yard. "Can you say why not?"

"I didn't know your Kayla. I didn't know my grandmother Betty or my mother Little Nettie." She stopped and drew a deep breath, then let it out slowly. "But I knew Uncle Terry, lived with him long enough to—" She stopped again. "I told you I wouldn't tell you how I know he's dead. That's really to say I can't tell you, 'cause I don't know how that part of it works. Not for sure anyway."

"That part of what?" he said from the foot of the steps and yet almost eye-level with her. "What is this 'it'?"

She looked at him for a long moment, her green eyes searching his face and not straying to either mosque or mountains.

"I don't know what to call it," she said at last. "Have you ever heard of some old granny woman having 'the sight'?"

"I've run across it in books," he said. "There's an old woman has it in a couple of Sharyn McCrumb's novels."

"I've read them, and it's kind of like that." Her gaze slid off his face and down to his chest. "But it's different, too." She closed her eyes and ran a palm back and forth across her forehead, then drank the last of her coffee, turned and set the cup on the porch floor as she'd done earlier. "And more," she said. "It's more than that."

When she turned back to him, he saw the girl in her face as he'd seen it the day before at his kitchen table. He found his shoulders hunched and relaxed them. He felt his jaw clenched and his hands stiff and relaxed them as well.

"Uncle Terry named it 'The Rumbles' when I was little. I don't have another name for it."

"It's all right."

"Big Granny always made me promise not to talk about it, and though she ain't here in body, it's hard for me to speak against her wishes."

"It's all right," he said again. He'd noted the phrase *in body* with a bit of a shiver but said nothing of it. His hands felt like they would shake, so he pushed them down into his pockets. He looked up from her face to the roofline and then to the still-bare trees above. "I'm gonna lose the light if I don't get out looking around." He dropped his gaze back down to her green eyes. "Do you want to ride with me?"

She stood and brushed the seat of her jeans. "No, not today," she said. "Maybe tomorrow or the next, if you don't find him before then." She leaned as if she might stumble down the steps to him, but she steadied. "I feel the need to stay here right now."

EIGHT

Gabriel Tanner

Dr. Jubal Kincaid and I did all the damage we could to the Pizzeria salad bar and buffet, same as we'd done on a fairly regular basis in the nearly fifteen years we'd known each other. Outside on the corner afterwards, I asked if he wanted to ride over to Avalon, but his afternoon was full with an advanced class in twentieth-century American music sandwiched between two student flute lessons. So, we parted on the corner, he to his office on campus and I to my office across the street to check for messages or breaking news. Finding all quiet, I locked the front door, flopped into my car, and drove south on Main Street, blowing the horn three times—*"I love you!"*—as I passed Eliza's salon. At the foot of the hill, I turned right onto NC Highway 209-A and crossed the bridge toward Piney Ridge. In the middle of the third right-turning switchback on the ascent to the ridgeline, a dirt-and-gravel driveway exited the highway blacktop and hugged the mountainside as it descended to the French Broad River. This terminated in a gravel lot just big enough for a school bus turnaround. At the far end of this the Andersons' stand-alone three-car garage stood with all three doors closed. The only vehicle in the lot was a dusty-windowed, cream-colored Chevy Equinox parked to the right, a blue solo canoe strapped to the roof and its grill nosed into kudzu.

I climbed out of the Honda and grabbed my camera, then tucked my notebook and pencil into my shirt pocket and turned away toward the island. Ahead of me, a short, well-manicured trail cut through bulrush, goldenrod, and stinging nettle and forked after twenty feet or so. The right fork led to a wide footbridge that spanned the forty feet of river water flowing between the Piney Ridge shoreline and Christabel Island. The left led to a hand-operated cable ferry for carrying vehicles and large deliveries bound for Avalon Cottage, the orchard, or the new wolf sanctuary.

The wooden footbridge was solid, and my steps reverberated between the island in front and the mainland behind. I kept arms stretched out and my palms dancing close to the rope railings on either side, my brain a little swimmy from the right-to-left movement of the current beneath. In the middle of the footbridge, I stopped and watched the river pass through the channel, the silt-and-rock bottom visible through knee-deep water, shallow enough for wading at most times, as was that in the main channel on the other side of the island, where another cable stretched from shore to shore without a ferry attached, the cable there probably unused for decades if not a century. I scanned for fish and caught glimpses of shadows darting between sky-bright riffles but couldn't get a fix on a distinct shape.

I turned and took a picture of the half of the footbridge between the island and me, catching a bit of the house beyond the trees. Then I pointed the camera upriver toward the south end of the island and snapped a picture of Christabel's headland that rose almost two hundred feet above the water. From there the island's ridge sloped downward past the midpoint, where this bridge connected, to the low-lying north end. I took a few more shots, remembering Mel MacOde once told me that, from a certain vantage point on his family's side of Five Finger Mountain, Christabel's undulating downward slope from south end to north end formed the shape of a woman lying full length on her side, raised up on her elbow with her head resting on an upturned palm. From the mountain in winter, he'd said, the rows of Avalon's leafless apple orchard looked like stitches in her skin.

"Bride of Frankenstein," Mel had said.

"Or maybe Mrs. Gulliver among the Lilliputians," I remembered saying.

At the end of the footbridge, I went down steps made of creosote-darkened railroad ties and landed on the island somewhere in the vicinity of the giant woman's waistline. A walkway of blue-brown sandstone slabs led me downward past a natural grotto and then upward again through a still mostly dormant English garden, at the edge of which I stopped and took some pictures of the house.

Although the building was larger than probably ninety-five percent of the homes in Madison County, it was called Avalon Cottage, a name that always suggested to me something cozier. I'd been here several times during my fifty-five years, but most of what I knew about the place I'd learned either during a third-grade field trip or from Caldwell Rowe's historical pieces for the paper. Avalon Cottage was completed in 1798 by two men named Hucks and Holcroft. They'd come from England and settled on the island with an idea of creating a utopian community—a Pantisocracy—in the mountain wilderness. But I suppose they weren't quite ready to abandon everything to do with the empire, because they built Avalon Cottage in the style of a spacious English country house, with slate tiles on the roof and the exterior walls limewashed white, far different from what the locals were building at the time. Then again, not many locals were around at the time to build much of anything. Hucks and Holcroft constructed their house out of local wood and stone: yellow birch, mountain maple, granite, limestone, marble. Dr. Rowe has cited this construction and its elevated position near the giant woman's hip as the reasons it was the island's only structure to survive the massive flooding of 1902.

Christabel Island and the Avalon compound had once been home to a thriving community of thirty to forty souls, particularly through the hundred years or so between the initial settlement and the 1902 flood, but the three modern-day Andersons had been the sole occupants since the late 1980s. The name Anderson hadn't arrived with the initial influx of English settlers that grew from a handful in 1798 to full strength by 1818. The first Spellman Anderson was a local boy from Piney Ridge. He landed on the island as a sixteen-year-old carpenter in 1855, and before the outbreak of the Civil War, he'd married Sara Landor, youngest granddaughter of William Savage Landor, and become a member of the Pantisocratic community known as Avalon. He watched the maneuvers and machinations of Johnny Reb and Hillbilly Yank from the shore of Christabel or from the partial roof of some building project but remained on the island with Sara and didn't join the war effort on either side. During the hostilities and their violent aftermath, the romantic idealism that had sustained Avalon for more than half a century faded, and Spellman II, the youngest of four, was born into a significantly diminished community in 1873. He was twenty-nine years old when the flood came that swept away the last vestiges of early Avalon, leaving behind only Avalon Cottage, Avalon Orchard, and the remaining Andersons: his mother Sara, two brothers, and a sister, all of whom had left Christabel Island for life elsewhere—or for the afterlife—by 1907. Spellman II shunned Avalon Cottage and built a one-room cabin a little toward the northern end of the island in which he lived the life of Robinson Crusoe for two years before abandoning Christabel altogether to seek a wife among the Runionites across the river. But by June 1910, he found and married Harriet Payne and returned to the island, the orchard, and Avalon Cottage, where Spellman III was born in 1911.

The front storm door opened, and Spellman Anderson IV stepped out with a man I didn't know but assumed to be the driver of the Equinox in the parking lot. As the two men approached along the flagstone walkway that led from the door, I met them in the middle of the front lawn.

"Gabe," Anderson said and extended his hand. "You missed lunch."

"Sorry, I got caught up at the office." I shook his hand and released it. "Dr. Kincaid and I overdid it at the Pizzeria's lunch buffet."

"Gabe," Anderson said again. "This is Austen Caine. Austen, this is Gabriel Tanner, who runs our local newspaper, the *Runion Recorder*."

I noted the size of Caine's hand and the strength in his grip. He stood an inch or two taller than my six feet. I guessed we probably weighed about the same, but his poundage was better distributed than mine, which tended these days to settle toward my belly, hard as I tried to direct it elsewhere. He seemed dressed for safari—brown leather lace-up boots; Dutch white long-sleeved shirt; sage-colored vest and matching trousers, both covered with pockets. A camera hung from one shoulder and a small backpack from the other. Blond-haired and blue-eyed, he looked to be around forty years old.

"Nice to meet you," he said. "I'm guessing our paths will cross some while I'm working in the area."

I started to ask what his work was when Anderson preempted me.

"Austen is the location scout of a film that is to be made in the county. He thinks that Avalon Cottage and Christabel could be used for some scenes."

"Oh yeah, the adaptation of the Ron Rash novel, right?" I said. "*The Cove*?"

"You know about it already?" Caine said.

"The casting agency sent me an email this morning." I glanced over their shoulders and thought I saw the tall silhouette of Ariel Anderson, only child, now an adult, of Spellman and his wife Randi, standing far enough back from the storm door to remain out of the light. "A press release calling for local extras and maybe an old wagon or two."

"I am sure they will find more than enough of our people to swell a progress," Anderson said.

I almost laughed but stopped myself. "I'm sure they will," I said, figuring Spellman Anderson IV should have this moment for his guest, but I could tell the "Prufrock" allusion that had crossed my mind earlier slid past Caine. "I bet we'll be seeing Dr. Rowe on screen. He's got the look."

"And the flair," Anderson said and turned to Caine. "Dr. Caldwell Rowe—on the history faculty at Runion State, an expert in our local past lives."

We followed Anderson up the incline toward the southern end of Christabel. The pathways he led us along moved cleanly through trees and undergrowth. Where we emerged into a bit of a clearing, sections of chain-link fence were visible, although much of it was carefully camouflaged among tree trunks and large shrubs.

"This is Wolfpen One," Anderson said. "A one-acre enclosure built for two." He stopped and scanned the area. "We have red wolves Iasion and Demeter. They are still fairly shy."

Caine and I snapped pictures, but I didn't see either of the wolves.

"Let's walk to the promontory," Anderson said. "Afterward, we will walk down to the orchard and visit Wolfpens Two and Three."

As we walked, I kept an eye on the enclosure, hoping to see the wolves, but they'd hidden themselves well. I looked closely at what I guessed was the "pool house" Spellman had mentioned at the extension meeting. I thought I saw something that might have been a mound of fur just inside one opening in the structure, but I couldn't be sure.

I also kept an eye on Caine, wondering how a film's location scout looked at places like this. Did he see things as they were and consider what might be done in a particular spot as it was? Or did he look for places that could be manipulated in some way to make them useful for the film? *Probably both*, I figured. Maybe Eliza and I could have dinner with him at some point, and I could quiz him about these things and how he got this gig. He walked with the camera in his hands and at the ready, poised for a quick shot. I felt more than a little camera envy and smiled to wonder what Freud would make of that.

"The new Samsung?" I asked.

"Yes, the NX1," he said. "What's yours?"

"Old," I said. "A 2009 Canon Rebel XSi. I've been trying to find enough headroom in the *Recorder*'s budget to get something new."

He lifted the camera to his eye and snapped a shot that appeared to be the back of Spellman Anderson in the foreground, his hands clasped behind him as he walked, and the headland beyond in the background. "If you can find the funds, you can't go wrong with one of these."

"I'll keep that in mind," I said. "And keep my fingers crossed—" I stopped, sure that I'd seen something move within a small copse of trees inside the enclosure.

"Did you see them?" Caine asked, following the direction of my gaze with his camera as Anderson stopped and turned around.

"I thought I saw something move over there by that little stand of trees," I said. "But I can't pick it out now."

Anderson faced the promontory again and, without a word, continued walking past the end of the enclosure and approached the edge of the cliff.

My third grade visit to the orchard hadn't included this spot, so I'd always wondered what standing on the headland would be like. I'd seen it from all angles—from Stackhouse Park below Runion, from the sidewalk outside Eliza's salon on Main

Street, coming north along the River Road and just passing the little village surrounding the Stackhouse mansion, from up on Piney Ridge, from a raft riding the French Broad from Barnard to Hot Springs. But I'd never experienced the dizzying closeness of the precipice, to stand on it and gaze from it back at those same vantage points, to lift my face to Five Finger Mountain and its Pulpit outcropping, which seemed surprisingly close and distinct—maybe a quarter mile away.

To my right as I faced Stackhouse and southward, a small cemetery filled a clearing among the trees. I made a quick count of some thirty stones and turned to ask Spellman Anderson about the graves, but he stood gazing down toward the slow-flowing water and seemed lost in his own thoughts. And then I turned to Austen Caine, who faced Runion and worked over a sketchpad with a pencil. I watched the drawing shape up to be the lower end of Christabel, the bridge, Stackhouse Park, and Runion. "That's pretty amazing," I said. "How long have you been working on that—like a minute and a half?"

"When you're scouting locations for sometimes hundreds of shots, you have to be quick about it." He flew across the page with his pencil, continuing to add small touches and lines almost faster than I could follow. "So, you're wondering why sketch when I have this great camera, right?"

"Now that you mention it," I said.

"It's kind of counterintuitive, I guess, but—" He paused to add something I couldn't decipher in the blank space to the left of Runion. "Even though it's my eye looking through the viewfinder, the lens sees things—" He paused again. "Let's just say that human vision sees the world differently from the camera lens."

"Okay," I said.

Anderson had turned from his musings over the river and now stood on the other side of Caine, looking at the sketch that seemed almost completed as far as I could tell.

"I can't really explain it," Caine said. "But it works."

"It has to do with space," Anderson said. "The lens locks the scene in its frame and takes all the air out of it so that it is flat. The eye takes in all the space beyond the frame and senses how Runion exists in a vaster, deeper landscape. Maybe senses how one place or another is more important to us. And I think the eye also senses the airspace, the distance, between here and over there, and that keeps the image from being flat." He stopped.

"Can you write that down for me?" I said.

He shook his head, seeming not to notice that I was half kidding. "This all comes from Ariel—" He stopped and glanced toward the trees that stood mostly naked but still prevented a view of the house. "Now, how the image that is sketched differs from the image that is photographed—that is probably a conversation you would have to take up with my child." As if he'd said all he could say on the matter, Anderson started toward a path that entered the woods on the east side of Wolfpen One, and Caine followed, returning the sketchpad to the small backpack as he walked.

I glanced again at the cemetery, took one last breathless look toward the cliff's edge, turned in a circle to take in the panorama, and then fell in behind them, making a mental note to ask Anderson or Dr. Rowe about the little cemetery and its graves.

After we saw even less of the wolves in Wolfpen Two, the home of Milo and Atalanta, than we'd seen in Wolfpen One, I excused myself to head back to the office, saying that this week's edition wasn't going to put itself together. Anderson and Caine headed for the larger and uninhabited Wolfpen Three on the north end of Christabel, and I cut through the naked orchard toward Avalon Cottage.

I wished as I walked that I knew the trees better. Eliza and I always bought Avalon apples at the fruit stand they maintained down by the Piney Ridge end of the bridge. Our favorites were their Ginger Gold, Fuji, and Honeycrisp, and I wondered which of the trees I passed between would be heavy with those varieties in a few months.

When I emerged from the orchard and approached the house, I didn't see or hear any signs of life, so I intended to cross the front lawn and go straight to the footbridge and then to my car. I was almost to the edge of the English garden when I heard a door open.

"Gabe?" Randi Anderson called. "Have you got a minute?" She stood in the doorway of the main entrance. She and Spellman were, I thought, about ten years older than Eliza and I and our group of friends. The two had met in the Lowcountry of South Carolina, when Spellman attended the Citadel and she was studying at the College of Charleston. Somewhere in her mid-sixties, she was tall and strikingly beautiful, with a heart-shaped face, silver-green eyes, and a beauty spot just to the right of a Grecian nose. Her hair was golden and fell in loose ringlets well below her shoulders. Eliza cut Randi's hair every few weeks and said the color was real and the ringlets were natural.

"Sure," I said and started across the lawn toward her.

"Ariel requests an audience," she said with a smile and a raised eyebrow.

I felt a stutter in my stride but avoided falling "face fo'mos'," as Mama James would've said, and followed Randi into the house and then immediately up a staircase that rose along the lefthand wall. At the top, we continued down a carpeted hallway that ran in the direction of the orchard, and I imagined that through the window that glowed coolly at the end I would be able to see the naked trees, Wolfpen Two, and the French Broad River beyond. But in the middle of the hallway Randi stopped and tapped on a door to the left.

"Ariel?" she said in a soft voice. "I have Gabriel Tanner with me."

"Come," a likewise soft voice said.

Randi Anderson turned the knob and pushed the door gently inward and stepped back, directing me into the room with a motion of her hand.

I stepped in and stopped and stood.

"Thank you, Mother," Ariel said from where she waited by the window that looked out on the low north end of Christabel, the 209-A bridge, and Runion on its hillside above the French Broad.

The door clicked shut behind me.

Somehow the light of day appeared concentrated, even captured, within the window frame. Very little seemed to pass that point to illuminate the dusky room, but I saw well enough to note shelves heavy with books and walls hung with paintings and maps. A rectangular table, one chair tucked under it, stood with its width against the wall to the left of the window. On it, an unlit candle, knobby with dried drippings, hunkered among haphazard piles of books and papers. *A medieval scholar's garret*, I thought.

Ariel's back was to me as she stood at the corner of the table and looked out the window, possibly watching her father and Austen Caine as they toured Wolfpen Three. In contrast to the Gothic feeling of the room, she wore a dark green t-shirt with the Avalon Orchards logo on the back and cut-off blue jeans. Long, dark brown hair hung straight and loose down her back. Her arms and long legs and feet were bare and surprisingly tanned. And she was tall, probably as tall as Caine, and powerfully slender.

She turned away from the window, and her brown-eyed gaze touched my face. "I will not keep you," she said, her voice clear and her annunciation precise. "You left Father's tour early, so I assume you must have engagements elsewhere."

"Deadlines," I said. "Always deadlines."

"I am sure."

I stood transfixed and somewhat surprised that I was able

to utter my three words, which, I realized, were actually just two words. Even in the room's gloom, she was as strikingly beautiful as her mother, but that quality wasn't the same in the two. Her mother's beauty partook of a girlhood of privilege in South Carolina's Lowcountry, tempered by a womanhood on a mountain island. Ariel's betrayed her mother's origins as well but once removed and framed with an ethereal aura of mystique. Part of what transfixed me was this rare proximity. I couldn't think of anybody in my circle—or anybody I'd even heard of in the last quarter century—who'd been this close to her, this alone with her.

"I will not keep you," she said again, as if understanding that I was distracted to the point of reverie. "I have something that I would like to give you." She turned to the jumbled table and lifted the corners of a couple of piles, searching. "Ah, here." She set aside a few loose sheets and a thin, old-looking quarto volume and picked up a sheaf of ribbon-bound, handwritten pages. This she handed to me.

"What is it?" I said as I took it from her.

"I cannot say exactly. I have an idea, but I thought you could, perhaps, look into it or share it with someone at the university."

I stepped toward the window, nearer to her, and I imagined that both our breaths caught slightly—but probably for different reasons. Without removing the faded ribbons, I tilted the document toward the cool light filtered by the window's single panes of thick glass and tilted my head back to look down through my bifocals.

The first page was a letter sent from Philadelphia—"Phil."—and dated December 15, 1800. The salutation that followed was simply to "Sir," and the remaining text was handwritten in a small, slanted, and somewhat loopy cursive. Curly flourishes at various points—the tails of the letters *g* and *y* in particular—decorated the page from top to bottom, dangling from lines of text like ball ornaments from a Christmas tree limb. Words that ended with *t* were decorated with a drooping, swooping embellishment of that letter's crossing. The combination of fading ink and deteriorating paper promised to make the reading difficult, especially for old eyes.

I blinked a time or two to refocus, glanced at a couple of the following pages, and returned to the first.

"Do you know who this 'Sir' is?"

Ariel stepped next to me to look down at the document as well. "If I were to venture conjecture, then I would say it is one of the men who built Avalon Cottage. Either Joseph Hucks or Thomas Holcroft."

I again tilted both document and head to read. I couldn't make out all of the words in a quick scan—a nervous scan with Ariel Anderson standing so close and looking on—but understood the first paragraph to be about a late autumn journey from Christabel Island across the state to a brother's place, an estate or plantation—I couldn't make out the name—near Edenton, on the North Carolina coast. After visiting there until early mid-December, the writer sailed north to Philadelphia, which is where he or she seemed to be from. Still feeling a bit nervous in Ariel's presence and needing to get back to the office, I skipped a couple of middle paragraphs and scanned the last. The writer requested that this "Sir" try to locate and send to Philadelphia a fascicle of manuscript pages written during the visit at Avalon Cottage. "If you recall," the letter read, "I was unable to find these on the morning of my departure and was forced to leave them behind." The one-page letter expressed a final urgency to recover the manuscript, emphasizing that it was needed as part of a book project, and then closed with the valediction "Adieu" and an elegant signature made up of two letters, *C* and *B*, and a short last name that also began with *B*—*Brenn* or *Bienn* maybe.

I looked up at Ariel. "I'm assuming the rest of this is the manuscript. Never sent to the writer?"

"It would seem not."

"All right, I'll give it a read. Maybe pay a visit to Dr. John Riddle at RSU." I tucked the document under my arm and then, figuring I might be sweating, removed it from there and pressed it to my chest. "If I find something fun dealing with local history, can I use it for the paper."

She moved to the door and opened it. "Of course," she said, "with approval."

"Of course," I echoed and passed by her, drawing in a breath of her mystery, and stepped into the hallway. When I turned to wait, supposing she would want to show me out, the door closed with a soft click. "Of course," I said again and turned and made my way along the hall and down the steps and out the door I'd entered without encountering any other occupants of Avalon Cottage.

NINE

The man went about his workday as normal, making his stops and completing his paperwork and other responsibilities related to each site. He took calls and made calls but enjoyed the quiet in areas where he had no signal and could do neither. In such dead zones, he could hear the naked body of Kandy Wood tilting this way or that with curves on the mountain roads, hear the whisperings of her skin against the tarp as the body jostled beneath. He sought out the longest and twistiest routes to each destination, and once arrived, he left her in the back of the vehicle while he met the people he needed to speak with, shaking their hands and, be they woman or man, feeling the warmth or coolness of their skin and fantasizing beyond that touch to what strength a man might have to resist his own death—*mano a mano*—or what strength a woman might call upon when she got her hands or arms or legs around his throat. He liked to toy with his men for as long as possible, letting them think that whatever was happening was what they most wanted: competition, play, foreplay. He would take control so slowly that they didn't see their destruction coming until it was too late. He liked to make women take him over and over to that liminal space between consciousness and unconsciousness, and when he could see the hope, even triumph, in their eyes, could see they believed they might get away alive, he would explode with animal ferocity and destroy them so quickly that hope gave way no further than surprise or shock and had no time to descend to despair.

He wondered how the pair left lying in the snowfield fared

this beautiful day, the fifth day in their resting place. He'd never tried the trick with the peanut butter, and he wanted badly to see if it worked. He understood that in this part of the world young male black bears would be just out of their long winter's nap, ravenous and aggressive, but he wondered if they might turn finicky as the meat decomposed and only lick away the peanut butter before moving on. He imagined the coming of coyotes and vultures. The carrion fowl would sit at their grim feast, paying little attention to the traffic passing on Pump Gap Road, now and then spreading and lifting their black wings to the warmth of the sun. But a wake of vultures in a field or a kettle of them circling overhead might rouse the suspicions of passersby and lead to early discovery of the bodies. *Better if coyotes fight over the meat*, he thought, tearing the bones apart from each other and dragging the pieces away from the roadside and into the trees.

By late afternoon, he was in Asheville, where he drove up Lexington to Patton and turned left. After a right on Biltmore Avenue, he entered the public garage at the corner of Biltmore and Eagle Street. He parked and got out and walked once around the rear of the vehicle, looking in the tinted windows, curious if he could see her. "I'll be back," he said and headed toward a stairwell. When he stepped from the garage's shadows onto the sidewalk, he checked the titles on the marquee of the Fine Arts Theatre and then walked to nearby Pack's Tavern.

He sat at the end of the bar where he could see the video monitors mounted around the barroom and most of the faces of drinkers and diners when they looked toward the screens. Nobody seemed to him completely engrossed in the one or several companions sitting at any given table or along the bar. Nobody went more than a few seconds without glancing up at this screen showing an MMA fight or that screen beginning a replay of the North Carolina and Duke season finale from the weekend just passed. He read the faces of the people and saw in some a pure and enthusiastic interest in the outcome of what they were watching. In others he saw no interest at all, even though these uninterested still glanced at the screens from time to time. Among the rest, he recognized, here and there, hints of obsession with the violence of the fights and the fighters or the traces of desperation or anger or exultation the basketball game provoked with each dunk and three-pointer and blocked shot. He knew the certain expressions to look for—an unfocused desire would do for a start or a smoldering passion turned toward the screens but not really connected to the physical competitions taking place on them.

After nursing his way through two draught beers from different local breweries, he ordered the fish and chips, a side Caesar salad, and a third beer from yet another local. He ate slowly and continued to watch.

Truman South sat at the bar in Pack's Tavern and nursed his third Modelo Especial, knowing that he needed either to slow down or eat something. Otherwise, he wouldn't be able to continue his walk to the arena for the Southern Conference championship between Western Carolina and Wofford, his alma mater. He'd driven up from Spartanburg earlier in the afternoon and checked in at the Hilton on College Street. Until he walked into the room, closed the door behind him, and put his bag down on the nearer of the queen beds, he'd been glad that his cousin cancelled at the last minute, even though it left him with a ticket that wouldn't be used. But when he sat on the end of the other queen and looked at his dark reflection in the flatscreen television, loneliness seemed to enter him like breath.

Accompanying this loneliness, like a smell that he couldn't quite determine to be good or bad, came a thrill at what he might get up to here in Asheville, away from home and on his own. He was three years divorced, for reasons his wife, Charlene, had loudly voiced but that he still didn't fully understand. Once he'd gotten steady on his feet again, he tried the dating scene in Spartanburg bars but with no success. Then he'd tried an online dating service. He swiped and scrolled through what seemed like whole schools of women's faces, pausing, he soon realized, only on the ones that reminded him in some way of Charlene. His own profile had been public just a couple of hours when he received his first message, and he was taken aback to see that it was from a man. He thought he must have checked an incorrect box—or failed to check a correct one—during the profile process and read the message with a laugh, believing it to be a joke. But before long, he was looking at other men's profiles, at first, he told himself, just to learn how he might improve his own but eventually simply looking.

Recently, he'd found himself strolling through a few Yahoo! Messenger chat rooms, fielding one comment and then another. He wandered into one, the name of which he didn't understand and couldn't remember. He hadn't been long in it when he received a message from another user—*dude turn the knob and come out of the closet...no shame in it anymore!* He read the message several times before he responded, *I don't know what you mean.* But he thought he knew exactly what was meant although not what prompted the user to send such a note. With the message box hovering over the active chat scroll, he sat until he could barely keep his eyes open, but nothing further had come. He'd shut down his computer and gone to bed.

He fell back on the Hilton's Serenity queen but couldn't fall into the nap he'd planned, so he freshened up with a shower, dressed in his Wofford black and gold, and left the room.

On the wall above the lefthand end of the Pack's Tavern bar, a brutal MMA fight pulsed from a flatscreen. He wasn't that interested in the sport, not like some of his friends, but the man who sat beneath the match was a different story, his supper and beer untouched in front of him as he worked over a napkin with an ink pen. Truman stared for seconds at a time, and whenever the man would look up and meet his eyes, he would glance away, up to the punches and kicks and grappling, then let his gaze drift down again.

He finished his third beer and decided not to order anything else, not another beer and not supper. He would have both after the game, whether Wofford won or not.

The bartender set another Modelo Especial in front of him and slapped down a napkin beside it.

He looked at the squat bottle, at the inked sketch of himself on the napkin, and then up at her.

"From your friend," she said and tilted her head in the direction of the man sitting beneath the MMA match, who stared at him with a smile and a raised eyebrow.

TEN

Plumer Reeves changed out of the clothes he'd worn all day and put on a green long-sleeved t-shirt and faded jeans. After he'd laced up his everyday hiking boots, he retrieved his high-powered binoculars from the top compartment of their chifforobe, along with a flashlight from the drawer of the nightstand on his side of the bed. He let the screen door bang closed behind him as he danced down the porch steps, then crossed the yard to the right, to the uphill side of his cabin, and entered woods in which the trees were still mostly absent of leaves. Once he was several strides beyond the tree line, he stopped and looked up at the light in the sky, then down to check his watch.

Twelve minutes after six o'clock.

He knew that he was leaving later than he should—perhaps later than was safe—but couldn't shake the sense of urgency to get even a brief look at the landscape surrounding Runion. The sun would set around seven-thirty, so, in order to have even a few minutes of decent light, he would need to reach the rock overlook on the other side of Five Finger Mountain in twenty minutes or less. He would be lucky to get home before full dark.

He set a quick pace along the faint trail that led from his place up to meet the Five Finger Pulpit public trail, over the peak, and down to the outcropping.

He'd spent the afternoon in places he thought Terry Goforth might frequent, and he'd spoken to as many of Terry's friends as he could find based on a sketchy list from Livvy. Over the course of these visitations and conversations, he learned that

Terry hadn't been to any of his favorite places or with any of his favorite friends since early afternoon the previous Tuesday, the same day that Livvy had last seen him. A bartender at Chunn's Tavern said that Terry had seemed somewhat agitated—not necessarily drunk—and was trying to get one of his buddies to ride with him over the mountain to Johnson City, Tennessee. Nobody was up for it, so he'd left alone.

The strength of Plumer's uphill stride and the spring in it surprised him. The light ahead and above seemed to grow apace, and he realized, also with surprise, that he was already nearing the crest of the ridge.

He wondered about Terry's pickup. As far as he knew, it still sat hidden somewhere—perhaps at a lonely pull-off on a dirt backroad around Runion, perhaps in plain sight in downtown Johnson City or Asheville. He pictured Terry at the wheel, just driving around, but his imagination couldn't hold a picture of him doing so for a whole week without contact with Livvy who believed him dead or the friends who didn't seem very curious regarding his whereabouts.

And that's sad, he thought as he crested the ridge and descended toward the outcropping that jutted from Five Finger some fifty yards further down. He covered the distance quickly and came to a place where the trail veered to the left and then angled right again to enter the amphitheater-like formation from the side.

A semicircular slope of stone fell from just below where the trail turned left and formed a grassy bowl of some twenty feet in diameter. The outside of this bowl seemed shaped like a pulpit where a sermonizer might stand and preach to the empty air high above the French Broad River and Christabel Island, to distant Runion and even more distant Lonesome Mountain.

Plumer sat for a moment on a rock like a church pew and caught his breath. Then he stood and stepped to the pulpit and took in the panoramic view with his naked eyes before resorting to the binoculars. He used Runion to orient himself, tracing the channel of the Laurel River, the tracks of Genesis Road to the right of town and Lonesome Mountain Road to the left. Then he looked through the binoculars and raised them to Lonesome itself, thinking he might be able to locate Livvy's house and imagining that, if he did, he could see her sitting on her front steps and looking directly back at him with no aid of magnification. The image thrilled him and shivered his shoulders.

He began a methodical scan of the landscape from the top of Lonesome, working his way down, side to side like following a switchback road. When he reached the first ridgeline of hills under the mountain, he scanned to the right until it met another ridge, and then he followed that until it seemed to fall into the French Broad. He traced the same ridgelines back to center, to Lonesome Mountain, and scanned ridges left to the river on that side, realizing he was probably following the Appalachian Trail as well.

On his third pass along a ridge to the left of center, he noticed movement. The light was still with him, but what caught his eyes looked like moving shadows—a slight stirring of blackness. He pulled his face back from the eyepieces, trying to keep the objective lenses in place. He blinked twice and then looked through the ocular lenses again. In a moment, he relocated the movement and was able to tell that it seemed to be in the air rather than on a hillside or along a ridgeline. *Vultures?* he thought.

He felt a momentary rush of sickly excitement even though he knew that if the movement was that of vultures, this behavior didn't necessarily indicate the presence of something dead beneath them. They behaved similarly every evening at this time when preparing to roost. Whether circling a feast or simply getting ready for sleep, they seemed worth checking out. So, he tried to count ridges to figure where he might begin his search the next morning, aware in the back of his mind that if they weren't interested in a carcass then they wouldn't be hanging around in the same spot waiting for him.

While his mind ran through these thoughts, he lost track of the shadowy figures. Then he realized he was losing the ridges to fading light as well and ought to start back. But before turning away, he let the binoculars hang against his chest and ran through a mental list of roads and backroads in that general area. *No further away than Silver Mine Road*, he thought. The area between Silver Mine and Runion on the French Broad was mostly forest and field, and the only road names he could come up with were Lovers Leap, Cook Trace, and Mill Ridge.

A breath of breeze caressed his back and chilled him.

He turned from the dizzying expanse of air and distance to the stone and grass of the natural amphitheater, the dirt and wood of the mountainside, almost expecting to find somebody standing at the mouth of the path or sitting on the stone pew where he'd sat to catch his breath a few minutes before. At the same moment that he found nobody there, he shivered with the sudden remembrance that the last time he stood here he'd stood with Kayla.

Two years had passed since they'd come up from the cabin and over the ridge, carrying a picnic lunch on the first day of spring. Beneath a fair sky, the temperature had already climbed into the mid-seventies by the time they finished their sandwiches and wine. Having grown giddy with good weather and horny with alcohol, they'd stripped off their clothes, piled them on the stone pew, and made love in the new grass.

Less than two months later, she was gone. . . .

He turned away from the ground where they'd lain until almost sunburned and looked again in the direction of Lonesome Mountain, surprised at how quickly it had faded into the darkening eastern sky. His mind returned to Livvy in her house across from the mosque, but the sensation that rose into his throat was not a thrill of hope or desire but a lump of guilt. He seemed to hear Kayla's voice playfully singing the wrong words of an old song by the Police—*"that girl is half your age."*

He pulled the flashlight from his back pocket, turned it on, and left that place.

ELEVEN

Gabriel Tanner

I spent the afternoon in the office, first cataloging and filing the pictures I'd taken on Christabel Island and then structuring this week's issue of the *Recorder*. I took an hour or so for general layout—front page, obituaries, crime blotter, advertisements—then edited and formatted the casting announcement for the local filming of *The Cove*. During a final hour behind the desk, I racked my brain to come up with something for "Gabriel's Trumpet," my weekly editorial, and failed. But given that this was a regular struggle and that something always turned up and turned out all right, I didn't worry much about it.

Eliza had an early evening, so we drove up to Iron Horse Station in Hot Springs for supper. She told me about her day, which had been filled with good clients, except for the one who always attempts to trim her own hair between appointments. She'd enjoyed the usual light gossip—she doesn't allow anything too serious in the shop—and provided the usual unofficial psychological services, for which my cousin Cutter always thought she should be able to charge.

I told her about my meeting with Plumer Reeves regarding the missing Terry Goforth and my lunch with Jubal, my walkabout on Christabel with Spellman Anderson and Austen Caine. If she was curious about Caine and the upcoming filming, her curiosity didn't survive the mention of my meeting with Ariel Anderson.

"Have you read what she gave you?" Eliza asked.

"Haven't had time yet."

"Well, what was she like?"

I chewed a bite of steak and took a sip of beer before answering. "She's very tall, for one thing," I said. "Taller than I am. And her speech is really precise and formal."

"And she's beautiful?"

"Yeah, I guess so."

"You'll be the talk of the town for getting so close to her."

"It wasn't like that."

"Like what?" she said and then let slip her bedeviling grin. "If your mind went to *that* just now, it must've gone to *that* when you were with her."

I felt myself blush and, at the same time, felt the rush of relief that our relationship, after what we'd been through together and apart and together again, always felt like solid ground no matter what landscapes we had at our backs.

As we passed along Runion's Main Street on the drive home, she took my hand and squeezed it, and I expected her to say something sweet or sexy or both.

"What do you think happened to Terry Goforth?" she asked.

I faltered for a moment. Then, as we drove past her salon, "I don't have a clue. It's creepy."

"Do you know him? He's a few years younger than we are, right?"

"Yeah, his mother was probably about our age. Betty Goforth?" I turned left onto Genesis Road. "I don't remember her. I know Terry by sight, but that's about all."

"Same," she said. "Betty Goforth sounds familiar, but I can't put a face to it. Maybe she left school before I moved here."

Back home and settled in the living room, after Eliza turned on the TV and immediately fell asleep on the couch, I updated the *Recorder*'s website until I couldn't look at a screen any longer. I closed the laptop and poured myself a glass of red wine. Then I sat down at the kitchen table with the manuscript pages Ariel had given me and started trying to read, thinking that if I wasn't able to get much out of them, I could at least tire out my eyes so that I might sleep better than usual.

Phil. December 15. 1800~

Sir

After a day of recuperation, this recent visitor to Avalon, though strangely rested in body, but enervated in mind and spirit, writes to inform you of a safe return to Philadelphia. Last night, I slept again in my own bed for the first time since leaving this city on the 2nd of September. The last steps on my jaunt to North Carolina and back were by sea from Edenton to Phil., and while I lay awake & awaiting sleep, my pillow seemed still to move as if my room rode unseen waves. Eventually, I succumbed to weariness and slept deeply & late, waking in a room & bed beached & still.

Our travel plans across North Carolina succeeded better than such often do. We departed Avalon Cottage, as you well know, on Monday, the 10th of November, and, before the month expired—perhaps some twenty days later—I found myself safely in the bosom of my eldest brother, Joseph, now a planter and permanent resident in Bertie County, where I spent some three weeks with him and his Brownrigg friends. He and my new sister-in-law, Sarah, own a large plantation they have named Point Comfort, located on the Chowan River.

During the duration of my visit, I enjoyed the reunion

with Joseph & the new vistas to which I was exposed. Yet, I grew inclined to moralize, and to engage in thoughts of a sable complexion. My dear eldest brother owns thirty-nine slaves. If I may claim I once entertained strong feelings of opposition to the practice, from a distance, I may certainly declare that, after two-and-a-half weeks' witness to said practice, I imbibed the most formidable prejudices against it, and could stand no more time in its presence. I know that you, dear friend, will have the opportunity to bring slaves to Avalon, yet I pray you will not so stain such wild beauty.

To conclude my travels and return to my beginning—of life, of these travels, & of this letter—I took ship at Edenton on December 10th, having left earlier than initially planned, and set foot again in my native city, yesterday, the 14th.

I wrote, during my sojourn at Avalon, several pages that told the tale of the dramatic series of events that absorbed all our faculties throughout much of October and early November. As you may recall, I was unable to locate these, on the morning of my separation from you, and was forced to leave them behind. Pray, have they been recovered? If yes, please forward them to me, at the Swords shop, No. 99 Pearl-street, in this city. If no, their fate is unexplainable by me.

Should my mind not be stolen by other stories, possibly I will write to you again in the new year. I need not say how agreeable I would find it to see a few lines from the master of Avalon Cottage.

Adieu,
C. B. B——

I stood up from the table and went into the kitchen to fetch our magnifying glass from the catch-all drawer. Seated again, I still was unable to read the name that followed the initials *C. B.* After just a few moments of trying, I felt a scratchy heaviness in my eyelids and lay the letter atop the other pages, neatened them together, and left the stack on the table with the magnifying glass on top. I yawned and pushed back the chair and stood again, gentled the remote from Eliza's hand, and turned off the TV. "Bedtime, Love," I said.

Then came a flurry of brushing and flossing teeth, followed by Eliza's changing of her work clothes for sleeping clothes and my shedding of the day and stripping down to next to nothing. We fell into bed and, after we'd kissed ten times for the tenth of the month, I turned off the bedside light. As usual, she was asleep again within moments. I didn't lie awake as long as I sometimes do, but my sleep was uneasy. I didn't dream bad dreams, exactly, but images seemed to play across the backs of my eyelids—the invisible wolves of Avalon, the French Broad River as I'd seen it far below the southern end of Christabel Island, Terry Goforth drunk and sprawled atop a picnic table somewhere, Ariel Anderson silhouetted against a hazily lighted window, the ad for Ramsey's funeral services that hadn't yet fallen into place in this week's layout, Eliza across the table from me at Iron Horse Station, the manuscript letter's cursive scrolling across a sepia map like a flightpath in an Indiana Jones movie. Finally, a couple of hours after turning off the light, I awoke and rose from bed, stepped into the cold outside to pee off the deck, and then sat in the darkened living room for several minutes before returning to bed to find Eliza breathing steadily and the maddening loop of incohesive images broken.

Tuesday, March 11

TWELVE

Truman South felt his wife beside him. Her sudden presence thrilled him, especially when he noticed she was naked beneath their thin cover. And yet that seemed wrong. "You're so cold, Char," he mumbled. "Where are your pj's?" He tried to roll toward her, to cuddle her to warmth, but he couldn't move and wondered why, as everything else seemed to be moving. He remembered their honeymoon when they took a train out of Greenville bound for New England, remembered what it was like to sleep in their rumbling, vibrating berth. "Come here, Char—"

Sudden stillness.

Quiet.

Then the air freshened, and she was taken, yanked away from him by a silhouette that appeared at the foot of their bed, a blackness against the starry sky into the depths of which he fell.

He began to regain consciousness as he felt himself being pulled by the legs from wherever he was lying, then lifted and gently draped across a shoulder. The sensation of these movements, combined with the cool, damp darkness and the quiet, seduced him into imagining that he was returning home late with his family after a short road trip to his cousin's in Sumter, imagining that his father carried him, that they would walk across the yard and up onto the porch and wait while his mother dug the key from her purse and unlocked the front door. In a few moments, he would be gentled into his bed in the room at the top of the stairs. His father would tousle his hair and go out.

His mother would undress him and somehow get pajamas on him and then tuck him in bed.

He heard boards underfoot for a moment, the trickle of running water below, and roused himself from these imaginings of a time long gone.

He'd been at a basketball game, he knew, an important game, amidst lots and lots of noise—clapping hands, screaming voices, stomping feet, pulsing music. He'd been at this basketball game with another man, somebody he met at a bar who'd accepted the offer of his extra ticket and walked with him to the U.S. Cellular Center.

After the game and the celebration, they'd walked together to the Hilton for a nightcap. He remembered growing nervous about what might happen between them in his room, but he'd been determined not to resist.

And then he was here, and he could smell that this man wasn't his father. And he could tell that his gentle mother was nowhere to be found in this world.

Fear began to fall from his belly to his brain, and he felt it shutting him down until he was roused by the sounds of boards underfoot again and a sticking door being shouldered open. Then he was sloughed off the other shoulder and dropped from what seemed a great height to land on a kind of mattress on the floor. He felt a leg lifted and the shoe and sock pulled off, followed by the other leg, the shoe, the sock, and then a tug on his belt. Darkness enveloped and filled him.

"The wages of sin," Truman heard himself mumble.

"Hmm?" a deep voice responded from above.

Truman opened his eyes to find a low light separating the surrounding dark from the blackness inside him and the man standing naked over him. "What was the score?" His head ached so that he closed his eyes again. "I can't remember."

"Fifty-six to fifty-three."

"My Terriers won, right?"

"Yes, you are the winner."

"Awesome." Truman smiled and slitted his eyelids to see the man's glittering stare descending toward him. His eyes and mouth flew open as he drew a gasping breath.

And then the man was atop him—knees straddling Truman's waist and hands wrapped around his throat so tightly that the breath he'd drawn never became a scream.

The man liked the feeling of his skin against the skin of the dying. This body beneath him felt in many ways quite different from the previous week's fat and hairy hillbilly hobbit. The torso and legs seemed almost shaved hairless by comparison and retained much of a slim but beer-bellied college-boy physique, even in its forties. Like the other, this body had been physically weak and too easily overpowered, which was, again, a disappointment. He wondered if he should devise a way either to use less of the drug that disabled them or to discipline himself to wait until the majority of the drug's effects wore off.

He liked the ache that crept through his hands in these moments, liked to watch the eyes sparkle with terror and then quickly begin to dull and lose focus. He had learned that he could relax his grip ever so slightly, reviving focus and terror in the eyes, prolonging without interrupting the progress toward death. Regardless of the size or gender of his catch, he took this portion of his work as a significant challenge to his strength—not the strength of his body in general, which he knew was overwhelming, but specifically the strength and stamina in his powerful hands. These unfortunates could be made to lose consciousness within seconds, but to take their lives from them required minute after minute of sustained, squeezing pressure and conviction that could not be relaxed.

And as he liked to do in the midst of this unrelenting process, he pulled his own consciousness away from the immediate physical sensations and imagined that he watched from the doorway what was happening in the room. He could look around and enjoy the setting as the struggle continued. He saw the burlap-curtained window next to the doorway in which he stood, the low ceiling, the walls papered with yellowed newsprint. He enjoyed the look of the potbellied stove that, with its grate missing, seemed to gape in horror at what was transpiring only feet away from it. He noted the positions of a table and an old oak chest of drawers he had moved earlier to pull up a section of the board floor. He caught the smell of damp earth rising through the hole that would soon receive the body of the dead—to lie again alongside its waiting mate. He turned to the battery-operated light designed like an old kerosene lantern and then to the wool-stuffed, stained, and moldy mattress atop which the two naked bodies—his own and Truman South's—created a horrifying, thrilling *tableau vivant* of brutish life and death.

And then he was back inside his own skin and skull and again aware of the painful cramping in his hands and his sweat-slicked inner thighs and buttocks against the sides and genitals of the body beneath him. He continued the choke for a few more seconds and then removed his hands from the throat. While his aching fingers slowly relaxed from their rigid curl, he slid back onto the still thighs and leaned down to press an ear against the almost hairless chest. For long seconds, he listened but heard no heartbeat other than his own. Then he relaxed in child's pose and fell into a brief and dreamless sleep.

When he awoke, he found his lantern gone out and a gray glow prowling in the fire-scorched burlap sack that partially covered the window. He rose stiffly and stepped away from the body on the mattress. At the edge of the hole, beside the stack of removed boards, he stood and worked through eight minutes of Tai Chi warm-up exercises while the light increased in the folds of the burlap. He circled his hips, swiveled and stretched his neck, fisted and relaxed his hands, and rotated his wrists to the rhythms of birdsong coming from above and around the shack.

The body remained supple enough to move easily, and the man maneuvered it next to the hole in the floor. He then spread the black and gold clothing over the dark dirt beside the body of Kandy Wood. On one shoe, he saw the small head of a terrier attached to a black-and-gold lace, which he undid and tossed lace and charm onto the pile of his own clothes. He then turned again to the body, noting the bruising beginning to appear at the neck. He knelt and worked an arm under the back and another under the thighs, noting the cool skin, and gentled it into its grave. He looked at the two of them together, Kandy and Truman, reliving the long minutes of their separate dying, and then began putting the boards in place above them. When he had repositioned the small chest of drawers and table so that these looked natural in their placement and not as if they were hiding something, he noticed that he had not dropped the man's white sneakers, one stuffed with socks and the other with underwear, into the grave, so he put them in the bottom drawer of the chest instead.

He understood from the locals that hunting seasons for most species except for coyotes, feral swine, skunks, and two or three others, were closed by early March, so he felt certain that no hunters would be near enough to hear the pounding of nails. Still, outdoor adventurers seemed to be everywhere in the area, not to mention that farming and fishing could be happening within earshot. In these mountains, he could not control where sounds might echo to and chose not to hammer the boards in place, just in case. He would be back soon to check on them and could seal their grave then.

He dressed, took a careful look around, and stepped outside into the clean morning.

THIRTEEN

Ariel Anderson

I slept poorly again. My restlessness was not inspired by fear and storm-driven anxiety, as was the case the night I read the newly discovered manuscript while, outside, Ulysses wrought itself upwards from bluster to blizzard. By half past six o'clock this morning, I walked out into much more seasonable weather, although the world was still cold and much darker due to the intervening weekend's pointless time change from Standard to Daylight Savings. No, long after the drifts of snow melted into the ground or evaporated into the air, I felt an unnerving accumulation of mystery hovering about Christabel Island and lurking in Avalon Cottage.

The minor mystery of the trespassing raccoon remained unsolved. Both Father and I made several trips around the circumference of Wolfpen Two but found no breach of the fence by which the ill-fated beast made its way inside the enclosure. The only possible means—barring a flying raccoon or a leap from a tree, no substantial branches of which extended over the enclosure's interior—seemed to be climbing the fence to go over the top or, perhaps, squeezing through the feeding window. And yet, no telltale tufts of fur, which seemed to us must be left behind in such an endeavor, suggested either. Added to the mystery of ingress was the mystery of motive, which we could not fathom. Surely the raccoon would have smelled the wolves, even if their scent had been somewhat masked by the snow.

The other mysteries, I did not share with Father or Mother. The mystery of the manuscript remained between Gabriel Tanner and me and whomever he might share it with to gauge its authenticity, veracity, and meaning. I wished I had made a fair copy before giving to Mr. Tanner a document of such intimate historical import to my Avalon, but nothing could be done about that after it left the island, unless I wished to reach out and ask that it be returned for copying, which I was loathe to do.

I alone bore the weight of the most troubling mystery of all. The sense of being the object of some watchful gaze had continued from my snowy walk through the orchard after my adventure in Wolfpen Two. The feeling became, several days later, pervasive, seeming to follow me into even my private spaces in Avalon Cottage. Each time I sensed surveillance, the attention impressed me as more malevolent and more immediate.

"Something wicked this way comes," I thought. Then unbidden into my mind came another phrase: *The Watcher*.

FOURTEEN

Plumer Reeves awoke into half-light, emerging from looping dreams of one moment twirling Kayla in a waltz beneath a sky swirling with kettling vultures and the next trying to follow Livvy through winter woods he found both familiar and unfamiliar. With every step from bedside to toilet to kitchen to coffee cabinet, the residue of this dreaming slid from his mind to shiver his spine, chill his thighs, and ache in his feet.

He pinched a filter from the stack and nestled it inside the top of the coffeemaker. Then he shook grounds into the filter and filled the reservoir with tap water and, in these simple processes, felt Kayla slipping from his waking life. But he didn't want to let her go. *Not this morning*, he thought. Her mysterious loss tugged at his breath and threatened to take it away—and maybe with his breath, his life.

He pulled a coffee cup from the cabinet and set it on the counter, took a small waffle from the box in the freezer and dropped it in the toaster.

He didn't cook real breakfasts anymore and hadn't since the day Kayla disappeared almost two years before. That morning, May 5, 2012, her forty-first birthday, he'd gotten up early to prepare French toast, scrambled eggs, and fruit that she could eat before dashing out the front door.

She was scheduled to work with students at Hot Springs Elementary, putting the finishing touches on their pottery projects and, in her planning period, prepping their end-of-year portfolios. By all accounts, she'd enjoyed a good day at school and then left her Jeep there and walked to the music teacher's home on Jackson Avenue for birthday drinks with her colleagues. She seemed lively and happy, her friends had later said, and she practically danced away down Jackson when it was near time for her six o'clock birthday dinner with Plumer at Iron Horse Station.

Her route would have been down Jackson Avenue to the righthand bend, just before the railroad tracks, where Jackson bent to become Andrews Avenue, which then followed along the tracks, passed over Spring Creek, crossed Bridge Street, and ran directly by the Iron Horse. According to witness interviews conducted in the days and weeks that followed, a passerby saw her approaching Spring Creek from the north, but nobody saw her make it to or across Bridge Street.

Plumer had waited for her an hour without knowing he was already that long into never seeing her again.

He stood up from his meager breakfast and rinsed his small plate and coffee cup and took up a dishtowel to dry them. In the corner of his eye, the door to Kayla's studio seemed rimmed with pulsing light. He tried to ignore the sense of beckoning, as he rarely went in there anymore, having slowly built up over many months a resistance to its pull. But this morning, that pull drew strength from the waltzing dream, and he couldn't resist. He returned plate and cup to the cupboard. Then he wiped his hands on the dishtowel and draped it over the divider between the two sides of the double porcelain sink.

He drew a deep breath and turned the knob and pushed open the door without stepping over the threshold.

As always in the daytime, from dawn to dusk, the room was filled with the light she'd loved, light that was not pulsing but perfectly still.

He told himself that the sense of pulsation had been created somehow between his heartbeat and his eyes. *Maybe lack of sleep?* he wondered. The room seemed just as he'd left it back at Christmastime, which, apart from the sheets used for dust-covers, was just as she'd left it over a year and a half before that.

Also as always, the room struck him as haunting instead of haunted. And the most haunting aspect was the covered easel that stood with its back to the door and its sheeted canvas facing the wall of windows.

He stepped over the threshold and around the easel. When he drew aside the covering to reveal the last canvas she'd faced with paintbrush in hand, his breath caught. He'd stood in this same spot and looked at the curious work many times, especially in the weeks and months that followed her disappearance. He'd looked for clues in the painting's foreground and background and found nothing that made sense. But this time the images startled him with an unsettling familiarity. He released his breath and leaned in.

The canvas held a night scene in woods, depicted mostly through rangy shades of blue. In the foreground stood two large trees, the one on the right twice the thickness of that on the left—both rendered in blue-black. Dark undergrowth rose from the canvas's bottom border to intervene between the eyes of the viewer and the bases of the two trunks that in turn rose beyond the top of the canvas. In the space between these trunks, a man stood facing the woods, his back to the viewer, and held up a blazing torch, which lit the inside edges of the foregrounded trees. He seemed to stand on the verge of a small clearing or ravine. Several feet above him, on a thick broken limb that jutted from the larger tree, Kayla had depicted the black silhouette of a crouching and apparently naked woman.

In the background, whether across clearing or ravine, two sets of glowing eyes, beasts on all fours, peered at the man from around the smaller trunks of two evergreens that mirrored the trees in the foreground, and to the right, at the margin of the canvas, the silhouetted upper body of a two-legged beast stood half hidden at the edge of some low-growing shrub.

Mountain laurel, Plumer thought, paying little attention to the threatening silhouette. *She loved mountain laurel.*

Back at center, tree limbs spiraled like a staircase up the trunks of the evergreens. Between their trunks and elevated above the four-legged beasts, a young woman sat on one limb, resting bare feet on the limb below. She glowed golden in an aura that seemed partially a reflection from the man's torch and partially an emanation from within herself. Long blonde hair flowed across her face and fluttered beyond her left shoulder, as if blown by a wind that also tugged at the tassels or tatters of her dress.

His breath caught again as the images suddenly sorted themselves into names and things they hadn't before. He remembered his dream of trying to follow Livvy through woods and knew that he was the man who stood and held high the torch. *I'm looking for her*, Plumer thought and then wondered which *her*. The crouched silhouette on the broken branch above him became Kayla. Livvy perched in the trees above Christabel Island wolves and radiated light through the dark woods. *It fits*, he thought. *It's like she knew.* The dark figure lurking near the righthand margin again caught his eye, but as of yet no name or word suggesting either identity or intent attached itself to that shadow. *Terry Goforth, maybe?* he thought. *Or the thing that happened to him?*

With the sheet drawn back over the painting and the studio door pulled closed behind him, Plumer left home for Runion. He drove down the mountain until he connected with 209-A and took that along Piney Ridge, descended through its switchbacks to the river and across the bridge, then parked on Mill Street next to the graveyard flanking the Runion Community Church. He walked up the east side of Main Street to the Town Hall and Jail.

Deputy Williemae Rider looked up from her phone screen when Plumer entered. "Good morning," she said. "Can I help you, sir?"

"Is Deputy Boyce around?" Plumer said.

"No, sorry, not right now. He's gone out on an errand and probably won't be back until eleven o'clock or after."

Plumer stood a moment and looked around, then returned his attention to Deputy Rider, whose heart-shaped face seemed framed in a softness he'd always found attractive in the few girls and fewer women he'd known. Her body—compact and full and so much the opposite of his Kayla—seemed liable to burst beautifully out of her uniform if she only moved a certain way. He took in her bright blue eyes and wondered if her light brown hair was pulled back in a bun or ponytail. "Maybe you can help me," he said and shut his eyes and opened them again. "Are you aware of a missing man named Terry Goforth?"

Deputy Rider smiled as if she knew his brief appraisal had come out in her favor. She laid her phone on the desktop blotter and stood. Her brown bun peeked out from behind her head when she turned and came around the desk to stand in front of him. "Yes, I heard about him," she said and touched the wavy hair just above her left ear.

"Anything in particular you heard?"

"Well, I probably shouldn't tell you this, but Davis—that's Deputy Boyce—is gone to look at a truck that might be Terry's."

"Where is it?"

"Now, I know I can't tell you that without getting my ass in a sling." She touched fingertips to full, smiling lips. "Sorry, I shouldn't have said that."

Plumer stared at the deputy. "I reckon not," he said at last. He put a hand in a pants pocket and pulled out the keys to his Jeep. "Will you ask Deputy Boyce to give me a call when he gets a chance?"

"Oh, sure," Deputy Rider said. "And you are?"

"Reeves. Plumer Reeves."

"I had a feeling you were, but I wanted to be sure." She leaned slightly forward, laying the palm of one hand on her breast and reaching toward him with her other hand. "I'm awful sorry about your wife disappearing and all. I hope you don't mind me saying so."

"That's all right. Thank you." Plumer took a step back toward the door and stopped. "Did you know her?"

"She was my art teacher when I was in elementary at Mars Hill. She seemed so nice."

Plumer pushed through the door and stepped out onto the sidewalk. His brain swirled with vertigo for a moment, so he reached out a hand and touched the top of a parking meter. As he steadied, he looked across the street at the *Runion Recorder* office and considered going over to ask if they used a police scanner and if they'd heard anything about the truck that might be Terry Goforth's. He took a deep breath and opted for patience, deciding he would go for a ride through the backroads where he had in mind to look for vultures and wait for Deputy Boyce to call.

FIFTEEN

Gabriel Tanner

Sometime in the night, I must've decided to write this week's "Gabriel's Trumpet" on the possible arrival of a film crew and the possibility that my readers might get to take part in the fun. When the alarm went off at six o'clock, the component pieces seemed laid out in my mind and ready to be typed up.

But not yet.

Eliza and I snoozed a bit and cuddled a bit, reluctant to throw off the covers and get our feet on the floor. Our hands seemed to wake up before the rest of us. But I wouldn't name the business they got up to *exploration*. That's for youngsters. We knew the terrain of each other's body as *home*, knew it so well that I would name the business of our hands *confirmation*—confirmation that we were still alive, still lovers. We coupled for the couple of minutes it took, and then we were out of bed. Eliza made coffee, and I hit the shower. By seven-thirty she was gone to open the salon. I pulled our unread copy of *The Cove* from the bookshelf and sat down with it and my laptop.

Cliché as it was, I wrote that Hollywood was returning to Runion in June, and while no information was yet available as to what stars would be falling around us, interested readers might get an opportunity for maybe fifteen seconds of fame. My first draft included some reference to the swelling-a-progress lines from "Prufrock," but by the third draft, the reference disappeared. I told readers a bit about the project—a film adaptation of Ron Rash's *The Cove*. I reminded them that Rash was Parris Distinguished Professor of Appalachian Cultural Studies at Western Carolina University and that his novels *Serena* and *The World Made Straight* had also been or were being adapted into films. While the latter included some scenes filmed in Madison County, my readers hadn't had the same opportunity to work as extras that they might have with the coming filming of *The Cove*. I provided a brief summary of the novel, based on its *Goodreads* page. I flipped through and found some Mars Hill street scenes that, if included in the screenplay, might make use of local extras. I closed by pointing them to the casting call available in this week's edition, then left the novel out on the table to remind myself to begin reading it as soon as I got a chance.

With my spur-of-the-moment editorial drafted and proofed, I decided I had a few minutes to return to Ariel's Avalon manuscript, so I cleared a space on the table, carefully set aside the letter I'd already read, and bent over the first page, my head slightly lifted to target the hard-to-read text with my bifocals.

Phil. to Avalon in North Carolina
September 2 to 26. 1800~

My dear Friend......

I am amused by the image I hold of you holding in your hand and reading this page and those that will follow. My desire to amuse you, in turn, will inspire me to record the passing scenes and not allow this journal of my jaunt into the wilderness to go unwritten. You will of course ask too much of me, but if I think of that—of how much I will fall short of your expectations—I will not write at all. The novelty of this journey to Avalon, which took over my life and took me away from you so suddenly, must not pass without record. To push my pen forward across these pages, you will serve as both muse and audience—both inspiration and reception.

To begin, we set out from Phil. early in the morning of the first Third Day, Sept. 2nd. I found myself in good company with Robert and Lavenia Allen. You met the Allens at Mr. Proud's a week before our departure. Also with us were Walter and Sarah (called Sally) Landor. These two, you did not meet, as they arrived in Phil. from Boston with only one day to spare before we took our road south to Baltimore. All are English. All have assumed from reading my sojourns into Mettingen and Norwalk that I am a great adventurer into wilderness. Excited by the prospect of this journey, and having envisioned a way in which I might include a visit to my brother Joseph, I did not correct their assumption, and attempted to travel as easy as if I make such sojourns every other month at least.

We traveled without need of a guide from Phil., to Baltimore, and to the capital, where we were referred to one we would find in the vicinity of Mr. Jefferson's vast estate in Virginia. This man, Casper Callaway, is nephew or cousin—I did not catch exactly which—to Richard Callaway, frontiersman and hunter, whom you may have heard of due to the adventurous and horrible tale of his death some twenty years ago at the hands of a Shawnee war party.

Our daily travel was arduous, in which we generally traversed over twenty miles betwixt sunrise and sunset—more miles each day as we traveled through the valleys east of the mountains, fewer in the mountains themselves. I wrote nothing beyond random notes during this time.

All through which we wandered was wood and waste. In the last days of the journey, we passed through scenes that seemed little more to me than a trackless wilderness of steeps and rivulets, a craggy and obscure path through brambles and thorns, on the other side of which, stretched more of the same, until we came in view, at last, of the shining walls of Avalon Cottage, on Sept. 26th, a Sixth Day. There we were welcomed by its inhabitants, who have been building their island paradise for two years and more. They are: Joseph Hucks and his wife Mary; Thomas Holcroft and his wife, also Mary (called Molly); James Ridgeway and his wife Theodosia; Thomas Douglas and his wife Jeanetta (Jenny), and a young man named Tait Douglas, orphaned nephew of Thomas D.

Thus, in the space of twenty-four days, some five hundred miles, and three paragraphs, I am in Avalon, Secret Island of Apples!

My eyes suddenly began to feel scratchy and tired again, more so than I could afford on a Tuesday when I needed to finish writing and proofing and laying out the week's edition for emailing by midnight, just over twelve hours away. I forced myself to set aside the manuscript and headed for the office. As I drove down Genesis Road, I wondered about the drama referenced in the unanswered letter that the manuscript's author had written to some "*Sir*" at Avalon Cottage, thinking nothing I'd read so far warranted describing as a "dramatic series of events."

I obeyed the STOP sign at the foot of Genesis Road and then turned right toward town. Thoughts of Philadelphia reminded me of late summer or early autumn 1989 when Lonesome Star played there at Chestnut Cabaret to kick off a tour of the Northeast in support of our single "Catch That Train" and the album that followed. Having one morning left Nashville earlier than anybody wanted to, we shared the bill that same evening with a group called Hothouse Flowers. Riding in a van and pulling a small trailer for our equipment, we made the trip with restroom and drive-thru breaks in about fourteen hours. I tried to imagine a twenty-four-day trip on horseback from Philadelphia to Runion in the time before roads, even before reliable maps, when a guide was necessary. As I made my usual U-turn at the north end of Main Street and rolled to a stop in front of the *Runion Recorder* office, I recognized that even our 1989 trip by roadmap seemed somewhat archaic from the vantage point of 2014 with its proliferation of GPS.

I was unlocking the front door of the office when I remembered my idea of showing the manuscript to John Riddle, a friend and Professor of English at Runion State. Early American literature was his specialty, and I thought he might recognize something in the journey to Avalon—one of the names mentioned in the Avalon community's origins perhaps. And, of course, history professor Caldwell Rowe would certainly have some insights. I shouldered my way through a front door that sometimes stuck but sometimes didn't. At my desk, I woke up my computer and emailed Dr. Riddle and asked for a meeting with him the next morning, if possible, briefly explaining the manuscript I had and how I hoped he might help.

With that out of the way, I opened the previous night's missive from Edie-Mac, in which she wrote only "good 2 go." One of her jobs was an end-of-Monday proofreading of all items in a given weekly edition's folder, after which, except for being loosely on call for rare last-minute Tuesday needs, she more or less had Tuesday and Wednesday off. I added this morning's editorial to the folder and then began going through everything piece by piece, giving each a final revision and proofing. All the while, in the back of my mind, four men and two women rode horses single file through woods, shadowed by dark figures—human and wolfish—far off among the trees.

SIXTEEN

A violent chill shook him awake, and he lay shivering in the silent dark. He felt swathed in cold—rough and hard at his back, smooth and soft at his left side, frigid breath on his right arm and in his face and down across his belly and thighs to his feet.

The next thing he felt was that his throat hurt badly, and he hoped he wasn't coming down with something. He heard her telling him that he should drink lots of fluids.

Then two thoughts came to him at once: that he was thirsty, thirstier and colder than he'd ever been, and that he didn't know who she was, the one speaking about fluids.

He hadn't moved since he awoke—couldn't move. But somehow without moving a hand to touch himself he knew he was naked. And he wondered why in the world he would be naked in such a cold place.

Then he wondered about the cold place and realized he didn't know where he was. The place was dark and smelled familiar—not good or bad, just familiar.

Then three thoughts struck him at once: that what he smelled was dirt, that he didn't know who or where he was, and that he wasn't in the dark alone.

Then all sensing and thinking stopped, leaving only a wheezing, mindless screaming until all went black again.

SEVENTEEN

Silver Mine Road, Plumer Reeves had judged, was the farthest point at which he could have seen the vultures—*If they were vultures.* He'd decided as he left the sheriff's office and drove out of Runion that he would go to that farthest point and work his way back through Mill Ridge, Cook Trace, Lovers Leap, and any smaller roads he couldn't remember that might run between them. If the birds were still gathered over some dead thing, he stood a good chance of finding them and whatever had captured their attention, but at the same time, he knew it was possible, even likely, that they haunted some forest or field not accessible along any of these roads into the hollers.

By one o'clock, he'd driven to the dead ends of both Silver Mine and Mill Ridge, as well as Baylor Run between them. Back at the intersection of Mill Ridge and Lonesome Mountain Road, he turned right toward Runion but in half a mile turned right again on Cook Trace, a wide-enough but unlined stretch of blacktop that followed Cook Branch upward as the stream splashed downward from the heights. Plumer lost himself for a few moments in driving and watching the woods and clearings for local fauna, particularly the bear and deer so rare a sight when he was growing up but seen more often these days.

A clearcut for power lines opened to his left, and he slammed on his brakes at the sight of three or four vultures kettling in the clear air somewhere between his vantage point and Hot Springs. He checked his rearview mirror to be certain he wasn't holding anybody up, but no other cars were in sight, behind or ahead.

The vultures, he guessed, might be gliding above the rise of Lovers Leap Road but not as far to the north as the Leap itself. Or they might be above Pump Gap Road, which rose from the French Broad to intersect with the Leap road where it looped north along a ridge and paralleled the Appalachian Trail to end at the Lovers Leap trailhead.

He found no safe turnaround on the side of the mountain, so he drove the last stretch to the parking lot at the end of Cook Trace. To his right, an access trail led upward to the AT, and to his left, the wooded hillside sloped sharply downward toward the next valley through which ran the first part of Lovers Leap Road. Directly in front of him, in the trees at the far side of the lot, stood a stone chimney—all that remained of the old Payne place. He probed his memory for the story, but with a mind full of vultures to pursue, he came up with only one rough detail: that the Payne house burned to the ground over one hundred years before, in the late nineteenth century, leaving the stone chimney standing as a soot-blackened Ebenezer. He shook off the feeling that image gave him—of himself as such a structure since his life had burned down with Kayla's disappearance—and focused on the feel of the steering wheel in his hands and the pedals beneath his feet, the sound of the pop and growl of his tires rolling over gravel. No other vehicles were parked in the lot, so he averted his eyes from the lonely chimney, turned in a wide circle, and hurried back down the mountain.

Once on Lovers Leap, instead of watching for deer and bear in the woods and fields alongside, he kept his eyes alternately on the road and the sky. The blacktop rose up from the valley, but the sky remained empty. Near the ridge, the road angled left—north—and leveled out, running along the mountainside just one hundred yards or so below the AT. He approached the intersection with Pump Gap Road and resisted the urge to take the left and return to Runion. As he passed, he glanced to see that the sky above that road remained as stubbornly empty of vultures as had been the sky above all the other roads he'd taken to this point. *Where'd they go?* he wondered as he drove on. Lovers Leap dead-ended in another small gravel parking lot, but this time, instead of turning around, he nosed his Jeep up to the lot's bordering split-rail fence and turned off the motor.

He walked along the short trail through the woods and thought about how he preferred his private overlook—mostly private anyway—on the other side of Five Finger Mountain from his cabin. But he decided that, being this close to the more storied Lovers Leap overlook, he ought to make a quick jaunt to the spot to take in the view and try to get a deep breath, something he just realized he'd denied himself all day as he drove the roads in search of vultures and Terry Goforth.

In a few minutes he stood among the jagged rocks of the promontory. He closed his eyes and tried to breathe in the distances that stretched into space around him—the distance upriver to the south, the direction of Runion, Christabel Island, and Five Finger Mountain, the distance directly over the river and past blue-brown ridges fading into the west toward Tennessee. He succeeded in drawing a few deep breaths, but when his eyes opened, they drifted—irresistibly, like the flow of the river below—to the north and Hot Springs, where Kayla was last seen. Although some distance away, he easily picked out the old school where she taught that last day. He imagined he could see her leaving her friends to walk down Jackson Avenue to Andrews, where she turned and walked toward him. He imagined that as she approached Spring Creek at her usual slow and dreamy pace, she stopped and waved up at him. *Hello? Goodbye?* He thought he heard a flying vulture's nasally whine and looked up, but when he didn't see anything and turned back toward Hot Springs, the tiny image of Kayla had disappeared.

He shook his head as he left the outcropping. In a few moments, he was back in the Jeep and on Lovers Leap. Pump Gap Road came up on his right, and he swerved into it and began an immediate winding descent toward the French Broad. Where the blacktop briefly leveled and straightened and the landscape opened up along a kind of terrace on both sides, he caught sight of several deer across a small meadow to his right, standing near the tree line and watching him pass. He gave them a nod and a little wave. "Hello, beauties." His voice was dry and raspy after having not been used since the sheriff's office that morning.

When he turned back to the road, he slammed on his brakes as a coyote flashed across the blacktop in front of him, a large vulture flying low and giving chase, harrying the coyote that hurried across a corner of the meadow and darted into the trees.

The vulture swerved away toward the deer that still stood watching the Jeep. Then it circled the meadow, following the tree line.

Plumer glimpsed the bird in his rearview as it flew low across the road behind him and disappeared. He looked again at the blacktop in front of him, attempting to process what he'd just seen. The coyote had carried something in its mouth as it ran away, and when Plumer froze the image in his mind, he realized that it looked like a human foot.

He eased the Jeep into NEUTRAL and set the parking brake as quietly as he could, twisted in his seat and looked between the trunks of a small stand of trees that stood on the other side of the road. He could see the wake of vultures, six or seven of them, at a grim feast. He saw a flash of gray-brown in the grass beyond the scene and understood that a coyote—maybe the same or maybe another—worked its way closer for another quick raid on the carcass of whatever it was, turning his mind away from the thought that somebody's foot had dangled from the coyote's mouth. *This close to the road*, he thought, *maybe a deer hit by a car*. He turned to look at the meadow to his right and found that those deer he'd seen at the far end had disappeared. He looked straight ahead again and unlatched his seatbelt, leaned forward to his right and retrieved his phone from the passenger-side floorboard. Then, turning again and keeping an eye on the wake that settled or flapped away a few feet, depending on the movement of the coyote, he opened his door, swiveled in his seat and let his feet alight on the pavement. He stood up and stood still, watching the movements on the other side of the trees. Standing outside his Jeep, he could hear some of what was happening as the vultures alternately hissed at each other and at the encroaching coyote. He heard other sounds beneath the hissing, but he tried not to think about what those might be. The birds seemed more focused on their feast and the coyote than on him, so he stepped lightly across to the opposite shoulder for a closer look at whatever was dead in the grass. Although he still couldn't see much in the way of details, he saw enough to know that these carrion critters were disemboweling, dismembering, and devouring a naked human body. His head swam with thoughts of Kayla, of finally finding her, and then shouting and waving his arms, he pushed his way through the undergrowth between the trees.

The vultures rose with a great flapping of wings that stirred the air so that Plumer could feel it on his face, and the coyote slinking not ten feet on the other side of the body disappeared as if by magic.

Suddenly alone with the dead, Plumer stepped forward and then stopped when he realized that the horror on the ground before him was composed of two human bodies instead of one. He stumbled a step backward, glanced at his phone's number pad long enough to press 9-1-1 with his thumb, and then raised the phone to his ear.

EIGHTEEN

Gabriel Tanner

I was in the middle of playing something like Tetris with blocks of advertisements, engagement and birth announcements, and overly sentimental death memorials when the scanner squawked to life with urgent calls about the grisly discovery on Pump Gap Road. Gruesome as such things can be, I always feel an excitement that makes me want nothing more than to race to the scene to see what's happening—or what's happened. But a Tuesday afternoon is about the only time that I feel glued to my chair and my computer as I race instead to meet the midnight deadline for the week's edition. So, as much as I was itching to get out of the office and into the field to document the discovery of two dead bodies, I knew the responsible thing was to keep my butt in the chair and try to get Edie-Mac on the case.

I pulled the phone from my shirt pocket and dialed her number.

"Gabe," she answered with a tight voice. "Please don't ask me to do anything. I'm on my way over to Greeneville for the evening."

"I think they've found Terry Goforth," I said. "His body, I mean. And somebody else as well, but I don't have the whole story yet."

She was quiet on her end of the call, and I thought she might have lost her signal. Then, "I'm almost to Tennessee already," she said. "Please, boss."

"All right, but if Eliza gets pissed at me for pushing the midnight deadline, I'm gonna blame you."

"I'm okay with that. This is just a really important trip."

"What's so important that you would make your old decrepit employer burn midnight oil he ain't got?" I paused. "Or what's more fun than photographing dead bodies?"

"I'll tell you on Thursday," she said, unfazed. "Thanks, Gabe."

Three beeps in my ear told me she was gone.

I took the time to save and back up my work, grabbed my camera gear, and hurried out the door. In the car, I made a U-turn in front of the Town Hall and Jail and headed out the north end of town toward Hot Springs. Once down on the River Road, I drove a quarter of a mile and turned right on Pump Gap, which began to rise not far past the skeletal remains of the old Twilight Reel Drive-In. I wound my way up the mountainside to a natural terrace where several vehicles were parked along the edge of the narrow two-lane with their emergency lights flashing red or blue or yellow. I eased in behind the black pickup truck of the local fire marshal and cut my engine, smiling grimly at the thought that I should have some emergency lights, too, although I couldn't say what color they should be. Nobody was likely to be on the scene who didn't know me, but I looped my PRESS lanyard over my head and got out of the car.

I stepped to the middle of the road and stood astraddle the yellow lines, raised the camera and took a shot of the vehicles and people cluttered on both sides of the pavement. When I took the camera down from my eye, I recognized Plumer Reeves leaning against the driver-side door of a Jeep, his hands in his pockets, standing sideways to me and facing the assembly gathered across the road on the other side of a stand of trees. I snapped a quick shot of his profile and then walked over. "Mr. Reeves," I said.

He turned. "Mr. Tanner."

"This gathering is your doing?" I asked. "You found Terry Goforth?"

He didn't respond for a moment. Then, "I'm pretty sure it's him, but he and the woman are quite a mess." He paused. "Vultures and coyotes."

"Do you know who the woman is?"

He swallowed so visibly that I guessed when he made this grisly discovery his first reaction might have been to be afraid, or even hopeful, that the body was that of his Kayla, missing now for close to two years.

"It'd be hard to recognize her, even if I knew her. But I don't have any idea who she is."

"Yesterday when you were in my office, I got an email about a woman missing from Asheville." I paused and tilted back my head to think. "Name was Dolly Ham if I recall rightly. Might be her."

"Might be," Reeves said. "Is it wrong to hope so? I mean, if she can't be alive?"

I cleared my throat. "Well, you can probably answer that better than anybody."

As I made my way toward the bodies of the deceased and the bodies of those that stood around them, a number of first responders and a handful of the local curious nodded and said, "Gabe." A chill ran along my spine when I looked beyond the center of attention toward the trees that stood where the terraced meadow ended and the wooded mountain rose again. Scattered among the bare limbs of those trees, a committee of vultures sat and watched the proceedings with what I imagined to be a mixture of jealousy, outrage, hunger, and disappointment. I stopped and snapped several shots of the vultures above and the ring of people surrounding Reeves's discovery below.

The outer ring of law enforcement onlookers standing some five to seven feet back from a Ramsey's Funeral Home graveside tent top included Sheriff Ponder Brigman, dressed as usual in a three-piece suit and cowboy hat, Deputies Davis Boyce and Carlton Mayhew, Fire Marshal Wilfred Farmer, and three others I recognized as NCSBI investigators but whose names I didn't know. The inner ring beneath the tent top was made up of only one busy person, Dr. Eleanor Rios, who circled the bodies alternately standing, bending, squatting, and standing again. With gloved hands, she poked and prodded the bodies, gently lifted one part or another, snapped photos from awkward positions. After a few moments, she looked up and saw me standing outside the ring of officials.

"Gabe, you eaten recently?" she said as she stood with a hand to the small of her back, and all those gathered around her turned to look at me.

"Nothing but coffee this morning," I said.

"That's good. You mind helping with a couple of photos?"

"You don't have an assistant for that?" I asked, knowing that she didn't. Edie-Mac and I had both gone through forensic photography and imaging certification for this very reason.

Dr. Rios didn't answer, only smirked, cocked her head to one side, and raised one eyebrow.

"Sure. I guess not." I stepped between Sheriff Brigman and Deputy Boyce and then stopped just beneath the edge of the tent top. I forced myself to look at Dr. Rios and not at the bodies that lay on the ground between us.

She was a sturdy woman in her mid-forties, solid with what I imagined to be strong bones and muscle—beautiful in her way. She wore a disposable crime scene suit that stretched tightly over her breasts and hips. Its hood down, the white of the suit matched her smile but was in stark contrast to lustrous almond skin, the almost black irises of her eyes, and the dark brown hair that fell in waves down over broad shoulders.

"You okay with this?" she asked as she pulled a pair of blue gloves from her back pocket and handed them across to me. "I know you're certified and all, but I doubt you've ever seen anything like this before."

"Sure, I guess." My gaze followed hers downward to the bodies, and my vision blurred for a moment when my stomach seemed to flip. But then both vision and gut settled into a tenuous but steady equilibrium.

All four eyes were gone, as were part of their noses and lips. Her small breasts had been shredded in jagged tears. Both bellies gaped open and seemed to be missing organs, but I hadn't studied biology in almost forty years and couldn't tell which those absent parts might be. I could more easily recognize the genitalia of the human male and female and easily recognized that no signs of them remained on these bodies.

Dr. Rios dipped her hand in a front pocket and brought out her phone. She touched the screen a couple of times and unzipped her body suit a couple of inches, somehow stuck the phone against the skin near her collarbone and began speaking. "The bodies are a well-nourished male and female, the male somewhat overfed, to be honest, and both appearing to be in their thirties or forties. No clothes or shoes appear in the vicinity, suggesting that the bodies were naked when dumped here." She dropped to her haunches like a mountain man. "Both show signs of decay suggesting that they've been deceased approximately a week to ten days, but if they've been lying here since before last week's blizzard, temperature fluctuations and snow cover will have affected the rate of decay. Both bodies also show signs of significant animal predation, largely in the areas of soft tissue, although the female is missing a foot. Said predation is most likely from vultures and coyotes, both of which are common in the area." She swiveled on her haunches and looked toward the committee of vultures still meeting in the trees. "Some remain in the immediate area at this recording." She swiveled back around. "There is evidence of bird feces on and around the bodies." She pointed at the heads or upper torsos of the dead, her index finger wagging back and forth between. "Gabe, bend down and take a picture of that, please."

I did as she asked and lowered my camera. "What am I looking at?" I could feel the outer circle of law enforcement folk leaning in to listen.

"Apparently manual strangulation with some big hands." She pointed to two circular discolorations on the front of each neck. "Thumb prints," she said. "From hands big enough to wrap all the way around. At least on her."

"How long apart do you reckon he killed them?" Deputy Boyce asked from behind me.

Dr. Rios stood up. "I can't say for certain just yet, Davis, but I'm guessing twenty-four to forty-eight hours." She came partway around the bodies to stand at their feet, looking them up and down lengthwise. "Again, I can't say for certain, but I'm guessing she died first."

I looked away to see Plumer Reeves standing by his truck and watching the proceedings. When he nodded, I returned the gesture.

"That man there's almost got to be Terry Goforth, ain't it?" the sheriff said. "So, there's a missing persons case closed."

The three NCSBI agents glanced at Sheriff Brigman and then returned their attention to the bodies.

"Any idea who that woman might be?" the sheriff asked. "Anybody know her?"

I sensed a slight shaking of heads among the agents and a slight roll of the eyes from Dr. Rios. "I got an email yesterday morning about an Asheville woman gone missing from Mars Hill," I said. "Dolly Ham was the name, I'm pretty sure." I turned to Deputy Boyce. "Did you guys get that?"

Davis Boyce wiped his palm across his mouth. "I ain't been in the office much this week," he said. "Carlton, did you see anything about a Dolly Ham?"

Deputy Mayhew looked back at me. "Was it a email or a FAX?"

"What is that brownish substance all over them?" one of the NCSBI agents asked. "Is that some byproduct of decay in the elements?"

"Or something left by the predators?" another asked.

"No," Dr. Rios said. "Believe it or not, I'm almost certain that it's peanut butter."

"What?" I said.

"Peanut butter," she said again. "Probably smooth and creamy."

"Kinky," Deputy Mayhew said, and everybody looked at him. "I mean, don't you think?"

"That's possible," Dr. Rios said after a moment. "But I'm guessing it was applied postmortem, after they were already placed here. Probably meant to attract critters." She stepped from under the tent top and waved in a couple of techs who would transport the bodies to Wake Forest Baptist Medical Center in Winston-Salem for autopsy. "So, yes, agent, something left by a predator, just not of the furry or feathered variety."

NINETEEN

Austen Caine parked his Equinox in the public lot behind the Runion Pizzeria and a few moments later stepped into the Town Hall and Jail.

Deputy Williemae Rider stood when he entered. "Can I help you, sir?"

"Is the sheriff here?" Caine said. "I wanted to introduce myself."

Deputy Rider came around the desk and stood in front of the visitor, whose six-feet-two frame loomed over hers at barely five feet. "No, sir. The sheriff keeps his office over at Marshall. That's the county seat." She hesitated. "But the sheriff—everybody but me, I think—is up on Pump Gap Road, at a crime scene."

"Really?" Caine said. "Is that the road with the abandoned drive-in movie grounds?"

"That's right. But I probably shouldn't have mentioned it."

"What's going on over there?"

"Now, I definitely shouldn't mention that, especially as I don't even know who you are."

"Austen Caine," he said. "I'm the location scout for a new film to be shot in the area this summer."

"That's cool," Deputy Rider said. "Who's gonna star in it?"

"Now, that's something I shouldn't mention." He smiled.

"Oh, you." She smiled in return and reached out as if to poke his ribs but stopped. "Well, what's this movie gonna be called? You can tell me that, can't you?"

"Well, I probably could, but I don't actually know what title they'll use. The screenplay is based on a novel called *The Cove* by Ron Rash."

"Never heard of it," she said. "Or him."

"Okay, another of Rash's novels called *Serena* was made into a movie coming out this year," Caine said. "With Jennifer Lawrence and Bradley Cooper?"

"Now, them I've heard of," Williemae said. "Jennifer and Bradley." Her blue eyes flared wide as she took the left side of her lower lip between her teeth and looked him up and down. "So, what does a location scout do?"

"I drive around looking for sites that might serve for scenes in the film."

"Really?" she said and thrust out her hand. "I'm Williemae Rider. Deputy Williemae Rider."

"Nice to meet you—is it Deputy Rider or Williemae?"

"You can call me Williemae, Mr. Caine."

"Austen."

"All right, Austen." She motioned him into a chair and then sat herself in one beside his. She threw her left leg over her right knee and leaned toward him. Her eyes flared wide again. "So, tell me, are you gonna use the old Twilight Reel in the movie?"

"No, I'm afraid not. The story takes place in this area during the First World War." He crossed his legs and relaxed in his seat. "Before there were drive-ins." He leaned toward her. "You should try to get in the film as an extra."

"Seriously? That would be awesome!"

"I think you would look good on camera," he said. "I don't have the details, but I spoke with the editor of your local weekly yesterday, and I think he's featuring a casting call in this week's edition."

"I know Gabe," she said. "I'll ask him about it if I see him, or I'll just look for it in the *Recorder*." She paused. "But I'm sure he's at the crime scene, too."

"Well, Williemae, now that we know each other, can you tell me what's happened?"

Her blue eyes flashed wide and then narrowed with a half-smile. "I see what you did there, Austen." She playfully slapped his knee. "You're smooth." She leaned toward him and lowered her voice. "A local man by the name of Reeves found two dead bodies in a field beside Pump Gap Road earlier this afternoon."

"Oh, wow, that's crazy," Austen Caine said. "I've ridden up and down that road several times over the past two weeks."

"I know, right?"

"Well, that's certainly interesting news." Caine stood up. "I'll avoid the area and find another time to introduce myself to the sheriff." He paused. "What's his name?"

"Brigman. Sheriff Ponder Brigman."

"Thanks, Williemae, I should be getting back to work now." He reached out his hand. "I really enjoyed talking with you."

She took his hand and held it. "Likewise, Austen. And I'll look for the thing about extras in your movie." She released his hand and patted the light brown hair above her left ear and then cupped the bun at the back of her head. "You should stop by and meet Deputy Boyce sometime. He might be better to know than the sheriff if you get what I mean."

"Boyce?"

"Yes, Deputy Davis Boyce. Sheriffs come and go with elections, but Davis has been a deputy forever."

He looked at her. "Forever?"

"Well, you know. Seems like." She laughed and leaned close. "I'd say he was a vampire if he didn't come out in the daytime."

"You have an interesting mind, Deputy Williemae Rider," Caine said and stood looking her up and down for a moment.

She laughed again. "Now, that's the first time I've heard that one. Usually guys find my other parts more interesting." She cupped her bun again and winked. "But I probably shouldn't mention that."

"Hey, how would you like to have dinner with me tonight?"

"Seriously?"

"I'm sorry," he said. "I probably shouldn't—"

"I get off at six o'clock. I can meet you somewhere by seven."

Caine stared down into her blue eyes and then blinked back to the moment. "How about Stoney Knob Café in Weaverville? I'll see if I can get a reservation for this evening."

"Fancy, that!" She wrote her number on the back of an office business card. "Call or text me, you know, if something comes up or if the reservation time is different than seven."

He smiled and winked, pushed through the door and stepped out onto the sidewalk, where he stood a moment with eyes closed and took a deep breath. When his eyes opened again, he stared across the street at the office of the *Runion Recorder*, then turned and headed for his vehicle.

TWENTY

Plumer Reeves knew that a formal identification had yet to be made, but he felt certain that he'd found Terry Goforth and that those at the crime scene aware of the man's disappearance felt the same. As he returned along Lonesome Mountain Road, he wondered what he would tell Livvy Goforth about how he found her Uncle Terry. Then he wondered if he would even have to tell her, given that she'd claimed to know he was dead and asked him only to find the body. He wondered if she would want details of the state that body had been found in and if she would be comforted to learn it hadn't lain in that cold grass alone.

In the span of three days, he'd come to understand she had much of the uncanny about her. Their conversations had been sprinkled with vague or not-so-vague hints at some sort of power she possessed. He still felt a bit dizzy when he remembered the first encounter with her at his cabin, during which she seemed to appear and disappear at will and to know things she shouldn't, like her uncle no longer walked among the living and which seat at the kitchen table had been Kayla's. Something also struck him as odd in the silent across-the-road communication between her and Dr. Baddour and the attendees at the Islamic Center's midday prayers. And what, he wondered, was the nature of the situation or condition or event that her uncle had referred to as "The Rumbles"?

He rounded the curve that brought the mosque and her house in sight, and there she sat on the front steps, coffee cup held between her hands, just as he'd imagined her that morning.

He felt yet again a kind of chilling dizziness at the sudden thought that he might really be imagining her seated there on the steps. "Hell," he said as he maneuvered the Jeep into her driveway and parked it. "I might be imagining her altogether." He took a moment to draw in a deep breath that steadied him. Then he opened the door and stood down out of the vehicle, walked around the warm hood and stepped up into the tiny front yard.

She didn't rise to meet him or shrink from his approach, just sat and watched him come.

Neither of them spoke until he arrived at the foot of the steps and faced her.

"You found him," she said.

"I did." He shoved his hands into the pockets of his pants. He watched her closely and made no move to ascend the steps. "I'm sorry—" He turned his face up to the sky. High up, a turkey vulture drifted without wingwork to the northeast, toward Virginia, and he wondered if it was one of those that carried in its belly pieces of Terry Goforth and the woman. He shuddered at this and let his gaze fall slowly to rest again on her.

"Who was she?" Livvy asked. "The woman in the field with my uncle?"

That she knew didn't surprise him. How she knew, he didn't ask, knowing that she wouldn't or couldn't say. "Don't know for sure," he said. "Gabe Tanner with the paper mentioned a woman name of Dolly Ham that's gone missing. Might be her."

Livvy shifted her coffee cup from both hands to the left and patted the step beside her with the right. "Come up and sit."

He did so, and they sat quietly together for several breaths.

"There'll be another, if there's not one already," she said.

"Another what?"

"Big Granny always said death comes in threes, which I take to mean there's gonna be either one more dead or two more pairs." She took a sip of coffee and offered her cup to him.

He took it and sipped. "I've heard something like that before," he said. "Let's just hope he stops at two or six and doesn't go on to twelve or twenty-four."

"He?"

"The man who killed Terry and that woman."

"What if it's an *it* and not a *he*?"

Plumer didn't know how to respond to that, didn't even know how to think about what she'd just said, so he took another sip of coffee and passed the cup back to her.

"Could be a *she*, I guess," he said at last. "To be fair."

After a while, when the sun was nearly down, he cleared his throat. "Do you want to know how I found him?" He knew that *how* was vague, that she could take it as the process of finding her uncle or the condition in which he was found, depending on the intensity or squeamishness of her curiosity, but that was Plumer's intention—to let her decide what she was ready for.

"Are you hungry?" she asked.

The question struck him as so incongruous that he laughed.

She turned a smiling, curious look toward him, and a breeze caught strands of her golden blonde hair and blew them across her face—in his direction. She gathered these and tucked them behind her left ear. "You haven't eaten since early this morning, so you should be," she said. "I'm guessing."

He looked at her, and as if awakened by the thought of food, his stomach growled.

Livvy apparently heard and smiled again.

"I toasted a little frozen waffle this morning," he said. "But I don't remember having anything since then." He felt and heard his stomach growl again. "So, yeah, I'm hungry."

"I can fry us up some pork chops and bake some biscuits, if that sounds good."

"Well, it sounds more than good, of course. But you don't need to go to all that trouble. Let's go down to Runion and split a pizza or get something at Rio Burrito." He paused to think. "I don't think the Stonehouse Café is open for supper except for Friday and Saturday."

"I might have some catfish or trout Uncle Terry caught a while back." She stood up. "I'll just fix something here, but you can go on to one of those places if you'd like that better."

"No, I wouldn't like that better," he said. "Nor even near as well, I expect." He stood up beside her. "You pick. Pork or fish. I'm happy to have either."

They turned together toward the porch and the front door, and she startled him when she took his hand in hers and led him inside.

TWENTY-ONE

Sunset still shone bright among the bare trees on the ridge across the French Broad as Deputy Davis Boyce eased his patrol car off Highway 251—the "River Road"—and down the short, sloped entrance and into the paved lot of Walnut Island River Park. Earlier in the day, before the discovery of the bodies on Pump Gap Road, he'd driven all the way to the Sams Gap Overlook on I-26 before learning that the abandoned truck there wasn't the one he wanted to find. But this time he had the license plate number, courtesy of Deputy Williemae Rider, and confirmed the pickup at the River Park to be Terry Goforth's even before he pulled into the second parking space to the right of it, leaving an empty space between.

Boyce sat for a moment and looked out across the greening grass and picnic tables to the gleaming river beyond, wishing he had a fishing pole and a bottle of whiskey. His patrol car and Goforth's pickup were the only vehicles in the lot, but he scanned the river's edge and the perimeter of the park to be sure no local residents were there on foot to fish in the twilight, as he would like to do, or walk laps in a setting more peaceful and safer than getting in their exercise along the narrow shoulders of 251.

When he was certain he was alone, he shut down his vehicle, opened his door, and got out. Even though plenty of daylight remained, he reached down and pulled his flashlight from the space between the doorframe and seat. Then he closed the door and stood looking at the old truck. The idea struck him that if he'd found it on his earlier outing, he would be looking at it as a clue, a starting point for setting out to find a missing person. But after the discovery of Goforth's body—he was all but certain it was Goforth's body—on Pump Gap Road, he recognized that this might be a crime scene, the ending point for the man's life. He tucked the flashlight under his left arm and slowly worked his hands into latex gloves as he walked twice around the pickup. He inspected the body for any dents or blemishes that stood out on the faded navy paint job or the rust, but nothing looked fresh.

He stepped closer and looked in the truck bed—a fishing pole without line or reel, some beer and soft drink cans bent in the middle, an empty and balled up pouch of chewing tobacco, a pile of cloth that, when poked around with a gloved finger, turned out to be a dirty t-shirt and a pair of dirty drawers. *Tighty-whities*, he remembered hearing somebody say. *Not so whitey though.*

With flashlight turned on, he leaned to look in the passenger-side window. Keys still hung from the ignition, and he wondered what kind of stress or distraction might have caused Goforth to leave them. He thought perhaps the victim had exited his vehicle without thinking that he might be leaving the river park by some other means. The upholstery on the seat, maybe a light blue at one time, was blue-gray with dust and wear. On the driver side, he saw it was ripped along several seams, revealing the yellowish foam rubber underneath. On the passenger side, he noticed relatively little wear and tear, mostly just the fading from dust and sunlight. He shone his flashlight into the passenger floorboard and saw a small pile of clothes and more bent cans. *PBR and Mountain Dew*, he thought. *Pretty typical.* He saw a tie-dyed T-shirt and a wad of denim. A bib overall strap and buckle loop lay across the toes of scuffed brown brogans that stood neatly in the center between the driver and passenger floorboards—one fully laced with leather and the other without a lace.

He gave one last tug on his gloves, snapped each at the wrist, and tried the passenger door.

It was locked.

Probably not many riding with the poor boy.

He shone his light on the bent cans again and then moved its beam to the driver-side floorboard, where he saw a matchbook lying partially open. He walked around the front of the truck, wondering if the driver-side door was also locked and thinking that the keys might simply be in it because Goforth accidentally locked them inside. *Happens all the time.*

He stopped by the front left headlight and stared into brambles fifty yards away at the south edge of the park. He remembered seven years earlier in 2007 when a major undercover investigation by the Buncombe County Sheriff's office and the NCSBI netted some forty men here, including a middle school teacher and a Holy-Roller preacher, who were regularly engaging in what had been termed "indecent behavior." Over time, apparently, such men had cleared out a secluded space in the thickest brambles and dubbed it "the Man Cave." A successful chain of whispers had spread word about the place, and its popularity finally led to complaints which in turn led to the investigation. Most of those caught were in their forties and fifties, but the whole batch ranged in age from twenty-six to eighty-five. While at least one among those arrested had come from each of the surrounding states—from South Carolina, Georgia, Tennessee, Kentucky, and Virginia—most had been from the area. Two of the charged hailed from Runion, he remembered.

Boyce put his left hand on the hood of Goforth's truck. *Men and their peckers*, he thought. *Wonder if that's got started up again.* He knew they'd done a controlled burn to raze the Man Cave, but he also thought it looked like much of the necessary brambles had grown back in the past seven years.

He tried the driver-side door, and it opened. The air that rose out of the interior smelled as musty as he'd imagined it would after looking at the faded upholstery. He leaned in with the flashlight and went over everything closely again. Then he fished the matchbook from the floorboard and stood up, leaving the door open. He turned off the light and lay it on the front seat.

The matchbook was from a place called Numan's over the mountain in Johnson City. On the inside cover, a jerky hand had scrawled in fading pen a *C*, an *E*, and what looked like *mas 157*. He could tell the writer had attempted another figure or two, but the ink must have run out. He lay the matchbook on the seat and picked up his flashlight, looked through the cab for a pen but didn't find one.

Dagnabbit, he thought and wiped a palm across his mouth again. Then he stepped around to his patrol car, called dispatch at the Buncombe County Sheriff's Office, and asked for a detective to be sent to his location. When he'd been assured that somebody would be there within the hour, he called NCSBI agent Bass Hampton and told him about finding the truck. Hampton said he would be there within the same timeframe. Deputy Boyce again got out of his vehicle and stood in the darkening air. He grabbed his jacket from the back seat and put it on. Then he wandered through the little park and along the river's edge and waited.

While Randi cooked supper and he still had twilight to see by, Spellman Anderson made two trips carrying luggage from Avalon Cottage across the footbridge to the gravel parking lot, where his Acura TL waited with its open trunk, which he closed after the second trip. He raised his eyes to the sky. The moon, in waxing gibbous phase, hung pale and well above Lonesome Mountain and the ridges to its southeast, and he looked from the mountains to his car, to the moon and back again. The Acura salesman had called its color "silver moon," but even though

Spellman thought both vehicle and heavenly body beautiful at this moment, their colors struck him as not really anything alike. He locked the car and turned back toward his island.

He stopped in the middle of the footbridge, continuing to look up at the moon and listening to water singing softly as it passed beneath him. Beautiful as the fading evening was, he could not shake a feeling of uneasy anticipation. Randi and he would leave soon for her native Charleston, a place both of them loved, and as always, they were excitedly anticipating their time there—visiting family, eating favorite dishes in favorite restaurants, walking the historic streets south of Broad and around the College of Charleston, her alma mater.

But he was uneasy about leaving Ariel alone. In the past eight or ten years, Randi and he had made these quarterly trips most often without their only child, who proved more and more reluctant to engage with the world beyond the shores of Christabel Island—even the world of extended family. Spellman had grown used to not having her with them. But the wolves had not yet arrived when they had traveled to Charleston the previous December, so this would be the first time leaving her with them.

Yet he had to admit that she was confident and comfortable with the wolves, more so than she should be perhaps. Her story about discovering the raccoon and then entering Wolfpen Two sent a shiver through him as he stood in the center of the footbridge, just as it had done every time it crossed his mind since she told it over breakfast the week before. Milo and Atalanta are beautiful animals, he had gently scolded her, but, domesticated or not, raised in captivity or not, they are wolves and wild at heart. Over his eggs, he'd decried the folkloric legends that made them into murderous monsters, but he could not shake from his mind images of glowing eyes at the edge of campfire light, of beasts *"red in tooth and claw."* He could not completely separate them from a mystical wilderness invaded by ignorant peasants wielding pitchforks and torches. Even though he had sworn to the locals that nightmarish howls in the night were very unlikely from his wolves, he had sometimes wondered, since the animals' arrival on his island, if he would somehow be more comfortable with them, as Ariel seemed comfortable with them, were they periodically to raise a Hollywood-worthy cry at the moon.

"How long before this stops being weird?" Edie-Mac asked her internet date, known to her only as Chuckey D, who sat across the table in a booth at the Greeneville Applebee's.

"How long before it starts getting weird?" he said and grinned.

She half smiled and looked out the window and danced her fingertips on the tabletop. Then she faced him again. "Really, I mean."

"I thought we were in pursuit of the weird."

"Well, there's this weird, and then there's the weird we want."

The waitress appeared at their table. "Get y'all something to drink?"

They ordered beers.

"Let's just relax and pretend we're on a blind date," he said.

He knew her only as Bylineal, and they'd decided early in their chat history to keep themselves pseudonymous as long as it felt right to do so. Recently, however, they'd discussed that they would exchange real names if this first face-to-face went well.

"I think real names will be the passwords to begin getting beyond this public weirdness," he said.

"All right," Edie-Mac said. "But just so you know, I think it's going pretty well so far."

"Agreed." He looked up as their waitress appeared and set their beers on the table.

They ordered and talked and drank and ate and laughed and drank and talked, and then some seven weeks after they'd first begun chatting and two hours after they'd first met in the parking lot of Applebee's, Chuckey D lay tied to the bed, naked and spreadeagle in Edie-Mac's room at Relax Inn.

The light from the bathroom fell across a body somewhat softer than the one in the faceless or headless pictures he'd shared. The exhaust fan rumbled and hummed a background to the TV's commentary as the Houston Rockets ran up and down the court with the Oklahoma City Thunder.

From the open bathroom door, she watched him harden and tense as she slowly put on her gear.

Williemae Rider enjoyed the lingering tastes of Stoney Knob's Oyster Caesar Salad and the lingering effects of too much sauvignon blanc as Austen Caine carried her, laughing, over his shoulder into the bedroom of his Weaverville Airbnb. But just when she thought she should have held him off long enough to excuse herself to his bathroom to pee and brush her teeth, she passed out.

He wondered how long he'd been conscious before he realized he was conscious, how long he'd screamed with only an airy wheeze coming from his dry mouth and throat—a throat that hurt worse than during intense childhood bouts of strep. He closed his mouth and tried to take deep breaths through his nose, but he managed only a couple before the smells and the darkness shook his breathing into voiceless screaming again.

When that subsided, he sent out ravens and doves along sensory nerves and received them back with reports of cold, nakedness, decay, dirt, and something unidentified next to him. This reminded him of a story from childhood about Noah lying naked and drunk in a tent and cursing his son for seeing him in such a state. He'd never liked Noah after that.

Now he lay naked and imagined himself looking up to see the sky as the striped canopy of a tent and a man—not his son, as he had none—looking down at him.

The screams that were not screams came again.

But he didn't lose his mind for long this time. He began remembering that he'd awakened earlier in this place, and while he still couldn't recall who he was, he recalled seeing a striped sky above him, maybe something like Noah's tent top. *Strips of light?* He saw no stripes this time. He briefly thought he might be blind, but he didn't feel blind. He felt only unable to see—darkness then, he decided, not blindness.

He tried to move his arms and failed. He tried again, and his right arm seemed to creak to life like unoiled machinery while his left remained pinned against him. His right hand then served as raven and dove—flitting over his chest and belly and genitals, probing for damage and firmness.

He raised his left leg to try and bring it within reach of his probing hand, but when his knee banged against wood, the leg sunk back to the cold, moist dirt.

The screams almost came again, but he gagged them with frustration.

After a few moments of failing to think, he raised his right hand and let it wander over the wooden ceiling close above him. He pushed and felt it give a little. He pushed harder and not only felt the give but also heard something creak above it.

He wanted his left hand to help, so his right floated across his chest to learn what held his left arm immobile. He touched the chilled skin of his left shoulder and bicep. He reached further and felt more chilled skin—not his. The shock of it raised him up so that he banged his forehead against the low ceiling, and he slid downward into blackness again before more voiceless screaming could come.

Eliza Tanner finished watching the recordings from the day—*Good Morning, America!*, *The Ellen DeGeneres Show*—and looked at the clock.

10:55.

She set the television to Channel 13 out of Asheville and, finding the station in commercial break, hurried to the bathroom to remove her make-up. Then she returned to her chair with a strand of floss. Before she settled in to watch the eleven o'clock news, she sent a text to Gabriel, asking if he was going to make his midnight deadline for the week's edition. While she awaited his response, she put her phone down on the chair's arm as the news report's opening music sounded. She heard her text alert over the television.

Just wrapping up, Love, his text read. *Home by midnight*. He followed this, as usual, with an emoji of a blown kiss.

Eliza responded with a chain of red lips and heart emojis before returning her attention to the news.

After co-anchor Larry Blunt guided viewers through the second story in the news lineup, a report on two men charged with drug trafficking after a bust that seized almost fifteen hundred pounds of marijuana, he handed off to Darcel Grimes, who introduced the story of two bodies found near Runion in Madison County. Grimes in turn handed off to a blonde female field reporter for more on the story.

Eliza immediately picked out Gabriel in the report's opening shot. She saw him beneath a tent top that must, she figured, cover the two bodies Plumer Reeves had found. She wondered why he was so close to those dead people, but as that shot returned every few moments, she realized that he was taking crime scene photos for one of her salon clients, Dr. Eleanor Rios, whose hair, Eliza thought, looked good despite being in the shade of the funeral home's tent top.

Without introduction or segue, the jowly face and bloated belly of Sheriff Ponder Brigman in his three-piece suit and cowboy hat filled the screen. The reporter asked a couple of questions, and Brigman responded with his usual campaign platitudes about crime and immigration, neither of which answered the reporter's questions.

"What a dumbass," Eliza said aloud and raised her hands from her lap and began to floss through her upper left teeth. After the report finished with the reporter's "Back to you, Darcel," Eliza switched to her upper right teeth. When she'd finished flossing there, she stopped and watched the weather. After the forecast of another day much like the one ending had been, she turned off the television and stood and walked to the dining room table, where Gabriel had left the document Ariel Anderson had given him. Eliza pulled out a chair and sat down, thinking she might scan through the handwritten pages while she finished flossing. She turned over a few of the loose leaves, then stopped and tried to read as she worked through her lower right teeth.

The handwriting was small and tightly packed on the pages. Much of it she couldn't decipher, and those parts she could read didn't make much sense to her. She knew she would need to go back to the beginning and read through if she wanted to understand, but she didn't have the time or energy for that just then.

"I need to get my eyes checked," she said aloud and wondered where her readers were. She couldn't put her hand on her favorites, but she found several pairs on top of the refrigerator.

Back at the table and working through her lower left teeth, she flipped some more pages. But when the readers helped her pick out *terror*, *unknown assailant*, and *desperate*, she decided she shouldn't be reading a spooky old manuscript while alone in a relatively isolated cabin at nearly midnight. She gently restacked the pages, got up from the table, and went to brush her teeth and hair.

When she came out of the bathroom, Gabriel was coming in the front door. They met at the back of the couch and kissed.

"Did you finish?" she asked.

"I did, with thirteen minutes to spare."

"Did you know you were on the news?" When he said he didn't, even though he'd noticed the WLOS 13 people there at the Pump Gap crime scene, she described the story as she'd seen it.

"Maybe I can find it on 13's website," he said. He stepped to the refrigerator, took out a half gallon of chocolate milk, and pulled a couple of swigs directly from the jug. "How fat did I look?"

"Oh, you looked plenty jolly." She laughed. "Just the kind of man I like to crawl into bed with."

Wednesday, March 12

TWENTY-TWO

Plumer Reeves sat at his kitchen table, staring at the yellow Formica tabletop without really seeing it, a cup of coffee held between his hands and cooling to cold. He wasn't sure how he'd come to be there.

The previous evening, he remembered, Livvy Goforth had led him inside her house and seated him at the head of her wormy chestnut dining table. She'd set a cup of coffee in front of him and stoked the fire in the cook stove. Then she disappeared for a few minutes, and when she returned, she topped off his coffee and began gathering cookware and ingredients for the meal she had in mind.

"Can I help?" he said.

"No, you just sit." She set a large mixing bowl on the end of the table opposite him and went about working up her biscuit dough.

She'd pulled her long blonde hair into a ponytail that fell to the middle of her back. She wore a threadbare and faded yellow cotton housecoat, through which he could see she wore a man's tank undershirt and some type of knee-length drawers or knickers. Beneath the hem of the housecoat, her calves descended sleek and strong-looking, and she was barefoot.

He couldn't help imagining that he was in for the night and couldn't help wondering what he was in for after she filled his belly. The thought struck him that the two of them could easily become clichés, the beautiful blonde half his age and the dapper-dressed but dirty old man twice hers. With this thought he again heard in his mind Kayla's voice singing the wrong words to the old Police song, *that girl is half your age.* He watched the muscles in Livvy's forearms flex and relax as she worked the dough with her fingers. Then he wiped his palms on the tops of his thighs and raised his eyes to her face and found her staring at him without expression.

She reached into the bag of flour and dusted a section of the table with it.

He cleared his throat. "I probably shouldn't be here."

She continued to look at him for another long moment. Then she lifted the mound of dough from the bowl. "I've told you I don't think age is such a big deal." She dropped the dough on the floured tabletop.

He shivered at the confluence of his thoughts and her words and at the puffs of flour dust that billowed toward him from around the dropped dough.

"Besides," she said. "I've already got your supper going." She leaned down on the biscuit dough, beginning to press it flat with open hands. "Tell me a story."

"What kind of story?" *Maybe how I found your Uncle Terry?* he thought.

She lifted the flattened round of dough and turned it over, again sending a wispy breath of flour dust billowing in all directions. "Any story. Just something to pass the time while your supper's getting fixed." She again pressed down on the dough with open hands. "Tell me about your place up on Five Finger."

"What about it?"

"Anything about it." She turned and, with a loud clatter, lifted a baking pan from a low cabinet near the stove.

As she cut and panned the biscuits, he told her about his cabin—the history as far back as he knew it, the people known to have lived there, the landscape that the cabin's presence tamed, the animals and trees he knew, the stone outcropping overlook on the other side of Five Finger's highest ridge.

As the biscuits baked and she grilled the pork chops, he told her about how the cabin came to be his, the work he'd done on it with his own hands, how he'd furnished it and arranged its interior to his liking.

And as they ate, he told her about how he'd met and courted Kayla, how her presence changed the place and him, how she disappeared from Hot Springs on her forty-first birthday and just two months into their twelfth year of marriage, how he'd left the place as she'd left it, how it felt abandoned and empty even though he still lived there.

He couldn't remember ever talking so much at one stretch, even to the wife he'd lost, and he wondered if Livvy had cast some kind of speaking spell on him.

When he finished his stories and wiped up the last of the red-eye gravy with his fourth biscuit, he no longer wondered what might happen between them after they'd eaten. He sat in a stupor, his mind dulled with food and exhausted with talk and the long day, from standing in front of Kayla's last painting in the early morning light, to riding the roads in search of Terry Goforth's body, from finding it and the other, to arriving at her place on Lonesome Mountain.

Livvy cleared the dishes from the table and put them in the sink.

Then she moved behind him and placed a hand atop each of his shoulders, not massaging but only resting them there.

And then her hands left his shoulders.

And then he felt their closeness and heat as they hovered near his ears without touching them.

And then fingers eased into the edges of his sight, and she cupped his eyes.

And then she'd pulled his head back to rest against her breasts.

And then he sat staring at yellow Formica instead of wormy chestnut, with no memory of what had happened between that table and this—no memory of leaving her, of driving home to his cabin, of climbing his front porch steps and entering, of making the cup of coffee now cooling between his hands.

TWENTY-THREE

Ariel Anderson

In March, in June, September, and December, my parents make their pilgrimage to the Holy City—Charleston, South Carolina—where my mother was born and spent her privileged girlhood and became a young woman. When they make these trips, they depart our river island after midnight, doing so for two reasons. First, they do not want anyone to see them leave. No one, if at all possible, is to know that the island is unguarded—that I am unguarded, as I attend them on these sojourns only in Decembers, if then. Second, they enjoy arriving in Charleston early enough to watch sunrise from The Battery. They drive down King Street in predawn light and park on Murray Boulevard, exit their vehicle and stand hand-in-hand at the railing, the rest of their world and its history forgotten for a time. Only when the sun is fully up somewhere over Fort Moultrie do they drive around the corner at White Point Garden to Mother's childhood home, the estate at 5 East Battery.

So it was that they left at one o'clock in the morning on the twelfth of March, and I spent the remainder of the night alone in Avalon Cottage. I am not one to frighten easily, but still the night passed in fitful sleep as I startled awake every few minutes at some sound or sensation, even those that were commonplace enough and never disturbed me before. I heard the natural pops and creaks of a two-hundred-year-old house and imagined a murderer's misstep in the dark parlor below me or the groaning of a stair as he attempted to ascend quietly. Then I was repeatedly caught off guard by the rumbling to life of the furnace in the basement or the refrigerator downstairs in the kitchen.

I remember two flash dreams, terrifying in their brief, ineffable intensity. In the first, I was in some pitch-black place, which felt like the library across the hall from my bedroom. I moved about without aim and once or twice brushed against someone or something that terrified me with an unearthly solidity that suggested an irresistible strength. Then, without a rational transition from my moving about, I found myself on a bed against a wall in the dark room, and someone else—someone I loved, I think—huddled there in the blackness with me. I buried my face against my beloved and whisper-screamed over and over, *'It's on the bed! It's on the bed!'* I felt death imminent before I startled awake.

In the second dream, a tall figure in trailing ecclesiastical vestments glided toward Gabriel Tanner, who backed away in voiceless, abject terror until backed against a wall. Mr. Tanner's face and body revealed a powerless, hopeless surrender to the inevitable as he grimaced and writhed with pathetic, terrified shame at the figure's approach. I took up the train of the vestments and pulled in an attempt to save him, at which the figure turned its shiny face—the uncanny face of a ceramic child—and directed its sightless gaze toward me. Again, I felt death was imminent, and again, I startled awake.

Each of these dreams sent waves of chills back and forth along all my limbs, up and down my spine, and across my scalp for long minutes before I could once more close my eyes.

In all my waking or near-waking moments, my mind swirled with some remembered or perhaps some misremembered detail from the old manuscript I had discovered, perused, and passed on to Gabriel Tanner. The year was 1800, and, according to the narrative, members of the Avalon community and at least one guest believed that *loup-garou*—a werewolf—wandered Christabel Island and the meagerly inhabited surrounding hills beneath a half-year span of full moons. The story found its horrific climax in a cabin in the woods behind Avalon Cottage, a cabin that would be wiped from the face of Earth by the catastrophic floodwaters of 1902.

Over two centuries later, another beast had arisen among us in the early days of March.

I felt it. Even as I lay abed in the darkness, restless between an uneasy waking and a haunted sleeping, I felt the gaze of a malevolent presence periodically focused on me, speculating about me in some context I refused to contemplate.

Our wolves felt it as well. Although they made no unusual sounds, I felt their agitation. In my mind's eye, I saw them pacing with their distinctive lopes along the fencing that bounded their worlds.

I counted it a mercy when the night ended, and I gratefully arose into the same civil twilight I imagined my parents standing in on Charleston's Battery. I imagined that as they awaited the sunrise, they watched in front of them a trawler chugging out toward Fort Sumter and the open sea for a day of fishing and to their left a high-stacked container ship and its colorful cargo clearing the Ravenel Bridge and entering Charleston Harbor via the Cooper River. So taken are they with these sights in such moments that early rising runners and dogwalkers would be passing unnoticed. Unusual for me that I felt a pang as I dressed, a longing to be there with them.

I passed over the red cloak I wear when feeding the wolves—having fed them the day before—and selected my green one to put on over a warm white cotton shirt and jeans. Removing the cloak from its peg revealed the leather satchel also hanging there, its contents a sketchpad and pencils, a well-worn paperback of Romantic poetry, and some meaningful odds and ends. I slung the satchel over my head and hung it on my shoulder, then went outside to greet the risen sun and my wolves. After passing the orchard and noticing hints of reviving life on a few branches, I climbed the hill to Wolfpen One. Demeter and Iasion were as I had imagined they would be, outside their structures and loping along just inside the perimeter fencing. They seemed neither skittish nor aggressive, but I detected a slight raising of the hackles—evidence of some agitation—as they passed by me without seeming to notice my presence. The wolves lapped me three times as I made my way from the gate on the lower side of Wolfpen One to the top and around to the gate again.

I confess that I felt an increasing sense of anxiety related not to my wolves and their agitation but to that sense of malevolent watchfulness seeming to emanate from the surrounding hills and hollows. I had begun to feel that this presence approached ever nearer the shores of our Christabel.

I stood and watched the pair of wolves approach again from my left, pass by me, and move along the fence to my right, the tip of Demeter's tail seeming as if it should tickle Iasion's nose as he followed keeping perfect pace with her steady gait. After they had passed, my left hand went to the lock, and the fingertips of my right lightly touched the keyring in my pocket. I could not tell in that moment if I wanted to open the gate and enter, locking myself in with them, or to open it and let them out to roam the island and sleep in the mudroom of Avalon Cottage.

I left the gate locked and returned along the west side of the enclosure, this time leaving the fence line at its highest point and continuing to the southern headland. Just to the right of the promontory, at the edge of the Avalon community cemetery, a boulder juts some four feet of its bulk out of the earth, and this I often used as an altar to Artemis. I lifted the satchel's flap and dug around inside. The first item I removed was a red and white bandana, which I spread across the level top of the boulder. Next, I took out a bear figurine carved in desert ironwood, a buck in basswood, and a dove in wood known as tree of heaven. The last items drawn from the satchel were three pearls, a chunk of quartz crystal, a cast-iron arrowhead, and my grandfather's Barlow penknife. Finally, I removed the wide silver cuff from my wrist. The figures and gemstones and bracelet I then spread out on the bandana, arranging and rearranging them until something told me a certain configuration was right for the moment.

I took a deep breath and raised my face to blue sky and white morning clouds. I spread my arms out over the stone altar, palms up. After slowly releasing my initial breath, I drew in a deeper one and spoke. "O Great Artemis, Goddess of moon and forest, of deer and owl, divine Wolf Goddess of the woods, thy praises I raise from this headland. You are my Hunter-Protectress, feeding and sheltering me in sunlit day and moonlit night. You have called to me, and I have answered in this early light—to await your wisdom, to be filled with your presence and spirit. I seek entrance into thy mysteries, a vision quest into thy ways. Hear me, Great Artemis." After this invocation, I prayed, "O Divine Mistress, I ask thee to inspire me with confidence and courage. I ask for freedom from doubt and fear, from abusive and violent man. Show me the strength I have in you. Show me the strength I have in you. Through every trial I face, show me the strength I have in you, and let me walk in beauty. I pray this now. I pray this now. With assurance and thanksgiving, I pray this now, O Great Artemis."

As the name of the Goddess expired to a sibilance between my teeth, intertwined howls rose into the air behind me. Although each separate howl might be forlorn and the two together might be the voice of wildness, the difference tone they created between them seemed to me the answering voice of Artemis herself.

I turned and saw that Demeter and Iasion had stopped their agitated circling at the top of their enclosure and stood still, staring at me with ears perked up. Although I could not see Atalanta and Milo from where I stood, I listened to their first howls on Christabel Island. A shiver ran along my spine and to the tips of my fingers and toes, but I knew Artemis had heard my prayer. I felt the shiver not as a response to fear, not like the shivers that had followed my nightmares, but as an excited anticipation. Something was coming, I knew, and I was glad that I anticipated it with resolve rather than dreading it with fear.

I felt the almond-shaped golden eyes of Demeter and Iasion watching me as I descended through the headland woods. Although the howling had not continued, I imagined as I walked beneath the trees that I would find Atalanta and Milo on top of their enclosure's central mound with heads thrown back and open snouts skyward in full-throated howls, their bodies silhouetted against cumulous clouds white as the moon.

But when I emerged near the southeast corner of the orchard, their movement immediately drew my eyes to them. They were doing just as Demeter and Iasion had been doing, loping along counterclockwise and in tandem just inside the fencing, and as they bent toward me out of the northernmost curve of their enclosure, I admired the minimal movement of their gait, which, I imagined, conserved energy and would allow them to continue for hours and hours and miles and miles.

When they rounded the southernmost curve and turned away from me, passing the gate I had entered that snowy morning a week before and then continuing their journey along the far side of the enclosure, I physically flinched as if from the clumsy bump of a gnat against my open eye. I turned my face downward and blinked hard twice. I paused for a moment to be sure my vision was clear and then looked up again.

A naked girl sat against a tree trunk on the far side of Wolfpen Two.

My breath caught in my throat and my mind froze, and I could feel the sudden quickened beat of my heart in both throat and mind—quickening initially at the presence of a stranger on the island and then at her nakedness in the cool morning and then at her absolute stillness. I forced myself to breathe again and closed my eyes. *Through every trial I face, show me the strength I have in you, Artemis, goddess.* I looked again at the girl and then again at the wolves.

Atalanta and Milo approached to pass me once more at the same steady pace. Certainly, they were aware of the presence of humans—one alive and one, perhaps, dead—but showed no signs. They neither altered their gait nor looked aside as they passed each of us in turn.

I watched them all the way around until the point where they passed her for a third time, and my gaze slid once more from the wolves in motion to the motionless stranger. And then I found myself moving forward, at first keeping the enclosure between her and me but then stepping to my right so that I could see without the interference of fencing. I continued to draw closer to what seemed an apparition until I was only a few feet from it.

The woman—for woman she was and not a girl—sat propped against a white pine that stood some twenty feet outside Wolfpen Two, between the enclosure's high fencing and the island's eastern shoreline. She was, or she had been, somebody I did not know, somebody I had never seen before. She appeared small, perhaps little more than five feet tall, with shoulder-length light brown hair and oddly tanned skin. Her feet splayed left and right, and her hands lay clasped in her lap, not bound but with fingers interlaced. A thin black cord that stretched across her open mouth and bit into her cheeks was tied around the tree and held her head upright. Eyes that must have been startlingly blue in life stared palely toward the heights of Five Finger Mountain.

Something in that stare reawakened in me the now-familiar feeling of being watched. She was not the Watcher, but I somehow felt as if she were watching the Watcher—or maybe as if he had put her here and posed her in such a way that she must look up to him with a kind of rapt adoration.

I turned in the direction of her gaze and lifted my own eyes to the heights of Five Finger Mountain. I sensed him there watching us, the dead woman and me. Watching intently but as distant as a lustful god on Olympus. I turned away, back to my consideration of the unfortunate and what I should do about her. *O Divine Mistress, inspire me with confidence and courage. Free me from doubt and fear.* With this prayer, I took a deep breath and did what I felt strongly I must first do even though I also felt I should not. I went around the tree and bent to inspect the tight knot that bound her, touching it only to assure myself that it was too tightly tied to unloose. Then I knelt and pulled from my satchel Grandfather's penknife to cut the cord. I would release her from her forced idolization of the Watcher on the mountain. When the cord was nearly severed, I held it in such a way that I gentled her chin to her chest rather than allow it to drop abruptly and unceremoniously. When I came back around the tree, I found that Atalanta and Milo had stopped their pacing and stood facing me with ears perked up as from the headland sounded the intertwined howls of Demeter and Iasion.

"Sister," I said to the dead woman, "I am sorry to leave you here alone again as he left you." I turned to the wolves. "Sister Atalanta, please keep her company, and Brother Milo, please keep watch." With that, I left her and hurried through the orchard toward Avalon Cottage.

TWENTY-FOUR

Gabriel Tanner

When I got to the office, I found John Riddle's response to the email I'd sent the day before.

> *Gabe,*
>
> *Guess you didn't remember we're on spring break. I'm in town but not in the office. Given what you said about the manuscript you're trying to figure out, I think we ought not look at it over bagels and coffee. Best to keep old paper away from such things. I'd like to stay away from my office, but my place is too much a wreck to meet here. So, I'll be in the ASA reading room on the fourth floor of the library at 9:00. Will that work? If I don't hear from you, I'll see you there then. (Maybe lunch after?)*
>
> *Looking forward to it—and to reading this MS you have.*
>
> *John*

His was the most recent email, having come in at 8:23. I closed it and figured I had time to do one or two things before I hiked over to the Peery-Lenburg Library on campus.

I scanned the list of unopened emails that had populated my inbox since I left the office late the night before. "Shit," I said when I saw Dr. Eleanor Rios's name. I'd forgotten to send her the photos I'd taken of the bodies found beside Pump Gap Road. "Okay, maybe time for just this one thing."

As I began uploading the images into a series of emails, I wondered why photos of the bodies seemed more difficult to look at than the bodies themselves had been. Was it the difference between having them removed to the far end of a camera lens up there on Pump Gap while from my desktop monitor they stared me in the face? Or the difference between hovering around the dead while surrounded by people, including several members of law enforcement, and then seeing them while alone in the newspaper office, where I recognized the possibility that I could hear the front door open and be more or less in the condition of those two dead people—minus the critter damage—within a matter of minutes and nobody the wiser for hours?

I sent the first, second, and third emails with their ghastly attachments to Dr. Rios before my mind swerved to a question: *Where's Edie-Mac?* I remembered that yesterday she'd been on her way to Greeneville, Tennessee, and that she'd said she would see me on Thursday. We had a killer among us, that much seemed plain both in the field up Pump Gap and in the photos I took, and of course my mind raced to the image of a faceless killer with hands around Edie-Mac's throat in some seedy, curtain-darkened motel room an hour away. I knew that it was just my imagination running away with me, but my elbows and knees suddenly felt weak. My stomach flipped. I pulled out my cell phone and called her. When she didn't answer, I waited for the tone and left a message. "Hey, it's Gabe, your boss, just calling to let you know that you've won Employee of the Month yet again." I paused. "But new rules for this award dictate that the value decreases the longer it takes for you to acknowledge and accept by returning this call." I paused again. "So, get in touch, okay? As soon as you can." After a third pause, I added, "Hope you're all right and having fun."

I must have dazed off in front of the computer, seeing but not seeing the image of two dead bodies while my mind raced through horrific scenarios that might leave Edie-Mac lying with a man like Terry Goforth in some mountain meadow or shallow grave between Runion and Greeneville. I startled back to the moment when the chimes rang to announce an incoming email. I opened it and read, *thanks for these. where are the rest –er*. I clicked to send the fourth, fifth, and sixth emails and attachments. Before sending the seventh and final one, I wrote in the body of the message, *Sorry for the delay, Doc. Let me know if you need these in another form as well. Edie-Mac can help me figure out how to do whatever you need when she's back in the office tomorrow.—gjt*. I clicked to send, grabbed the folder with the Avalon manuscript, and hurried out of the office for my meeting at the library.

Dr. John Riddle, Professor of English, sat in the reading room of the Archives of Southern Appalachia, his shoulders slightly hunched, his hands clenched together with interlaced fingers and held between his thighs, his face hovering over the folder open on the tabletop in front of him. When he'd read through roughly the first half of the manuscript, he turned to me. "Gabe, have you read this whole thing?" Before I could answer, he turned to the Collections archivist, who sat at the reading room's reference desk. "Jen, what are your thoughts about copying this?"

Jen Bingham came from behind the desk and joined us at the reading table. "To be honest," she said as she took a seat, "since it's not a part of our collection, you can copy it however you want to." She leaned forward and seemed to study the paper. "But I'll be happy to scan it and send you out with a digital copy to print from."

"Perfect," John said. He turned to me. "Okay?"

"Okay by me," I said and pushed the folder to Jen, who carefully gathered the pages together, rose, and disappeared down a hallway. "What are you thinking?"

"I didn't get to the end, of course, but it's shaping up to be quite a story." He sat back in his chair for a moment. "It reads like fiction, but given the letter that came with it, I don't think we're supposed to understand it as that." He folded his arms and leaned forward with his elbows on the table. "Fiction in 1800 usually tried to read like fact or at least founded on—"

"What about the signature on the letter?" I interrupted. "Sorry. Could you recognize it?"

"I have an idea," he said. "Didn't I say?"

"Not that I heard."

"Well, maybe I just thought I said it out loud."

"One of those absent-minded professor moments?"

"Probably that or having lived alone too long," he said. "I'll need to do a little research, of course, but the first person that came to mind when I looked closely at the signature, especially with the mention of Mettingen and Norwalk in those first pages, was Charles Brockden Brown."

"Never heard of him," I said.

"Most people haven't. He was a novelist and a magazine editor. One of those American writers you probably won't run across unless you wind up doing graduate studies in early U.S. literature. And maybe not even then if you don't dig into his time period." He sat back in his chair again and yawned. "I try to do a little bit with him every semester either as an endpoint to the colonial and federal period or as a proto-Romantic."

"You mean like a forerunner of Poe and Hawthorne?"

John Riddle uncrossed his arms and slapped his palms down on the tops of his thighs. "By God, you do remember the class you took with me." He chuckled. "What was that, twenty years ago?"

“About that,” I said.

“I would imagine that Poe read him, but I don’t know that for sure. Hawthorne certainly did and even mentions Brown a couple of times in his short works.” He raised a hand to his chin and stroked his beard for a moment. “I’d bet Poe read him. Brown’s stuff has a bit of Poe’s madness in it. Moreso than Hawthorne’s, I think.”

Jen Bingham returned to the table with the folder sealed in a large ziplock bag that enclosed a flash drive as well. “Here you go, Dr. Riddle,” she said. Then she turned to me. “Gabe, scanning and the drive are on the house if you’ll try to get the folks over at Avalon to donate this to the Archives.”

“Thanks, Jen,” I said. “I’ll talk to them about it.”

John and I exited the reading room and stopped at the top of the library’s four-story staircase.

“Shall we meet for lunch in an hour or so?” John asked. “I’m going to step into the stacks and see if we have a biography of Brown. The author of the manuscript mentioned a brother Joseph in eastern North Carolina. That’s something I don’t know about, but maybe a Brown scholar confirms that.”

“All right, I’ll go back to the office and print out three or four complete copies for us.” I started down the stairs, then stopped and looked up as he was turning away. “I need to talk to Rio Burrito about some advertising. Will that be okay for lunch?”

TWENTY-FIVE

Plumer Reeves's kitchen had brightened with the advance of morning by the time the sounds of an engine revving and of tires humming over the blacktop on Highridge Road shook him from his stupor. He rose stiffly from the table, poured the remainder of his cold coffee down the drain, rinsed the cup, and set it in the sink. He decided that he could use some movement to loosen his joints and clear his head, so he changed again into his green long-sleeved t-shirt, faded jeans, and everyday hiking boots. He pressed his palm against the closed door of Kayla's studio as he passed on the way from their bedroom to the front porch.

In the woods, he stepped between the laurels that mostly hid his private trail from passersby on the public trail to the overlook called Five Finger Pulpit. He glanced down the slope to his left. He could see through the trees some sort of light-colored vehicle parked at the Pulpit Loop trailhead. He also caught a glimpse of blue that he thought might be a second vehicle parked on the other side of the first, even though he'd heard only the one. Still not bright-minded enough to be overly curious, he turned right to follow the trail across the peak.

He slowed as he descended toward the Pulpit itself. Remembering how he and Kayla used the overlook from time to time, he didn't want to barge in on some bare-assed tryst in progress. He continued quietly downward until he was twenty feet from the top rim of the overlook's bowl and the point where the trail bent left to enter the bowl from the side. Then he stepped off to his right as quietly as he could in the dried leaves underfoot and found a hiding place behind a forty-year-old white oak. He peeked around the trunk, and his breath caught.

The man stood on the Pulpit rock, dangerously close, Plumer thought, to the edge. He wore hiking shoes and khaki shorts but no shirt. His blond-haired head was bare as well. In profile, his chest and back and left arm appeared hard with muscle and strangely tan for March.

Weight rooms and tanning beds, Plumer thought.

The man stood steady and casual on the edge of a view that sometimes—although rarely in hazy recent years—stretched all the way to Asheville. His right hand appeared to be in the pocket of his shorts or akimbo on his right hip, and his left hand held a monocular scope to his left eye. He seemed focused on something in particular and didn't move his lens back and forth across the landscape as Plumer had done with his binoculars two evenings before.

After watching the man's uncanny stillness until he felt anxious, Plumer decided not to disturb him and stepped quietly back to the trail and turned uphill toward the peak. He reached the point at which he could manage one last glimpse of the Pulpit and turned to see the man still standing just as he had been. He shook his head at the strangeness of this and continued over the peak, thinking that a banana sandwich and a nap might make him feel more himself after this and the other the strangenesses of the past twenty-four hours—seeking a dead body and finding two, talking and talking to Livvy Goforth, finding himself at home without knowing how he came to be there.

The man lowered the scope from his eye and turned from the cliff's edge just in time to see the fellow who'd been watching him disappear up the trail. He'd known he was under surveillance from the moment the spy stepped into the dried leaves beside the beaten path, and he wondered who his visitor might be and why he chose to hide and watch rather than join him at the overlook. Had he come hoping to find the Pulpit vacant so that he might carry on some tryst with woman or man or god? Or simply find some solace in solitude? Maybe, he thought, his presence had caused the fellow to abandon a suicidal plunge down the mountainside.

He'd kept an ear trained on the fellow's departure while he devoted the rest of his concentration to what passed on Christabel Island. The scope didn't bring the activity there as close as he would like, but he could watch well enough the increasing ant-like swirl of activity around what he had wrought in the night.

TWENTY-SIX

Several floorboards in a back corner of the shack lay askew, revealing the hole where he'd lain beside her for he didn't know how long. He'd shivered his way up from the cold and damp, through the opening he'd made between the boards, and curled into himself beside the hole to try and get warm. In the pale gray light of early morning, he shivered partly from the cold, partly from the chilled flesh that had pressed against him in the hole, and partly from words that seemed to crawl on all fours through his addled mind—*grave*, *tomb*, *handsome stranger*, *monster*, *murderer*, *strangler*, *lover*, *corpse*.

At last, he rose to all fours and then reached into the hole, trying not to look at her face, and pulled out his gametime hoodie and gold slacks. He sat cross-legged on the floor and held these in his lap and cried over the dirt on them. When his sobs subsided, he struggled to his feet, clutching the clothes to his chest and using the table to brace himself. He spread the hoodie and slacks on the tabletop and brushed away the dirt and mud as best he could, then folded them carefully. He wondered about his shoes and socks and underwear and turned and stood at the edge of the hole, alternately looking for them in the darkness beside the pretty woman and at the droplets of blood welling from the thin skin of his naked knees. As he teetered there above his resting place, he could feel splinters in the meat of his toes.

He picked up his clothes and clutched them to his chest again, and then, as if he suddenly remembered where he'd put his shoes, he bent and opened the bottom drawer of the chest and removed them. With two fingers hooked inside the heels, he straightened up and let his gaze roam over her body from painted toenails to open eyes. Fixing on her face, he tried to remember her name and then wondered if he even knew it. He remembered some TV show in which a man and woman had spent a wild night together without either knowing the other's name. He tried to recall if they had made love in the muddy chill beneath the boards or maybe, at least, held hands against the cold and darkness. He gave up on trying to remember her name when he realized again that he couldn't remember his own. Thinking he should say something, maybe thank her for keeping him company or invite her to leave the place with him, he drew a breath and held it a moment before letting it out, not knowing what to say and fearing that anything he came up with would come out as nothing but a wheeze.

Clutching clothes and shoes to chest and belly, he waggled two free fingers at her and turned and used the same fingers to open the door and stepped out onto the rickety porch. He watched one car roll past on the dirt road just the other side of a ditch that divided the front yard, faces looking at him open-mouthed from the passenger-side windows. He saw its brake lights shine for a moment and then heard gravel clunk against the undercarriage when the driver floored it.

He wondered who was in that car and where they might be going.

He wondered where he might be. He couldn't recall ever visiting this place before or standing on this front porch looking across the wild grass and the ditch and the dirt road.

He wondered why he was here, wherever he was, and if the ditch might have some cool water running through it and if he would be able to find his car from here.

He wondered what time it was and what day it was. He wondered if he'd missed checkout at the Hilton and would have to pay extra.

He marveled for a moment at how he could wonder all this and not even know his own name.

He closed his eyes against the coming tears and stifled his need to cry after only two sobs. Then he went down two cinderblock steps, crossed the yard and the bridge over the ditch, oblivious to the trickle of running water underneath, and stopped to stand beside a tree at the edge of the road.

TWENTY-SEVEN

Gabriel Tanner

John already sat at a table and was thumbing his way through an old book when I arrived with the photocopies of the MS and the advertising paperwork I needed Pablo McCormick, Rio Burrito's owner, to look over and sign and, I hoped, return to me with his payment. "Find what you were looking for in the library?" I asked.

"Nothing up to date," he said. "But looks like it contains the information we need." He handed me the book. "It's from 1949."

I looked at the spine, but the gold lettering seemed to have faded into the book's textured burnt orange cloth. I flipped to the title page and read, *Charles Brockden Brown, American Gothic Novelist* by Harry R. Warfel. The facing page held a woodcut image I assumed to be of Brown. According to it, he appeared to be in his forties or early fifties, balding but with what looked like a good bit of short-cropped hair growing far back on his pate, large eyes and nose. The high collar of a dark coat wrapped around the back of his neck, and his clean-shaven chin was firmly set above a ruffled shirt front. The initials "T.C." appeared in the lower lefthand corner. "Gothic indeed," I said and glanced up from the page. "Looks to be about our age."

"Actually, he didn't make it that long. Died of consumption—tuberculosis—at thirty-nine."

I again studied the picture and wondered if the glancing eyes were blue or brown or green, wondered if they were faded with disease. Then I closed the book and laid it on the table.

We went to the counter and ordered our burritos, filled our drink cups, and returned to our seats to wait.

"So, you think this is our author?" I asked.

"I might check another source or two to confirm, but yes, I think Brown wrote your Avalon manuscript." He opened the book and flipped through the pages for a moment, then stopped and scanned. "Listen to this," he said and read, "'Joseph, the eldest brother whose residence was in'"—he turned the page—"'Edenton, North Carolina, visited in Philadelphia and Princeton, New Jersey, in the summer of 1800.'"

"So, older brother heads north for a visit in the summer, and younger brother returns the visit in the fall?"

"Something like that, I suppose." John sipped his unsweet tea. "We had another book, a brand new collection of Brown's letters, in the library's reference section. No letters between the first of September that year and the fifteenth of December, which squares exactly with the dates he gives in the Avalon letter asking if his manuscript has turned up."

"Seems like confirmation to me."

"Yes, it does, especially with the mention of Mettingen and Norwalk I pointed out earlier." He snapped his fingers. "The volume of letters included a historical essay that I meant to check, but I got hungry and in a hurry. It might have information like Warfel's in it. I'll go back for another look before I head home."

We leaned away from the table as Pablo delivered our orders.

"For Dr. Riddle," he said and set down a basket overflowing with a large burrito half wrapped in foil and surrounded by a mound of chips. "And here's yours, Gabe." He set my own piled-high basket in front of me.

"Thanks, Pablo." I picked up the envelope I'd brought from

the office and handed it to him. "Before I get food on this, can you take it and look it over if you get a minute? I'll come find you when we've finished here."

"Sure thing," he said and left us.

We settled into eating, and after a few bites, John wiped his lips and took another sip of tea.

"The collection of Brown's correspondence also included a sample image of a holograph letter. The handwriting looked pretty much like what I was reading this morning. When I go back and check the historical essay, I'll compare that sample page with what you've printed out." He picked up his half-eaten burrito and then stopped, holding it between basket and mouth. "If this Avalon manuscript is indeed Brown's narrative of a previously unknown southern sojourn, it'll make a great article or conference paper."

"Well, if you'll write a version for our Runion folk, I'll put it in the *Recorder*," I said. "Not that you need another publication, I'm sure." We both continued eating, and I imagined that he was wondering about what the rest of the manuscript might hold and thinking about possible thesis statements, about research he would need to do, the conferences or journals where he might present or publish. For my part, I was curious about the unread portion of the story as well and what it might contribute to the *Recorder*'s offerings on local history. What little I'd read in the manuscript seemed interesting and light enough for my readers, but language in the letter that accompanied it gave the whole a sense of foreboding.

After John left to return to the library, taking the manuscript copies with him, and I concluded my business with Pablo, I pushed through Rio Burrito's front door and stepped out onto the corner of Main and Mill Streets with Edie-Mac on my mind. I stood facing across Main and looking at the front of Eliza's salon while I dialed Edie-Mac's number and put the phone to my ear. When I'd listened to her outgoing voicemail message, I simply said, "Let me hear from you, please," and disconnected the call. I dropped the phone in my pocket and crossed the street. "The Whole Enchilada" by Keb' Mo' greeted me when I opened the door, and Eliza danced away from her lady's head and kissed me.

"You just came from across the street, I smell," she said.

"I had some business with Pablo."

"And some lunch." She returned to stand behind her styling chair. "Did you bring us anything?"

I held out my hands, empty and open. "Just came to get your order."

She laughed. "We're good."

Her client turned toward me then, and I saw that it was Martha Buckner, whose hair Eliza had been taking care of for well over thirty years.

"Hey, Martha," I said. "Sorry to interrupt."

She smiled and winked and turned back to her image in the mirror.

"Have you heard from Edie-Mac?" I asked Eliza.

"No, should I have?"

"I've been calling, but I haven't gotten an answer," I said. "Just makes me worried after what we found yesterday."

"It's her day off, right?" When I nodded, Eliza added, "I'm sure she's okay." She danced away from Martha and kissed me again. "See you at home later," she said and went back to her work.

I headed up the sidewalk to my office. When I unlocked and pushed through the front door, the police scanner was going crazy. I heard a lot of distorted orders barked between clipped and cryptic reports.

Something had happened on Christabel Island. Something or somebody had been seen in the vicinity of Hipps Mountain. Nothing was clear beyond these garbled sound bites.

I pulled out my phone and dialed Edie-Mac one more time.

When the call went to voicemail again, I said, "Hey, still waiting to hear from you." I paused as if she might answer. Then, "Listen, something's going on over in the Hipps Mountain area. I can't tell what it is, but if you're coming back from Greeneville this afternoon, keep an eye out, okay?" I collapsed into my chair and tossed the phone onto my desk blotter. I'd planned lots of work with my advertisers, and now something was happening at almost opposite ends of the county while my help was *incommunicado*. I couldn't decide which direction to go, so I sat twirling a pencil, glancing at my phone, listening to the scanner, and waiting for clarity.

After a while, I heard no more about whatever had been seen on Hipps Mountain. I hoped that Edie-Mac would be on her way back from Tennessee in the afternoon, if she hadn't returned already, and that she would hear my message and take a look around. The few sporadic bursts from the scanner seemed all about Christabel. Little detail came across in these bursts, but I got the sense that something bad had happened—something on the scale of the previous day's Pump Gap Road discovery, maybe even worse. I turned to my computer and brought up those programs and documents I would later need to work on the advertising accounts. I wanted them to pop up in front of me as soon as I returned to the office and jiggled my mouse. I stood up, already tired and nervous, and waited a moment to steady myself. Then I grabbed my phone and camera bag, along with the folder containing the original Avalon manuscript, and headed for my car.

But I got only as far as dropping into the driver's seat before the phone vibrated. I squirmed to draw it out of my pocket, checked to see who was calling, and immediately answered.

"Hey, boss, you called?" Edie-Mac said.

I almost ripped into her for not calling me back sooner, but I checked myself. "You doing all right?" I asked. "How was Greeneville?"

"I'm okay and headed back," she said. "Greeneville was weird, but that's just what I needed it to be."

"I'm not sure I want to know what that means."

"That's good, because I can't tell you until you're younger."

"Meaning?"

"I can't tell you."

"Well, I guess I'll just have to live with not knowing, 'cause I sure ain't getting any younger," I said. "Did you hear my messages?"

"My generation doesn't listen to messages, especially on our day off. What's up?"

"Where are you right now?"

"Let's see," she said. "I'm on 107, just passing the Nolichucky Substation."

"Well, you really are just now headed back, aren't you?"

"That's what I said, boss."

"Okay." I started my car. "Do you know the Hipps Mountain area before you get back to Belva bridge?"

"I do," she said. "You're gonna make me work?"

"It's probably nothing, so just a drive-by will do. Something came across the scanner earlier. A garbled burst about somebody seeing something. And it was only the one mention of Hipps Mountain and then nothing, so it's probably just that."

"Nothing?"

"Just drive a mile or so up the mountain. If you don't find anything, go on home, and I'll see you tomorrow."

"You've got it, boss. If I don't have a signal up there, I'll text you soon as I can."

"All right, something's going on over at Avalon, so that's where I'm heading." I checked my side mirror and pulled out onto Main Street. "Hang on," I said and tooted my horn as I passed Eliza's salon and then coasted down toward the bridge to Piney Ridge.

I felt a sudden pang of uncertainty about sending Edie-Mac

alone to Hipps Mountain. It was one of those areas that exist on the periphery of most communities like Runion, communities thought to be happy and secure. Hipps Mountain and its canopy-covered, dead-end dirt roads was a storied place of rough terrain and rough denizens, a place fugitives disappeared into and where others—so the stories go—sometimes just disappeared. But it was broad daylight, a plain Wednesday in early March.

"You still there?" Edie-Mac asked.

"Yeah, sorry," I said. "Listen, on second thought, don't worry about Hipps Mountain. Don't go up there. Just get home safe, and I'll see you tomorrow."

"You're acting weirder than normal, gramps," she said. "What's up?"

Just then, the phone vibrated between my hand and ear, and I glanced at the screen to see a text from Dr. Rios—*need you or e-m on christabel with camera asap*. I put the phone back to my ear as I turned right onto the bridge. "Runion is weirder than normal," I said. "Get home safe, okay?" I barely heard Edie-Mac asking what I meant as I disconnected the call.

Rolling slowly across the bridge, I thumbed Dr. Rios's text and then the microphone icon for dictation and sent, "On my way." Then I dropped the phone in the passenger seat but continued rolling slowly on the bridge, looking south and scanning the undulating ground of Christabel Island.

TWENTY-EIGHT

Ariel Anderson

I stood at the window at the end of Avalon Cottage's upstairs hallway and watched through a spyglass as the group of men circled the women beneath the tree—the dead one I had found and the other dressed in a white garment of some sort that covered her from head to toe. Atalanta and Milo had resumed loping along the fence, snouts always pointed forward as if they took no notice of the intrusion of humans, and in my mind's eye, I saw Demeter and Iasion likewise engaged in Wolfpen One. The men seemed as wary of the wolves as they were interested in the goings-on concerning the body of the dead, and they stood in postures that allowed them to keep an eye on both.

I understood their feeling, the desire not to turn their backs on immediate danger. We differed, however, in what we considered the more dangerous or threatening. Certainly, they believed the danger to be my wolves, while I had found it difficult to turn my back on the woman. I was not concerned about ghosts or revenants, but she represented the threatening presence of the uninvited unknown. Perhaps my terrifying dreams of monstrous things in the night indicated some subconscious awareness of evil's having come ashore at Avalon.

This thought, along with the idea that the evil might still be on the island, had pursued me as I fled through the orchard after discovering the body. I knew that something must be done, that someone must be contacted and allowed to come and take care of the dead. My first idea was not to stop at the house but to pass it by and make my way to Runion. But I had not left Christabel in more than a year, and I had not found my feet on Runion's Main Street in more than a decade. *Recluse* came to mind. *Recluse!* I was halfway across the footbridge to the Piney Ridge side when I stumbled to a stop. In the absence of my wooden footfalls, I heard only my breath and my heartbeat and the busy whisper of water beneath me. Try as I might, I could not force myself forward. After what seemed far too long, I backed away until a foot found the first step down from the bridge, and then, again on the island's solid ground, I turned and ran to the house, the skirt of my cloak whipping around my legs.

Once inside with the door bolted behind me, I hurried to my father's study, where he kept a cellular telephone "for emergencies." To my knowledge, he never used it, depending always on the one my more modern mother carried. I found it in the desk drawer where he had promised it would be when, a year or two before, Mother had shown me how to turn it on and use it. I took the thing from its hiding place, and to my relief, it immediately came alive.

In the drawer with the telephone was a sheet of paper with three numbers written in my father's hand. They were Mother's number, that of my grandparents' home in Charleston, and that of the Runion constabulary with the name Deputy Davis Boyce beneath.

The authorities had come *en masse* but not all at once. Over the course of an hour after I completed my emergency call, our parking area across the footbridge slowly filled with vehicles—various shapes of vehicles arriving to the various songs of their sirens and skidding to a halt in clouds of dust lit by flashing lights of similarly various colors. They gathered on the lawn and milled around while Deputy Boyce came and spoke to me through the kitchen's screen door.

I stood where he could not see and told him what I had found and what I had done. When he asked, I gave him permission for the crowd to cross the orchard along with two admonishments—"Be careful of the orchard trees" and "Try not to upset my wolves."

"Yes, ma'am," he said. "Okie dokie."

I had cringed at the colloquialism, hung up my cloak, and then gone upstairs to set up the spyglass and keep watch over the proceedings.

Gabriel Tanner soon joined the crew surrounding the women. Instead of standing around with the men in suits and uniforms, he approached the women with camera in hand and began taking photographs, apparently under the direction of the woman in white. She and Mr. Tanner circled the dead. She pointed her finger to this or that, and he pointed his lens. She moved the body slightly this way or that, and he crouched down and moved close with the camera to his eye—limber, I thought, for a man of his age and size.

After a time, the woman in white stood abruptly and said something to Mr. Tanner, at which he let his camera hang from the strap around his neck. He secured a cover to the lens and stepped away as she motioned to two people—a woman and man—in navy blue uniforms. These came forward with a stretcher and prepared to move the body while the woman in white stepped to one side and began removing her suit. When the dead had been carried a short distance aside, another small group of women and men, each wearing a jacket with NCSBI on the back, moved forward and began examining the tree, the ground around it, and the grass, stone, and sand beyond to the edge of the French Broad's eastern channel. The postures and gestures of Deputy Boyce and two others in uniforms like his expressed significant agitation. Surrounding them, a man in a suit and western hat and three other men in NCSBI jackets maintained the same formation they had held throughout the proceedings and seemed to make attempts now and again to mollify Boyce and his fellow deputies.

When Mr. Tanner and the dark-haired woman—no longer in white—began helping the two in navy blue return across the orchard with the stretcher, Atalanta and Milo disappeared into their den.

I continued at the spyglass for a few minutes more until I heard a knock at the kitchen door. I quietly descended the staircase and peered into the kitchen and saw that it was Mr. Tanner. "Come," I said.

He no longer wore the camera around his neck, and he carried a folder in his hand.

I invited him to sit, indicating the seat at the end of the kitchen table, near the door, and I took the seat at the opposite end. Unused to speaking to people other than Mother and Father, I said nothing more.

Mr. Tanner cleared his throat. "I'm sorry about the morning you've had," he said. "That must have been a shock."

I nodded.

"I've brought your manuscript back," he said and opened the folder, which contained the loose pages and the black ribbon. "I didn't want to try to retie it." He slid the folder across the table to me. "I've got a digital file for making hard copies, so you can have this back now." He paused. "The university's Archives of Southern Appalachia would like to add this manuscript to their holdings if you and your family are interested in donating it."

I nodded again and pulled the manuscript toward me and looked down at it, noticing that it seemed none the worse for wear since leaving the library upstairs. I then looked at Mr. Tanner. "Have you read the whole of it, sir?"

"I haven't gone through all of it yet. Most of it. Dr. John

Riddle and I looked over much of it this morning. He's learned that—" He stopped for a moment. "At least he's pretty sure that the author is a Philadelphia writer named Charles Brockden Brown. He's excited about that, I think."

"I know Brown," I said. "Have you read him?"

"I haven't," he said. "But Dr. Riddle tells me that Hawthorne and Poe read Brown, and I've read them."

"Two or three volumes of his work—English and American editions, I think—are shelved in the library upstairs," I said. "I read them some years ago. *Wieland* and *Ormond*, as I recall." Although I had not thought of either work in some time, I remembered both vividly, and I immediately saw how the situations Brown narrated corresponded, to some extent, with my own. Both told the stories of young women—namely, Clara Wieland and Constantia Dudley—haunted by hidden men—namely, Carwin and Ormond. I stood up and stepped toward the stove. "Would you like some tea, Mr. Tanner?"

"Sure, thanks," he said and then asked, "Did the founders of this place keep diaries or any records of visitors? I'm sure Dr. Riddle would love to be able to confirm that Brown was here."

I nodded a third time but did not turn away from the sink where I filled the kettle. With my mind's eye I scanned the shelves of the library, which held precious little holographic material in the hands of the original builders and occupants of Avalon Cottage. In fact, I had been surprised to uncover the manuscript that then lay on the table, and I suspected that Father did not even know of its existence. "I am certain our library has no such holdings," I said at last and set the full kettle on the stovetop. "Documents of that nature would be locked away in Father's study."

"Speaking of your dad, does he know what's happened today?"

I almost pointed out his transposition of *Father* to *dad* but let it go unnoted. "Not unless Deputy Boyce or some other among the authorities notified him. Mother and he arrived in

Charleston only this morning, having driven overnight, and I do not like the idea that they would immediately attempt to return because of this situation, which seems well in hand." I gathered our tin of Earl Grey, the strainer, and our Brown Betty and grouped them beside the stovetop. "I'm sure you understand, Mr. Tanner."

"Sure," he said again. "And please call me Gabriel."

I felt him watching me, but the feeling was not the same as that associated with the Watcher. Nor did his attention feel inappropriate. I understood that I must be an item of some curiosity to him—to all the Runionites. As I set the kettle on the stovetop, I realized that over the course of our two short visits in the past week and my horrifying dream the previous night, I had spent more time with this man than with anyone except my parents since my last trip to Charleston two Christmases before.

Gabriel cleared his throat. "The authorities will need to interview you. Would you want your dad here for that?"

I turned from the countertop and moved to stand behind my chair. "I am capable," I said. "But I would prefer to speak only with Deputy Boyce. Is that possible?"

"It might be, but he's pretty out of sorts right now."

"Why? Does he know the dead woman?"

"Yes, he does," Gabriel said. "It's Williemae Rider, one of his fellow deputies."

"Oh, my," I said and turned away. As I removed the top from the teapot, I said, almost to myself, "He has killed a law enforcement officer?"

"He?" Gabriel said behind me. "You know who did this?"

"I do not know him, but I have felt him watching us." I turned again toward Gabriel, wondering if I should tell him of my recent nightmare, the one in which he appeared. But I added only, "All of us."

He leaned forward and placed his hands flat on the table and spread his fingers. "What do you mean?"

"It is a feeling I have had most strongly since last week," I said. "A feeling that something wicked—something malevolent—is acting among us and surveilling all we do."

The kettle began burbling toward its screaming whistle, and I turned and removed it from the stovetop. As Gabriel sat behind me without speaking, perhaps mulling over what I had just said, I poured a small amount of the boiling water into the Brown Betty, swirled it to warm the pot, and then emptied it in the sink. I spooned loose leaves of Earl Grey into the teapot, covered these with steaming water from the kettle, and replaced the lid to let the tea steep. Then I took down two mugs from the cabinet in front of me.

"If I may make a suggestion," Gabriel said, "you might try to avoid speculating about that when you speak with Deputy Boyce."

"Speculating about what?" a gruff voice said.

Gabriel and I turned to see Deputy Boyce's grizzled visage framed in the kitchen screen door.

"Sneaky as ever, Dagnabbit," Gabriel said, an attempt at lightheartedness that failed.

"Come," I said and turned to take down a third mug.

TWENTY-NINE

Edie-Mac Lane turned right on the wide dirt-and-gravel road that zigzagged up the tightly packed switchback curves of Hipps Mountain. She took note of driveways as she ascended but saw none of the houses to which they led. *Hiding in hollers*, she thought. Beside most of these driveways stood mailboxes—a few simply blank, a couple with stick-on gold letters and numbers, some with hand-painted names such as Hipps, Shelton, Wallin, Rice, and Gosnell. She picked up her phone from the passenger seat, saw that she had one bar of signal, and dropped it in the seat again. She met no other vehicles on her serpentine rise toward the top. When she could tell she was nearing the blue sky, the road forked. She took the righthand fork and continued until it ended in what she figured was probably called something creative like the Hipps Mountain Turnaround, and she shuddered with a little thrill at all the wanton weirdness that surely went on there most nights, imagining that the ground beneath the trees and undergrowth edging this backwoods cul-de-sac would be littered with a wide variety of alcohol vessels and used condoms.

She rounded the turnaround and parked. *A freaky scene for Chuckey D and me.* She thought of some kinky things they could get up to in the back of his van and imagined some Lester-Ballard-type character creeping out of the woods to peep at them through the window while he yanked himself out through the unbuttoned fly of his overalls and seeded the back tire. Her breath caught, and she picked up her phone again, wanting to tell her new friend about this place, and saw she then had no bars of service. Knowing she could sit there and run such scenarios through her mind the rest of the afternoon, she tossed the phone back into the passenger seat and put her vehicle back in gear.

She left the cul-de-sac and, after descending a short distance, made the hard righthand turn to take the nameless lefthand fork she'd bypassed on the way up. This bent steeply downward, switching back and forth just as her ascent had done. As she rode the brake, the thought struck her that this could be another driveway, but it seemed wider and more used than the driveways she'd passed earlier and no mailbox suggested it led to a single dwelling. At the bottom, the mostly dirt road straightened somewhat through a narrow valley where the mountainside steadily gave way on the left to form a deeply shaded cove.

As her eyes followed the receding wall, she first noticed a small creek that crossed the level ground of the cove and then seemed to disappear under the solid base of the hedging mountain. She slowed, wondering where the water might come out and imagining a beautiful, high waterfall somewhere on the mountain's other side.

The next thing she saw was a shack of weathered gray boards that stood in the deepest shade of the cove. Trees growing at an angle from the wooded slope above looked as if they must someday lose their purchase and crush the rusted tin roof and all beneath it. The shack appeared to be a one-room affair, small with a single visible window and door. The old boards of its covered porch lay warped and out of line, reminding her of a smile full of bad teeth. Cinderblock steps led down to a grassy path that in turn led to a weathered wooden bridge that crossed the creek.

The last thing she noticed was the naked man, and she skidded to a stop, raising a cloud of dust that swirled around her CR-V.

He'd been partially hidden by a tree beside the road, but at her approach, he stepped into full view and smiled. Thinning red-gray hair stuck out from the sides of his head like the wig of a clown. Although his face seemed deathly pale, his cheeks blazed as if reddened with rouge and his neck seemed strangely dark. A thin left arm clutched to his chest folded clothing of mostly white and black and gold. The right arm crossed beneath the left to help hold the clothes, and he gripped with the fingers of that hand a pair of sneakers that dangled beside his hip. His beer paunch and thin legs appeared as ghostly gray-white as the underside of a catfish.

Edie-Mac sat with her foot firmly on the brake and stared as the naked man stared back, smiling. She glanced in her rearview mirror to confirm she had no space to turn around, and as she returned her gaze to the strange apparition ahead of her, she tried to imagine backing back up the way she came and didn't see how she could.

"Shit," she said.

The man hadn't changed his expression since he cracked his smile. He hadn't made any move to cover himself.

"Shit, shit, shit," Edie-Mac said. She made sure her doors were locked and then eased her foot off the brake to let her vehicle roll forward. Approaching him slowly, she cracked her window enough to speak through, raised up, and turned her face toward the opening. "Hey, I'll be right back," she said. "Stay there, okay?" When he responded only enough to turn his head and follow her with his red-eyed gaze, she stepped on the gas pedal and hurried herself away, watching the man in the rearview until she lost him when she rounded the next turn. She thought she would follow any driveway that offered itself, but when the road dead-ended in a turnaround similar to the previous one, she realized she was alone in the wilds of Hipps Mountain with a naked and probably crazy man.

She swung through the turnaround and came to a stop.

Instead of imagining another kinky scenario with Chuckey D, she sat thinking what she should do to escape the strange real-time scenario she found herself in—what she could do to help the naked man or help herself get safely away. She looked at her telephone again. "Shit."

After a few more moments, she double checked all her mirrors. When she felt certain she was alone at the turnaround, she popped the CR-V's back hatch window, unlocked her door, jumped out, and hurried to the rear of the vehicle. There, after looking around once more, she lifted the window and reached into the cargo area and retrieved her pink gym bag. She then hurried back to her seat and locked the door and tossed the bag into the backseat. She sat another moment, running through the plan in her head. A minute later, she took a deep breath and let it out, put the CR-V in gear and started rolling back toward the cove.

He hadn't moved.

As she'd done when she first entered this hidden valley from the other direction, she stopped. She felt to be sure all her doors were locked and then rolled forward until the back passenger-side door was in front of him. She stopped again, put the CR-V in PARK and set the emergency brake. From the master controls at her left hand, she cracked the back passenger-side window a couple of inches.

"Hey, there," she said over her shoulder. "Are you okay?"

The naked man—she realized he was shorter than she first thought—neither moved nor changed his expression.

"Sir, can you understand me?" She undid her seatbelt and climbed from the driver's seat to the passenger's.

He nodded.

She settled on her knees, facing the rear, leaned and took her keys from the ignition and pushed them down into her back pocket. She then reached into the backseat and pulled her pink gym bag onto the console between the front seats and unzipped it. She settled down on her haunches and dug around in the bag while keeping her eyes and a reassuring smile focused on the man. "I don't have a signal up here," she said and pulled a mini cattle prod from the bag and laid it beside her right calf in the passenger seat. "But I don't want to leave you here while I go call somebody." She removed her handcuffs from the gym bag and put them in her lap. "Will you come with me?"

He nodded again.

"So, I'm gonna open the back door now, okay? Is that all right?" When she saw another slight nod, she rose to her knees and said, "All right." She unlocked the door and pushed it open.

The man ducked his head just a bit and peered inside.

"All right," she said again, "step closer."

He did as he was told.

"I don't mean to be mean, but I've gotta handcuff you, okay? I just need to be safe, all right?"

His smile dimmed, and he didn't nod his agreement.

"You might even like it," she said and laughed. "I know I do."

His smile brightened again, and he took a half step forward.

"Now, hold on," she said. "Can you put down your clothes and shoes?"

After a moment's hesitation, he leaned inside the CR-V and lay his dirty clothes in the center of the backseat and set his shoes on top of them.

"Good, thanks," Edie-Mac said. "Okay, take the grab handle above the door with both hands, okay?" When he did so, she deftly cuffed his left wrist, looped the other cuff over the grab handle, and cuffed his right wrist. "All right, now, be a good boy and stand right there." She unlocked the front passenger-side door, climbed out, and stepped behind the man. "Hang on, there's mud." She wiped flecks and clumps of drying mud from his buttocks, and the backs of his thighs. *I hope it's mud*, she thought.

When she'd settled him in the backseat, she opened the rear hatch window again and got her camera. She took a couple of photos of the man as he sat and stared blankly straight ahead. She closed both passenger-side doors, turned, and photographed the shack across the creek. Then she crossed the bridge and stepped up on the shack's porch, taking photos along the way. Finally, she lowered the camera from her eye, pushed the front door open, and stood in the doorway surveying the dimly lit single room. She didn't enter but photographed a mattress on the floor, a small table and two chairs, a chest of drawers, a pot-bellied stove, and jumbled floorboards beside a dark hole beneath the back window.

Again behind the wheel of the CR-V, she took the mini cattle prod in her lap and started the engine. When she put the car in gear and began rolling forward, she looked up in the rearview mirror. "So, we've been kind of intimate," she said. "What's your name?" She watched his face fold in on itself and then stretch into a voiceless howl.

THIRTY

Gabriel Tanner

I'd offered my chair at the table to Deputy Boyce, but I stayed at Ariel's request and stood leaning against a kitchen countertop with my arms folded over my chest. As I listened to the interview, the back and forth of it, my gaze moved between what Boyce wrote in the notebook that lay on the tabletop in front of him and what passed across Ariel's face as she answered the questions put to her. Given her inexperience dealing with off-islanders like Davis and me, she remained remarkably steady in both mannerism and voice. I watched and listened to Davis, too, wondering if he was as intimidated by her beauty and composure as I found myself to be.

"You say the wolves howled this morning, but, as far as you know, they didn't during the night," Deputy Boyce said.

"Yes."

"You didn't hear them at all?"

"No."

"How do you reckon them two in the pen by the crime scene acted when he was leaving—" Boyce's voice choked to a stop but recovered quickly. "—when he was leaving her like he done?"

I expected to see Ariel cringe at the syntax, but what I saw, despite her calm, were hints of kindred emotions: indignation and empathy.

"I imagine that they lay quiet in their den, alert and watching."

"They wouldn't attack?"

"No, why would they?" Ariel said. "If this man is as emotionless as his actions suggest, he probably aroused only their curiosity." As Boyce wrote in his notebook, she continued. "If he left her there without displaying any agitation—such as rage or desperation—and did not pay any particular attention to their presence, they would have responded likewise."

Boyce scribbled another line and then looked up. "Any idea why he came here?" he said. "Why he left her here?"

I wondered if Ariel would mention her Watcher. When Boyce had eavesdropped on my suggestion that she not speculate about this entity in her interview, I'd passed it off as a reference to the old manuscript that lay on the table in front of her, the narrative of which, so far as I'd read, suggested something similar as having gone on in the early days of the Avalon settlement.

"None," Ariel said.

The deputy closed his notebook but kept a forefinger in it to hold his place. "You recall anything else out of the ordinary happening recently?"

The way the reclusive Ariel met and held the deputy's gaze surprised me.

"Every day tends toward the extraordinary here at Avalon," she said. "Even when one has lived here all one's life." She lay a hand on top of the manuscript, as if it were an example of what she meant. But when she continued, she didn't reference it. "One week ago, the morning after the Ulysses storm, was a scheduled feeding for the wolves. When I arrived at Wolfpen Two, the scene of this morning's—" She paused for breath and a thought. "—activity, I discovered a bloody mess in the snow and learned, after some investigation, that a raccoon had somehow entered the enclosure and fallen prey to Atalanta and Milo. My father and I searched thoroughly for the beast's means of ingress but found nothing."

Boyce stared at her for a moment, then flipped his notebook over again and bent over his scribbling. "Is there a coon population on Christabel?" he said without looking up.

"No."

My phone buzzed in my pants pocket, and I dug it out and looked at the screen. When I saw that Edie-Mac was calling, I excused myself, my gaze briefly lingering on Ariel's face to confirm she'd be okay if I stepped away for a moment, and then went out through the kitchen screen door and onto the front lawn.

"Hey," I said.

"So, I went ahead and rode up Hipps Mountain."

"Didn't I tell you not to do that?"

We both knew the answer to that, so she didn't respond.

"Okay, okay, I should've known," I said and wondered if I had, in fact, known that the best way to get her up the mountain was to tell her not to go. "Did you find anything?"

"About what you'd normally expect," she said. "Except for the naked man."

"What?"

"Yeah, he's in the backseat of my CR-V right now."

"What? What do you mean?"

"Okay, focus with me for a minute, boss." She spoke with the tone of playful condescension she liked to use with me and proceeded to describe her detour and her discovery of a naked man outside a shack on the Hipps Mountain spur, how she'd secured him with handcuffs in the backseat and driven away from the shack, how when she got back to the main road she'd called Tallent Health Clinic in Runion for advice. Then she called the Runion Sheriff's office, but nobody answered.

"I called the Tallent folks back, and they're gonna try to find somebody to be there when they let me in at the Back Street door of the clinic."

"You are truly crazy, Ms. Lane," I said. "You got pictures of the scene, I hope?"

"Keep your hair on," she said. "Yeah, I have things under control." She paused and said something to the man in her backseat. "So, what's going on there?"

"It's bad," I said and quickly told her where I was and why.

"That's unbelievable, Gabe."

"Yeah, more on that when I see you, but we'd better get off here so you can keep an eye on your passenger."

"Probably a good idea," she said. "See you in a few."

"Wait, why do you have handcuffs?"

Three beeps told me she'd already ended the call.

THIRTY-ONE

Plumer Reeves sat in a rocker on the porch of his cabin and tried to finish reading *The House of the Seven Gables.*

> *. . . They transfigured the earth, and made it Eden again, and themselves the two first dwellers in it. The dead man, so close beside them, was forgotten. . . .*

His drowsy afternoon attention grabbed hold of such passages but soon twirled away again like a mini cyclone gathering dead leaves and dust from a roadside. His mind swirled with Livvy and Kayla, the two bodies found in a field off Pump Gap Road, the stone-still and half-naked man standing on the Pulpit that morning. He bent eyes and mind to the page for another attempt to finish the penultimate chapter, then raised his head at the sound of a vehicle coming along his driveway but not yet in sight.

An off-white SUV rounded the laurel thicket that hid the cabin until the last moment—a Chevrolet model Plumer couldn't immediately name with a shadowy man behind the wheel and a blue canoe strapped to the roof. The Chevy rolled to a stop at the edge of the yard, and the driver cut the engine.

Plumer wondered if this was the same vehicle that he'd seen earlier through the trees, parked over at the Pulpit Loop trailhead. He remembered thinking that the blue was probably a second vehicle parked on the other side of it but thought it could have been the mounted canoe instead.

The driver's door opened, and the man stepped out. He ducked back inside for a moment, then stood again and hung an expensive-looking camera around his neck. He pushed the door quietly closed as if not wanting to disturb the peaceful setting or Reeves's reading or as if used to coming and going with a practiced measure of stealth.

"Mr. Reeves?" the man said.

"Yes." Plumer dog-eared his place in the Hawthorne novel, closed it, and held it in his lap a moment before setting it on the porch banister. He wondered as the man crossed the yard if he could be the one he'd seen standing precariously close to the edge of the Pulpit rock. He was dressed differently—*sharply*, Plumer thought—in a wide-brimmed khaki boonie hat that shaded his face, sage vest and long trousers, a long-sleeved white shirt, and brown leather lace-up boots. Plumer thought as he rose from his rocker that—given the blond hair curling from beneath the hat, the man's size, and the vehicle and canoe—this was probably the same fellow, but he couldn't be certain.

"My name's Austen Caine," the man said. "Do you mind if I speak with you for a few minutes?"

"Come on up and have a seat." Plumer indicated the rocker beside his own, which he lowered himself into again as Caine came up the steps. "And I'm Plumer."

"I'm glad to hear you say it," Caine said, seating himself in the rocker and reaching across to shake hands. "I would've said it like *plumber*."

"And you would've been like most people."

Austen Caine apologized for his intrusion and launched into a brief explanation about his work as location scout for a film to be shot in the area later in the summer.

"I've heard something about that," Plumer said.

"Have you read a book called *The Cove* by Ron Rash?"

"Heard of it but haven't read it." Plumer took the Hawthorne novel down from the porch railing. "My tastes tend to skew toward the nineteenth century."

Caine tilted his head to see the title. "And I've never read that," he said. "But I think we were assigned *The Scarlet Letter* in high school. That's by him, right?"

"It is."

Caine sat for a moment and looked into the woods across the yard and up the hillside to their right. "In *The Cove*," he said, "there's a cabin I picture to be a lot like yours that's the central domestic setting. The main character, Laurel Shelton, lives in it with her brother." He lifted the camera from his chest and then turned to Reeves. "Do you mind?"

"Go ahead."

Caine stood, held the viewfinder to his left eye, and took several photos of the surroundings from the perspective of the porch. Then he sat back down. "Anyway, I've already looked at the towns in the county and at a lot of river locations, so I'm devoting the next few days to finding places that could be the home of the Shelton siblings." He turned in his seat and took a photo down the length of the porch and turned back. "A young woman I met in Runion yesterday suggested that I might want to see your place here and gave me directions."

An image of Livvy's face with blonde hair blowing across it appeared in Plumer's mind. He couldn't quite interpret the look in her eyes before the image faded. He also couldn't imagine her having been in town yesterday, much less talking to a stranger like this Austen Caine. "What young woman would that be?"

"She was in the sheriff's office." Caine raised his face to the porch ceiling for a moment. "Williemae Rider was her name. Deputy Williemae Rider."

"I've spoken to her but can't say I know her," Plumer said.

"She was a pretty thing, a small blonde," Caine said. "Feisty."

Plumer again caught the fleeting image of Livvy Goforth's

face and again wondered at the curious look in her eyes. "Well, I don't go to town that much," he said.

Caine rocked back and forth a couple of times and then abruptly stood, leaving the chair rocking on its own. "I shouldn't take up more of your time, but I was wondering if I could get some interior shots."

Plumer stood as well, taking note that his visitor stood almost half a foot taller. "I haven't picked up or made the bed," he said.

"I'm just looking at layout and structure," Caine said. "No judgment, I promise."

"All right." Plumer directed him toward the front screen door.

Inside, Austen Caine took photos of the living room floor, walls, windows, and ceiling. He did the same in the kitchen and the bedroom, seeming careful in the last not to include the unmade bed.

As they stepped back into the kitchen, Caine turned toward the closed door on their right. "What's in this room?"

Plumer raised his hand and pressed his palm against the wood. "That's off limits, Mr. Caine," he said. "My wife's painting studio."

"Is that the wife that went missing—" Caine stopped. "I'm sorry, I—"

"Sounds like I need to have another chat with Deputy Rider," Plumer said.

Caine grunted something like a chuckle. "Good luck with that because she talked a mile a minute."

Outside on the porch, Caine took a couple more photos of exterior windows and the length of the porch again, this time from the opposite direction, toward the rocking chairs. "So," he said as he lowered the camera to his chest, "do you think you'd be willing to have your place considered as a possible setting in the film?"

Plumer looked out across the yard. "I don't know." He smoothed down his beard with a palm. "It would depend on what that entails—how many days I'd lose my privacy, what changes they'd want to make to suit themselves, what's going on around the place at the time they want to film. Stuff like that."

"What do you mean about what's going on around the place?"

"Well, I'm acquainted with a number of the critters that live around here, and they trust me. I have to consider them, too."

"I see," Caine said. A puzzled look crossed his face, and then he shook it off. "Do you have a phone number you can give me?"

Plumer recited the number. "My phone stays in the Jeep, so if I'm not driving when you call, just leave a message."

"I think you've got potential," Caine said. "The place, I mean. As a setting." He offered his hand. "Thanks."

Plumer felt the strength in the man's large hand. "Don't mention it."

He watched Caine descend the steps and cross the yard, climb into his vehicle and take the camera from around his neck and set it in the passenger seat. He pointed to indicate how Caine should turn around and then waved when the man waved. He walked to his rocker, stopped, and listened to the Chevy until the sound faded.

Something about the visit muttered like a grouch holed up somewhere in his brain, but he put it down to the uncomfortable moment in front of Kayla's studio door. He took his seat again and found his place in Hawthorne's novel. "Let's see if I can knock out the end of this," he said aloud, wondering at the same time who he was talking to and if he should offer to loan the book to Livvy when he finished it.

THIRTY-TWO

When Edie-Mac Lane slowed on Lonesome Mountain Drive and turned left into Back Street, she saw Deputy Carlton Mayhew, a nurse practitioner, and a CNA waiting outside the open rear door of Tallent Health Clinic. "Shit," she said, and the naked man handcuffed in her backseat giggled. She'd been hoping to arrive unattended so that she could remove the handcuffs and hide them away, but now she braced herself for raised eyebrows and sarcastic questions.

As soon as she brought the CR-V to a stop and shoved the gearshift up to PARK, Deputy Mayhew yanked on the locked door.

"Hang on," Edie-Mac said. She stretched across the passenger seat, felt around for the lock button, found it, and pulled it up. As Mayhew opened the door, she said, "Sorry, the electronic locks don't work anymore." She hopped out and hurried around the back end. "Hang on," she said again. She pulled the small key from a pocket of her jeans, unlocked the handcuffs and backed away as she tucked the key back in the pocket along with the cuffs.

With Mayhew keeping a close watch and shielding the process from passersby on Lonesome Mountain, the NP and the CNA carefully helped the man out of the backseat and got him covered with a light blue examination gown. Mayhew held the door for the three to enter and then followed them inside, leaving Edie-Mac alone. She spotted a parking space toward the opposite end of Back Street, behind Cowart's Department Store, and moved the CR-V there. As she was returning, the clinic's rear door opened again.

Deputy Mayhew reemerged and stopped to stand in the middle of Back Street and rubbed his face hard with both hands. "What a fucking day," he said at last.

Edie-Mac stopped beside him and put a hand on his shoulder. "I'm sorry about your colleague," she said. "I didn't really know her."

"I just can't believe it." He started to run fingers through his black hair but stopped halfway with the hand atop his head. "I just can't fucking believe it."

"Dr. Rios was there?"

"Yeah."

"And?"

"Her prelim was that Williemae was strangled."

"That's how she was killed?"

"She thought so, but she said the autopsy would need to confirm that."

"Is she here?"

"What? No, they've taken her on to Wake Forest."

"No, I mean, is Dr. Rios here?"

"Oh," he said. "No, but she's on her way back." He covered his eyes with both hands for a moment and drew a sharp breath, then let his arms fall to his sides. "She was heading to Avery County when we called her about your friend in there."

"Did you notice his neck?" Edie-Mac asked, rubbing her upper arms with her palms as the midafternoon cooled. "I think he might have been strangled, too."

"That was also the prelim on yesterday's bodies," Deputy Mayhew said. He dropped his gaze to the ground. "What the fuck is going on around here?"

By five o'clock in the afternoon, the temperature had dropped into the mid-forties. The man found on Hipps Mountain had been examined and sent on to the hospital in Asheville for observation and testing. Deputies Boyce and Mayhew had interviewed Edie-Mac Lane about her discovery on the Hipps

Mountain spur. Boyce told her she could go home and directed Mayhew to go to the shack and check out the scene. As the two exited the rear door of the Town Hall and Jail to Back Street, Mayhew stopped abruptly.

"One more question," he said. "Off the record."

"Here it comes," Edie-Mac said with a grin and then didn't wait for the question. "Okay, the handcuffs are for personal use. Of a sexual nature. And nobody else's business. But really, all women should be encouraged to carry a pair or two." She dug in her pocket for the keys to the CR-V. "I'm surprised you guys didn't ask that in the interview."

"Well, it wasn't my place," Mayhew said. "And I don't think Davis is thinking too clearly right now."

"I was wondering about that when he told you to go to Hipps Mountain by yourself." She clutched her keys inside a fist. "I don't think that's a good idea."

"Why?"

"You know perfectly well why," she said. "If you think for a minute, there've been four attacks and three deaths, all apparently strangled. If it's the same man doing this and he's the one who left my little guy for dead in that shack—" She stopped. "I'm coming with you."

"I probably shouldn't let you ride in the patrol car."

"Then I'll drive," she said and began backing away toward the CR-V. "Come on."

Deputy Mayhew looked at her and then turned to look at the closed door behind them. "I guess that would be okay." He started to follow her. "Will you tell me more about a lady's need to carry handcuffs with her?"

"The old writing dictum is 'show, don't tell.'" Edie-Mac winked, turned, and began walking faster toward her vehicle. Then she called over her shoulder, "Now, come on, it's getting colder by the minute."

THIRTY-THREE

In the Town Hall and Jail's interview room, Dr. Eleanor Rios covered the table in plastic and spread out the foundling's dirty clothes on top of it. Deputy Boyce stood with his back against a wall and watched.

"Looks like we've got a Wofford Terriers fan," Dr. Rios said.

"They played in the basketball tournament last weekend in Asheville," Boyce said with a dry voice. "I think I heard they won the conference championship on Monday."

Rios patted the pants on the table. "There's something here," she said and dipped fingers into a pocket. "Not a wallet." She pulled out a money clip that held a few bills, a Hilton key-card, and a driver's license. "Truman South. Looks like he's from down in Spartanburg."

"That's where Wofford is."

Rios looked up at Boyce but didn't say anything.

"Sorry, Doc," Boyce said. "You know where Wofford is." He wiped a palm across his mouth. "I can't get my head straight since this morning, El'nor." He took off his cap, slapped it against his thigh, and put it on again. "You got any ideas?"

"I'm thinking that you might be able to use Truman South in some way." She stood up straight and then pressed her fists into the small of her back. "I got measurements from the bruises on Mr. South's neck, and I'm betting they'll be strikingly similar to those on the necks of Mr. Goforth, Ms. Ham, and Deputy Rider." She began readying the clothes for folding and storing in evidence bags. "My guess is that our man made a mistake here that he didn't make with the others. He must have thought that Mr. South was dead when he left him. Surely, there's something actionable in that."

"Gotta be," Boyce said. He again wiped a palm across his mouth. "I'll think about that in the morning." He lifted the evidence bag they'd used to carry the clothes from the clinic and held it open.

Dr. Rios finished carefully folding the items—jersey, pants, underwear, socks—and put them in the bag. When she picked up the shoes, she stopped and looked at them. "There's a shoestring missing."

"I saw that," Deputy Boyce said. He stared at the pair of shoes the doctor held in her hand, one with a shoestring and one without. "One of Terry Goforth's brogans was missing a string, too."

THIRTY-FOUR

In Cowart's Department Store, Austen Caine stood in front of shelves piled high with neatly folded dark blue bib overalls and wondered if he should buy a pair or two before he moved on from this place.

A bell jingled as the front door opened.

"Hey, Georgette," Julia Cowart said.

"Time for our daily, honey," Georgette Penland said as the door jingled closed behind her.

The two of them laughed and launched into an over-the-counter gossip session, beginning with the story that earlier in the day had made its way across the river from Christabel Island—that Deputy Williemae Rider had been found dead, murdered, her nude body tied to a tree beside one of Spellman Anderson's new wolf pens.

"Aren't the Andersons visiting her people down in Charleston?" Julia asked.

"Spellman and Randi are," Georgette said. "But I heard Ariel stayed back and found the body first thing."

"Poor girl. To wake up to something like that."

Caine continued pretending to shop for overalls and listened while they ran down the various bits of information they'd heard since first getting wind of the story.

While Julia had known Williemae a little bit as a customer, Georgette knew only who she was and had never spoken with her. They agreed that neither knew much of anything about her past and nothing about her family, then blessed all their hearts and wondered what the world was coming to.

Caine's stomach growled as they veered off into a discussion of the homemade fried pies laid out on the counter by the cash register, "mostly from canned apples this time of year," Julia said, "made by a woman from over around Burnsville." His breath caught when the women's conversation turned abruptly from the fried pies to a "nude man the girl that works with Gabe at the paper" had brought into town from over Hipps Mountain way.

Their talk dropped to whispers until Georgette laughed. "Lord, you wonder if that movie company won't go somewhere else with all the craziness going on around here."

"It's like we're going Charlotte crazy," Julia said.

"Or crazy like Atlanta." Georgette laughed again.

Twenty minutes later, distracted by a troubled mind and a grumbling belly, Caine found himself alone in a booth at Runion's Stonehouse Café, hardly remembering how he came to be there. He had a bag from Cowart's sitting in the seat beside him and a waitress standing by his table.

"Ready?" she said.

While he waited for his order of a rare hamburger steak and extra crispy fries, he tried putting finishing touches to two sketches he'd been working on before going into Cowart's. He'd sketched, first, Plumer Reeves's yard and the exterior of his cabin, including two empty ladder-back rocking chairs on the porch. Catty-corner to the cabin, he'd sketched the interior floorplan—living room, kitchen, bath, and bedroom. Beyond the door to what Reeves called his wife's off-limits painting studio, Caine drew three question marks and left the space open without outlining exterior walls. But try as he might to focus on these sketches, the conversation he'd overheard in Cowart's Department Store—especially the news of a strange discovery on Hipps Mountain—kept pulling his mind away and setting his heart racing.

"Hamburger steak, rare, and extra crispy fries?" the Stonehouse waitress said.

Caine flinched back to the moment and looked up at the waitress's face and then her nametag. "Yes, Reta," he said and pushed his sketches across the table.

"Sorry to startle you," she said as she put down his plate.

"I guess I'd gone somewhere else for a minute."

"Sure you don't want anything to drink besides water?"

"Maybe I better have some coffee to focus my mind. Pour it to go?"

"All right," Reta said. She cocked her head to the side and looked down at his sketches. "Is that Plumer Reeves's place?"

"As a matter of fact, it is," Caine said. "I was by there this afternoon to talk with him."

"It's a good likeness."

"Thanks."

She turned away and was quickly back with his coffee. She looked down at the sketch again. "I don't know nothing about art, but there's a loneliness about your picture that's like the place itself."

"Thanks," Caine said again. "Hey, Reta, have you heard anything about a person being picked up on Hipps Mountain this afternoon?"

"Yeah, we've all heard about that by now." She opened her mouth to say more but seemed to catch herself. "I better let you eat before it all gets cold."

"What did you hear?"

"Edie-Mac from the paper found him standing by the road outside a little shack, buck naked and carrying his clothes bunched up in his arms." When the small bell above the door rang, she turned. "Y'all sit anywhere, and I'll be right there." She looked down at Caine again. "He seemed crazy's what I heard. Not a stitch on and couldn't speak a word."

"What happened to him?"

"Nobody knows, I reckon. They had him at the Tallent Clinic first, but I think he's gone on to the hospital in Asheville by now." She pulled her order pad from the pocket of her smock, tore off his ticket, and laid it beside his sketches. "I'll check back with you in a few minutes." She turned toward the new arrivals. "How're y'all this evening?"

Caine waited long enough for Reta to take the new orders and disappear into the kitchen. Then he fished forty dollars from his wallet and laid the bills on top of the ticket, gathered his sketches and left the café with his coffee but without touching his food.

THIRTY-FIVE

Gabriel Tanner

After Deputy Boyce left to meet Edie-Mac and the man she'd brought to town, I hung out with Ariel Anderson and finally suggested that she shouldn't stay on Christabel by herself that night. I offered the spare room at our house on Genesis Road and hoped that Eliza would be all right with that. Ariel said that she needed to check on the wolves and that she would think about my suggestion while she did so. She put on a green cloak, and I stood in the front yard and watched her go up the hill toward what her father had called Wolfpen One. When she disappeared into the trees, I strolled around the orchard side of Avalon Cottage and called Eliza at the salon. I could see her building from where I stood and imagined her putting down her shears and wiping her hands on a towel before she picked up the phone. But she didn't answer, so I figured she had her hands in somebody's hair and couldn't stop what she was doing. I left her a message, dropped the phone in my pocket, and walked a short distance toward the island's northern lowlands.

As I skirted the edge of the woods that divided the western channel of the French Broad from the orchard and the empty Wolfpen Three, I noticed Spellman Anderson II's bachelor cabin standing on a low knoll back among the trees. Curious about its condition after, I figured, being left mostly to itself over the past century, I walked into the woods for a closer look. As I made my way through some fifty yards of river birch, white pine, and a variety of oaks, I passed three stone foundations that had survived the 1902 flood and, with the cabins that sat atop them long washed away, now served like oversized landscape edging for beds of younger trees.

Spellman Anderson II had built his cabin within the confines of a fourth foundation that served like the outer wall of a fort or castle. This stone fortification and the rise of the small knoll had protected the old cabin from subsequent floods and might do so for as long as the waters never again reached the devastating levels of 1902, when the building built atop this earth and stone had been drowned and completely washed away.

An opening on the east side of the foundation-cum-fortification led to a door on that end of the cabin.

I cupped my hands around my eyes and looked through wavy panes of glass mounted in the upper half of the door. The single room was empty except for an old chair sitting sideways to the rear window.

For reading, I thought. *Some Anderson still comes here.* I reached down and tried the doorknob, the mechanics of which worked smoothly, and the door opened easily and quietly. I stepped inside and felt a chill deeper than the one that was rapidly coming on outside as early evening approached. I crossed the clean wood floor—*swept clean, kept clean*—to inspect the chair. *Grandfather's cabin and Grandfather's chair*, I thought, considering this probably a place sacred to Spellman Anderson IV.

The chair's wood was a warm brown all over except for the arms, especially the outsides and the ends of them, where many fretting or sweating or resting hands had turned them a much lighter color, almost yellow. The seat and the upper portion of the back were covered with a thin red-brown leather secured in place with brass rivets spaced an inch or so apart and in good shape except for a ragged half-moon torn away at a sitter's crotch. In the leather of the back, the words *Eine Einnerung* were stamped.

"A memory," I remembered aloud and startled slightly at the sound of my own voice in that place. I looked out through a clean, wavy pane of the window and into the woods behind, where nothing moved but a few early leaves and early birds. I turned in a circle and saw the same through all the other windows—one in each wall except that with the door—and then startled again when the phone suddenly buzzed in my pocket.

"Hello?"

"What're you doing?" Eliza's voice smiled in my ear.

"Well, I'm standing in a little one-room cabin in the woods behind Avalon Cottage," I said. "Looks like at least one of the Andersons uses it as a reading room or a getaway."

"You're still on the island?"

"I am."

"Is all the excitement still going on around poor Williemae?"

"No, that's over," I said. "But Edie-Mac found a naked man up on Hipps—"

"What?"

"That's about all I know so far," I said. "Maybe we can learn more this evening."

"What in the world is going on around here, Gabriel?" Eliza said. She paused. Then, "Who's there on the island with you?"

"It's just me and Ariel."

The line went quiet for another moment, and I could hear one of my old songs, "Best I've Ever Seen," playing in the background.

"Is she there with you now?" Eliza said.

"No, I suggested that she shouldn't stay by herself tonight, so she went to check on the wolves and think about it." I could tell that Eliza was thinking about me being on the island alone with Ariel and not really listening. "Hey, listen, Love, how would you feel about inviting her to stay with us tonight?"

"Why?"

"Well, like I said, I don't think she should stay here alone. And I can't think of anybody better than us for her to hang with." I paused, and when she didn't say anything, I decided to dig a deeper hole for myself. "Maybe we could have John Riddle and Jubal and Caldwell over later and—"

"Don't you think that might be a little overwhelming for her?"

"Possibly. But probably no more so than what she's been through today."

In the end, Eliza decided it was a good thing for us to do, at least the part about providing a refuge for Ariel. She even suggested that I bring the recluse to the salon where the two of them could meet and maybe even do a cut and style if such seemed desirable, while I went ahead and straightened up our place.

"It's in the low forties all of a sudden," Eliza said. "You should turn the heat back on when you get there."

"All right," I said. "If I can convince her to leave, we'll be at the salon in a few minutes." I saw Ariel coming through the trees toward the little cabin. "Okay, Love, let me get off here and see if I can get off the island before sunset."

"Bye, I love you," Eliza said and hung up before I could say that I loved her, too.

THIRTY-SIX

By the time Edie-Mac maneuvered her CR-V onto the Hipps Mountain spur, she and Deputy Mayhew had bantered so much about the handcuffs and her other toys that they considered making quick work of his investigation, taking everything inside the old shack, and spending the night there. But they grew quiet as she navigated the descending switchbacks and then rolled to a stop where the dirt road bottomed out at the southern mouth of its narrow valley. Although the sky above them still held the radiance of early evening, deep twilight darkened the short straightaway that ran ahead between steep walls of tree and stone. In a slight recess to the left, the shack stood lightless and ghosted like an abandoned gatehouse to a forgotten realm beneath the mountains.

Mayhew startled when Edie-Mac spoke. "He was standing right up there by that tree." She turned and looked at him. "Why'd you jump like that?"

"A little on edge, I guess." He nodded forward. "Do just what you did when you found him."

"Why?"

"I don't know. It just seems like the thing to do."

She rolled slowly past the shack and the tree next to which the naked man had stood, then drove on to the turnaround, describing all she did and thought as she turned and headed back. She stopped at the tree and put the CR-V in PARK, cut the engine and described how she got the man in the back seat.

"All right." Mayhew opened his door and stepped down

onto the dust and gravel of the road. He stood scanning the scene until Edie-Mac joined him with her camera and the mini cattle prod. He looked down at the prod and then at her face.

"I don't know," she said. "I ought to have something, don't you think?"

Mayhew smiled and pulled a small flashlight from his belt. "Let's have a look hereabouts first."

They saw nothing around the base of the tree and no marks in the bark within reach of somebody standing on the ground. Following the focused beam, they moved to an area between the roadside and a ditch from which they could hear the small sounds of running water.

"Big enough to park a couple of cars," Mayhew said as he moved the beam back and forth. "Looks like at least one vehicle has pulled in here recently."

They avoided the faint tracks visible in the dirt and crossed the weathered bridge over the ditch.

"You said you came over here after you got him in the back seat?"

"Yeah, I took some pictures. Went up as far as the doorway but didn't go in."

They stepped up on the porch.

Mayhew looked at the electric prod again. "Did you bring those cuffs, too?"

Edie-Mac patted a back pocket. "I saw an old mattress on the floor beneath that window."

He swung his flashlight beam to the window, raggedly curtained on the inside with burlap. "Weird there's still panes." He returned the beam to the doorway. "You didn't go in?"

"No, just as far as the threshold. There's an old pot-bellied stove and a chest of drawers to the left. A little table to the right. Over by the back wall a bunch of floorboards have been taken up and left a dark hole." She paused and shivered. "Shades of Poe's 'Tell-Tale Heart.'"

"Who's what?"

"You probably read it in school and just forgot."

"Yeah, probably," he said. "Stay behind me."

They moved together to the threshold, and he swept the single room with his flashlight.

"Stay here." He took a step into the shack and shone his beam over the mattress. "Bet there's been a bunch of nasty behavior happen on that."

"Bet you're right," she said, her voice at his ear and her breasts at his back.

"I thought I told you to stay on the porch."

"You did." She pressed closer to him. "But I'm a bad girl."

"Hold that thought." He stepped farther into the room.

She moved with him and perched her chin on his right shoulder. "Want me to tickle you with this prod?"

He chuckled. "Not yet." He turned the flashlight beam on the wallpaper of faded yellow newsprint. "That's actual newspaper," he said. "Wonder if we can find dates."

"Deputy Mayhew, your date's right behind you—" Her breath caught. "Somebody's in that hole."

THIRTY-SEVEN

Gabriel Tanner

The six of us—Dr. John Riddle, Dr. Jubal Kincaid, Dr. Caldwell Rowe, Ariel Anderson, Eliza, and I—sat satiated with pizza and wine around our tidied dining room table. Eliza and Ariel had arrived just as I put the finishing touches on the clean-up. The professors arrived soon after. Once we decided on the pizzas we wanted from the Runion Pizzeria, Jubal and I jammed some on flute and guitar while we awaited delivery. As we ate, Caldwell entertained us with stories of the Avalon community's history, and as we drank the last of the wine, he drew Ariel into a conversation in which they compared notes on that history from the outsider's and insider's perspectives.

She seemed like a sheltered, sleeping child suddenly awaking to find herself in some boisterous foreign setting—maybe a pub on a Friday night in a village in Ireland or Germany or the Czech Republic. She'd allowed Eliza to cut her hair and shape it up into a style that looked great on her, and I congratulated the stylist with secret winks and caresses. Ariel had borrowed from my closet a Runion State sweatshirt I'd outgrown around the middle but hadn't yet been able to part with and sat among the Runionites almost as if she were the one that was Irish, German, or Czech and dropped into our little Appalachian community.

When the table was cleared of all food and drink except after-dinner coffee for those who wanted it, John brought out the four copies I'd made of the Avalon manuscript. "With Ariel's permission, I thought we could entertain ourselves with a live reading of something written on Christabel Island two hundred and fourteen years ago." He looked at Ariel. "What do you think?"

She said nothing at first but looked at each face in turn, then cleared her throat and sat up straight. "I have found parts of it unsettling. Frightening even," she said in a quiet but precise voice. "This, however, seems exactly the appropriate gathering with which to attempt such a reading." She stopped and nodded at John.

"Thank you, Ariel. I think it'll be fun." He slid one copy to her, kept one for himself, and distributed the other two to the couples—Jubal and Caldwell, Eliza and me. "We'll probably stumble over the handwriting here and there, so when stumbles occur, if anyone knows the word, go ahead and say it so that we can keep moving." When we all nodded, he said, "As long as we don't get stuck on a word or in a discussion, we should be able to finish this by nine-thirty. Any questions?"

Caldwell Rowe spoke up. "What are we reading?" he said. "By that I mean, where did it come from and who wrote it?"

We all turned to Ariel.

"Toward the end of February," she said, "I was exploring the attic in Avalon Cottage as I have enjoyed doing periodically throughout my life. I discovered this document secreted away in a desk that has always been up there. I cannot say if I explored a place I had not before or if I simply explored more closely. In one low drawer brimming with minutely handwritten theological treatises, I located a false back, discovered only through feel, which, I imagine, very few people have stooped to investigate over the past two centuries and more. Beyond this false back, I found a remote second section of the drawer and in it a stack of papers the mice had mysteriously passed by. When removed, the stack was found to be comprised of more than one hundred pages, in the middle of which I found the original of these pages before us bound with a single black ribbon."

"If I may," John Riddle said and put down the coffee cup from which he'd just sipped. "The author was at first unknown, but after some research in our library and on the internet, I'm ninety-nine percent sure that the Philadelphia novelist Charles Brockden Brown wrote this." He stopped for questions, as if he were in his literature classroom and then proceeded. "The top page is a letter from Brown to somebody at Avalon. I can summarize that for you." He did so, briefly describing Brown's journey across North Carolina in the late autumn of 1800 and his return to Philadelphia. "So, on the morning he had to depart and head east, he couldn't find his narrative of events written during his stay with the Avalon community, which was newly established at the time."

"Obviously, the Avalon recipient of this letter did not return Mr. Brown's manuscript to him in Philadelphia," Ariel said. "I do not know if it remained lost, perhaps until I found it, or if it has remained hidden, intentionally hidden, all this time."

"I suspect the latter," John said. "But let's get started." He shuffled Brown's letter to the back of his stack of sheets. "I'll read the first page or so and then—let's go clockwise starting with Gabe—we'll read a page or a paragraph at a time. Whatever you feel like when it's your turn."

"Can we pass our turn on to the next reader if we don't want to read?" Eliza asked, and Jubal nodded his approval of the query.

"Certainly," John said. "Reading like this is rough on the eyes, especially at this time in the evening." When we were all bent over our copies, he began reading Brown's description of the journey from Philadelphia and into the wilds that had come to be our home over two hundred years later. He concluded Brown's introduction, reading, "Thus, in the space of twenty-four days, some five hundred miles, and three paragraphs, I am in Avalon!"

Everybody shifted in their seats, and I began the next page.

THIRTY-EIGHT

Avalon
September 27 to 30. 1800~

But soft! I seem to hear you say. An island? In the mountain wilds? Yes, I answer, yes! To dispense first with geographical particulars, the island—the community's enchanting name for it is Christabel—rises in a deep bend of the river known as French Broad. According to Mr. Ridgeway, the shape of this island is the same as the bend itself. Comprised of some forty-four acres, Christabel's western shore curls into the mountainside, separated from it by a small channel of clear flow, sparkling and melodious day or night. The eastern shore appears to turn its curved back to the larger channel and the mountains rising beyond. The northern end of the island flattens and narrows, seeming to enter the French Broad's flow like sand sluicing through an hourglass, while the southern end rises to a high headland that terminates in a frightful double-tiered drop to rocks and the river below.

The air above and around Christabel is filled with the unending whisper of the French Broad. I rarely hear the voice of my native river, the Schuylkill, be so persistent and insistent. I think it must be that here the mountains that stand all around the island pass the river's talk back and forth between themselves in perpetual colloquy. This murmuring takes up residence in every ear and, entering at the edges of windows and keyholes of doors, soothes or irritates each waking or sleeping mind—sometimes by turn within the same mind.

Gabriel stopped and slid the manuscript copy they shared in front of Eliza. "Your turn, Love," he said.

"All right." She picked up the top page, squinted at it a moment, and then began.

An apple orchard is planned for the island (Avalon!), but, at present, that remains in the future. As of now those in residence are consumed with securing shelter for all. The main house is complete and named Avalon Cottage. In addition to this, four other structures are mostly finished and already inhabited. They stand inside a grove that grows behind—or north of—the main house. These dwellings are occupied by the Ridgeways, the Douglases, the Allens, and the Landors. Avalon Cottage is occupied by the Huckses and the Holcrofts, who seem generally considered the leaders of this venture in Pantisocracy.

As a temporary guest, I have been provided bedding and a couch in the community's library on the second floor of the main house. As you might expect, knowing me as you do, I took the excuse of needing to recover from my arduous journey—in truth, as much reason as excuse—to spend these first days in the library, where I have slept to my heart's and body's content and refreshment, reading long and desultorily through almost all my waking hours. What slim remains of my time there be, that exist after these pursuits, I have spent dining in company or alone, walking the island, from southern headland to northern cape, and writing very little.

Before Ariel could pick up the narrative, Caldwell cleared his throat. "John, in all three sections we've read so far, Brown has addressed some person by 'you.' Do we know who he was writing this for—or writing to?"

"I can't say for sure. It's possibly Rebecca Linn, who was the younger sister of his future wife Elizabeth." John reached for his coffee cup. "He seems to have addressed a number of things to her, including a similar travel piece I ran across called 'A Jaunt to Rockaway' that I found in one of his old biographies." He looked at a page of handwritten notes he'd laid alongside his copy of the manuscript. "A couple of Brown scholars, Battistini and Weyler, have suggested Brown's tendency to fictionalize everything he wrote, from letters to scientific articles to political pamphlets, so the sense of a particular audience could simply be a literary conceit."

"Very interesting," Caldwell said. "Very interesting." He turned to Ariel. "Sorry to interrupt, Ms. Anderson. My curiosity—"

"His curiosity and sense of wonder are among his most useful and lovable traits," Jubal said with a wink and an under-the-table maneuver with his left hand, something that caused Caldwell to blush. "Sorry, Ariel. Go ahead."

She nodded and began to read, the archaic language and cadence of Brown's words sounding similar to the way she naturally spoke.

Avalon
October 1. 1800~

How quickly change the forms of being!

In the space of four days, life has progressed from a weary but welcoming arrival in Avalon, joining and enjoying its venerable Bucolics ("remote from the bustle and troublesome constraints of the great world"), to a vexatious and repulsive watchfulness at the approach of monstrous terrors beyond our control or comprehension.

Some one in the company at Avalon, it is rumoured, will likely metamorphose into murderer in the shadows of tomorrow night's full moon!

This means, of course, that it is just as likely that some one in the company will become a murdered victim.

It began with a whistling at midnight. This first came to me in a dream in which a mock-bird sat in darkness on a barren bough and poured forth a simple Scots air. When large eyes, red and malevolent, slowly opened behind the singer's back, I startled awake. My own eyes opened to the moonlit darkness of the library. Yet, the mock-bird's song continued, and for a moment, I felt caught between dreaming and waking. Gradually, I became aware that I was indeed awake and hearing some one somewhere outside.

Whistling upon a midnight! The shocking and hideous incongruity of it pulled me up from my couch and drew me to the east-facing window. Although the moon, one night short of full, lit the Avalon grounds, the casement's thick crown glass obscured my view. What I could see froze me for a moment. Even after a month away, my expectation at a window is that Phil. is on the other side—Second and Chestnut Streets. I found myself unwilling to throw open the sash and expose myself to the mountainous waste and bring my presence to the attention of the whistler, whose activity, at this hour, bore the stamp of lunacy.

Ariel trailed off at the word *lunacy*, and Jubal Kincaid took up the narrative.

The other inmates of the house must have been awakened as well, but without my trepidation. A voice brusque with sleep and irritation—that of Mr. Hucks—spoke into the wild night and chastised the whistler. "What is the meaning of this untimely performance, sir?" Mr. Hucks waited only briefly for a reply. "Halloo! Who be ye? Show yourself!"

The whistled air finished, leaving only the eternal murmur of the French Broad. All else was quiet moonlight.

Made more confident, perhaps, by the commanding voice of Mr. Hucks, I eased open the sash and let my gaze roam over the midnight shimmer and shadow of the lawn and garden below, the woods beyond.

"Show yourself!" again cried Mr. Hucks. "Are you still there? Halloo!"

At first, the absence of response continued, but then came, to my ear, a sound that chilled the blood in my veins—an absurd growl that sounded low and threatening for a moment and then stopped.

"Mary, fetch me my fowling-piece," said Mr. Hucks with exaggerated volume.

I could hear his voice both rumble beneath my feet and scatter into the darkness without. Then, its echoes yielded to a renewal of the growling, this time more urgent and insistent, but of only short duration, before it rose to a terrifying howl of maniacal laughter that I thought must make the silent mountains shudder.

Mr. Hucks did not discharge his firearm. I imagined his face and mine and that of Mr. Holcroft—in the second-story apartment across the central hallway from mine—all moonlit and framed in our windows.

Caldwell Rowe cleared his throat again, adjusted his glasses, and continued.

This horrific cachinnation was likewise of short duration, and stopped abruptly, as if he who laughed wished to study our reactions or as if he had inadvertently frightened himself.

I am not sure what Mr. Hucks could observe from his lower vantage point or what Mr. Holcroft could see with his apparently weak eyesight, but I, at last, espied a figure, within the shadowed margin of the woods beyond the garden, a figure upright but hunched, so that its true height and form were difficult to descry at a distance. I could not tell if what I saw was man or beast or some incongruous and ludicrous mixture of these. As I stared down from my window, I imagined that the figure's large eyes—I felt they must be large—steadfastly met my own astonished and widened orbs, and another droll growl began as it straightened, perhaps in defiance, to its full height.

"There!" cried Mr. Holcroft. "At the edge of the woods"—he paused, perhaps to squint to sharpen his vision—"just nigh the willow!"

But still Mr. Hucks did not fire his weapon.

The man—for man I believed it to be—rushed forward from the shadows and into the moonlight, as if he would attack the house. Then he stopped, haply as if in a moment of indecision. He turned, then, and, with a sidling lurch, disappeared once more into the shadows.

I listened, but heard nothing of its retreat. Stunned by the events just passed, I could not move from my window.

Mr. Holcroft said, "It's gone, whatever 'twas," and must have left his window open, for I felt my face flush to hear his Molly and him return to their creaking bed. A few mumbled exclamations rose to my ear from the Hucks's first-floor window before it closed.

"Can you imagine?" Eliza said.

"A world without security lights," Caldwell said. "Or even flashlights."

"Christabel still uses no outdoor lighting," Ariel Anderson said. "When night falls, the island is dark except for the lights within our house. Father likes to live as close to a natural life as possible, and I approve." She stopped herself. "As close as possible without being inconvenienced, of course."

"All right, we're back around to me," John Riddle said.

Keeping my eyes on the moonlit grounds below, I fumbled to grasp the sash, before getting hold of it, pulling it inward, and latching it. I turned slowly, to face the shadows of the library. I stood as if made of stone, unable to traverse the darkness to my couch, unable to reason down my perturbations. With the appearance of a fool, I am certain, I moved to my right, keeping my back to the bookshelves, until I stumbled my way into the desk chair.

And here I have remained, upright and awake, until enough of dawn arrived, to allow me to record these events, in the early light of . . .

Avalon
October 2. 1800~

I spent next day in observing each face and deportment among those around me, as they went about their daily duties. My energies, however, were wasted. Shadow had hidden the droll physiognomy of our extraordinary visitant, and the hunched, mis-shapen form, whether made thus by nature or design, was not to be seen among us.

The intercourse of the day, enthralled as it was to the bewildering and stupefying visitation of the previous night, in no way prepared us for the horror that hunted the island and even our habitations, when darkness fell again. The Hunters-Moon appeared to rise at the same instant as the sun set, and in the evening dusk, an aggressive, grim Artemis forcibly wrested the day from Helios and commanded Hecate pour down night, from the mountain holds. The inhabitants of Christabel fled to our chambers, where soon we heard what seemed strangely concomitant with the failing twilight—a savage yell, part howl and part roar, that was echoed, on all sides, by the abruptnesses with which this valley of shadow is surrounded.

"I'm with Eliza," Gabriel said when John paused. "Can you imagine?"

"I mean, that sound?" Jubal said. "In that darkness?"

Gabriel hunched his shoulders, leaned over the manuscript, and read.

The howling continued as night deepened. It seemed to emanate from a different direction each time—from the northern reach, from the eastern shore opposite Avalon Cottage, from the southern headland—as if the beast paced, in a frenzy, back and forth, up and down, from one end of Christabel to the other. And it seemed to come perceptibly closer each time, as if it closed the gap between itself and us with each pass from end to end.

The patience of this creature! The wariness! I said to myself as I stood in my darkened library apartment, near the eastern window—but not too near, perhaps two steps back—and, as I listened to these periodic, unholy howlings, watched a thick mist rise from the distant river channel and creep, as slowly as the beast, towards us. The baying ceased at the same time as the fog enveloped the garden, and crept across the lawn. This impenetrable mist lay low upon the island, perhaps two fathom thick, and I looked from my window as if from a high precipice—the ground like a cloud-benighted valley far below me, and above me, the mountains etched darkly against the moonlit sky.

Other than hearing the dismally loud, and violently explosive, discharge of a musket close at hand, and, soon afterwards, a muffled and distant snarling and shouting, I have no direct knowledge of what happened as midnight approached. The circumstances, as I was able to collect them the following day, from the actors and witnesses, were these.

"My eyes feel like they have sand in them," Eliza said. "But I'm gonna go ahead and read." She blinked hard twice. "This is crazy."

Gabriel scooted a little closer to her and wrapped her right arm in his left. "I got you, babe," he said.

Eliza rolled her eyes and shook her head and read.

When the fog had crossed the cottage-lawn, and wreathed the lower floor of Avalon Cottage, Mr. Hucks had thrown open his east-facing sash—"In order to hear any mischief I could not see," he exclaimed later. After the howling had ceased and only the muted hush of the river reigned for a time, he heard the muffled sound of halting footsteps approach. He could see no one, at first, embarrassed as the lawn was by swirling mist, but then, with the sound of one footstep more, a form began to take shape in the fog.

"A wildness of ruffled mane appeared to float around a head and hunched shoulders," recalled Mr. Hucks. "With yet one more footstep, methought glowing yellow eyes emerged from the obscurity of face, and hands, curled like claws, raised and reached toward the open window. At the same time, a low growl rumbled in the creature's throat. I shouldered my musket. When the growl increased in vigour, I did not employ the usual niceties of old English hospitality, and, stimulated by terror, I suppose, fired upon our visitant." Here, he stopped a moment and patted the knee of Mrs. Hucks. "When I regained my senses, after the dismally loud report from my weapon, I flew to the window and looked out, but I could neither see nor hear anything on the lawn."

Mr. Holcroft and I had then descended to the lower floor, where we met Mr. Hucks, lit lanterns, and, huddled awkwardly close together, went out to inspect the lawn. We found no body, and no blood suggesting that Mr. Hucks's musket-ball had not found its target.

Ariel didn't wait for interjections but continued the reading relay.

Halloos reverberated through the fog, followed by the tread of several feet that sounded from the edge of the lawn. Vague and indeterminate orbs of light appeared in the mist, and soon, we assembled in the midst of the lawn. with the inhabitants of the cabins, that stood among the grove at the rear of Avalon Cottage.

"Where are the Ridgeways?" asked Mr. Holcroft.

The gathered lifted lanterns, and peered in each face. Then, as one, we turned, and proceeded in the direction of the cabin occupied by James and Theodosia Ridgeway. The night was even more obscure beneath the trees, and our group kept close together. As we approached the cabin, we heard a door creak open and then closed, and suddenly James Ridgeway loomed out of the fog-deepened darkness.

Never a man of kind visage, and often heedless of propriety, Mr. Ridgeway stood before us with coarse, uncombed locks, naked to the waist, wearing only wide trowsers of tow cloth, without stockings or shoes. A smear of what appeared to be blood painted his left cheek, and three scratches extended from his left shoulder, to the center of his bare and capacious breast, joined halfway along by a fourth bloody scratch.

Mr. Hucks thrust his lantern forward for a better view. "By Jove! Ridgeway," exclaimed he. "Are you quite all right?"

"Yes, quite well," answered Mr. Ridgeway.

"And Theodosia," asked Molly Holcroft.

Mr. Ridgeway squinted in the light from the lanterns. "She is abed and resting," said he. "She received a shock, and experienced a sudden fit of madness, brought on by the—"

"May we see her?" interrupted Mary Hucks.

"Be still, Mary!" cried her husband. He turned back to Mr. Ridgeway. "What of the blood?" He indicated that on the man's face and breast.

"All mine, fortunately," said Mr. Ridgeway. "Her madness erupted in unexpected violence. To restrain her required some violence by me. My wounds are from this, but, fortunately, it drew none of her blood."

"Is she in need of a woman's attentions?" asked Molly Holcroft.

"No," said Mr. Ridgeway. "As I said, she is abed and resting. You may possibly see her tomorrow."

With that, he turned, and in a few moments, we heard the door of his cabin creak open and then closed again.

Ariel fell quiet.

"Well, that's suspicious as hell," Eliza said. "Don't you think it's one of the Ridgeways?"

"My money's on the husband," Gabriel said. "Ariel, don't tell us, okay?"

Ariel gave a slight nod and an even slighter smile.

Jubal looked across the table at John. "You said this guy wrote novels, right? Are they like this?"

"I haven't read all of them," John said. "But I read two for my PhD comps. *Wieland* and *Edgar Huntly* are pretty wild rides, but I can tell you about them later, if you're interested." He straightened the pile of pages in front of him. "Are you going to read?"

"I think I'll pass and just listen," Jubal said.

Caldwell straightened in his chair, adjusted his glasses, cleared his throat once more, and began reading.

Avalon
October 3-25. 1800~

On the following day, and for several days after, Theodosia Ridgeway was not seen by me. I believe the women of Avalon ministered to her, but they were unable—or unwilling—to discuss her condition. Then, she was among us again, appearing hale, active, and cheerful. Mr. Ridgeway, on the other hand, exhibited a dejected, gloomy sadness, a condition that seemed to decline, as his wife's vitality increased....

I wrote the above a few days after the events of the Hunters-Moon, and now, more than three weeks have passed without a word written here, when I had intended to take exact and daily note of every particular of life at Avalon. I have found, that in daily taking part in every particular, I am transformed into a complete pioneer—a back-woodsman, half civilized, half savage, too exhausted at night to lift my pen. I wonder at myself for this failure of my plan, but I ask how I might empty on the page a mind already emptied by corporal labour.

Avalon
October 26-30. 1800-

Our spirits improved—excepting that of Mr. Ridgeway—through the progress of October's various modulations of beauty in earth and sky, but toward the close of the month, as leaves began to fall, the general spirits fell with them. As an outsider, and younger than most of Christabel's inhabitants, I had developed a delicate friendship with the orphan Tait Douglas, a young man not many years younger than I, and without whom I might have been miserable, throughout my sojourn at Avalon. It was from him that I learned how, in the previous six or seven months, the community had been hounded by a were-wolf, a loup-garou, *or some such monster. The terror began around the appearance of the Worm-Moon in March, he recalled, as winter ended. No person from Avalon had as yet been harmed or murdered, but the same cannot be said among the widely scattered habitations in the mountain dells. One back-woodsman, Tait said, suffered serious wounds from an attack, and one's wife had apparently died from fright at the approach of the monster. The howls heard beneath the Hunters-Moon, and several moons before, had become the harbinger of horror, and even the anticipation of them, caused the spirits of all my fellows to wane as the moon waxed toward full, and threatened to dissolve me to a jelly.*

"Keep going if you want to," John Riddle said. "You've got a good voice for this piece."

Caldwell nodded and continued.

Avalon
October 31-November 1. 1800~

Perhaps for the benefit of me, but certainly for the benefit of themselves as well, the Avalon folk attempted to hold a Celtic celebration of harvest and summer's end. The name of this festival, I was taught to pronounce but not spell. As explained to me by Robert Allen, with whom I travelled from Phil. to here, this celebration involves the lighting of bonfires and the wearing of costumes, to ward off ghosts. One would think that the latter practice would be relished by Christabel's inhabitants, but the were-wolf seems considered by them, to be too dissimilar to a ghost. At any rate, a bonfire was the most they could manage, and above its leaping flames, the man in the silver moon smiled, one night short of full, and radiant with indifference....

Next night, when the Beaver-Moon rose at the end of All Saints Day, our hearing and our hearts were again assaulted with the same horrible howls of wolfish spleen, echoing between the nearly perpendicular hill-sides. Despondency and horror took possession of the souls of Avalon, which lay prostrate and powerless within us for a time. All inmates of Avalon Cottage gathered in the large ground-floor apartment of the Huckses. We did not speak, but sat and gazed at the fire, which failed to warm us.

"I hope the others remain safe," said Molly Holcroft at last. According to plans, the others—the Ridgeways, Douglases, Allens, and Landors—were to gather in the spacious cabin occupied by the Douglases, but no sooner had Mrs. Holcroft spoken, than a commotion at the front of the cottage served as an herald of the arrival of all the others except the Ridgeways. We moved from the Hucks's apartment to the communal parlour, across the hall.

"But where are James and Theodosia?" asked Mary Hucks, when we were all settled and quiet again.

"They did not gather at the Douglases' with us," said Sally Landor. "We stopped at their cabin coming here, but it was empty."

John Riddle jotted something in the right-hand margin of his copy of the manuscript and then sipped his coffee before picking up the narrative.

At length, when we had been settled for a time, and the wild cries had come no closer, Mr. Hucks grew agitated, and lifted his musket from across his lap.

"Gentlemen," said he. "We can sit awaiting our fate no longer. Mr. Holcroft, will you fetch your fowling-piece, and remain here in defence of our property and people?"

The men of Avalon—weapons in hand—rose as one to follow Mr. Hucks out into the night, which was once more becoming obscured by the mists, that often embarrassed the island. I accompanied them, although I had no musket, and carried only a pen-knife as a means of defence and offence. We went first to the cabin of the Ridgeways, and found the spot still deserted.

"Mr. Brown," said Mr. Hucks to me, "as you have no fire arm, will you consent to remain here, should James and Theodosia return in need of assistance?" He then addressed Mr. Landor. "Walter, please, give Mr. Brown your lantern."

Almost as soon as the sound of their tramping faded away through mist and trees, the crack of a twig disturbed the stillness and wounded my bosom's frail and delicate peace. I went to the window and saw, to my horror, a fog-shrouded figure approaching, with a distorted and halting gait. I at once recognized the droll creature that had haunted us beneath the Hunters-Moon. It growled and fretted, and kept its shoulders raised up about its ears, and carried its hands like claws. I could not turn away my eyes from it, but as it drew closer, to the opposite side of the window, I backed away, with slow, stumbling steps, to the opposite wall. The mis-shapen creature seemed to bow, then to hover, before it crashed through the window, and was in the room with me.

The monster was Theodosia Ridgeway!

All sat quietly for a moment.

"I stand corrected," Gabriel said. "Not the husband then." He clasped his hands together and buried them between his thighs, then hunched over the manuscript in front of him and read.

And yet it was assuredly not her. That was plain enough. I barely remarked that she was naked to the waist, and that what remained of her dress was in shreds around her legs. All of my attention was absorbed by her strangely monstrous carriage and clawed fingers. The wonted lustre of her eyes was lost in madness. Up from her exposed breast, a rumbling growl issued between blood-stain'd lips, that were drawn back to bare the teeth. When my trembling hand found the pocket of my fustian coat, she sprang and crushed me against the wall at my back. She threw me to the ground, and fell upon me. She tore at my face and throat as if she would claw out my eyes or rip out my windpipe. We rolled upon the floor of the cabin, but like Antaeus, she kept getting stronger the longer we wrestled in such a manner. Her mad exertions began to wear out all my strength, so that her clawing hands secured a purchase on my throat, and she began to strangle me. Try as I might, I could not loosen her gripe or get a similar hold on her throat, and I could feel my life drain away. I read in her eyes, that she knew I was dying, and that this thrilled her.

He slid the manuscript in front of Eliza, who immediately began reading.

My fading brain conjured one last thought, that was less intention than desperate frenzy. Rather than use my hands to pull pathetically at hers, in an effort to save myself, I let go. The increased strength in her hold almost palsied my courage. I was well nigh subdued: The lapse of another moment would have placed me beyond hope. My hands met at her back, as if I would embrace my own murderer. My fingers desperately worked to open the pen-knife I had drawn from my coat-pocket, as a darkness began to creep in at the edges of my vision, which was filled with her horrible, gloating visage. My stroke, when it came, was desperate and at random, but it served all too well. The strength fled from her gripe, and the wolfish madness fell from her face. As my vision cleared, I pushed her aside, where she lay as if struck by lightning, the blade of my pen-knife buried in her heart—

Those gathered around the table sat stunned, all staring at the manuscript copies on the table in front of them.

Then Jubal Kincaid looked up and across the table at John Riddle before turning to Ariel Anderson. "This really happened, right?"

Ariel nodded.

John gathered up his pages and tapped them on the tabletop to neaten the stack. "As I said earlier, Brown tended to fictionalize most of what he wrote, even in a private capacity." He looked at Ariel. "But, yes, I think we're supposed to understand that this actually took place just over two hundred years ago."

Ariel nodded. "It is almost finished," she said.

Avalon
November 2-7. 1800~

The Avalon folk were, at first, slow to believe my story, that the taking of Theodosia Ridgeway's life was necessary for the preservation of my own. Tasked to prepare Mrs. Ridgeway for interment, Jenny Douglas and Lavinia Allen were especially against me, and took every opportunity, for the better part of a day, at least, to show their displeasure. Their ire, however, was somewhat mollified, as the bruises on my throat, became increasingly vivid. Then, the Third Day following, the evening of November

4th, I was absolved from all censure, when the body of James Ridgeway was discovered, on the spacious ledge, several feet beneath the lofty and precipitous cliff edge that abruptly ends the southern headland. The throat of Mr. Ridgeway bore the same bruises as mine, and his face and body many more horrible wounds besides.

Thus it was early in the life of Avalon, that a portion of Christabel Island must be allotted as a burying ground, and that the bodies of James and Theodosia became the first to be committed to that hallowed earth. A man named Roland Gunter, newly arrived from Bad Schandau, in Germanic Saxony, by way of Bristol, in Bucks County, Pennsylvania, to settle one of the surrounding mountains, was discovered to have surveying skills. He was invited to Christabel, to lay out the burying ground, not far from where Mr. Ridgeway was found murdered. Mr. Hucks and Mr. Holcroft, then, determined where the graves of the Ridgeways should be dug, and they supplied Tait Douglas and myself with a spade.

Nov. 7th—a Sixth Day. The Avalon folk buried James and Theodosia Ridgeway. I stood somewhat aloof, for reasons easily guessed. It was a solemn occasion, and changed the nature of the community, as death always does. I suppose some wondered, as did I, what the next full moon might bring, but I will not be here to see, as I leave on the morning of the coming Second Day. Tait has promised to write to me periodically, and keep me informed of what passes in the life of Avalon.

THIRTY-NINE

In his cabin halfway up Lonesome Mountain, Deputy Davis Boyce stretched out in his recliner and stared at the blank screen of his television. He'd set a new bottle of Old Crow and a tumbler on the TV tray beside his chair, but he hadn't yet begun drinking. The day had run long and stumbled well into the night. Three times he'd called Dr. Rios to Runion from wherever she was or wherever she was going—for Williemae; for Truman South; for the unknown young woman discovered in the Hipps Mountain shack, lying in the grave Mr. South had apparently fought his way out of. Boyce shuddered in his recliner at thoughts of the clawing and kicking and pushing to rise, thoughts of escape from the darkness of unknowing and from the cold touch of the dead.

Across the darkened TV screen, images of the life and death of Deputy Williemae Rider played like a true crime documentary—her interview day with the idiot sheriff, who would have preferred to hire her as a secretary; her compact and admirable body, her light brown hair and blue eyes and smile so bright and sparkling; her laughter at herself during her first days on the job; her barely subdued excitement over her first arrest; her face across the lunch table at the pizzeria, a dab of red sauce at the corner of her mouth; her naked and brutalized body tied to a tree on Christabel Island; the crying eyes and collapsed faces of her parents when he delivered the death notice.

Sleep, Boyce knew, would come by only one means this night, like so many others—the tumbler of whiskey, filled and refilled, rising and falling, until he passed out where he sat. After a sharp intake of breath and a slow release, he picked up the bottle and tilted it for his first pour.

Dr. Jubal Kincaid and Dr. Caldwell Rowe lay in boxers and t-shirts beneath light cover in the dark bedroom of their house on Lonesome Mountain Road, just beyond the Runion State University campus. They lay side by side on their backs, Jubal with his left leg thrown over Caldwell's right thigh.

"Another interesting evening at the Tanner house," Caldwell said, his voice soft and thick with sleepiness.

"That was fun, wasn't it?" Jubal said. "It really was like a séance or something, like you said." He pulled his beefy arms from under the cover and laced his fingers beneath the back of his head. "What did you think about that story? As a historian, I mean."

Caldwell lay with both hands flat atop his barrel chest. He drew a deep breath in through his mouth and blew it out through his nose. "Certainly interesting. Given the source, it reads more like a Gothic novel than a history, but it fills some gaps in our knowledge of the Avalon community." He fell quiet a long moment before continuing. "I'd like to know more about the Ridgeways and the wife's psychosis."

"What, you don't believe she was a werewolf?"

Caldwell heard the grin in Jubal's voice. "Hardly," he said.

"You have an early class, so I'll shut up." Jubal lay staring at the ceiling a long moment. Then, "But wasn't Ariel intriguing?"

"She certainly was." Caldwell breathed deeply again. "Goodnight, Love," he said as he slowly exhaled.

"Goodnight, Love," Jubal said. "I think I'll write some music for her."

"For Ariel?" Caldwell slid his left hand from his chest down to his belly. "What, a flute piece or something else?"

Jubal snored.

Caldwell grinned and floated his right hand from his chest to the inside of Jubal's left thigh. "I wish I knew how you do that," he said.

He lay wide awake in a hospital room, startled by the whiteness of the bedding and the light from the machines. The doctor had told him that his name was Truman South and that he was from Spartanburg, South Carolina, and that his clothing indicated he was a Wofford University Terriers fan. Truman whispered these facts over and over to himself, trying to feel some connection to them. So far, he felt nothing except for the Terriers. He knew somebody bad had done something bad to him, and he wondered if a policeman was stationed outside the door for his protection. He wondered why he would remember that from some television show when he couldn't remember his own life.

He looked down at his right hand, the fingers of which kept opening and closing in a steady rhythm around the housing of the call button. He watched this with some curiosity, then closed his eyes and lay his head back on the pillow.

But the darkness behind his eyelids became the darkness in which he'd been left for dead, and his eyes flew open.

The black silhouette of a man filled the doorway to his room.

When his eyes pulled away from that terrible vision and small green and blue lights on the ceiling became glittering eyes descending toward him, his thumb pressed the call button over and over as he screamed his voiceless screams for a nurse and for help.

Livvy Goforth sat at the table in her kitchen lit by a single candle. She stared into the flickering flame, which, by turns, seemed to lean toward and then away from her as if in response to gentle inhalations and exhalations much slower than her own. On the roughhewn beam-and-plank ceiling directly above, shadows of faces seemed to shimmer together and dissolve in succession—women bearing resemblance to one another and to Livvy, Uncle Terry as a young man, a clear image of Plumer Reeves that stayed steady and lingered long. Livvy didn't look up at any of them except the last. But when Plumer's face faded and another formed in its place, a face with vague features that shapeshifted between man and monster, Livvy's eyes flared wide and then narrowed. Without lowering her gaze from the shadow-haunted ceiling, she reached out and extinguished the candleflame between her fingertips.

Thursday, March 13

FORTY

Austen Caine blinked hard against the building pressure of a headache as he navigated Highridge Road by moonshine and the low glow of his SUV's fog lights. He'd slept too little in the previous forty-eight hours, but to his mind, sleep stole time he didn't have. And he'd eaten too little since his filet mignon at Stony Knob Café almost thirty hours before. And then earlier that morning, he'd stood too long squinting in the sun. He blinked hard again and told himself that his headache resulted from this combination of unhealthy behaviors. Although he'd claimed otherwise in order to leave his plans open, he'd finished his scouting of locations for filming *The Cove* and needed to leave the area as soon as he could. He had no good reason to stay. Despite the headache, he half smiled at the thudding tramp of that phrasing through his mind—*no good reason to stay.*

He looked down and checked the trip odometer and slowed, looking left for the track that entered the woods. He'd found it by accident earlier in the day, thinking it would take him somewhere—maybe one last location discovery—before learning it was a track that dead-ended some twenty-five yards off the blacktop. *Maybe an aborted driveway*, he thought as he spotted it in the dark. He stopped a few feet beyond and reversed to back into the darkness beneath the trees. Just before he killed the fog lights, he judged the front of his vehicle to be about twenty yards from the near edge of Highridge. He turned off the engine and disabled all the interior lights and got out. At the rear of the vehicle, he opened the hatch and took out the folded tarpaulin. Leaving the hatch open, he moved to the front of the vehicle, where he shook out the tarp and spread it so that it hid reflecting surfaces from the top of the windshield down to the headlights and bumper.

He wanted to strip naked, but his plan had him hiking a quarter mile along the road. The thirty-degree weather didn't bother him, but the soles of his feet weren't conditioned for walking that distance on asphalt and gravel and whatever else he might step on. He unbuttoned his shirt but kept it on and returned to the open rear of the vehicle, where he took a high-powered flashlight from a storage compartment and slid it handle-first into the utility pocket at his thigh.

He stopped to consider if he'd forgotten anything, but his mind was too crowded—*dangerously crowded*, he thought—with headache and obsession and anticipation. Through the stand of dark tree trunks, he could see the blacktop clearly beneath a waxing gibbous moon three nights short of full. He understood he would be exposed walking there, but the ground beneath the trees was absolutely black. He reasoned that he might as well walk on Highridge by the light of the moon as walk through the woods with a flashlight. His aching mind made up, he cracked his neck and knuckles and set out.

Some five minutes later, Caine slowed and stepped off the road and entered the shadowed driveway. He picked his way carefully along to avoid the noise of snapping twigs, of scuffed or kicked pebbles, of a tripping stumble over half-buried stone or exposed root. At the edge of the yard, he stopped and studied the dark cabin in its clearing beneath the moonlit sky.

A breeze like breath moved through the boughs of those trees dressed in evergreen needles or in buds and new leaves. Winter-naked limbs of late-leafing trees clicked together. Trunks creaked as they swayed. Something far down to the right whistled for two seconds and stopped. From the left, up the mountainside in the direction of the path to Pulpit Rock, came the sharp scream of a red fox. Something winged its way from the treetops above him to those behind the cabin.

He bent and removed his shoes and socks and set them together on the sparse grass. Then he slid off his shirt and dropped it atop the socks and shoes. After another moment of listening and watching, he padded across the yard and stopped at the foot of the front steps. Then, testing each board for telltale creaks that would stand out from those of the surrounding tree trunks, he went carefully up the steps and across the porch. He slowly opened the screen door, hearing the hum of tension in the spring but no rusty squawks, gripped the front door's knob and turned, somewhat surprised but pleased to find it unlocked. He opened the door, likewise pleased to find it moved quietly on its hinges, then stood and listened for movement from the direction of the bedroom.

All remained quiet.

His headache seemed to have grown worse when he crossed the threshold, so he closed his eyes for a moment and massaged his temples. After twice blinking hard again, he stepped carefully to his left and crossed the kitchen.

No sooner had the eyes of Plumer Reeves flown open at the sound of the creaking floorboard near his bed than they were blinded by the powerful beam of a flashlight directed at his face.

"Don't move," the man growled through gritted teeth.

Plumer raised his left hand to shield his eyes, but the light pulled away and swung once around the room until the flashlight's metal casing cracked hard against his fingers, and then the beam bore into his eyes again. He let his eyelids flutter shut as he cradled his left hand in his right.

"Don't move, and keep your fucking eyes open," the man growled, spit sizzling between his lips and clenched teeth. "Or I'll crack your skull next."

The pain in Plumer's hand brought tears that he wanted to squeeze away, but he forced himself to open his eyes to a squint. The piercing light blurred, awash in pooling tears that then began to seep from the corners of his eyes and run toward the place where his hairline met his beard.

"Now roll over toward me. On your stomach. Keep your face to the right and your eyes on the light."

Plumer did so as best he could with the throbbing left hand.

The beam followed his movement until he was on his belly.

"Hands behind your back."

When Plumer complied, the man gripped his wrists together in one hand and set the flashlight on the nightstand and directed it at his face. And then the man was on top of him, straddling him, immobilizing his arms between hard-muscled shanks and somehow sitting on his head. He felt some type of cord being wrapped around his wrists.

The man tied off the manacle with a grunt and climbed off of Plumer and the bed. He lifted the flashlight from the nightstand.

Plumer felt the quilt and sheet thrown off his feet, felt another cord begin to wrap around his ankles.

The man cinched the second knot with a grunt. "Stay there," he said with a huffed chuckle, picked up the flashlight, and left the room.

Plumer tested the strength of his ligatures and found them tight. He could feel that his hands were already numb. He could see the peripheral glow of the flashlight moving on the portion of kitchen ceiling and wall—on Kayla's closed studio door—visible through the doorway of his bedroom. He heard a cabinet open and close. Another opened, and he heard the clatter of dishes.

Then the man returned to the room and laid a saucer upside down on Plumer's back between his bound arms. "Lie still," he said and balanced a plate right-side up atop the saucer. He positioned two delicate cups on the edges of the plate.

Plumer could tell by the clatter that these were pieces from the fancy china set Kayla's mother had given them and they'd only used when her parents came for supper.

"These fall and break," the man growled, "I'll bash your fucking head in." Then he left the room again.

In the kitchen, more dishes clattered. The refrigerator door opened and closed. Something danced and then spilled into a dish.

My Grape-Nuts, Plumer thought.

The refrigerator opened and closed again. A drawer opened, and silverware clinked. Chair legs scraped the floor. Then a spoon ticked against the bowl, and jaws crunched cereal with a steady rhythm.

While Caine ate, between the thunderous crunching in his head and the waves of headache, he listened for the clatter of movement from the bedroom. But he heard nothing. He hadn't used drugs on his man this time and yet had subdued him easily. He liked the feeling and decided that if he got away with it all and escaped these mountains he would push himself and push himself until he either found the place and peace to stop or finally encountered somebody who pushed back hard enough to overwhelm and destroy him.

After he finished a second helping of cereal, he left the spoon in the bowl and set both in the sink. When he turned around, his eyes fell on the closed door of the missing wife's painting studio—*That's off limits, Mr. Caine,* he remembered Reeves saying. He listened to the quiet for a moment and then stepped to the studio door and reached for the knob.

"Don't go in there," his captive said from the moonlit darkness of the bedroom.

Caine paused.

"Please."

He turned the knob and stepped inside and closed the door behind him.

Plumer heard no response to his plea and no sound of movement. Yet he knew that the man had gone into Kayla's studio.

He imagined the quick play of the flashlight beam around the room, revealing a few canvases hung without frames and more gathered in groups on the floor—some finished, some unfinished, some blank. The room was mostly windows, and the reflection of the flashlight beam from these, he hoped, would sting the man's eyes as his eyes had been stung.

He imagined Kayla as a ghost at her easel in the center of the room, unaware of the intruder looking over her shoulder, painting as she always had in bursts of quick strokes interrupted by long minutes of staring at the canvas or out the windows.

He imagined golden beams of moonlight angling through those windows into the room like the strands of blonde hair that often blew across Livvy's face, a face that seemed somehow to be looking at him now, seeing his predicament, its expression inscrutable.

Caine pointed the flashlight at the canvas he'd uncovered on the easel, the beam revealing the painting in parts: the woman in light at its center, the man with his torch, the silhouette of another woman hunkered down on a broken branch in the tree above him. Then he noticed the glowing eyes in the darkness beneath the torch-lit woman. *Wolves?* He thought it curious that Plumer Reeves's missing wife had imagined wolves long before they were brought to Christabel Island. Did their presence here make the woman above them Ariel Anderson? He let the beam drift over the painting, through the trees, until it brought to light a man standing half hidden in the shadows to the right of the central figures.

It's me, he thought. *She painted me.*

He clicked off the flashlight when a noise seemed to come from the painting, a noise that he knew couldn't come from there but must come instead from somewhere beyond the studio's closed door. It wasn't the clattering and breaking of dishes that he'd anticipated if Reeves somehow freed himself from his bindings or made any serious attempt to do so. He held his breath and listened and heard it again—a noise part thump and part whoosh. He couldn't imagine what might make such a noise, and at the same time, he knew he wasn't imagining it.

He left the painting uncovered and moved quietly to the door, put his ear to the wood and listened.

Again, the noise.

And again.

Then Reeves coughed, and the balanced china rattled.

The noise sounded yet again.

Caine returned the flashlight handle-first to his utility pocket. Moonlight grew in the room as his eyes adjusted to the absence of the flashlight's beam, and he reached for the doorknob and turned it, then carefully pulled the door open. He could see nothing in the kitchen, so he stepped quietly out of the studio and stood listening.

He lifted the flashlight from his pocket, pointed it at the bedroom doorway, and clicked it on. He saw Reeves's eyelids snap shut and his face flinch away and heard again a slight rattle of china. Caine ran the beam along the length of Reeves's body and saw that the ligatures on his hands and feet appeared to be secure. He clicked off the light and heard the noise once more, this time seeming to come from the front porch or the yard beyond. He pocketed the flashlight again and padded softly across the kitchen and into the living room, where he stood just inside the screen door and peered out at the moonlit yard and woods.

He stayed there until several minutes had passed since he'd heard the noise, feeling his confidence and resolve begin to lift him again. At some point, he'd heard talk about Ruffed Grouse drumming at night. He had no idea what that sounded like, but he wondered if that might have been what he'd heard. After listening through a few more steady breaths, and then listening for any sound from Reeves, he pushed open the screen door and stepped out onto the porch.

His plan had been to secure Reeves, return to his vehicle, and drive back. He would load up the bound man and haul him somewhere else—maybe to Christabel Island, where he could take possession of Ariel Anderson as well or back to the spot where Reeves himself had discovered the bodies of Terry Goforth and Dolly Ham.

He looked at the sky and saw no hint of dawn through the trees, but still he felt an urgency to get back to business. He clambered down the steps and strode across the yard. Then he stopped, squinted at the darkness, and took the flashlight from his pocket.

His shirt and socks and shoes were gone.

He stood staring at the sparsely grassed ground where he knew he'd left his things. Then he remembered the fox he'd heard when he arrived. *Damned foxes*, he thought. He glanced around the moonlit yard to be sure the thief—or thieves—hadn't simply moved the stuff from here to somewhere nearby, but he didn't see anything.

Nor did he hear anything among the night sounds akin to the thump and whoosh that had lured him from the studio out into the yard. Whatever had made that sound seemed to have disappeared like his things. Then, as if to taunt him, the fox screamed again, but this time he couldn't get a fix on the direction it came from.

He picked his way along Reeves's driveway, testing what lay underfoot. With each step away from the cabin, his headache somewhat eased so that more of his sensory awareness went to feeling every sharp point that seemed anxious for him to put his weight on it. He didn't think that anything had broken the skin, but certain footfalls felt like he was crossing a bed of thorns. When he finally stepped off the driveway and onto Highridge, he stood and relished the cool smoothness of the asphalt. And yet he knew that to hurry barefoot across such a surface for a quarter of a mile could be as abrasive as walking all night in socks lined with twenty-four-grit sandpaper.

Although the ache behind his eyes dissipated as soon as both feet were on the blacktop, it left some aftereffect affecting his vision. He could see clearly what was directly in front of him: the moonlit stretch of Highridge down to the first bend, ridgelines adjacent to Lonesome Mountain, the silver-dark sky above. But wherever he wasn't directly looking swirled with shimmering shadows, eruptions of murky radiance, and ghosted tableaus of memory. Along his way to that first curve downward and to the right, he tried to turn quickly to catch the remembered images—helping his father dig graves; sitting alone in a seat on the school bus, a gravedigger's son, powerless and ridiculed and bullied; arriving home one afternoon to find his mother and uncle fucking on the couch while his father sprawled naked and passed out in his favorite chair; sitting alone in a dark theater with Hollywood flickering across his face; sketching the world as he saw it, drawing it as he would make it. He thought if he could capture and confront these images with the clarity of vision leading him forward down the mountain, then he could somehow erase his vulnerabilities to strong women and weak men and aberrant desires.

After a time of walking on blistering feet, half naked in the cold and surrounded by swirling, dizzying darkness and flashes of light and memory, he flinched from a blast of bright golden radiance in his left periphery. Before he could turn toward it, he thought he felt a rumbling through his stinging soles and up into his shins. He stopped in the middle of the road and vomited the cereal he'd eaten at Reeves's kitchen table. Hot spew splattered on his bare feet and kept him retching even after he was empty. When at last he straightened up, his vision seemed normal again, and the feeling of something like vertigo had gone. The night was darker, and he realized that the moon had set. He didn't know where he was or how far down from the Reeves place he'd come, didn't know if he'd missed the dead-end spur where his vehicle sat hidden or if it still waited somewhere ahead of him. He stepped aside from the mess he'd made on the asphalt and looked up the dark mountain, feeling it more likely that he'd come too far than not far enough, but when he took a few steps back in that direction, the abnormal vision and the headache threatened relapse. He stopped and stood shivering, then turned and started downward again, considering the hint of rising light on the eastern ridges and wondering where he might hide for a while to pull himself together.

Since the flashlight beam briefly flared in his eyes and then disappeared, Plumer hadn't heard a sound from the man who'd broken into his home, bound him on his bed, ate his Grape-Nuts, and violated the sanctity of Kayla's studio. He had no sense of how much time had passed. He thought he might have slept but then wondered how he could have with the aching in his arms and legs and the full-body tension of keeping the dishes balanced on his back. As the pain in his limbs intensified, he began to grow concerned that the restraints might be doing significant damage to the nerves and circulation in his hands and feet.

Again, as he'd cautiously done several times, he tried to pull his feet apart without upsetting the china. He rotated his wrists, pulling and pushing in hopes of loosening the knot securing his hands. At one moment frustration got the better of him and some jerking movement caused a clatter that seemed to him loud enough to be heard up on Pulpit Rock. He stilled and then huffed a half laugh through his nose with the realization that his first fear at the noise was of breaking Mrs. Logan's wedding gift instead of bringing back the violent man who had put him in this situation.

He heard a dull thump somewhere toward the front of the house. *On the porch?* And then in the absolute quiet, he heard the spring on the screen door hum with tension when the door opened. He closed his eyes and could feel more than hear the footsteps crossing the kitchen. He opened his eyes again but realized that he didn't want to see the dark form fill the bedroom doorway, so he turtled his neck and turned his head away to face the back wall of the bedroom. He wanted to close his eyes again but somehow couldn't. He wondered if, when the end came and he went into that darkness, he would find Kayla waiting for him.

The floorboard beside his bed creaked. Something metallic clicked, and then the manacle on his wrists fell away and his arms flopped to his sides. After a rustling movement, the cord binding his feet did likewise.

"Stay still," Livvy said. She dismantled the china stack on his back and reassembled it on the nightstand. "Can you roll over?"

Plumer stifled a sob of relief and tried to roll over, away from the edge of the bed. His arms still felt weak, his hands numb. He turned his head to see her shape standing in the darkness and leaning over him.

"Here, let me help." Her hands were warm on his stiff arm when she lifted and pushed to help him. As he rolled away from her, she mounted the bed on her knees. "How do you feel?"

"Where—" Plumer started and coughed.

"Slow," she said.

He swallowed hard. "Where is he? What time is it?"

"It's about half past six. Gone down the mountain. He won't be back." She touched his arm and chest and thigh with warm hands. "Are you hurt?"

He swallowed again and took inventory. "Hands and feet are

numb," he said. "Some bones in my left hand are likely broken." He winced as he tried to close that hand but couldn't. "More than likely, I'd say." He swallowed a third time. "I'm thirsty."

"Let's get you upright, and then I'll get you a glass of water." She guided the swing of his legs toward her, and as she helped him sit up, she backed off the bed and stood in front of him. "You steady?"

He nodded. *Embarrassed*, he thought. "Thirsty."

She left his bedside without a word.

He heard a cabinet open and close, heard water sluice from the faucet. And then she was back. He raised a hand to take the glass.

"You can't hold it with numb hands," she said. "Let me."

He lifted his hands as if to steady hers as he drank, but he had no feeling at all in them.

She set the glass on the nightstand. "Do you need to pee?"

He did and felt like a child. "But I don't think I can—"

"Let me—"

"What? No, I can sit and do it." Even in the dark, he could see that she smiled down at him.

"I ain't offering to hold your goober while you make water," she said slowly. "Let me have your hands."

He felt his cheeks blaze but held up his hands to her and hoped that she couldn't see his embarrassment in the dark. He kept watch on the doorway, listening for sounds in and around the cabin, as one by one she held each of his hands and feet between both her hands and massaged them, pressing with a warm fingertip here and there. He thought he could hear the soft sound of her lips moving and of a singing breath, but he couldn't be sure. The moment he dreaded—when the rush of blood and feeling returned to his broken left hand and awakened the maddening prickling and tingling sensation elsewhere—never came.

She removed her hands from him, patted both his knees, rose, and stepped back. "Now you can go pee," she said.

Not until he stood over the toilet did he realize that he had no pain in his left hand. He raised it in front of him while he peed and saw that the fingers and knuckles showed no sign of being cracked with the man's flashlight, no swelling and no abrasions. And when he finished and flushed, he wondered at his hands as he washed them, then looked at himself in the mirror over the sink. "Damn," he whispered.

"You need to eat," she said from the kitchen. "And then nap after."

As he dressed for breakfast in a long-sleeved t-shirt and crisp bib overalls, the embarrassment of her having seen him mostly naked struck him, but that feeling quickly gave way to the greater mortification of her having seen him so helpless—and then having helped him. These feelings lasted only as long as it took to step out of his bedroom and into the kitchen filled with the sizzling of sausage and the scrape of scrambling eggs, the aroma of baking biscuits, and the radiance of her golden blonde hair and sunflower-yellow blouse. He lay a palm against the closed door of Kayla's studio—wondering if the man had closed it or if Livvy had—and then took his seat at the table.

When all was ready, she served them and sat in the chair closest to his.

"Thank you," he said. "For everything."

They ate without speaking, and when they'd cleaned their plates, he stood and served them second helpings of eggs and sausage and refilled their coffee cups. Then he sat again and looked at her.

"How did you come to be here?" he said.

"I can't explain that to you."

"Can't or won't?"

"Does it matter?"

"No," he said and covered her right hand with his left for a moment. "It doesn't."

She moved her hand to take up her fork again and cut into

a sausage patty. "I just wish I could've come to Terry when he needed help."

When they finished eating, he washed the dishes while she sat and drank coffee. Then he went to the living room, set the hook-and-eye latch on the screen door, closed the front door and locked it, and returned to the kitchen.

"I could use that nap now, I think," he said. "But what if he comes back?"

"He won't," she said. "Can't."

"How can you know that, Livvy?"

She stared at him with the same inscrutable expression he'd imagined earlier in the darkness. "I ought to get back," she said.

"Stay," he said. "Please."

They straightened the bedding and lay down on top of it, fully clothed and side by side, hands held between them, and slept.

FORTY-ONE

Ariel Anderson

I awoke before dawn, rose from the strange bed I had been given, and dressed. I could hear Gabriel snoring in my many moments of wakefulness during the night and again as I prepared to leave, and I wondered how Mrs. Tanner slept through such monstrous noise. I thought that if we became friends, I would ask her. I felt I could not face participating in—interrupting—their morning routine, so I left their home as quietly as I could, thinking I should leave a note but knowing not what to write on or with or, in fact, what to write beyond the thanks I expressed to them before retiring after last night's reading of Mr. Brown's Avalon manuscript.

Such a strange and wonderful event for me. I appreciated the Tanners' thoughtful hospitality, inviting me beneath only the third different roof I have slept under in my life. I was pleased to meet all in attendance. The trio of professors seemed a singularly talented group. Philologist, musician, historian—I was unsure how to act in such company. I could not but wonder what they thought of me as the living representative, if not a direct descendant, of the community in which the horrific story we read together unfolded. To hear it aloud from such diverse voices, with the interjected reactions, questions, and discussions, was both thrilling and chilling.

At the base of Genesis Road, on which the Tanners live, I crossed the highway that leads up into Runion and proceeded to traverse the bridge by which I thought I might arrive home not long after sunrise. Yet I stopped in the midst of my passage over the French Broad and took in the view of Christabel Island. I do not believe that I had ever taken the opportunity to stand and leisurely examine my home from such an objective perspective.

Christabel seemed a living thing to me from that vantage point. Its undulations from the lowlands on the north end to its highlands on the south seemed somehow to suggest that a voluptuous, giant woman lies on her side in the river tide, her exposed body encased in rich soil—the taper of her feet in the north, the power and fulness of broad, strong shoulders propped up on an elbow in the south. Although I could not see from where I stood, double cliffs dropped from the southern headland—the first a sheer drop of some twenty feet from the altar stone where I worshiped Artemis to the prominent and stony Ridgeway's Ledge, the second a sheer drop of more than one hundred feet to jutting and jagged rocks that divide the river into its smaller west and larger east channels.

I imagined Avalon Cottage as if built on Christabel's waist, just beyond the swell of her hip, where I saw its roofline and three east end windows on the upper floor. I saw the outline of vacant Wolfpen Three and some fencing of Wolfpen Two—the area where the monster, the Watcher, left the body of that unfortunate policewoman—but nothing of Atalanta and Milo. Interposing trees prevented my seeing Wolfpen One and its inhabitants, Demeter and Iasion.

I was just before continuing my way across to the western shore of the French Broad when I realized that the sun was risen earlier and higher than I had anticipated. As it ascended the sky, I watched its first rays slowly bathe Christabel, illuminating the island from the western shore to the eastern. My heart swelled so at the beauty of my home that I must linger just a few moments longer. And it was in this lingering that I saw something curious: a sudden glint of light flashed forth from the grove behind Avalon Cottage. A second glint followed, and then all became as before. It was as if a random beam of sunlight had, for just a moment, found its way through the grove's boughs to a piece of reflective metal or a pane of glass. Then either something in the boughs had moved and interrupted the momentary gleam or the shiny surface itself had moved. Although I could not know with certainty which of these had occurred, I knew the phenomenon probably came from my great-grandfather Anderson's cabin, which had stood in the middle of those woods for more than one hundred years and was now used primarily as my father's place for reading and reflection. I wondered then if my parents had made an early return from their sojourn in Charleston.

I suddenly became aware of the increase in vehicles slowing past me and realized that the inhabitants of this outside world were waking up and that, to them, I was something of a spectacle—perhaps even a spectre—standing on the bridge. So, I gathered my green cloak about me, lowered my gaze to the concrete underfoot, and hurried to the other end, where I found the old path that would take me along the base of Piney Ridge to our footbridge. At a certain point along that path, Great-grandfather Anderson's cabin came into view through the trees across the narrow river channel to my left. I stopped where I could best see it and observed it carefully and thoroughly. The thought of Mr. Brown's danger two centuries and more before, when he was attacked and almost murdered by Mrs. Ridgeway, came unbidden to my mind. I drew a calming breath and could see nothing amiss, and yet I could not rid myself of the feeling that something was, in fact, amiss. I continued to follow the path for some one hundred yards, and by the time I approached the footbridge, I had convinced myself that the uneasiness I felt was a residual effect of yesterday's gruesome discovery at almost this exact time and my pleasant but unsettling off-island experience now coming to a close.

The restoration of my peace of mind seemed to await my first steps upon Christabel's soil, the return to my wonted setting and habits. But I froze in place and was rendered momentarily breathless as I was about to mount the steps up to the footbridge. There on the sandy ground was a single print of a man's naked right foot. I stooped and looked at the impression in the sand and then straightened and looked all around. I could see no one. Looking down again, I thought it must have been made by a large foot, but, of course, I had precious little experience with the naked feet of men. After a final examination of the print, I straightened again and hurriedly crossed to the island and did not slow until I was safely inside Avalon Cottage with the door locked behind me.

When I had caught my breath somewhat, I removed my green cloak and hung it in its place. Yet I became so quickly chilled that I donned the red cloak, which I wore to feed my wolves. I took up the same seat I had occupied the day before in conversation with Gabriel Tanner, first, and then Deputy Boyce. With neither of those gentlemen to talk to, I talked, as I had often done as a child, to myself, to the four walls of the kitchen, to the ghosts of Avalon.

"The denizens of Piney Ridge and Runion often fish along that riverside trail," I said aloud. "Father permits it."

"Very true," I answered myself. "And they often fish barefooted."

"Very true as well."

"And I have watched many individuals engaged in fishing who might have left such a footprint."

"Yes, you are right, of course. But in mid-March? In cold weather?"

I had no response to that and fell quiet.

This play, however, made me feel better, so I gathered what I needed to offer tribute and praise to Artemis and, after donning my red cloak, went out of doors again, visited the cold larder to stock my feeding satchel and set out through the orchard en route to Wolfpen Two.

Yet I soon slowed almost to a halt in the orchard's center. Images of the mysterious blood-stained snow from a week or more past—blood of the raccoon—and of the brutalized female deputy from the morning before almost caused me to retreat to Avalon Cottage, maybe even to return to the Tanners' cabin on Genesis Road. I forced myself forward, however, not shying away from my memories and imaginings but welcoming them and turning them over in my mind. I could not, at first, understand how either of the poor things had come to be there. That someone—I believed one person to be author of both mysteries—had accessed the island by our driveway or the wooded path I had just taken, crossed the footbridge, and passed across our lawn unnoticed seemed unlikely. While his movements during the raccoon incident might quickly have been erased by a falling, drifting snow, I found it difficult to believe that he could cross the width of Christabel with the deadweight of a woman, create the horrific scene I discovered at the tree, and then leave, all without leaving behind some trace—more than a single footprint—that at least one of the previous day's many investigators would have noticed.

So, I looked the short distance beyond Wolfpen Two to the island's edge and the eastern channel of the French Broad. The water there was fairly shallow and slow-moving, but I thought how difficult to wade it carrying a wriggling raccoon in a sack or a dead body over one's shoulder with the slippery river rocks under one's feet. I traced the ancient cable that extended from our eastern shore to the Runion side. This might have provided access had the flat-bottom ferry it once guided not rotted and drifted away ages before. The idea of a canoe landing then struck me forcibly, and I shuddered at the realization of how possible, even probable, that was.

Still musing about these bloody oddities of recent days, I stopped at the edge of the orchard and watched Atalanta and Milo lope counterclockwise around the inside perimeter of their enclosure. This suggested to me that they were yet again perturbed. I observed them closely for any turning of heads at a certain point or any shying from a certain portion of the fencing, but I saw nothing of the sort. Receiving from them no indication of the nature of their perturbance, I scanned the area and still saw nothing. Then I recalled the flashing reflections seen from the bridge and turned to look toward the grove that hid my great-grandfather's cabin. All appeared still there as well, but I resolved to visit the place in the afternoon.

I delivered fish to the pair in Wolfpen Two, food they ignored as their pacing continued. Keeping my eyes averted from the tree to which Deputy Rider had been bound, I turned away and started up the slope toward Wolfpen One and the south headland. There I found Demeter and Iasion engaged in the same obsessive revolutions. Nothing I could see seemed to warrant this behavior in both pairs of wolves, but I trusted their senses far more than my own and urged myself to remain alert.

After I served more fish to Wolfpen One, I climbed to the headland and prepared my altar to Artemis. The very moment when I concluded my opening oration as usual with "O Great Artemis," I found my strength and senses overwhelmed by an oracular vision. My body from head to toe twisted and contorted as I fell forward onto what had been my hands and transformed into a wolf—not the hunched shoulders and clawed fingers and snarling visage of Mrs. Ridgeway but an actual wolf with dun fur and yellow eyes and extravagant senses of hearing and smell. And then I was running shoulder to shoulder with Atalanta and Demeter, the three of us flanked by Milo and Iasion. We ran at speed through woods, glimpsing ahead of us our prey, also transforming, glimpse by glimpse, between furred stag and naked man. Just when I had closed the distance and was about to lock my jaws on a naked trailing right foot, I awoke, lying on my back beside my altar boulder and looking up at the cold blue sky. I quickly overcame the odd sensation of having four legs and stood upright, feeling a clarity about what I must do without an understanding why.

I picked up my satchel and gathered the figures and gemstones and bracelet I used in my worship of Artemis. Then, after a glance aside at the Avalon cemetery and a deep breath drawn, I returned to the gate of Wolfpen One, which I unlocked and swung open and left it so. I hurried down through the headland woods, not looking back over my shoulder to learn what Demeter and Iasion might make of the open gate. I unlocked Wolfpen Two, left its gate open as well, and hurried through the orchard to Avalon Cottage.

FORTY-TWO

Gabriel Tanner

Eliza kissed me awake before she left to meet one of her early standing appointments. "The coffee's on, and Ariel's gone," she said.

I must have dozed off again, because by the time I sat up with "Ariel's gone?" Eliza was gone as well. I ached and groaned myself out of bed, peed and washed my hands, and poured a cup of coffee. Then I turned and leaned against the counter and stared at the neatly stacked sheets of the photocopied manuscript that still lay on the table where Eliza and I had sat during the group reading. The story it told ran through my mind in the voices of the night before—our different abilities at deciphering the handwriting, different talents for dramatic voicings. But through all this, I could hear the singular voice of Charles Brockden Brown speaking to us from across more than two centuries. Somebody had said after the reading—Caldwell, I think—that it was like a séance, and it was. The manuscript was the medium that channeled Brown and the early Avalon community into our cabin on Genesis Road.

I finished my coffee, washed the cup and those left from the reading party, shaved, brushed my teeth, and hit the shower. As the hot water splashed against the top of my head and ran in rills down my back and chest, I wondered what a penknife was.

A quick, naked Google after I dried off informed me it was just a basic one-blade pocketknife. I dressed and dug around in my old Camel cigarettes jewelry box—a brand-loyalty gift from my smoking days—and found the Barlow knife I carried as a kid. I dropped it in the pocket of my jeans with a certain feeling of nostalgia, thinking that I should make a run over to Christabel at lunchtime to check on Ariel.

I drove directly to the printer's and picked up the hard-copies of this week's edition and from there went to the office. As I unlocked the front door, the RSU carillon sang through its nine o'clock chimes. Neither Edie-Mac nor the RSU interns had shown up yet, so I unloaded the bundles into the front room and then sat down at my desk to await the crew. When I jiggled my mouse, the screen came alive with the advertising programs and documents I'd left open the previous day when called to the crime scene on Christabel Island.

"Shit," I said and looked up as Edie-Mac appeared in my office doorway.

"Top of the morning to you, too," she said. "Yours is that good, huh?"

"What? No, it's fine," I said. "I just got a reminder of work I didn't get done yesterday."

"Accounts?"

"Yeah."

She turned and looked toward the street. "Well, they're gonna have to wait, boss. I see the kids trooping down Lonesome Mountain from campus." She squinted. "Looks like we'll only have three this week."

"Oh, yeah," I said. "It's spring break, so we're lucky to have three."

She disappeared from the doorway, and in a few moments, I heard the printer whir to life.

"Hey," I said, "while those address labels are printing, will you make some coffee?"

"Did you have some already this morning?"

I didn't respond.

"I'll take that as a yes," she said. "Should I call Eliza to ask if you can have more?"

"Shit," I said again as the front door opened and the interns clamored in.

Only one of our three helpers from RSU's Department of Journalism had a car, so while I went into the hinterlands—Spring Creek around to Hot Springs and into the Laurels—where students who didn't grow up in those parts would likely get lost or worse, the three interns would deliver the local papers and then make the Marshall to Mars Hill run. Edie-Mac asked for the Alexander to Weaverville route because she wanted to take a trip into Asheville to try and see the man, Truman South, she'd brought down from Hipps Mountain the day before.

I would get to Christabel, but it would be the afternoon. Not that Ariel needed me to check on her. She'd probably enjoyed enough of my company and that of the outside world I represented to last her another decade. Still, I would get there to check on her, whether she liked it or not.

I locked up the *Recorder* office and sent the interns and Edie-Mac off with delivery maps in their hands and their vehicles heavy with the week's edition. I drove to the Post Office and dropped off the many copies we'd just labeled for mailing to subscribers along the highways and into the hollers of Madison and nearby counties, as well as to all but eleven of the lower forty-eight states, and to Alaska and Hawaii. Then I drove south on Main Street, blowing the horn three times—*"I love you!"*—as I passed Eliza's. Down on the River Road, I slowed past the bridge to Piney Ridge. I could see across the French Broad to Christabel, see the tree where we'd stood around the brutalized body of Williemae Rider, see the enclosure just beyond, which, from this distance, appeared empty of wolves, see the budding orchard and Avalon Cottage on the far side of its apple trees. Then I sped on toward Marshall, where I turned right in the middle of town and headed over the French Broad into Sandy Mush, already tired at the thought of this route that would take me throughout the west and north of the county and around to Wolf Laurel before I emptied the back seat and trunk of my share of our deliveries.

FORTY-THREE

Plumer Reeves awoke to the smell of fresh coffee—coffee he hadn't risen to make himself—for the first time in almost two years. He lay on his side fully clothed, bearded cheek resting on his open right hand, his left hand tucked between his thighs. He traced with sleepy eyes the imprint of her head on the pillow beside his and then rolled onto his back and breathed deeply, stretching and flexing various parts to confirm only the normal aches and pains and listening to Livvy Goforth move around in his kitchen. He swung his legs off the bed and sat on the edge of the mattress, pushed up to his feet and stood still for a moment. When he was sure he was steady, he walked out of the bedroom and into the kitchen, pressing a palm against Kayla's studio door as he passed it.

"Morning," Livvy said. "Going on afternoon."

He yawned. "How is it your coffee smells better than what I make myself?"

"I couldn't say." She lifted the carafe from the maker and began filling two cups she'd already taken from the cabinet. "How do you feel?"

"Surprisingly fine, thanks to you."

With only the hint of a smile, she handed his cup to him. "You hungry?"

He held the coffee beneath his nose and breathed in its aroma, then exhaled across the surface to cool it. "I don't think so. That breakfast is still with me." He took a careful sip. "Delicious," he said.

They sat at the table together in the same seats they'd taken earlier that morning.

"You need to call the sheriff," she said. "Let them know what happened."

He nodded. "It's embarrassing to admit."

"Nothing to be embarrassed about," she said. "You lived through it, and that's more than Uncle Terry—" She stopped.

He felt his face redden. "Of course," he said. "I'm sorry. I wasn't thinking."

"I didn't mean it like it sounded," she said. "You didn't go looking for such trouble."

When they finished their coffee, neither moved to refill the cups. They sat quietly together and looked at the dregs, and then he looked at her until she met his gaze.

"You knew I was in trouble," he said.

"Yes."

"Do you sense all the troubles people around here get into?"

"No."

Plumer considered this. "Do you know the name of the man who attacked me?"

"No," she said. "Do you?"

"I have a suspicion, but I'm not for sure."

"I know a way we might find him out or get enough so the law can."

"How?"

"Get your shoes on while I wash up," she said. She stood and gathered the cups and turned to the sink.

When they were in the living room together, he bent to a knickknack shelf and began lifting some of the items to look under them and digging his fingers into others.

"What're you doing?" she asked.

"Looking for my key to this door," he said. "Kayla and I never locked it, so she didn't have a key with her when she—" When Livvy didn't react, he didn't elaborate. "Ah, here it is."

He locked the front door behind them, and they turned away from the cabin. Livvy started down the steps, but Plumer froze at the edge of the porch.

"What's that?" he said.

"What's what?"

"There at the edge of the yard."

"What it looks like, I reckon," she said. "A pile of boots and socks and a shirt."

"I wonder why he didn't take them with him."

"Maybe he couldn't find them in the dark."

"Maybe." Plumer worked the key onto his keyring as they crossed the yard to his Jeep. She seemed startled when he opened the passenger-side door for her but nodded her thanks and climbed in. Behind the wheel and buckled up, he took his cellphone from the dash and flipped it open.

"Let's drive a little ways down the mountain before you call them," Livvy said.

"All right." He started the engine, turned around in the yard, running over the pile of clothing backward and forward. He could feel her looking at him as he drove the short driveway. "I probably shouldn't have done that," he said as he stopped at the edge of Highridge Road.

"Probably not," she said.

"Down?"

"Down."

When they'd descended Highridge a quarter of a mile, she touched his hand that rode atop the gearshift knob. "Pull off to the right here."

He did so, put the Jeep in neutral, and set the parking brake, leaving the engine running. "What's here?"

They opened their doors and got out and met at the front of the Jeep.

"His vehicle's sitting back in there," she said.

"He in it?"

"No," she said and stepped to where the turnout entered the trees. "I don't know where he is exactly, but I know he's not here."

He wanted to ask her how she knew some things and why she didn't know others, but instead of asking questions she wouldn't answer, he stepped into the shaded track behind her. He saw the vehicle some twenty yards in, and after a moment of confusion, he realized that the front of it was covered. When they reached it and Livvy yanked away the tarp, the shock he felt surprised him, even though he'd already suspected.

"This is Austen Caine's," he said. "He came by to see me yesterday afternoon."

"Who's he?"

"Said he was a location scout or something for a movie somebody's making around here this summer. Said he thought my house might make a good spot for a scene or two." He paused and swallowed. "I felt like he might be my visitor last night, but I couldn't be sure."

"So, he's the one that killed Uncle Terry."

"Looks like it. And the woman we found with him. Probably more besides."

She gave him a long look and then turned and walked slowly around the Equinox. At the rear of the vehicle, she stopped and stared long into the open back. "He was here," she said.

"Caine?"

She shook her head. "Uncle Terry." She looked another moment. "You were meant to be in here, too, I reckon."

His mind whirled with a burst vertigo at that realization, and he nearly fell backward into the undergrowth.

Livvy steadied him with a hand on his shoulder as she hurried past, walking back toward the road and his Jeep. She bent without breaking stride and picked up the tarp and dragged it along behind her. "We'll mark the spot with this," she said as he followed. "So those that come for it can find it easy."

FORTY-FOUR

After Edie-Mac dropped off her last bundle of the *Runion Recorder* at the Newbridge Hot Spot on Weaverville Highway, she turned right out of the potholed parking lot and headed toward Asheville instead of back toward Madison County and Runion. Figuring that Gabriel might still be without a signal in the narrow and shadowed valleys of the Laurels, she sent him a text to say she'd finished her deliveries and was going to visit Truman South in the hospital before she went home. She fed Against Me!'s *Transgender Dysphoria Blues* into the CD player and rolled down the window and nursed a Highland Gaelic Ale she'd poured into her Starbucks insulated water bottle as Weaverville Highway became Merrimon Avenue. By the time she was on the south side of Pack Square, the street she drove had changed from Merrimon to Broadway to Biltmore.

She parked in a space deep in the hospital's garage and, a few minutes later, walked down the hallway toward Truman South's room, where she found Deputy Carlton Mayhew blocking the doorway.

"Well, hey, you," Deputy Mayhew said. "What's up?"

She craned her neck to see past him and could make out Truman's shape in the bed. "I just thought I'd drop by and see how he is," she said. "Is that allowed? How is he?"

Mayhew ran fingers through his black hair. "It's allowed, I reckon," he said. "He's about the same as when you found him yesterday, if not a little worse."

"Worse?"

"Davis sent me up here to see if I could get some sense out of him—" He stopped. "Let's go over here." He took her by the elbow and directed her back to a small lounge near the elevators before he continued. "Apparently, the bastard that did this showed up last night and traumatized him all over again." He slicked his hair with a palm. "The nurses said he started hitting his button around eleven o'clock. When one of them got there, she found Mr. South under his covers and talking gibberish, and this big man was standing in the shadows over by the window."

"Oh my god, that's crazy."

"It don't seem like he was attacked again. The nurse got to the bedside before she even noticed the guy in the room with them. Said he didn't answer when she told him visiting hours were over, just stood and stared at the bed for a minute and then took off."

"Poor guy."

"Hey, you want to try talking to him?" Mayhew grinned. "Maybe y'all have like a bondage bond from them handcuffs yesterday."

"I don't know, do you feel like we have a bondage bond today?"

"Touché," Mayhew said.

Edie-Mac stood up. "I can try, I guess."

When she took his hand, Truman South flinched, but he didn't pull away. His face folded in a momentary grimace but then relaxed, and his eyes fluttered open.

"Hey, you," Edie-Mac said as she bent over him and smiled. "Remember me?"

He stared at her with a blank expression, but he followed this with a blush and a shy grin.

"You do remember me," she said.

He nodded. His grin broadened, and his blush deepened.

She asked him the usual hospital questions—was he comfortable, did he sleep, how was the food, was he hungry, was he thirsty.

He responded with nods and shrugs and stares but said nothing.

"Have you had any visitors other than Deputy Mayhew and me?" she asked.

His eyes flared wide. "Do you have your handcuffs?" he said with a wheezing voice.

"What?" Edie-Mac said with a half laugh.

"If he comes back, put your handcuffs on him."

She looked across the bed at Mayhew, who returned a raised eyebrow and an almost imperceptible nod. She looked down again at Truman's expectant expression. "I sure will," she said. "Can you tell me who he is, so I'll know who to handcuff?"

Truman shook his head, and a puzzled look passed over his features. "No name."

"You don't remember his name?" Deputy Mayhew said, at which Truman flinched and squeezed Edie-Mac's hand.

She looked at Mayhew with her own raised eyebrow and pursed her lips. Then she turned back to Truman with a smile. "You don't remember his name?" she said. "He didn't tell you his name?"

"No name," Truman said again.

"That's all right," Edie-Mac said. "We know he's big and scary and mean. Can you remember anything else about him?"

Truman's face lost all expression, and it seemed to Edie-Mac as if he might be falling asleep.

"He makes pictures," he said.

Again Edie-Mac looked at Mayhew and then back down at Truman South. "You mean like with a camera?"

Truman shrugged and closed his eyes. "Makes pictures."

A knock on the open door startled all of them.

"Hello, hey, sorry, I'm Dr. Blackmore," the man in the doorway said. "Would you folks mind stepping out for a few minutes while I take a look at Mr. South?"

Edie-Mac squeezed Truman's hand and felt him squeeze hers in return before she let go.

"He makes pictures?" Mayhew said when they were in the hallway.

"I don't know what that means," Edie-Mac said.

"I wonder if he meant like movies. They used to call them picture shows, didn't they? There's that guy who's been around looking for locations to shoot a movie this summer." He pulled a small notebook from his uniform shirt pocket and flipped through a few pages. "Austen Caine," he said.

FORTY-FIVE

Caine woke and lay still and listened. In the warmth, he felt the recovery of strength in his arms and legs and core. But when he flexed his feet, he almost gasped at a feeling like his soles were pulling apart in jagged red lines from toes to heels. Mostly just blisters, he knew, but he also knew he would need to treat his feet in some way and use them carefully for a time. In their present condition, he doubted they would carry him back up the mountain to retrieve the vehicle he'd somehow lost track of in his confused descent from Plumer Reeves's place. He'd realized in those moments when the sky above the eastern rim of mountains had begun to grow steadily lighter that he had no time and was in no shape to do anything other than find the nearest hidey-hole he could. He'd gritted his teeth and plunged off Highridge Road and into the downhill slope of woods he hoped would bring him to the parking area across the narrow western river channel from Avalon Cottage. He soon lost his footing and slid downward through a jungle of kudzu but found himself exactly where he'd hoped. Ignoring the pain in his feet, he crossed the parking area and the footbridge and, as the sun rose, made his way straight to a cabin Spellman Anderson had shown him during their walking tour of the island a few days before. He'd been surprised how quickly, once inside, the pain in his feet had flared up and his last strength had faded. His resolution to stay in this cold and bare space faded with his strength, and he hurried out again. He found the front door to Avalon Cottage unlocked and stepped inside, where he stood and listened for any sound from Ariel Anderson but heard nothing. Thinking she must not yet be awake or had spent the night elsewhere, he tiptoed quickly and quietly to the other side of the kitchen, then stopped and looked back expecting to see bloody footprints, but the hardwood floor was clean.

With a pillow and a covering of two quilts found on a shelf in a large closet attached to what appeared to be Spellman and Randi Anderson's bedroom, he crawled into and stretched out on a narrow run of floor between a low hedge of shoeboxes—Mrs. Anderson's one indulgence in this reclusive island life, he figured—and the wall of the closet, where he lay hidden under the canopy of a rich assortment of hanging dresses.

Just as he settled into this cozy, impromptu pallet bed, he'd heard somebody enter the kitchen and lock the door. He'd thought it must be Ariel Anderson, perhaps returning from feeding the wolves or from being away overnight. He heard her speak—the hum of voice only, nothing intelligible—and wondered if she might be talking to her parents in Charleston. But he remembered neither thinking nor hearing anything after that.

A low rumble began and continued somewhere inside or underneath the house.

Oil furnace, he thought, waking to the moment, not sure how long he'd slept.

He stretched again as best he could in the cramped space, careful not to groan or grunt or stretch all the way through the wounded soles of his feet. Again he listened but still heard nothing apart from the distant rumbling of the furnace. He slithered quietly from his hiding place, leaving behind the pillow and quilts for somebody to discover later. As he stood, he smiled to himself at the thought of the horror such a discovery would inspire. He stripped off his pants and underwear, tossed them onto his hidden bedding, and carefully went through Spellman Anderson IV's clothing in search of anything that would fit.

None of the button-up shirts would work in shoulders, chest, or biceps. Likewise, no pants would fit waist or thigh or length of leg. Eventually, he bent to the bottom drawer of a bureau against the back wall of the closet. There he found a maroon College of Charleston sweatshirt and—oddly out of place, he thought—a pair of stretchy green polyester joggers. Thin as Anderson was, his feet were big, and Caine found thick socks and hiking boots that fit well enough.

He gathered up these clothes in his arms and set them atop the bureau. Then, wearing only two pairs of socks, he worked through his eight minutes of Tai Chi, keeping quiet as he moved between the "his" and "her" sides of the closet. Just as he neared the end and closed the lotus flower into two fists, he heard movement overhead and stopped and let those fists fall to his sides.

Footsteps . . . strong . . . decisive . . . the upper hallway . . . descending stairs . . . quiet again.

He imagined this beautiful young woman as tall as he padding down the hallway toward her parents' bedroom and his hiding place, imagined her opening the closet door and standing naked in front of him, imagined toppling her backward onto her parents' bed and finding her throat with clawed hands.

He heard her moving about in the vicinity of the kitchen, then heard a door open and close. He waited and listened for two quiet breaths and then opened the closet door and moved across the bedroom to the east-facing window. She entered his field of vision, her face and body shrouded in a green hooded cloak, and he watched her cross the lawn to his left and disappear into the trees.

To the cabin . . . where I would have been.

He remained standing at the window, where he knew she must surely see him on her return, and he was half determined to wait for this when a movement that was not her returning caught his eye.

She was also being watched from the edge of the woods to his right.

He squinted against the sun-and-dust-bright light that bathed him and peered into the shadows where the grass met the trees at the bottom of the southern headland.

A wolf . . . no, two wolves. How—?

He turned and looked left again and imagined seeing her emerge from the woods, imagined watching her retrace her steps across the lawn, imagined her raising her piercing eyes to meet his, those eyes widening first in admiration of him and then in terror and hopelessness when she heard the wolves growling across the dewy grass with no time to turn and run before they were upon her.

FORTY-SIX

Ariel Anderson

From the corner of my eye, I saw Demeter and Iasion emerge from the trees to stand at the edge of the lawn. Yet I did not turn my face and look at them directly. I kept my head bowed and moved steadily forward, sensing from them only a watchfulness that seemed neither malignant nor threatening and congratulated myself on the good sense shown in wearing my green cloak instead of the red that might set their bellies and throats growling.

I sensed other eyes watching me, however, a more ravenous gaze, and wondered where Atalanta and Milo might be. The two of them, I thought, had recently tasted the blood of a living thing when they tore apart that hapless raccoon, and they had seen and smelled the blood of a human when the murdered woman had been left bound to the tree just beyond the edge of their enclosure. They had witnessed the depravity of the man—the Watcher—who had somehow brought both live raccoon and dead deputy to the shores of Christabel. Demeter and Iasion had sensed these things, I am sure, but they did not have the direct experience of them that Atalanta and Milo had.

I shied away from considering the gaze that I sensed might be that of the Watcher lurking somewhere nearby. Breathing prayers to Artemis for protection, I raised my eyes to take in the surrounding woods and then turned my focus on the cabin. As I did so, I could not but think of the narrative read around the Tanners' table the previous night. The structure I approached was not the same one from which Charles Brockden Brown had watched the monstrous advance of Mrs. Ridgeway, that one having been washed away over one hundred years before. Yet in some ways, these were the same woods—many of the individual trees being the same, only two hundred years older. I resisted the mad urge to impersonate Mrs. Ridgeway's wolfish behavior, fearing that such a change might turn my wolves against me.

I stepped through the opening in a former structure's crumbly foundation work—serving as a low wall that surrounded and protected the cabin—and stopped in front of the door and turned to my right. Through the budding grove, still mostly winter-denuded, I could see the bridge over the French Broad, where I had stood just after sunrise and saw the flashes of light from the opening and closing of this very door, which, upon turning back to it, I found securely closed but not locked. We never had reason to lock it. A look through the door's wavy windowpanes revealed that portion of the interior visible from my vantagepoint to be undisturbed. Before entering, I stepped back and examined the ground, remembering the footprint I had found earlier. I saw no sign of such again, but the soil at the cabin door was of a different consistency and leaf-strewn.

I opened the door, entered, and looked around.

No dirt or leaves marred the mat beneath my feet. The board floor was likewise clean. At the far end of the interior, the reading chair Father and I used in warmer weather sat in its usual position—sideways to windowpanes that wanted cleaning after the winter weather. The cabin was otherwise pristine. With an outside temperature hovering near forty degrees, the cabin's interior held a distinct chill felt to the bone, despite the sunlight filtering downward through the "bare ruined choirs" and wavy, water-spotted glass.

I pulled my cloak more tightly around me and stepped outside again and found myself face to face with Atalanta and Milo. The pair stood shoulder to shoulder not thirty feet away and stared at me with what seemed a single yellow gaze. I lowered my eyes and stooped my shoulders and stood as still as possible. After a few moments, during which none of us moved, I drew a deep, calming breath and took a slow step forward.

They, just as slowly, stepped backward but neither growled nor bristled.

We repeated this careful choreography until I was past the low wall and stood in the path that led out of the grove, at which point I made a slow bow and turned toward home. Self-consciously unhurrying, I walked away, listening for movement behind me—I heard none—and aching to step into the sunlight brightening the lawn. I emerged from the grove and found that Demeter and Iasion were no longer in sight. Still keeping my shoulders stooped and my eyes lowered, I walked more quickly across the grass and around the corner. I tried to remember the good reasoning I must have had that morning when I released the wolves, but nothing that made any sense came to mind. I shuddered at what might happen if the authorities returned with more questions or if Gabriel stopped by to inquire after my wellbeing. As I approached the front door, I determined that I must call to inform him of what I had done and then must call my parents to let them know all that had transpired since their departure. I dreaded both calls. If I could keep Christabel to myself for one more night, I thought, the next morning might find the Watcher caught and the wolves returned to their dens and waiting to be fed.

At the kitchen door, I turned and scanned the lawn, the visible portion of the orchard, the wooded hillside of the southern highland, but I saw no sign of wolves or trouble. I entered and closed the door behind me and set the lock. When I had removed my cloak and hung it on its peg, I turned to go to

Father's study and retrieve his cellular telephone. As I passed the hallway that led to my parents' suite, I sensed movement in the shadows there, and my breath caught in my throat. Yet before I could turn to investigate or defend myself, I felt a frightful blow against my head, a blow that dropped me downward into darkness.

FORTY-SEVEN

Gabriel Tanner

When I rolled out of the last holler in the Laurels and had a signal again, I called Eliza at the salon. "Hey, Love," I said when she answered on the third ring. "How's your day?"

"Not bad," she said. "Just finishing up my apple and peanut butter before my next one. How's yours?"

"Just heading back to civilization."

"Where'd you eat lunch?"

"I haven't had it yet, but I've been thinking about Bojangles in Mars Hill."

"Eat light, okay? Cutter and Rendy have appointments at four-thirty, and we're all going to dinner after I finish them."

"Of course," I said. This was a standing date with my cousin and his wife that I almost never remembered but was always ready for.

"Where are you?" she asked.

"Just coming out of Wolf Laurel and getting on the interstate to come back your way." I glanced at the digital clock on the dashboard and saw 12:17. "I should be back in town around one o'clock."

"I won't finish with them until six-thirty or so."

"All right, that'll work. I can spend the afternoon with my advertising accounts."

"Don't eat too much at lunch, and don't snack this afternoon."

"Got it," I said. I'd been thinking about adding a couple of Bo-berry biscuits to my usual Bojangles order but began trying to push that thought off my tongue and away from my belly. "Where are we eating tonight?"

"Rendy said something about Stoney Knob. Can you call and make a reservation?"

"Seven o'clock?"

"I think that'll be okay," she said. "Or as soon after that as possible. Maybe seven-fifteen or seven-thirty?"

"I'll call it in," I said. "And when I get back to town, I think I'll run over to the island and check on Ariel before I get into the accounts." I waited for her consent but heard only Pink's "Just Give Me a Reason" in the background. "You there?"

"Yeah, sorry, I was looking for a comb I need for my next lady."

Pink and the sounds of Eliza's search continued while I drove and listened.

"Oh, here it is," she said.

"Good." I wondered if she'd heard what I said about going to Christabel Island. "I'll see you at the salon by six-thirty, Love."

"Okay. Tell Ariel I enjoyed spending time with her last night." She paused. "Here's my next one. Bye."

When she ended the call before I could respond, I dropped the phone in the passenger seat and tried not to think of Bo-berry biscuits.

As I'd done on Monday afternoon, I stopped in the middle of the footbridge to Christabel Island and watched the clear stream of the French Broad's western channel pass beneath me. The electric bank sign on the Marshall bypass had indicated that the temperature was forty-one degrees, but the air felt colder here above the water. I stood facing upriver in the direction of Stackhouse, Barnard, and Marshall, and breathed in the subtle hints of spring greening, rich mud along the banks, and something musky I couldn't place. To my right, the circular parking area for the Anderson family and Avalon Orchards seemed lonely with only my Honda parked against the wall of kudzu on the far side of it. And that loneliness made me wonder what it must be like to be Ariel, to grow up in this place without siblings or same-aged friends or television or means of escape other than books and daydreams. I supposed that she might have a car behind one of the three closed doors in the garage at the end of the parking area, but I doubted it. Even though she was twenty-six years old, I guessed that neither Spellman nor Randi had taught her to drive. To my left, I could take in Avalon Cottage and allow my eyes to range all along the island's western edge. But I couldn't see either wolf pen from where I stood, and as I turned to continue across the footbridge, I wondered what the wolves might be doing in their enclosures on such a beautiful, chilly afternoon on the cusp of spring.

When I stepped down from the island end of the footbridge and began to descend the rough stairway of railroad ties, I found myself almost overwhelmed by a longing for six-thirty, when I would be with Eliza, Cutter, and Rendy, ready to carpool to a good meal and the good fun we always made together. But the longing faded, and a chill shuddered through me that seemed more than my body's involuntary response to the cold. I'd seen and photographed and written about dead people lots of times over the years, but very few of those had been murdered and they'd certainly never come at the rate of three bodies in two days. And none I could remember had died in the ways these had—such face-to-face brutality. The intimacy of it sent another shudder through me, and when my mind's eye turned aside from imagining those deaths, it fell on Brown's manuscript pages we'd read the night before—a city boy in the wilderness, a malevolent moon, a wolfish woman's madness, salvation by penknife.

I felt myself becoming panicky and stopped at the edge of the Avalon Cottage yard to take a few calming breaths. My left hand dug into my jeans pocket and pulled out the old knife I'd dropped in there before I left home. I hoped it hadn't cracked the screen of my phone sometime during the morning. The feel of it in my hand seemed both reassuring and ridiculous. Like most people, I reckon, I've had my superhero fantasies of saving the day with wondrous strength and skills I don't normally possess. And like most, I've daydreamt revenge fantasies—or fantasies of enacting righteous retribution—in which I take out those I believe have wronged or shamed me or somebody I love. But the reality was that I'd never been in a fight, not even in elementary or high school. If Ariel's Watcher found us here on Christabel, I would be as helpless at defending her and myself as young Brown in the clutches of the madwoman Theodosia Ridgeway, giving in and giving up as he did, and saved—if like him I might be saved—by nothing but a lucky strike.

I again felt panic rising and laughed it out in the still midday. When this laughter, so out of place there in that moment, creeped me out, I stowed away the old knife, in a back pocket this time, tucked bearded chin to gray-haired chest, and hurried across the yard toward the front door.

FORTY-EIGHT

Livvy reached across the center console and touched Plumer's thigh. "Stop," she said, leaving the hand where it lay as he braked to idle in the middle of Highridge Road, a thousand feet or so from the right-hand turn that would take them down to the French Broad River and across the bridge to Runion. She lowered the window and sat looking down the steep and wooded hillside that fell away on their right.

"What is it?" Plumer asked.

"He left the road here and went down through the woods."

"Caine?"

She nodded and tucked strands of blonde hair behind her left ear.

"I think it's time we call the police," Plumer said. "The Andersons are even more isolated than I was."

Livvy nodded again.

Plumer dialed the number, put the telephone to his ear, and eased his foot off the brake. When he heard the voice of the female deputy he'd met Tuesday morning, he almost disconnected the call, but then, as the Jeep rolled forward, he listened to her information and the invitation to leave a message and waited for the tone. "Yeah, this is Plumer Reeves from up on Highridge Road. Listen, a fellow I believe to be named Austen Caine attacked me in my home in the middle of the night, and I think he might be causing the Andersons some trouble on Christabel Island right now. You should check it out. This guy's dangerous." He disconnected the call and lay the phone on the seat between his thighs as he swung into the right-hand turn to descend from Piney Ridge to the river.

"Who was that?" Livvy asked.

"Voicemail."

"You know how to get to that island?"

"Yeah, there's a driveway a couple of curves down from here, or we can go to the bottom and take a path along the riverbank." When Livvy only nodded yet again, he cleared his throat. "I'm thinking we park at the west end of the bridge and walk from there. That way they don't even have to know we're around if it's not necessary."

After multiple switchbacks brought them down to the river, Plumer eased the Jeep into the dirt turnout, where at certain times of the year he'd seen Mr. or Mrs. Anderson—sometimes even both at once but never their daughter—lounging underneath a tent top behind a table or two piled with boxes of apples. He cut the engine and sat staring straight ahead across the expanse of bridge and the river moving right to left on either side of it, yet almost unconscious of what he saw as his mind's eye flinched from the night's repeated blindings by a flashlight. He flexed his left hand, feeling again a ghost of crunching pain but feeling, at the same time, amazement that he felt no actual pain after the miraculous healing—he didn't know what else to call it—performed by the young woman sitting in the Jeep with him.

"Don't make more of that than it deserves," she said, without turning away from her window and the riverbank path beyond. After a moment, she looked at him. "What do you think?"

"If anybody's watching for us, they'll see us." He dropped down from the Jeep and closed his door quietly. He walked around to the passenger side. "But I don't know why they would be," he said as he closed her door. "Watching for us, I mean."

"All right." She moved without sound to the head of the river trail.

He followed her over the embankment and down to the

water's edge, keeping his eyes on moccasin feet that disturbed nothing—no pebble loosened to roll away from her, no miniature avalanche of dirt from underfoot. Again, his mind swirled with vertigo at the uncanniness of the way she moved through the world. He raised his gaze to steady it on her back and kept it there until they were a few feet along the path.

The deep and unbroken voice of the river's broader eastern channel filled the cool air, but the water passing through the narrower western channel, within feet of their path, made only the barest burble. Beneath its surface, shadows of elusive size and shape flitted hither and thither in silence. Above, a bird or two, or a squirrel or two, mirrored these movements in the overstory. The March light seemed murky, even without the canopy of leaves that would, during the next two months, develop to keep both sides of the channel in constant deep shade onward into October.

To their left, on the opposite side of the quiet water, the northwestern portion of Christabel Island lay thickly wooded and hushed. They passed along the path, glancing every few steps at those woods, both watching, Plumer thought, for the first appearance of some Avalon structure: a cabin in the gloom, perhaps, or the roofline of Avalon Cottage in the sunlight beyond. Eventually they saw both, the cabin first and then the house, and slowed their pace. Plumer didn't know if he'd expected some sort of movement around the place, but the absence of it, the absence of any little ordinary movement to suggest all was well, vexed him.

Just before they emerged from the shadowing woods near the Piney Ridge side of the footbridge, Livvy stopped and waited for Plumer to come up alongside her.

"What is it?" he asked quietly. "Is he here?"

"Yes, I think so." She stared toward Avalon Cottage, mostly visible from where they stood.

He wondered how she could know, how she could sense the

man, wondered if Caine had visited her place like he'd visited his own the previous day, wondered if she could sense his presence because some residue of her uncle's life and death haunted the man's mind or lingered on his skin. He figured that asking her would be pointless, that she would say she didn't know or that she would say nothing at all. A sudden wave of frustration at her enigmatic nature washed over him, but this was followed and obliterated by a wave of anger at the memory of what the man had put him through a few hours before. The humiliating tension of dishes balanced on his naked back. Ridiculous indignation at stolen Grape-Nuts. The outrage of the man's casual trespass into Kayla's studio.

"I'm going over there." He started past her but stopped when she palmed his chest.

"Ssshhh." She jutted her chin in the direction of Avalon Cottage.

He looked at the house—its dark windows and one visible doorway—and saw nothing amiss except for the strange stillness that bothered him. But when he let his gaze drift away from the house toward the shadows between the front lawn and the mostly dormant English garden at the end of the footbridge, he saw them.

Two wolves stood side by side in those shadows—a distorted mirrored image of Livvy and himself standing likewise in the last shadows of the riverbank path.

"They've gotten loose somehow," Plumer whispered.

"Or been let out for some reason."

The wolves stood still with snouts slightly lifted, and Plumer wondered if they sniffed a breeze he couldn't feel, like the one that seemed constantly to float strands of Livvy's hair across her face.

He was suddenly struck with how much this tableau echoed Kayla's last painting. He stood among trees near the edge of a divide—perhaps a ravine in her imagining but the French

Broad's western channel in this setting. From the opposite side, wolves watched him. Livvy was present but beside him instead of with the wolves. A dark woman—not Kayla—wasn't in the trees above, as in the painting, but in the old house, and the sinister figure so threatening at the edge of the canvas had become an actual danger.

The wolves lowered their snouts, bared their teeth, and raised their hackles.

Although he couldn't hear their growls, Plumer thought they must be growling. He felt a freezing shock just imagining the sound and the first sudden steps of their attack. He wondered if they would cross the footbridge to get at Livvy and him or leap the channel in a single bound. A shudder ran through him, and she touched his arm.

"Be still," she whispered.

He tried to remove expression and tension from his eyes and mouth, shoulders and hands. The standoff seemed to go on for long minutes, but when the wolves suddenly calmed and he felt himself breathe again, he knew it could have lasted only a few moments.

Then the wolves turned their heads toward each other, almost touching noses. The one on the right spun away and loped into the woods that covered the rise to the island's southern headland. The other followed close behind.

"What do you think?" Livvy said for a second time when the wolves had disappeared.

Plumer startled at her asking and realized that he'd been thinking of her as the leader of their reconnaissance mission. He stared after the wolves for a moment and then turned his gaze on Avalon Cottage. "I think I wish I paid more attention to the comings and goings around here," he said. "If Caine is in there, we have to figure he's holding at least the Anderson daughter—"

"Ariel."

He looked and nodded. "At least Ariel, if not the whole family." He smoothed his beard with spread thumb and forefinger. "Could he handle all of us if we just walked up and knocked?"

"With a gun."

"He didn't have one last night."

"He might've found one in there, I reckon," Livvy said. "What about the wolves?"

Plumer shook his head. "Do we know how many they have?"

"Four, I think."

"No telling where those two went," he said. "But the others might be still locked up."

"Might be."

They moved together toward the near end of the footbridge. After a few steps, they were holding hands and released the clasp only when they mounted the bridge to cross it in single file. Halfway over to Christabel, Livvy tapped him on the shoulder. Plumer stopped and turned back to see her point downriver, the direction from which they'd come. He saw a single sheriff's car speeding over the French Broad from Runion to Piney Ridge, its blue lights twirling but no siren he could hear.

"Should we wait?" Livvy asked.

"I don't know," he said. "Better not." He took another step and stopped. "What if they're not coming here? They could've misunderstood my message and be on their way to my place."

Livvy nodded, and they continued to the Christabel side of the footbridge. They crossed the garden and stopped and stood where the wolves had stood and took a closer look at Avalon Cottage and its surroundings. Both caught their breath at the same time, and their hands found each other again.

Two wolves—*two different wolves*, Plumer thought—stood at the near edge of the dormant orchard. Gleaming eyes glanced at Livvy and Plumer for only a heartbeat before returning to stare at the house.

"They don't seem interested in us," Livvy said.

"I'm okay with that." Plumer heard the pop and grind of gravel under tires from high up the Anderson's hillside driveway. "Sounds like we'll have a deputy or two here in a couple minutes, but I still don't think we should wait." When Livvy didn't respond, he turned to look at her.

She stood still with her eyes fixed not on the wolves but on the house.

The mostly winter-barren tree limbs overhead and the naked flower bushes around them began first to tremble and then to shake.

"Livvy?" Plumer said, seeing her as the stone-still center of all the sudden movement. *The Rumbles?* he thought. Behind him, he heard the growl and pop of dirt and gravel as the patrol car skidded to a stop. He turned away from Livvy long enough to see Deputy Davis Boyce rise out of the driver's seat, to notice for the first time the car parked on the far side of the parking lot, then looked again at Livvy, who remained motionless in the middle of the quaking flora. As he heard Boyce's footsteps on the bridge, he turned to see that the wolves seemed to stare at her as well. "Are you all right?" he said without taking his eyes from the wolves. "Livvy?"

FORTY-NINE

Gabriel Tanner still lay face down and motionless at the kitchen end of Avalon Cottage's central first-floor hallway, and Ariel Anderson—half naked as her captor had her when interrupted by Gabriel's knock at the kitchen door—knelt beside him. She braced herself with her right hand on his lower back and dabbed at his bleeding head wound with the same damp dishcloth she'd used on the crown of her own head and the gash above her right eye.

Austen Caine stood above them, clenching and unclenching his fists. Although he outweighed her by at least fifty pounds, Ariel was as tall as he, and the exceptional strength of her resistance had frightened him, a sensation that elevated his excitement to new heights before the interrupting knock and the need to deal with the intruder, who had been easy to subdue when taken by surprise. But Caine wondered what kind of challenge the newspaper man might be when he came around—if he came around. He'd never had both his woman and his man together and alive at the same time, and while the situation tightened his throat and groin with thrill, he found himself confused about how to proceed.

Caine's confusion increased with the sudden return of the headache from the night before. Half-remembered images of past degradations and perpetual obsessions taunted him from the blurred and trembling periphery of his tunneled vision—father, mother, uncle, abusers, lovers, victims. He looked down and could clearly see only the profile of Ariel's head and shoulders and breasts. He could tell that her hands busied themselves around the newspaper man's body, but without taking his eyes from her, he couldn't tell exactly what she was doing to minister to him.

"He's alive?"

Ariel dabbed again at Gabriel's head wound. "You needn't have struck him so hard."

"He interrupted us," Caine said. "Come away from him now."

She didn't move.

"Come away."

At that, she rose from her knees and got her feet underneath her but remained crouched at Gabriel's side. "I dare not," she said.

Caine felt a wave of anger crest and crash in his mind, and he bent to grab a handful of hair. "Come!" he growled.

She sprung upwards as he pulled, and they staggered backwards toward the window at the end of the hallway, the light from it glinting on the blade of the opened pocketknife that had appeared in her right hand. She cut a deep gash in Caine's upper arm, but when she drew back for another strike, he caught her wrist. As they crashed to the floor with her atop him, he slammed her hand against the wall, and she dropped the knife. The jolt likewise loosened his grip on her wrist, and she wrenched free. He moved to block her from retrieving the blade, but she only feigned that attempt and slipped through the opening in his guard and wrapped her hands around his throat and tightened.

He relished these moments, when his woman brought him to the threshold of unconsciousness and began—he could see it in her eyes—to believe that she could win, that she would survive the night and his intentions. But this woman attacked with ferocity and power, and the idea flashed through his fading mind that he was the one who might not survive. He saw nothing of triumph in Ariel Anderson's eyes. Instead, as she snarled something over and over through gritted teeth, he saw a raw and determined savagery, as if she gave no thought to her own survival and thought only, if she thought at all, of his destruction.

"Show me the strength I have in you. Show me the strength I have in you. Show me the strength I—"

A loud knocking at the kitchen door reverberated through the hall, distracting her enough for Caine to buck her off balance and upwards on his body from his belly to his chest so that she first lost her leverage and then her hold on his throat.

Voices sounded in the kitchen.

She scrabbled for a hold and he for an escape. He knew by the sounds they made that the new intruders stood in the hallway's entrance, trying to make sense of what they saw—the fallen newspaper man and the struggle taking place further along the hall from where he lay. Just at the moment when she attempted to lock naked thighs around his head, he squirmed away and scrambled to his feet. He looked once toward the three people filling the hall doorway, then turned and leapt past the young woman as she reached for the pocketknife and in two more strides crashed through the window at the end of the hallway to sprawl on the cold grass of the side lawn. He struggled to his feet and took three steps toward the orchard and the river's shallow eastern channel but stopped and stared.

Two wolves stood with heads lowered and eyes glowering, each at the near end of a row of apple trees—hackles raised, teeth bared, growls filling the air like the explosive headache that filled his skull.

FIFTY

Ariel Anderson

I reached the shattered window and thrust out my upper body in time to see Austen Caine disappear into the woods that rose to Christabel's southern headland. I looked at Atalanta and Milo and noted their agitation. They looked back at me and seemed to calm somewhat. Then, as if I had communicated some command to them, they turned and followed Caine. Watching them go, I listened as behind me the two strangers, a woman younger than I and a man older, ministered to Gabriel Tanner while Deputy Boyce telephoned for an ambulance.

For a moment, I scanned the orchard and the hillside rising from the French Broad's eastern shore, aware that this place would never be the same for me. I felt different. I had ventured into those unknown hills on the other side of the river and spent an enjoyable evening with the Tanners and their pleasant friends. The leaving of narrow bounds I had prescribed myself for as long as I could remember, the opening of myself to company, to companions, other than Father and Mother and the wolves—these were mere glimpses, intimations, of possibilities to be realized in both people and places beyond Avalon Cottage, within the walls of which I suddenly wondered if I would ever feel isolated and protected again.

When a cool breeze pulsed through the broken window, I

remembered I was naked from waist to feet. I turned back to the hallway and hurried into my parents' suite and retrieved the britches and boots the man had forced me to remove before Gabriel Tanner's timely interruption. Fully dressed again, I returned to the hallway, retrieved the penknife from the floor where I had struggled with Caine, carefully stepped past my fallen friend and his caregivers, and entered the kitchen.

"You all right, Ms. Anderson?" Deputy Boyce asked in a tight voice as he clipped his telephone to his belt. "Did you see where he went?" He took another device in hand.

I stepped past him as well and took my red cloak from its peg. "He has fled toward the highland, and two of my wolves follow him."

"What?"

"The wolves are free," I said. "For the moment."

"Saw that when we got here," Deputy Boyce said. "How'd that happen?"

"I released them."

Boyce stood and stared. "Why—" He stopped.

"I will also follow Austen Caine to see that no harm comes to them."

"Now hold on, young lady," he said. "I gotta call us in some backup."

As I donned my cloak and changed boots, he spoke to a fellow Runion deputy—ending with "Go by the beauty shop and tell Eliza. Tell her gently, Carlton, and give it a positive spin"—and also to the Sheriff's office upriver in Marshall. When I left by the kitchen door, he was on the telephone again to some authority higher than the Sheriff, I gathered by his tone. Movement to the right caught my eye, and I turned that way to see Gabriel Tanner's ambulance hurry into our car park, its twirling red lights diffused in an afternoon that had clouded over since my walk across the river bridge just after sunrise. As I passed into the trees, I heard Deputy Boyce utter a curse or two to punctuate his shouts for me to come back or "wait up."

The early spring woods provided little protection from the eyes of either man or wolf. I realized with a start that my red cloak was perhaps not the better of the choices available, and yet it, too, was of a color representing Artemis. Wrapped in it, I felt a kind of power. I knew it could likewise arouse in the wolves a level of hungry aggression that might prove useful. In that moment, if I chose to keep moving forward, all that was left for my protection was stealth, to move uphill as quietly as possible.

I stopped often and held my breath. The commotion at the house faded as I progressed further from it, so I listened forward for any sound of man or wolf—or of man and wolves engaged in desperate and deadly combat. I closed my eyes, the better to hear, and heard my own inner voice rise into my mind. *Through every trial I face, show me the strength I have in you, Artemis, goddess.*

FIFTY-ONE

Livvy and Plumer rose from Gabriel Tanner's side to make room for the EMTs. The two stood a moment in the kitchen until the doorway was clear, and then they stepped outside onto the lawn, where Deputy Davis Boyce already stood with hands on hips and stared into the woods.

"Goddamn, I hate to go up in there without backup," he said, seemingly more to himself than to them. "I mean, goddamn wolves for crying out loud."

"She's up there alone with him," Plumer said. "And them."

"I know," Boyce said. "I know." He wiped a palm across his mouth. "Dagnabbit to hell."

A growl of dirt and gravel came from the gravel lot as Eliza Tanner's car skidded to a stop. She sprung up from the driver's seat and in moments was across the footbridge and crossing the brown bowl of English garden. By the time she reached the edge of the lawn, the EMTs were rolling Gabriel out through the kitchen door. "Gabriel!" she shouted and hurried across the lawn.

Sitting up and strapped in for the bumpy ride to the ambulance, he was awake, and although he had blood and the beginnings of bruising on his face, his eyes were clear.

The EMTs stopped and waited.

When Eliza reached his side, they kissed.

"Sorry, Love," he said. "Guess you better cancel those reservations at Stoney Knob."

"Hush," Eliza said and wiped something from his cheek.

Some signal passed between them, and she slowly turned and looked toward the three standing on the lawn.

Livvy pushed a strand of golden blonde hair behind her ear. "He's all right," she said.

"Eliza, you go on with him to get checked out," Deputy Boyce said. "Leave the keys in your car, and we'll make sure to get it back to your house." Then he turned without another word and strode toward the edge of the woods.

"He's all right," Livvy said again.

"He really is," Plumer said with a nod. Then he and Livvy followed Deputy Boyce into the trees as, behind them, the EMTs and Eliza gentled Gabriel's gurney across the lawn.

Deputy Boyce turned to see the two following and stopped to wait. He patted his sidearm lightly against his right thigh, his forefinger outside the trigger guard.

"Do you have help coming?" Plumer asked.

"I thought Deputy Mayhew'd be here by now," Boyce said. "Not sure how Eliza got here ahead of him."

"Well, what about that young female deputy I met Tuesday morning?"

Davis Boyce glared from behind his eyeglass lenses. His lips remained closed but working, and the muscles in his throat seemed to spasm. Then he steadied and spoke in a terse voice barely above a whisper. "Reckon y'all wasn't down from your mountains yesterday." He looked over their heads in the direction of Avalon Cottage and then in the direction of Runion, the muscles in his jaw working. "We found Deputy Williemae Rider murdered yesterday morning, her body desecrated and left for Ms. Anderson to discover just yonder on the other side of the orchard."

Plumer stood with eyebrows raised and mouth slightly agape, as if trying to understand the words he'd just heard.

Livvy said something under her breath.

Boyce tapped the pistol against his thigh three quick times.

"It ain't for certain yet, but I'm figuring that son of a bitch up the hill here is the one that killed her and left her there." He turned abruptly to continue his climb toward the headland.

Plumer and Livvy looked at each other and then followed, again joining hands a couple of steps along the way.

FIFTY-TWO

Ariel Anderson

I know not what Austen Caine believed he might accomplish by fleeing to Christabel's escarped headland. As I approached along the eastern edge of Wolfpen One, I began to hear the growls and snarls of wolves and man. I imagined Caine with his back to the precipice, the wolves slowly closing and forcing him to the very verge. I wondered at their behavior—those wolves—and would not have believed it were I not hearing with my own ears their agitation and anger. These creatures were raised among humans and if not tame then nearly so. Father had made certain of this. The inhabitants of Wolfpen Two, Atalanta and Milo, growled thus at me that snowy morning of the raccoon, but I had encroached on their territory with a kill at stake. They might have some particular knowledge of Caine or some intuition about him, having no doubt seen him trespass with the raccoon and later deliver and defile the body of the female deputy who fell victim to him. But Demeter and Iasion had no such experiences to associate Caine and bloodletting. Perhaps, then, Atalanta and Milo somehow inspired them with a grievous sense of the man.

When I at last achieved a vantage point from which I could espy the spot where I imagined a pitched battle taking place, they were not there. Still, I heard them clearly, and after a few hurried steps more, I saw them in the headland cemetery.

Austen Caine stood, as near as I could tell, atop the grave of Theodosia Ridgeway, the woman I had recently learned was the first monster to foul the atmosphere and grounds of Avalon. With his back not nearly so close to the edge as I had imagined and hunched in an attitude of defense, he confronted first one and then another of the four wolves arrayed in front of him. His face glistened with sweat, and the skin of it burned red. His eyes were dark slits, and his lips curled back to reveal his teeth. Beneath ill-fitting clothes I had never seen my father wear, Caine's body appeared like an arrow nocked and drawn in a straining bow, ready to fly toward any wolf that dared advance.

Demeter stood nearest me in front of the boulder I used as my altar to Artemis. Her forepaws were spread in front of her, and her forelegs extended low, almost touching the ground. Hackles raised above hunched and lowered shoulders. Her haunches gathered and taut.

Milo and Iasion displayed similar postures, but I could see their intent eyes and bared teeth. Iasion's tongue flicked out at quick but random intervals.

Atalanta paced the tight perimeter of their semicircle with head lowered, eyes likewise intent, almost glowing in broad daylight, with shoulders likewise bunched beneath bristling hackles.

Neither man nor wolves appeared to take notice of my presence.

I lurched nearer and stopped, breathless with a commixture of fear, curiosity, anticipation. Then, as had happened that morning, the sensation of transforming into a wolf momentarily overwhelmed me, and I envisioned myself joining the others in their deadly cluster. Yet, unable to master their patience and maintain my distance, I attacked and tasted Caine's blood on my lips, felt his muscles yield to my canines and his bones crack between my jaws.

And then it was there interposed a shimmering apparition

between man and wolves, and as the latter's bristling and growling immediately increased, my beastly reverie shattered at the intrusion of a single thought—*the risen specter of Theodosia Ridgeway!* I tried to shape the pulsating iridescence into the form of a woman. My eyes and mind and imagination refused. The more I focused, the more she flickered and appeared but a trick of the light.

I thought of the method by which I sometimes contemplated stars in the night sky or examined the substance of vague figures in the dark of the orchard and thus averted my vision, letting my gaze drift toward the pacing Atalanta. Figment of imagination or not, a woman indeed took shape. She hovered on the tensions that vibrated through the cemetery, monstrous as the man and brute as the wolves. From the center of a floating mane, large yellow eyes appeared at first directed—Janus-faced—toward each side of the stalemate, but then they revolved away from these opposite directions to fix directly on me. I felt a shiver of something akin to madness pass through my body from scalp to soles. Whether generated externally by those eyes or internally by my own fevered brain, I could not tell. Terror took hold as the figure's hunched shoulders appeared to square to me and hands curled like claws reached out.

Awareness of sudden movement to my right and somewhat down the hill then interposed between the specter and my horror, and with some difficulty, I pried my eyes from the *danse macabre* and broke the spell.

Deputy Davis Boyce had emerged from the tree line, weapon in hand. He stopped and stood with mouth agape and eyes wide behind the thick lenses of his eyeglasses so that I wondered if he also saw the shade of Mrs. Ridgeway.

Behind him, still in the mixture of broken light and shadow beneath the sparse overstory, I saw those two who, like Gabriel Tanner, had served as blessed interruptions to whatever mad plans Austen Caine intended to enact on me beneath the ancient roof of my hallowed Avalon Cottage. I knew neither of their names and had seen neither in my life before I looked up from my struggle with Caine to see them standing in the hallway door. The man was somewhat older than I, perhaps by ten or more years, as well as shorter and more slightly built. A searching intensity characterized his face and frame. Dark hair and beard and eyes lent his countenance a brooding quality, and I was taken aback by the dangerous emotion revealed in the set of his eyes and jaw and shoulders and hands as he stared in the direction of Austen Caine.

By comparison, the expression of the young woman, whose bearing and looks struck me as like those of a heroine from an eighteenth-century novel, was calm as she took in the strange cemetery spectacle. Her hair was the blondest I had seen in my limited experience of the world beyond Christabel's shores, and strands of it continually wisped across her face as if caught in a breeze. She did not blink at the wisps, and when she pulled the strands aside and tucked them behind an ear, her lips appeared to move to some purpose but without any voice that I could hear.

FIFTY-THREE

With his tunneled vision, Austen Caine could clearly see only one wolf at a time—the one to his left, the one to his right, the one in front, or the fourth pacing the perimeter. As he faced each in turn, the others became snarling dun blurs, a grating and growling soundtrack to his headache. Then a voice began to speak from deep inside the rumbling pain behind his eyes. He couldn't make out the words, but he felt the thrumming rhythm of them, their urgency like a chant or an incantation.

Other voices, guttural and whispery, slowly rose to mingle with the first and then to thicken above it.

Should we wake Ham up? The voice of Uncle Claude. *Him sleeping, this feels wrong or like—*

Hush now. The voice of his mother. *Don't you start thinking and go limp on me.*

A snore, long and stuttered.

Just feels wrong, Trudy.

Hush now.

The two voices began to thin and sink beneath the chanting of the first.

Pretend he's watching. His mother, speaking over Uncle Claude's naked shoulder, her words echoing and fading. *He's watching.*

And then these whispered voices and the reverberating rumble of his father's snore were gone, leaving only the monotonous chant that continued unbroken except during pauses for breath.

Caine pulled off Spellman Anderson's sweatshirt and a chill teased his skin to goose bumps, a sensation that overrode—for one agitated heartbeat or two—the relentless pain behind his eyes. He flung the maroon sweatshirt with its blood-stained arm at the wolf to his right, which first sprang backward and then lunged forward in mock attack before resuming its position.

A red blur hovered some distance beyond that wolf, and he risked a moment's attention to look directly at Ariel Anderson. She stood tall and tantalizing, taking in his confrontation with her wolves. Although he couldn't tell from the cast of her eyes exactly what she was looking at with such an expression of fearful wonder, he felt his skin prickle more intensely at the thought that maybe it wasn't the wolves or him. Maybe she saw or sensed some other presence among the living gathered in the cemetery. Maybe the chill he felt was more than that of the March air on the headland above the river.

When the chanting voice paused for breath, a sudden and differently toned snarl burst into his mind and pulled his eyes from the statuesque young woman to the largest of the wolves, a male, he believed, and probably the most immediate threat. He couldn't see any alteration in the big beast's demeanor to explain the altered sound, so he turned his tunneled vision to each of the other three in succession but likewise detected no changes in them.

More human blurs hovered at the top of the trail he'd taken up from Avalon Cottage, but before he could turn his attention to those, he heard again the odd snarl as a contorted human face—teeth bared, lips pulled back and trembling, yellow eyes wide with madness—flashed across his limited field of vision. He flinched, and the growls surrounding him swelled at the movement. The face was that of a woman, he thought as he slowly held out his open hands to try and calm the beasts. Yet the face was not that of any of the women who had, alongside the men paired with them, filled his mind the past few days—not Dolly, not Kandy, not Williemae, not Ariel. Not his mother, always there. Not any other he could remember.

Caine blinked away the afterimage of the unknown face and shook the echo of its snarl from his head, but the tedious drone of the incantation remained.

A woman's voice?

He raised his gaze to one of the newly arrived human blurs, and Deputy Davis Boyce came into focus—the brown cap with SHERIFF embroidered in gold thread, its bill darkening the thin-lipped, white-whiskered face, the service weapon held against his right thigh. Caine had kept an eye out for Boyce during his time in the area, but he hadn't met this man who looked old and tired. As the deputy wiped his left palm across his mouth, his face seemed to dissolve into that of another, not the snarling woman he'd just imagined—*surely imagined*—but Williemae Rider as Caine had bound her to the tree outside the wolf pen, her dead eyes staring up into the hills. After a breathless moment, her stare awakened and fixed on him just before the face reconfigured itself to that of the wizened deputy.

Caine turned from that man's glaring stare and found himself under the much different scrutiny of Plumer Reeves. He could tell that Reeves knew who'd attacked him during the night and guessed what the intention behind that attack had been. Caine's desire was to make this mountain man and Ariel Anderson his next pairing, but he'd failed to take either. He felt an ache in his hands and a sudden single throb in his loins at the thought of the final chokehold he'd never locked around the man's beardy throat. When Reeves broke eye contact and turned his face aside, Caine's gaze followed.

He'd never seen the young blonde woman until she appeared in Avalon Cottage a few minutes before. He didn't know her name or understand her connection to this moment and this gathering. He took in her bright hair, strands of which floated across her face as if touched by a breeze, her pale brow furrowed with consternation or concentration, her eyes too distant and narrowed to tell their color. When his gaze slid downward to her mouth, he saw the lips moving, and his breath froze as that movement synced with the voice of his headache. She was the one speaking some kind of spell into him, and he wondered if his failure to take Reeves in the night was somehow her doing. Stunned, he watched the lovely face grow round and whiskered as it morphed into that of the fat and hairy hillbilly hobbit he'd recently left slathered with peanut butter in a snowy mountain meadow.

He remembered that face red with dying as he choked life from the pitiful man, but then yet another face bloomed red with anger and loomed larger and closer until it blotted out the young woman and Reeves and the deputy. The lips parted in a sneer that bared the teeth. The sneer became a snarl, and the teeth became fangs. The face—quickly closing the distance between itself and him—became a hybrid of wolf and yellow-eyed woman.

FIFTY-FOUR

Plumer Reeves turned from Livvy Goforth back to the scene playing out in Avalon cemetery and couldn't tell exactly what he was seeing.

The big female that had been pacing in front of Austen Caine hung in midair as it leapt toward the half-naked man. But the wolf didn't attack alone. An iridescence, something wraithlike, seemed to swirl around its outstretched body, a palpitating shimmer that rode the beast and blurred its outline. Although Caine seemed momentarily lost in some kind of trance, he managed to spin partway to the right and raise his left arm. When his elbow connected with the attacker's snout, the she-wolf flinched backwards in mid-flight but not before that strange iridescence transferred from beast to man. It spun up his arm to wreathe his shoulders and head. Caine's face flew open in horror before collapsing in a grimace. Then all four wolves attacked, and he sank beneath a growling, jerking mass of fur.

Plumer stood stunned, unable to think anything except that Caine shouldn't have taken off that sweatshirt.

Beside him, Deputy Boyce said, "Oh, shit," and raised his gun and stumbled forward.

Beyond the deputy, Ariel Anderson cried, "Hold!"

Plumer couldn't tell if she shouted at Boyce or the wolves.

Caine suddenly rose to his feet—for a moment shed of both wolves and wraith—and stood with bloodied torso and arms and nearly naked legs. He fended off his attackers as they snapped at his hands and the strands of the green joggers. Then he was on the move, backing out of the cemetery as the wolves fanned out and pursued.

Just before he would have bodily backed into Ariel Anderson where she stood seemingly transfixed, Caine spun behind her and wrapped his right arm across her breast and the other low across her belly. He lifted to keep her between himself and the wolves, which hesitated and then one by one began randomly lunging, clearly intent on driving Caine and his human shield toward the cliff's edge.

Plumer surged forward with Boyce and Livvy alongside him as the trio brought up the rear behind the wolves. Plumer watched Ariel Anderson's face. She looked nothing like his Kayla, but something in her unearthly calm in this mad moment—as if she imagined how she might paint this scene instead of how she might escape or might die—likened the two exactly. He saw her right hand dip into the folds of her cloak and then reappear. Both hands came together below Caine's two-armed grip, and Plumer saw the flash of something narrow and silver.

The shimmering wraith reappeared as if from behind Caine and spun around his head at a dizzying speed. His grip on Ariel loosened enough so that she turned in his arms. The wraith's spinning expanded to take in Ariel's cowled head as well, and she and Caine teetered on the edge of the cliff, briefly looking like drunken lovers. Caine's face flew open again as if in surprise or pain or ecstasy. When Atalanta suddenly leapt, this time at Ariel's red-cloaked back, and dug her teeth into one of Caine's forearms, wolf, woman, man, and wraith disappeared over the brink.

Thursday, April 3

FIFTY-FIVE

for *The Runion Recorder*

GABRIEL'S TRUMPET

(from the Editor's desk)

RUNION—Those of us who live along the French Broad River in Madison County, NC, are no strangers to moviemaking. We've provided settings and services for such films as *Loose Cannons* (1990), *My Fellow Americans* (1996), *The Hunger Games* (2012), and more, including *A Good Baby* (2000), filmed at Stackhouse—barely more than a fly rod's cast upriver from Runion.

Along the way, we've hosted such stars as Alan Arkin, Gene Hackman, Dan Aykroyd, Dom DeLuise, Jack Lemmon, James Garner, and Jennifer Lawrence. Many downriver in Hot Springs fondly remember their Bridge Street interactions with DeLuise.

While these films have portrayed some scenes of comic and cinematic violence, we are also, unfortunately, no strangers to real violence. We've long been known statewide as "Bloody Madison," a nickname sadly well earned from the Civil War's Shelton Laurel Massacre in 1863 to the horrific murders of Nancy Morgan in 1970 and the Gahagan siblings in 1983.

In fact, your humble editor has just recovered from a brutal attack that bloodied his crown and put him in the hospital for a time, keeping him away from this office and these pages for three weeks.

By now, you've learned that preproduction for another film—an adaptation of Appalachian author Ron Rash's 2012 novel *The Cove*—brought real violence amongst us in the form of one Austen Caine, the film's location scout and, allegedly, a serial killer.

Four people are dead, two of whom belonged to our Runion community—Mr. Terry Goforth, 41, of Lonesome Mountain and Deputy Williemae Rider, 22, of Runion.

Dolly Ham, 36, appears to have been Caine's first area victim. Ms. Ham lived in New Bridge, but she disappeared from the Ingles parking lot in Mars Hill on Sunday, March 2. Witnesses who came forward say she was beside a buggy return with a man matching Caine's description. The two of them talked loudly but friendly, attracting some attention but raising no alarms among those grocery store staff and patrons who happened to be in the parking lot.

Her autopsy report suggests she probably died by strangulation that night or sometime on Monday, March 3.

Ms. Ham's body was found alongside that of Mr. Goforth in a mountain meadow adjacent to Pump Gap Road. Goforth had been last seen alive in Runion on the afternoon of Tuesday, March 4, and probably died, also by strangulation, a few hours later.

Although Goforth's truck was located at Walnut Island River Park in Buncombe County (a site recently infamous for clandestine liaisons of a sexual nature between men of the region), evidence found inside the vehicle points to Numan's, over the mountain in Johnson City, TN, as the place where Goforth might have initially encountered his killer. Authorities believe that after this first meeting the two rendezvoused at the river park, where Caine allegedly murdered Goforth as Winter Storm Ulysses bore down on the area.

Indications suggest Goforth's body and Ham's were left

together beside Pump Gap before Ulysses got well underway that night of March 4.

Kandy Wood, 24, of the Barnardsville area, appears to have been Caine's third victim. Mrs. Wood was last seen Sunday, March 9, at Cowboy's, a bar located on the Old Mars Hill Highway between Mars Hill and Weaverville. Owen Macdonald, bartender at Cowboy's, and a handful of Sunday afternoon patrons identified Caine from a photograph and claimed to have seen him talking with Mrs. Wood briefly before the two of them left the bar together.

A second male victim, Truman South of Spartanburg, SC, was taken while in Asheville to attend the March 10 Southern Conference Tournament championship game between Western Carolina and Wofford. Caine drugged Mr. South and took him to an abandoned shack on Hipps Mountain, where the killer proceeded to strip his victim naked and then strangle him. Thinking South dead, Caine then laid him under the shack's floorboards beside the naked body of Kandy Wood. Sometime on Tuesday, March 11, however, Mr. South miraculously revived, and by the following afternoon, he had escaped his grave.

The RECORDER's own Edie-Mac Lane found Mr. South on a Hipps Mountain roadside and delivered him to Runion's Tallent Health Clinic, from where he was transported to the hospital in Asheville.

Ms. Lane escorted Deputy Carlton Mayhew to the shack outside which she'd found Mr. South. There the two eventually discovered the body of Mrs. Wood.

Truman South remained in the hospital for more than a week, during which time he provided local and state authorities with what information he could, his recollection apparently somewhat sketchy due to the physical and mental trauma suffered at the hands of Caine.

South is recovering at the home of his ex-wife in Spartanburg.

Next, the body of Deputy Williemae Rider was discovered on Christabel Island early on the morning of Wednesday, March 12, having been last seen at "end of watch" on the previous day. Town Hall and Jail security footage shows Austen Caine entering the sheriff's Runion office on the afternoon of March 11 and engaging Deputy Rider in a brief but friendly looking conversation (security footage does not include sound), while the other deputies attended the Pump Gap Road site where the bodies of Goforth and Ham had just been discovered.

Authorities do not know if Rider and Caine were previously acquainted but speculate that the meeting resulted in a date arranged for the evening. Subsequent investigation located Rider's vehicle at Stoney Knob Café, where witnesses among the staff said she and Caine occupied a table for two hours beginning at 7:00 PM.

Where Rider and Caine were between the time they left her vehicle in the restaurant's lot and the time her body was found on Christabel Island is unknown, but they were likely at an Airbnb Caine apparently used as a base while performing his legitimate duties as location scout in Madison County.

Austen Caine seems to have intended the worst for three others among us, but his killing spree ended before he could complete those plans.

His final fall—an actual fall—concluded a string of failures to achieve apparent aims. He appeared in Truman South's hospital room in Asheville late on the night of March 12, seemingly determined to finish off South, but whatever intensions he had were abandoned when he was confronted by a brave nurse and fled the room.

An invasion at the home of Plumer Reeves of Highridge Road then occurred in the early morning hours of Thursday, March 13. Mr. Reeves was assaulted and bound before Caine, for unknown reasons, again abandoned his intentions and fled the scene.

Authorities believe Caine then descended Five Finger Mountain on foot and made his way to Christabel Island, where he broke into Avalon Cottage around sunrise. Several hours later, Caine attacked Ariel Anderson, whose parents were away to visit with Randi Anderson's family in Charleston, SC.

At this point, I inadvertently but fortuitously interrupted the attack on Ms. Anderson and received two significant blows to the head with a blunt object—a nineteenth-century cast iron door stop in the shape of a man's boot. This left me bloodied and unconscious in Avalon Cottage's first-floor hallway.

Before Caine could fully return his perverse attention to Ms. Anderson's person, a second interruption occurred in the form of Livvy Goforth of Lonesome Mountain (victim Terry Goforth's niece), Reeves, and Deputy Davis Boyce. Ms. Anderson launched a counterattack with a penknife she found in my back pocket as she ministered to me in my prone and unconscious state. Her assailant escaped through a window at the end of the hallway and, pursued by wolves, fled to the headland at the south end of Christabel Island.

Yes, dear reader, you read correctly: "pursued by wolves." Perhaps having some intuition about the violence her afternoon would hold, Ms. Anderson had, earlier that morning, released all four lupine residents at the new Avalon Wolf Sanctuary—by name Atalanta, Demeter, Iasion, and Milo.

According to eye witnesses (I was with my wife in the back of an ambulance on the way to the ER in Asheville), the strange and exciting climax to Austen Caine's reign of terror took place at the double cliffs on the southern end of Christabel Island. Caine had again taken Ariel Anderson captive and held her as a human shield while the four wolves forced him—and her—toward the precipice. When they were at the edge above Ridgeway's Ledge, Atalanta emitted a ferocious growl and leapt forward. All three—man, woman, and wolf—went over the cliff.*

The other three wolves reportedly went to the edge, looked down for a moment, and then, as if satisfied, turned and loped away to be found later, believe it or not, in their respective pens.

When the wolves abandoned the headland, the humans present—Ms. Goforth, Mr. Reeves, and Deputy Boyce—ran forward to witness the result of the fall.

At the foot of the short cliff, Caine lay dead, the back of his head crushed by a large stone. (I suppose he thus became the fifth person to die.) Ariel Anderson stood over him, his body having broken her fall. She held in her hand the open and bloodied penknife she had previously taken from my unconscious person. The autopsy showed the knife had penetrated Caine's spleen, a painful but non-fatal wound that possibly facilitated the fall. Ms. Anderson, of course, faces no charges for the stabbing.

The wolf, Atalanta, who suffered a broken foreleg, had limped to the edge of the ledge where she lay down and watched subsequent proceedings peacefully. She was later sedated and transported to The Valerie H. Schindler Wildlife Rehabilitation Center at the North Carolina Zoo, where her broken leg was set. She will remain in Asheboro until her injury heals. According to proprietors of the Avalon Wolf Sanctuary, plans are to return Atalanta to the pen she shares with Milo sometime in mid-May.

A source in local law enforcement reports that Austen Caine's movements as a location scout for other films are being backtracked, and cold cases of murder and assault in those locales—particularly involving pairs of female and male victims—are being reviewed.

*EDITOR'S NOTE—During my interviews with those involved in this scene, I picked up some hints that

> another entity, neither human nor wolf, participated in Caine's demise. Nobody made specific claims, but some sort of spectral presence seemed to haunt the way in which they described what they saw.
>
> Having recently read a 200-year-old story of violence and madness in the early Avalon community, I wonder if a woman named Theodosia Ridgeway had something to do with how events played out that afternoon on Christabel's southern headland.
>
> A story for another time, I suppose.

"If there was a ghost involved in all this, I hope she stays over on the island." Eliza folded the *Runion Recorder* and let it fall to the floor. She turned off her reading light and rolled to her left side, burrowed her left arm under her pillow, and lay looking at me where I sat propped up against my pillows and the headboard. My body shaded her eyes from my reading light, and she reached and cupped her right hand over my bicep. "That's quite a story we lived through," she said. "Good job on your 'Trumpet.'"

I looked at her and smiled. "Glad you liked it." I returned to my reading for a moment, then closed the book and laid it on the nightstand. "I felt like the ending was a little abrupt, but I ran out of space."

"You wonder what goes on in the mind of a monster like that." She lightly massaged the skin and muscle of my upper arm. "You haven't got to campus to talk to Jill."

"Not yet. I've just had so much to catch up on at the office."

"Well, she had an appointment today, so I asked her about some of the things we've been wondering."

"And? What'd she say?"

"I won't remember all of it, but I did ask about why he always wanted a woman and a man together." With the nail of her forefinger, she gently traced the perimeter of a mole on the inside of my upper arm.

"And?" I said again.

"She told me she couldn't know, of course, without interviewing him. But such—I can't remember the word she used—behaviors, I guess, tend to go back to childhood." Eliza kept her hand on my bicep but partially rolled and turned her face to the ceiling. "'It all goes back to your damn childhood,'" she said, mimicking the voice of RSU's forensic psychologist. "Which I already knew." She rolled back again to face me. "She said I could tell you but it's definitely off the record." She paused. "So, if she had to guess, she'd say something traumatic—sexually—happened between his parents. Like he saw them making violent love or something like that. And he started connecting violence with arousal. Maybe the two naked bodies were his parents, and he was his little self." She paused again. "Or maybe the two bodies were his mother and somebody else, and he was either his little self or his father." She chuckled and patted my bicep. "It was hard to follow with my music playing. I should've turned it off, but you know I can't do that."

"I know," I said.

"You should still go talk to her."

"I will when I get a chance."

She slid her palm lightly up to my shoulder and down along the length of my arm to my wrist, then pulled back her hand and tucked it under her cheek. "I'm sorry I got a little jealous about Ariel."

I smiled again. "Did you?" I lay my right hand alongside my hip and rubbed the hem of the sheet between forefinger and thumb.

"She's beautiful," Eliza said. She reached toward me and rubbed the swell of my naked belly for a moment. "And seemed very taken with you."

I sat up straight, and Eliza withdrew her hand. I twisted and rearranged my pillows and turned on my right side, facing her. "Did you ever read Homer's *Odyssey*?"

She spread her hand across her forehead and sniggered. "Lord, Gabriel, I don't remember. Did we read it in Mrs. Tolley's class senior year?" She reached out to tug lightly at the hair in the center of my chest. "That's going on forty years ago." She smiled and teased a nipple to hardness with her fingernail.

"Just know—" My breath caught for a moment before I could finish. "You are—and you've always been—my Penelope." Then with a grinning growl, I reached out and pulled her to me.

Sunday, April 20

FIFTY-SIX

Easter Sunday morning, Plumer Reeves stood in the Five Finger Pulpit as civil twilight brightened toward day. His idea had been to witness the quotidian spectacle from high above the Runion-area graveyards where learned pastors and rabid preachers were gathering sleepy-eyed and yawning congregants to hear resurrection sermons. Then, when the sun was up, he would begin reading the novel he'd tucked in the back pocket of his overalls before he left the cabin. He thought he might try something from the twenty-first century for a change, so he'd visited the Runion Public Library and come away with a borrowed paperback of Ron Rash's *The Cove*, wondering even before he returned to the Jeep if the book's relation to recent traumatic events might prejudice him against it.

His mind suddenly swam with vertigo, and he was glad he wasn't standing on the outcropping as Caine had done that day more than a month before. He wanted to believe that his swimming dizziness was a response to the vast emptiness that fell away below and hovered eternally above his line of sight between the Pulpit and that point on the distant ridgeline where the sun was about to breach. He wanted to believe it had nothing to do with the memory of a flashlight beam playing across the walls and floor of his cabin as he lay trussed up on the bed with pieces from his in-laws' wedding gift of china stacked on his back, his left hand throbbing from what could only be broken skin and broken bones. He wanted to believe it wasn't due to Livvy Goforth—the mysterious ways she moved through the world; her healing touch and incantations; her "Rumbles," whatever those actually were.

At the moment the sun began to rise, his gaze slid left of the brightening spectacle, to the north of it, to where her small board-and-batten farmhouse stood across from the mosque, to the top of the front steps where she so often sat. He tried to picture her sitting there in faded blue jeans and an old blue sweatshirt, her hands around a cup of coffee, her face partially hidden behind strands of blonde hair that danced across it.

But she wasn't there.

He pulled the book from his back pocket and sat down on the Pulpit's stone pew, opened it to the Prologue and read,

The truck's government tag always tipped them off before—

The sunlight touching his brow and eyelashes winked, and he looked up, expecting to see a hawk or turkey vulture gliding north or south along the horizon line.

But none was there.

He smiled to himself, lowered his gaze to the book in his lap, and continued reading.

"Mr. Reeves?"

He knew as soon as she spoke—the tone she took—she was harkening back to their first meeting, when she'd come to him on another Sunday to ask if he would find her uncle Terry—her uncle Terry's body. He closed his book, and a grin appeared in his beard as he looked up to find her standing at the end of the Pulpit path, not hiding behind azaleas this time but as open to him as a piece of sunlight sky in faded blue jeans and a blue "I ♥ Madison County, N.C." sweatshirt. Vertigo again swirled his mind for a moment when he recognized that she was dressed exactly as he'd just tried to picture her.

"I don't mean to intrude," she said.

"How'd you know I'd be here?" He stood. "Or is that one of those things you can't tell me?"

She laughed. "You weren't at your place, but your Jeep was. So, not that much of a mystery."

"Fair enough," he said. "Please, come in." He again sat down on the pew and patted the stone beside him. "Welcome to the Pulpit."

She skirted the edge of a bed of bright spring grass that spread in front of the pew and took a seat beside him.

They sat together for a time without speaking. He scanned the horizon, looking for nothing in particular now that she was with him. She sat straight-backed with her palms planted on the stone alongside her thighs and her head bowed toward the lush and inviting grass.

He still had no understanding of her "Rumbles" or her "sight" or whatever other gifts she possessed, and he wondered if she could somehow sit in the Pulpit and envision Kayla and him making love that first day of spring over two years before. He felt his cheeks redden beneath his beard, chanced a glance at her, and reddened more deeply to find her blushing as well.

He looked down and seemed to see Kayla there like a mist among the leaves of grass. His breath caught, and her voice came to him again, playful but distant—*that girl is half—*

"I've told you more than once I don't think age is such a big deal," Livvy said and abruptly stood and brushed off the seat of her jeans.

Plumer stood up beside her, bent and picked up the paperback, then straightened and returned it to his back pocket. "Maybe we should go to the house."

"Maybe we should."

They took the trail up and over the ridge, and as they descended toward his cabin, they found themselves holding hands for the first time since the dark days of Austen Caine. When they entered his yard, their hands separated, and he pulled his keys from a pocket as they climbed the front steps.

Once inside with the door locked behind them, they went into the kitchen.

"How about an Easter brunch?" she said. "You've got eggs and such?" She grinned. "And Grape-Nuts?"

"Always Grape-Nuts if nothing else," he said. "But I want to show you something first." He took her hand again and led her to the closed door of Kayla's studio. He put his free palm against the wood and looked at her, a feeling as if unseen fingers were gently closing around his neck.

"Are you sure about this, Plumer?" Livvy asked.

He cleared his throat, and the sense of constriction eased. "I am if you are."

She squeezed his hand. "Show me."

He turned the knob and stepped into the studio, drew her inside and closed the door behind them.

Tuesday, May 6 – Wednesday, October 8

FIFTY-SEVEN

Ariel Anderson

The day had been all a-romp with mid-spring life and activity in the orchard. We Andersons spent the morning eradicating weeds and trimming grass from beneath the apple trees. After lunch, Mother whiled away the post meridian in Runion—thrifting for summer at Aslan's Den, refreshing our reading lives at the Runion Public Library, and restocking our pantry from Whitson's grocery. Father and I continued working in the orchard—some pruning among the elder trees to open their canopies to breath and light, some basic training of the younger trees.

All the while, Milo sat outside his den and watched with apparent interest, a curious tilt to his head.

Perhaps for the first time since mid-March, Father and I conversed easily as we worked. Mother and he had been put terribly out of sorts at learning of the horrific events that took place whilst they were away in Charleston, but I believe they had been even more upset at both Deputy Boyce and me because we neglected to apprise them of the situation during the whole of their absence. Yet tensions had slowly subsided to allow us finally to be, during these days in the orchard, together as we had always been.

Deputy Boyce and the Tanners came to dine that evening, as if to confirm all was well again, and soon after their departure, my parents, exhausted, retired early.

As midnight approached beneath a perfectly halved moon, fitting for the birthday of Artemis, I made my way uphill through quietly greening woods toward Christabel's headland. The only sounds as I climbed were my footsteps punctuating the ancient drone of the French Broad. I fancied the night scented with the perfume of my Huntress—heavy notes of flora and earth, a subtle admixture of fauna from Demeter and Iasion. I felt the wolves watching as I moved past their enclosure, unsure how close or how far away they lay or sat or stood as still as the dark and followed me with eyes and nostrils. To think of them was to think also of Milo and Atalanta—of him enclosed below, solitary and waiting; of her caged somewhere miles from Avalon, healed and anxious to return.

Home soon, my love, I thought.

At the tree line, I paused to catch and steady my breath and survey the moonlit scene beyond the shadows enveloping me—the grassy edge of the precipice, the altar stone of Artemis, the cemetery of Avalon. The place—all of it—appeared restful, its peace recovered, like my parents' steady tempers, after the deep and jarring disturbance of Austen Caine.

I drew a calming breath and left the shadows beneath the trees and crossed the headland grass to the altar. With hands palm down atop the stone, I stood and looked upriver to the south, where a lamp burned in a second-story window of the Stackhouse mansion and the moon's light played on the bosom of the French Broad as she entered the bend the mansion overlooked and then flowed around Christabel toward Runion. I withdrew my hands and looked left toward the hollow of Genesis Road, where the Tanners lived, then looked behind and took in the silent lights of town—streetlights, a flashing yellow traffic signal, a few lighted windows along Main Street, and more such windows stacked atop one another in the university campus buildings higher up the hillside.

As I turned back toward Artemis's stone, my gaze lingered

a moment over the spot on Ridgeway's Ledge where Caine had died—died, in one sense, to save my life. Having recently read Mr. Brown's narrative of his brief stay with the early Avalon community, I understood how the outcropping came by its name, and I wondered if James Ridgeway, murdered by his wolfish wife, had lain dead in the same spot on the ledge over two hundred years before. Had he gone over as Caine and I had—pushed by a wolf? I raised my gaze to scan the landscape surrounding me and doubted if anything besides the moonlit river and the contoured silhouette of the mountains against the ever-changing unchanging sky looked as it did when Theodosia Ridgeway became a monster beneath the full moons of 1800.

I recalled my mind to the moment and spread the red and white bandana atop the altar, consecrating it with bear, buck, and dove, with pearl and quartz, with arrowhead and penknife. I drew a deep breath and turned my face up to the bright half moon. "O Great Artemis, Goddess of deer and dove, divine Wolf Goddess of the woods, thy praise I raise from this headland. You are my hunter-protectress, strong and wise, feeding and sheltering me in sunlit day and moonlit night. You have called to me, and I have answered upon this headland, Lady Artemis. I wait to be filled with your presence and spirit. I seek peace in the bed of thy mysteries. I pray you influence my dreams and bless my sleep with the same freedom from fear I see in the stars that twinkle in the sky. Through every trial I face, show me the strength I have in you. Hear me, Great Artemis."

I sensed a presence behind me, and an arm snaked around my waist, confining my left arm against my side. Another wrapped around my throat, and I felt my feet leave the ground. Lifted and unable to breathe, I raised my one free hand to claw at my attacker but scratched only myself.

"Come away!" a breathless voice said. *"Come away!"*

I could not tell if Caine's words came from inside my mind or from some vast distance. I seemed to see the altar stone recede into darkness. The prayers to Artemis that only moments before hovered and shimmered above the stone likewise faded and decayed into chaotic babble.

"Come away!"

I felt myself moved bodily to the precipice, not the precipice above Ridgeway's Ledge but that high above the ragged stones at the base of the southern headland. Unseen hands seemed molesting me everywhere at once, but when I swiped at the offending, probing fingers, my hand connected with nothingness.

"Come away!"

I shuddered and moaned at my helplessness in the clutch of my tormentor. While his arms held fast, the invisible hands roamed freely, somehow parting and discarding my clothing. Terror threatened to overturn my very sanity, and my mind desperately grasped at prayers that came easily only moments before.

"Come away!"

I caught hold of a phrase—*Through every trial I face—*

"Come away!"

—show me the strength I have in you—

"Come—"

"Release her!" a second voice said, its tone commanding, its cadence grave.

Artemis! I sang in my mind or cried aloud, I know not which. *Goddess!* I felt myself freed, not released to plunge to the river below but flung aside to the spot on Ridgeway's Ledge where Atalanta had lain to protect her broken foreleg. I rolled over and rose to hands and knees to see my attacker and my savior.

No one was there.

I marveled at this only a moment before I shuddered again, this time from brain to tailbone. Groaning, I clawed the grass for purchase, a hold to keep myself from tumbling backwards over the precipice as I felt my entire body twisting, contorting, transforming. Then everything stilled, and I stood on all fours in a night alive with sounds and scents and the light of a full moon.

In the middle of the broad ledge, where the stone that had taken his life was embedded, Austen Caine wrestled with the figure of a female that seemed somehow both human and wolf—decidedly not Artemis. They snarled and snapped in ferocious struggle, as the advantage between them seemed to shift with every blink of my eye.

Before I could stop myself, I lunged forward to join the fray between those shades, those ghosts, or whatever they might be. I found myself likewise snarling and snapping, biting hands and fingers and arms of flesh and blood.

Then Caine slipped away from us and rose like a spider up the short cliff wall and disappeared over the precipice onto the headland. Mrs. Ridgeway—for that is who I believed my companion to be—easily bounded upward and disappeared as well. I followed, and we sprinted shoulder-to-shoulder in pursuit of Caine as he entered the woods. The fencing of Wolfpen One did not seem to exist for us, and we passed through the upper side of the enclosure and through the lower before Demeter and Iasion had time to do more than prick up their ears. In a few more moments, we burst out of the headland woods—first Caine, then Mrs. Ridgeway and I—and sped through the misty orchard's wide central avenue.

In my peripheral vision, I imagined I could see, to my left, my parents watching our moonlit passage with horror from their bedroom window in Avalon Cottage and, to my right, Milo sitting outside his den and following our progress with great curiosity. Directly ahead, Caine, clearly visible in the full moon's light, fled toward the north end of the island. I knew not what he believed he might do there outside of splashing into the shallow river and swimming away from us, and I was surprised when he did not make it even that far.

His bare feet encountered the sandy strand, and he stumbled and sprawled face foremost. We lay back our ears and increased our speed. He had only time enough to turn onto his back before we were upon him. Unlike our battle on the headland, the fight seemed to have gone out of him, and he only wept as we ripped open his throat and bowels and tore him limb from limb.

Then, with Austen Caine dead at our feet and our muzzles red with him, Mrs. Ridgeway and I threw back our heads and bayed at the full moon just entering the trees on the western ridges above us. I threw back my head a second time, but before I could howl again, she attacked, gripped my exposed throat between her jaws, and bowled me over onto my back. My first instinct to resist with equal violence was throttled with increasing pressure and pain at my throat and an intense growl deep in hers. I relaxed into submission and rolled my eyes upward to where only the last sliver of full moon remained in the ridgeline trees. As it began to disappear and my eyesight began to darken, Mrs. Ridgeway quivered back and forth between wolf and woman—my throat alternately clamped between wolfish teeth and gripped in choking hands. At my last moment of consciousness, I saw her clearly a madwoman and heard the stars sing out joyfully at finally having the sky to themselves.

I awakened with a gasping start to find my throat free of the stranglehold and the night's half moon fading in the predawn sky. I lay naked and alone on the edge of Ridgeway's Ledge, my clothing scattered about. Had I entered some feverish dream state to encounter Theodosia Ridgeway and Austen Caine? Could Artemis be the author of such an experience? I could not tell, but I knew I could not remain where and as I was and let the day come on. The good relations with my fellow inmates at Avalon Cottage would again suffer from a mystery such as this.

I arose against the complaints of strangely sore muscles and joints, gathered my clothing, hoping nobody from Stackhouse watched through a spyglass, and dressed myself. At the altar of

Artemis, I whispered a brief closing prayer and returned the rudiments of worship to my satchel. After last glances aside at the haunting emptiness of Ridgeway's Ledge and the shadowed cemetery of Avalon, I hurried down through the woods, aware of Demeter and Iasion sitting atop their den and watching.

Mother and Father were still abed, so I crept in and changed to my red cloak for feeding the wolves, relieved that my overnight outing—and whatever actually happened during it—would go undiscovered. Later that morning, Atalanta returned to us, her foreleg mended, and she and Milo sat together companionably and watched as we Andersons continued our routine spring work in Avalon Orchard.

Over the week that followed, the moon waxed from half to full. Beneath that Flower Moon, I slept without dreams until I awoke, for no apparent reason, sometime past midnight. I arose and wrapped myself in a robe and felt drawn to the window. The day had been quite warm, and I had left the sash open. Just as Thomas and Molly Holcroft might have done when this room was theirs two hundred years before, I looked out on an island ghosted with moonlight.

Movement among the apple trees caught my eye. Two figures seemed playing at a game of tag. I started at the thought that Atalanta and Milo had escaped their enclosure, but then I recognized that neither were these figures wolves nor were they playing the games wolves play with each other.

They soon revealed themselves to me as Caine and Mrs. Ridgeway, the pursued and his pursuer both shades and silent. I could not always see them, but at times they burst through the near row of trees and, in clear view, came to grips in desperate struggle for a few moments before breaking apart again and resuming the chase. All the while, my mind supplied their howls and growls, their gnashing of teeth and cries for mercy, and my face alternately blanched with fear and reddened with passions I felt in my breast and nethers but could not name.

Thus we three spent the remainder of that night—they in constant, desperate motion and I motionless at my window. At the first faint glow of astronomical twilight in the eastern sky, they dissolved, and I was released from my trance. I watched the next night and the next, but they did not return until the night of June's full moon—the Strawberry Moon. After that, I watched their fearful engagements beneath the Buck Moon, the Red Moon (largest of the year), and the Harvest Moon.

Early October brought the Hunter's Moon, and this time, feeling something ominous in the name of that lunar event, I went downstairs and out of the house and stood at the threshold between yard and orchard until they appeared. Beneath the full white orb, the shades of Caine and Mrs. Ridgeway fought their most vicious battle hitherto. I stood there without cloak or boots, nearly naked in the night, and throbbed with desire to join them. Yet I was rooted in place like the apple trees that seemed likewise watching. Even when the first blush of twilight bloomed above the eastern ridges, they raged on, those two eternal combatants as I had come to think of them. I felt—rather than saw—the moon setting at my back, and I involuntarily shuddered and cried out in the dawn light. Both turned bloodied, rapacious gazes on me and disappeared.

I never saw them more.

Acknowledgements

Thanks first and always to Leesa, my one and only.

Thanks to my monthly workshop cohort Tamara Baxter and Tess Lloyd.

Thanks to my amazing, hardworking, and creative colleagues —present and past, here and gone—in the Department of Literature and Language at East Tennessee State University.

Thanks to my colleagues in the Charles Brockden Brown Society, particularly Philip Barnard, Robert Battistini, and Karen Weyler, for allowing me to delve deeply enough into Brown's work to help me imagine a story he might have told in the autumn of 1800.

Thanks to writing friends and writing inspirations who agreed to read the completed work and provided kind words about it—Andrew K. Clark, Whiskey Leavins, Bobby Mathews, Peter McDade, Mark Powell, Ron Rash, Cathy Rigg, and Charles Dodd White.

Thanks to the late great Shaun Power (1957-2024) for his beautiful, haunting, inspiring artwork, particularly "Shaun's Strange Land," the piece that, with the kind permission of Shaun's wife Tricia Shepherd Power and son Wayne Power, graces the cover of this book.

Thanks to Madville Publishing for making *Avalon Moon* a reality. The book is better because of acquisitions reviewer Mike Hilbig, line editor and proofreader Liz Evans, and cover designer Jacqui Davis. That *Avalon Moon* has entered the world at all is due largely to Kim Davis, editor, project manager, and Director of Madville Publishing.

About the Author

MICHAEL AMOS CODY was born in the South Carolina Lowcountry and raised in the North Carolina highlands. He spent his twenties writing songs in Nashville and his thirties in school. He's the author of the novel *Gabriel's Songbook* (Pisgah Press 2017) and the short story collection *A Twilight Reel* (Pisgah Press 2021), winner of the Short Story / Anthology category of the Feathered Quill Book Awards 2022. Cody's novel *Streets of Nashville* (Madville Publishing 2025) was named a Finalist for the Best Thriller Book Awards 2025 by bestthrillers.com and won the Independent Press Award 2026 in the category of Thriller. Cody lives with his wife Leesa in Jonesborough, Tennessee, and teaches in the Department of Literature and Language at East Tennessee State University.

About the Author

[illegible]

ALSO BY MICHAEL AMOS CODY

Streets of Nashville

a novel by Michael Amos Cody

ISBN: 978-1-963695-17-5 paperback $22.95

ISBN: 978-1-963695-18-2 ebook $9.99

"Streets of Nashville is one of the year's best thrillers" — BestThrillers.com

A BOLD THRILLER—Kirkus Reviews

www.ingramcontent.com/pod-product-compliance
Lightning Source LLC
LaVergne TN
LVHW030916080826
845145LV00013B/2926